LORE

of the

TIDES

ALSO BY ANALEIGH SBRANA

Lore of the Wilds

LORE
of the
TIDES

ANALEIGH SBRANA

MAGPIE

Magpie Books
An imprint of
HarperCollins*Publishers* Ltd
1 London Bridge Street
London SE1 9GF

www.harpercollins.co.uk

HarperCollins*Publishers*
Macken House,
39/40 Mayor Street Upper,
Dublin 1, D01 C9W8
Ireland

First published by HarperCollins*Publishers* Ltd 2025
1

Designed by Angie Boutin
Part-opener page background texture © dmutrojarmolinua/stock.adobe.com
Part-opener page sun icon © Valedi/stock.adobe.com
Chapter-opener jellyfish art © Alisles/stock.adobe.com
Map by Virginia Allyn

Analeigh Sbrana asserts the moral right to
be identified as the author of this work.

A catalogue record for this book is available from the British Library.

ISBN: 978-0-00-868539-3 (HB)
ISBN: 978-0-00-868540-9 (TPB)

Printed and bound in the UK using 100% renewable electricity by CPI Group (UK) Ltd

MIX
Paper | Supporting
responsible forestry
FSC
www.fsc.org   FSC™ C007454

This book contains FSC™ certified paper and other controlled sources
to ensure responsible forest management.

For more information visit: www.harpercollins.co.uk/green

To every Black reader who grew up looking for themselves on the fantasy shelves, this one's for you

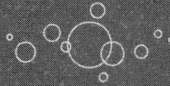

PART ONE

THE
LAVENDER LARK

CHAPTER 1

The earth pitched and shifted beneath Lore Alemeyu as panic clawed up her throat, thick and choking. Oh gods, was this another earthshake?

She couldn't see. The room was dark, black as a new moon night. Were towering shelves about to crush her—the ceiling above poised to crack in two?

"Finndryl?" Lore rasped, offering the name into the darkness like the small candle of hope it was. Her throat was raw and scratchy, her tongue dry from thirst.

Silence answered, punctuated by the howling of a storm, the rustle of branches in the wind.

Were they not just together in the hidden garden? With Ember the fox? No, Ember the moth.

Wingbeats fluttered delicately upon her shoulder. Lore brushed aside curls to nudge the fox-turned-moth, but there was no sweet moth nuzzling her throat.

A phantom memory.

Lore shook her head. Her thoughts seemed to drift, as though they existed apart from time. A fog, swirling her memories and scattering them like birdseed.

The room oscillated again. Prickling vines of fear climbed

up her spine. Lore reached for her magic but felt no familiar warmth—no ignition of *Source*.

It was night, she should be able to call on her magic. Unless . . . unless her grimoire was gone.

It had been months since she'd been without her grimoire. An ache crested within her as she realized what it meant to be without it—as though she were missing a hand.

Dread twisted in her gut, tighter than the tangled sheets clinging to her trembling limbs. She extricated her legs from the sheets and placed bare feet on the floor, holding on to the bedpost for support as the room spun around her—a dizzying kaleidoscope of blacks and smears of grays.

She swayed on her feet against this unceasing, sickening, rhythmic sway.

An earthshake would be over by now.

Lore's stomach heaved, her chest constricting. She pressed the back of one hand to her mouth, scrunching her eyes shut and urging her stomach to settle. Though her thoughts were slow turning, like a stagnant swamp, this was not an earthshake. There was something decidedly *other* about this motion; it was unfamiliar.

Lore stretched out an arm, searching in the suffocating darkness. Scrabbling for purchase, she brushed her fingertips along the smooth surface of a table until she found an oil lamp and the cool, rough texture of a flint striker.

A spark. A flicker of flame. She spun the knob, adjusting the wick length. In the sudden swell of light, a door came into focus.

Lore stumbled toward it, only to collapse against it; her legs felt insubstantial, the weakness a horrifying echo of the wildwood, of when poison had coursed through her veins delivered on the sharp edge of an Alytherian guard's sword. But unlike that time, Finndryl wasn't by her side.

She clasped the door handle with trembling fingers. Twisted. The handle did not yield. Locked. Of course it was locked. There seemed to be no doors willing to open for her without an insufferable amount of effort.

Lore surveyed the unfamiliar room as despair coiled around her heart, a serpent tightening its viselike grip with every passing second.

The chamber seemed a cruel mockery—a lavish cell gilded with silk cushions, plush rugs, polished floors, and velvet curtains. A bloodred vase bursting with flowers—dahlias, peonies, and dripping displays of lilies of the valley—which had begun their descent into decay. Their once sweet perfume now hung heavy in the air, cloying and oppressive.

She lurched toward the window, ripping aside the thick curtains to unveil the truth. Sunlight, harsh and unforgiving, flooded the room. But it wasn't the comforting warmth of a familiar dawn. This was a relentless glare. Lore's breath hitched as her eyes adjusted.

The view crashed over her like a rogue wave, stealing her last vestiges of hope. Where there should be earth, trees, and hazy mountains was a churning sea of foam-capped blue.

She'd thought the sound was branches brushing against the window, but no, the swishing sound was the hum of water.

Lore was on a ship, and there was no land in sight.

Time stood still as it all came crashing back to her at once.

The tower. The fight with the steward. The women and children. Katu and Milo . . .

She closed her eyes, whispering a prayer that Grey and Isla had managed to lead the women and children to safety.

She flinched at the memory of betrayal in the garden. He'd betrayed her. Asher had . . . gods. The truth of who he'd been all along. The lies he'd spun, weaving them around her as though he were a spider—and she'd clung willingly to his web.

"Sleep, for now. Tomorrow, we sail in search of Auroradel, *the Book of Sunbeams."*

He'd mentioned sailing, just before she'd lost consciousness.

And he'd done as promised—that whispered threat. He'd abducted her, absconded with her grimoire, and trapped her in an inescapable prison. She was at his mercy, this stranger, this male whose heart was unknown to her.

A heart that could only be as grim as the storm clouds gathering on the horizon, slowly eating up the sunlight.

She turned, stumbling to the table, gripping the bouquet. She strangled the stems in her hand, not caring that some were barbed with thorns. Though the flowers had wilted, the thorns remained sharp, biting into the soft flesh of her palms. The fog in her mind, the persistent panic—those last few moments in the garden, what had been done to those women, Asher's betrayal. Each thought dug into her like another thorn.

Lore pressed her face to the opening of the vase and retched.

Minutes or eons passed before the sound of a lock sliding free clanged through the room, drawing Lore from a labyrinth of wrenching guilt and recrimination. The door made no sound as it arched across the rug. Lore swallowed a bout of nausea at the sight of his form silhouetted in the curved doorway.

She was surprised he'd waited so long.

He wore black fighting leathers shined to a gleam. Two vast wings erupted from his shoulder blades—sleek black-and-gray feathers like those of an eagle, so large they obscured all beyond the door. Where two gorgeous antlers should have sprouted from his head, there were instead short-cropped, shining coils. Where a scar should bisect one eyebrow were smoothly manicured, un-marred brows. And in place of the thoughtful, mischievous face of a grounder, a lower caste of dark fae, the lowly soldier who had abandoned his post to defend, shield, and shelter Lore . . . was the cold and aloof face of Lord Syrelle.

He strode through the door, his cruel eyes drawn to her straight-away as though he knew exactly where she would be—squeezed into the sliver of space between the bed and the wall.

"Come to gloat?" Lore called as she heaved herself into a standing position. She pressed her hip to the carved siren at the tip of the bed-post; her knees were weak still, and her arms were preoccupied with the vase pressed firmly to her chest. She didn't dare place it down; the fluidity of the ship was unnatural, and her body rejected the constant fluctuation. Though it wasn't just motion sickness that had forced her to expel the entire contents of her stomach into the vase; it had to do with him as well.

She was, it seemed, sensitive to treachery.

The glow of the oil lamp cast dancing shadows upon his cheeks, playing with the black-and-gray feathers of his widespread wings. Lore was glad she'd cinched the curtains tightly closed earlier, blocking out the light of day and the bloodcurdling view of continuous blue; she didn't think she could stomach an uninhibited sight of him. She shifted the vase to one arm, ignoring the sloshing of its contents.

"Mouse," he breathed.

That term of endearment, spoken by the wrong face, with the wrong timbre.

"Don't you dare call me that." The sound of Lore's palm con-necting with Syrelle's face fractured the room, surprising them both. Syrelle hissed as his face jerked sideways. His hand flew to his cheek, massaging the smooth skin beside his left eye. The nerve of this male—he had the gall to sound *relieved* to see her.

Her chest heaved as she gulped in breaths through clenched teeth. Shit. She'd told herself, while she'd waited for him, crouched between the wall and the bed for some semblance of stability . . . heaving into the vase . . . to keep her godsdamned head. The easi-est way to escape was to play along at first . . . to not give in to her emotions. Lore shook out her hand. Her palm throbbed. Just as the memory of Asher throbbed.

"I'm glad to see you are awake," he said, turning back toward her slowly, his dark eyes meeting hers. Rivers of red snaked through the white of his eye. She'd burst a blood vessel. His gaze roamed over her as if checking that she was unharmed, whole, before snagging on the vase clutched to her chest with one arm. The corners of his lips tugged downward into a frown, and his brows knitted together in concern. "You will adjust to being at sea soon enough."

"I won't be doing any adjusting. I demand you turn this ship around. Take me home."

He continued on, as though she hadn't spoken at all. "I regret having to sedate you these last few days. It was necessary to dose you with solace-root while we arranged our journey. I felt it would be less . . . difficult for you . . . to sleep through the preparations."

Solace-root . . . that explained the weakness in her legs, the confusion clouding her thoughts. Lore swallowed back a wave of nausea. There was nothing left to expel anyway.

Lore opened her mouth to demand, once more, that Syrelle turn the ship around, when a voice interrupted from the shadowed hallway. "Commander Syrelle, should I inform Lady Coretha that the human has awakened?" A guard, by the looks of her uniform.

Syrelle's gaze never wavered from Lore's face even as he addressed the guard behind him. "Of course, Cecil, we must apprise Lady Coretha. But first notify Cook that Lore will be in need of sustenance."

"But I am to tell the lady straightaway—"

"Cecil, you will first go to the galley, then inform the Lady Coretha." Syrelle's tone allowed no room for dispute.

"Yes, of course, Commander." The guard bowed at the waist before retreating down the hallway, her footsteps imperceptible.

"Commander?"

Lore hadn't known much about Lord Syrelle before. Of noble birth, he'd seemed important, important enough to allow for the transport of a human outside of Duskmere for the first time in living history. She'd thought him a scholar maybe, that his interest in the contents of the cursed library was simply to appease curiosity or a thirst for the sequestered knowledge. The high steward's deference to him hadn't seemed out of the ordinary; Wyndlin Castle was devoid of all other nobles. She hadn't realized that he was a commander.

She hadn't known anything at all, though, had she?

Syrelle rubbed the back of his neck. "Ah yes. *Commander*, though you, of course, need not address me as such. *Syrelle* is just fine. Or"—he hesitated—"*Asher* if you prefer—"

Never would she call him by that name again. The name of the kind soldier who had risked everything for her. The name she'd whispered against his lips.

"*Commander* doesn't suit you." She raised her chin. "It seems as though you missed your calling. With acting like this, you clearly belong in the theater."

"It wasn't all an act," he voiced quietly.

"Oh, thank the gods. Is this the act, then? I was afraid you had lied to me for months, that you had tricked me into being your pawn— risked my life for your gain. But if it wasn't all an act, then I suspect you'll let me off at the next port? I should like to go home."

He winced, managing to twist his face into a perfect semblance of regret. Lore wanted to clap at his performance, but she still had the vase in a vise grip. The cool porcelain might be the only thing keeping her from screaming like a banshee and clawing his eyes out.

"I admit, I waited too long to tell you the truth, but I can explain—"

She wanted nothing more than for him to explain this all away. To change back into Asher, to pull her into his arms and tell her that this was a bad dream. That he hadn't made her fall for a lie.

But she couldn't stand to listen to any more of his dishonesties; it would only carve his betrayal deeper into her bones, and the burn was already excruciating.

Since waking up, she'd had time to think as this ship sailed farther and farther from home, from her people. She'd decided that she would not give him the privilege of lying to her ever again.

No matter what he had to say, it could only be more untruths.

"—I'm sure you've a perfectly reasonable list of fabrications ready in that irrational mind of yours, but I would prefer to skip all that. Where is Finndryl? Where is my grimoire? What happened to Grey, Isla, and the women and children?"

She wanted to ask if Isla knew, if she knew the truth about "Asher," but she was too cowardly. Afraid the answer would damn another friendship. And she wouldn't trust it anyway, not if it was him who spoke it.

"Finndryl, I imagine, is still resting. We had to dose him with more of the solace-root than you." Lore's mind reeled. Finndryl was here? On the ship? *She wasn't alone!* And yet, that meant like her, Finn was captive. Syrelle continued, "And Grey and Isla have safely returned with all the prisoners to Duskmere. All accounted for."

Safely returned.

Safe.

Syrelle took a step toward her, though his large form still blocked the exit, she noticed bitterly. "I am glad to say that my uncle, the king, has given his word that he will make no move upon Duskmere until we have returned with the sister book to *Deeping Lune*— *Auroradel.* You need not worry for them while we search. And it will give us enough time to devise a plan on how to dissuade him from any sort of retaliation—"

"How benevolent of you, to pretend to care what happens to those in Duskmere." Lore's eyes burned with tears. She yearned for the luxury of trust. Hungered to collapse with relieved sobs that she had been victorious in this at least, in getting them all home. If only she could confirm his claims that while she'd been putrefying under the effects of solace-root, the women and children were back with their families. That right now, through community, they could begin to heal from the ordeal.

"I have always cared. Not many Alytherian nobles realize the hardships your kind have faced, sufferings caused by my uncle. I've always longed to make things better."

Lore rolled her eyes. "I remember when you came into the shop that time—looking for my aunt. Searching for a pawn to enter your cursed library. Now I know you were truly after . . . what did you call the grimoire? *Deeping Lune*? You didn't care about us then, and you don't now." She huffed a bitter laugh. "You certainly didn't care for *my* well-being when you made the deal with me—you couldn't have known that the library's curse would spare me. You risked my life on a whim."

"I had been *mostly* sure that you would not be harmed—yes, I know how bad that sounds—but I also knew that it would be worth the risk." Syrelle looked around the room then. As if afraid someone might be listening in, he closed the door behind him, softly, as though he were forbidden to be alone with her . . . and Lore wondered: If he was her puppeteer, pulling her strings, who was pulling his?

"'Worth the risk'? I could've been slaughtered just by entering the library—sacrificed merely to appease your avarice. But what is the sacrifice of one human when the inherent power, innate privilege, and many, *many* freedoms you were *born with* weren't enough to subdue such . . . such *relentless* ambition?" She seethed, rage erupting from her despite her commitment to remain levelheaded. Lore risked much by letting anger cloud her judgment, and she still felt encumbered by the persistent fog of the solace-root. She exhaled a shaky breath, extinguishing the heat in her voice, until she knew that her words would crackle with ice. "Yes, I suppose it was worth the risk for *you*, who bore none of it."

Syrelle winced as though her words cut like knives. "The risk . . ." He ran a hand through his cropped coils and glanced at the closed door, as if making sure it hadn't opened behind him without his knowledge. "The risk was never for my gain, but something far bigger than me . . . than you . . ."

She wanted to scream at him to stop talking, to end these lies, but she resisted. The more Syrelle talked, the less he reminded her of Asher and the more knowledge she gained. Instead of begging him to stop talking . . . she needed to keep him talking, so that she could harden her heart so she could survive this.

He continued, his voice heavy, "My uncle, the king, has lived far longer than any dark fae should, and his power . . ." He trailed off, a flicker of fear like burning embers showed in the coal black of his eyes. "It surpasses even my grandfather, who created two grimoires that defy the very laws of alchemy." His voice lowered even further, until Lore could barely make out what he said. "There are things in play you cannot fathom, things I couldn't share with you as Asher, because Asher wouldn't have known them."

"And, what . . . you wish to enlighten me now?"

He shook his head. "Not just yet; the threat is too great. Lady Coretha or her guards could be listening."

Lady Coretha—the person the guard had gone to inform about Lore waking. Wait, *her* guards?

Lore twisted her face into a confused expression. "I thought you were commander?"

"Commander, yes, but aboard this ship, I am Commander in name only. I didn't manage to bring any of my cabal with me. Those crewing the ship are loyal only to the king." His voice held a bitter edge. "He has sent my cousin, Lady Coretha, on our journey to protect his interests—we are, of course, seeking the grimoires as gifts for him."

Lore's mind shuttered. The grimoires were not for Syrelle at all . . .

"You would find the grimoire . . . complete the set . . . and gift them to the king? Does he not have enough?" Aghast, her voice rose an octave. "Is he not in control of an entire kingdom already?"

"You weren't wrong—what you accused me of just now. Only, the one with an unceasing lust for *more*, it was never me—but the king. That's the thing about power, Lore, is that for those who seek it, there can never be enough." His expression was grave, earnest. "I have hurt you, lied to you, betrayed your trust, and I am sorry for that. I will apologize for my betrayal for as long as there is breath in my body, and I know, yes, I know you do not wish to hear this, I know that you don't wish to hear anything from me just now, or even see my face—and trust me, I do not blame you one bit . . . I would despise myself if I were in your boots—just know, I could never have helped you to unlock the secrets of *Deeping Lune* as . . . as myself."

She had been right. Him admitting to his wrongs did not make her feel better, she hurt *more* somehow. She'd wanted to avoid this because she was filled with so much rage it was like plugging a geyser with earth. She could feel the dirt dampening her anger, shaking and shifting, ready to explode apart by a scalding torrent of devastation and hatred. Briefly, she considered scratching out his eyes, ruining his true face. She tightened her grip on the vase, her fingers itching to toss its contents, or at least throw the vase at him. She resisted. Barely.

Oblivious, he continued, his words rushed. "My original plan didn't play out. I tried, but I could not make *Deeping Lune* unlock for me. When I changed the plan—told my uncle that there was something wrong with the grimoire, that I had a plan to unlock its secret using a human, he accepted it. He was irate when he discovered that not only had the magic been unlocked, but that I had withheld that information. When he learned the truth in the tower, that you, a human, had access to the magic . . . his reaction surprised me. He was furious, scared about what it meant for a human to have access to magic . . . he . . ." His tone was grave. "The king wanted to eliminate the human race altogether."

Terror shuddered Lore's breath. And her removing the grimoire from the library . . . they risked the king becoming even more powerful . . .

"I knew that I couldn't keep the knowledge of your bond with *Deeping Lune* from him forever—and when Isla and I discovered the steward's repulsive plot with the women and children, my priority became to put a stop to the Tower Project, but, Lore . . . and I am fearful admitting this . . . I used the unfortunate circumstances as an opportunity."

Lore felt bile climbing up her throat. How could the abduction of women and children—and the sick use they had planned for them—benefit *him*?

He continued, "I had to know . . . I had to be sure that you could do it—could use your powers to extract your people, that you were powerful enough to make it happen. For only through your strength and mastery of *Source* will we find the Book of Sunbeams."

"You think . . ." Lore opened and closed her mouth in shock, not believing what she was hearing. "You think that, after everything, I would search for this other grimoire *willingly*? That I would place another weapon into your hands and then . . . what, stand aside as you reward the very being who has imprisoned my people for *generations*? The king who even now must be persuaded not to annihilate us?"

Lore swayed on her feet. It was worse than she thought. Everything was worse than she'd thought. Syrelle's betrayal seemed inconsequential to this threat on Duskmere.

And it was all his fault.

If he had never tricked her into the library, things would still be bad, but the king wouldn't be on the hunt to acquire two monumental weapons . . . her people wouldn't be facing extinction.

Syrelle closed his eyes for a moment, pinching the bridge of his nose as if he knew exactly what she was thinking. "I wish I could open up to you completely, tell you the entire truth—but if it were relayed to the king . . . the results would be not just my death, your people's . . . but yours as well, and I will never let that happen. Just know that my intentions will benefit you and all of Duskmere. Do not fight me in this—together, we can find *Auroradel*; I will be able to fix everything."

How would finding another powerful source of magic—one that would be detrimental if placed in the king's hands—fix anything? "You want me to search for the book so that you can 'fix' this mess you made? As though the continuity of my entire race were a castle made of blocks, and they tumbled?"

He nodded solemnly.

"No." Lore clenched her teeth so hard she was afraid her molars would crack. "I won't do it. I won't be your puppet any longer."

She needed him gone. She needed him out of her life. This was a nightmare. This was a terrible, horrible nightmare. She would wake up from this, she could—

"Mouse—"

"Call me that one more time, and I'll break this vase across your face and use the shards to carve out your deceitful tongue."

Syrelle swallowed, anguish crossing his expression momentarily. Lore meant it.

Syrelle was bigger than her, stronger, faster, and his magic did not rely on the moon, nor a spell book, so she might not be able to achieve her threat, but she would try her hardest, and it was clear by his pained expression that he knew that.

"You didn't disclose how hostile she is, Syr." A high, lyrical voice spoken from behind Syrelle cut the tension in the room. "Nor how insolent. Should we have her bound and gagged?"

Lore cut her eyes behind him, where a beautiful female stood in the doorway.

Lore hadn't heard it open, and, judging by the expression on Syrelle's face, neither had he.

For the first time, fear crossed the depths of his dark eyes—just for a moment—real, raw terror, just before his face hardened into an apathetic mask.

Was he wondering how much the female had heard? Had it been enough to condemn him?

"Try to bind me, harpy, and you'll regret it," Lore spat out.

The female laughed, the sound effervescent as a bubbling brook.

Lore had heard that laugh before.

She studied this newcomer. Same lustrous, mahogany skin. Sharp, elegantly painted nails. Long braids that swayed when she stepped farther into the room. The small, brown wings sprouting from behind her were new.

The other fae from the apothecary.

The one who'd accompanied Syrelle, searching for Aunty Eshe all those months ago.

She'd been so rude about the conditions of Duskmere, complaining that the muddy streets had ruined her slippers.

Lore had convinced the female to pay ten times what a book was worth. She'd planned to use the funds for new boots for the twins. Lore had been so proud. And then the earth had split open, devastating Duskmere.

Had that been in this lifetime?

It seemed as if that day had happened to someone else entirely, so altered was Lore. She felt as though she were a husk of that person—a ghost. She felt like she had less power now than she did then, because now she knew what it was to be powerful, and she'd had it ripped from her grasp.

"You dare threaten me? I should have you whipped." The female's laugh was shocked, delighted.

This was a game to her. Lore's life and all the lives trapped in Duskmere were a game. What a despicable female.

"I would love to see you try, spoiled brat," Lore retorted.

"Syr, I thought surely you would have taught this feral creature some manners, with all that time you insisted on spending with her."

"Coretha, there will be no further threats to Lore. She's still under the effects of the solace-root."

Coretha . . . so this was Syrelle's cousin.

"Have I mentioned how exasperating you are to insist the human must *choose* to locate the book? Surely she isn't so stupid—she must know that choice is an illusion. If the king wills it, it must be done." She tossed her braids behind her shoulder and heaved a dramatic sigh. "I thought even the scum of Duskmere would realize that."

Syrelle growled. "I'm sure you have better things to be doing than minding me. Leave us."

"Oh, there are a plethora of things I would rather be doing than being on this ship, period. But Uncle said you weren't to be alone with the human beast. You're untrustworthy now . . . or have you forgotten that you've fallen so out of favor? I can't leave you; the king's orders must be followed." She cut her eyes at Lore. "Something you should be relaying to your pet."

Pet? "You—" Lore started, but Syrelle cut her off.

"Coretha, at least wait outside. You are hindering my plans." He recalculated. "The *king's* plans."

"Fine, but he expects results—and fast. He won't wait forever before taking matters into his own hands." She backed into the hallway and leaned against the wall, her wings fluttering as she watched the two of them, her expression giddy.

Lore didn't have to know the female nor the cousins' dynamic to know that something had changed—and recently. Coretha liked having power over Syrelle. It seemed that Syrelle had made a grievous error by withholding information from the king—his leash had been shortened, and he was clearly unaccustomed to it.

The guard from before cleared her throat. She'd returned with a plate of food. The aroma made Lore heave into the vase.

"Are you unwell?" Syrelle asked.

Lore's shoulders shook with laughter as she wiped saliva from her lips.

Was she unwell? She didn't think she'd ever been *more* unwell. Not even when she was close to death from being poisoned. Or when the steward was whispering all the terrible things that he wished to do to her, his decrepit knee pressed to her chest.

"I'll feel better when you and your deplorable cousin have left my presence."

"I see. I'll leave you to eat. You need your strength. Someone will be by shortly with water to wash up . . . and a new vase. There are clothes in the wardrobe. Please make yourself comfortable."

The guard placed the plate of food on the table.

"Tonight, when the moon is high, we begin our search."

Syrelle closed the door behind them. Someone slid the lock into place.

Lore was left alone.

She wilted to the floor, wishing that for just a moment this fucking ship would stop its rocking. She pressed her forehead to the cool floor.

Betrayal settled like stones, heavy within Lore's chest.

If she wasn't careful, the weight of it would tear through her lungs, leaving her unable to breathe. She had known a great deal of suffering in her life: oppression, grief, helplessness. All of it dwelled behind her ribs, piling up like pebbles, weighing her down. But this was a new type of ache, one she was not accustomed to—the agony of loving someone who was not who they had pretended to be.

Lore clenched her hands, one upon each thigh, digging her fingers into the delicate skin in an effort to distract from the pressure crushing her bones. This anguish felt so dense—how was it not dragging the ship down to the depths of the sea?

The physical pain of her nails carving moons into her thighs grounded her for a moment, just long enough to pull in a thread of breath. To focus on her fury instead, kindling that ember of rage until it ignited, melting the hurt away, if only for a moment. Lore had practice with this at least: When faced with grief, she would choose anger.

Her desire to escape this ship with Finndryl and the grimoire would have to be disregarded.

Syrelle wouldn't rest until he found *Auroradel*.

And she had no doubt that he *would* find it. With or without her. And she knew that the worst thing that could happen would be him finding it. Whether he chose to gift it to the king or bind it to himself, either would be disastrous.

She would have to stay—she had no other choice. She must find *Auroradel* and bind the grimoire of the sun to her before Syrelle could.

Only then could she enact her vengeance.

Only then would Duskmere be free.

CHAPTER 2

L ore was dipped in ink. Her palms were smeared with darkness that slithered up her wrists in tendrils.

Deeping Lune, Lore's grimoire, sat open before her, its pages as empty as the day she had found it.

She glanced away from the blank parchment and surveyed the commander's quarters. Syrelle's office, which was a large space separated from his sleeping quarters by a tapestry hung from rafters in the ceiling, was dark today. The moon concealed itself behind a thick layer of cloud. Lore wished she, too, could hide.

By now, she, her legs, and her stomach were accustomed to the unceasing motion of the ship, the steady rhythm of the colossal vessel carving through the waves. The first week at sea had been rough—there were a few days she'd forgotten what it felt like to eat a meal and not meet its contents again a bell later as she vomited into a bucket.

But she wasn't used to, and probably would never grow accustomed to, the sight of the male before her.

"Look again, Lore. I know you can do this," Syrelle said as he pushed a wooden bowl filled with water toward her, carefully avoiding the grimoire, which lay open upon his desk. Lore's gaze snagged on the bandages wrapped around his fingertips. Syrelle had made the mistake of touching her grimoire again, and the burns hadn't yet healed.

Good.

Lore ignored the bowl of water.

She wouldn't scry for him today. Not until he gave in to her demands. He was convinced that she should use her magic to locate *Auroradel* for him. Locate the lost Book of Sunbeams. A magical text that drew power from the sun itself, the sister book to her own *Deeping Lune*. He wanted her to peer into the water, turning it into a mirrored surface to show *Auroradel*'s location.

It had been a mistake to tell Syrelle, then masquerading as Asher, that that was how she'd located Grey when he was imprisoned in the palace, drowning under Queen Riella's vicious whims. Syrelle was convinced that scrying was the best way to pinpoint the exact location of *Auroradel*. He had a hunch which continent his grandfather had hidden the grimoire on, but that was it.

So far this evening, Lore had stubbornly held to the silent treatment, but enough was enough. "I wish to see Finndryl," she hissed.

Syrelle gritted his teeth. "Not this again. I told you, once you successfully find the location of *Auroradel* on the map you will be allowed to see him." Syrelle sounded weary of this dance, but Lore remained unfazed.

"And I've told you, let me see him, and I'll scry for *Auroradel* again."

Finndryl was somewhere on this ship, and Lore was desperate to see him. To confirm with her own eyes that he was all right. That Syrelle, or Coretha, or any of the awful dark fae aboard this ship hadn't mistreated him.

Syrelle had brought Finn on this journey for no other reason than to "protect his assets." *Deeping Lune*—the grimoire that he insisted was his, though it belonged to Lore as much as the blood that filled her veins belonged to her. And though Syrelle didn't say this, he didn't *have* to: Lore herself had been reduced to one of his assets. He felt he'd made her what she was: a human with the ability to cast spells—to harness magic, known as *Source*—and so she, and all her abilities, belonged to him. Now all Syrelle had to do was successfully mold her into exactly what he wanted her to be: a compliant puppet to be used in whatever way he chose.

In his demented mind, anyway.

"Locate *Auroradel* for me, and you can have just about anything you desire."

He was a stubborn musician, piping the same notes over and over.

Lore rolled her eyes.

"My magic is more accessible when he's around," she lied. "Something I discovered when you left me in Tal Boro." Syrelle's mouth twitched, he didn't like that she kept mentioning Finndryl or her time spent in Tal Boro, the town beneath the Canaan Mountains that bordered the Alytherian Empire and the Queendom of Rywandall. "You must've known, somehow, that he could teach me what you could not. It will make it easier to—"

"Perhaps a more potent spur is required to inspire the human's cooperation." Coretha's cruel, lyrical voice butted in from where she leaned on the edge of a carved wooden stool in the corner of the room.

Gods, Coretha was a constant plague.

"If you wish to find *Auroradel* before we arrive on the shores of Ma Serach . . ." *Ma Serach? Had Coretha just let slip their destination?* ". . . it's clear that pain will motivate more than whatever . . . this is." The female gestured to the desk, the bowl of water, and the open grimoire.

Lore stiffened. *Pain?*

Syrelle bared his teeth, his sharp canines flashing, before closing his eyes momentarily to gather himself. Composed, he addressed his cousin, "As I've said before, Lore is not to be harmed."

Lore met Coretha's sneer with a glare of her own.

She may have been afraid of her all those months ago in Duskmere, but Lore was no longer the scared human. She'd been personally responsible for three fae deaths. She wouldn't lose any sleep over increasing that number by one.

Syrelle's wings unrolled slowly until his feathers covered the entire length of the bay window behind him and the tips of the feathers brushed the low cabin ceiling. "Coretha, if you or anyone else on this ship so much as touch a single curl on her head, I will bind your arms and wings and throw you over the railing of the *Lavender Lark*. We crossed into the Dread Abyss last night—how long do you think you'll last in the ocean before Takuma swallows you whole?"

Coretha rolled her eyes and pushed off the stool, shaking out her own pair of wings, though they were a songbird's compared to Syrelle's predatorial breadth. "I'm sure the king would love to hear that his heir has been thrown to her death by his least favorite nephew . . . Need I remind you that you are *tenth* in line?"

Syrelle's lips drew into a hard line. "You aren't heir yet, Coretha. You'll do well to remember that. And either way, Takuma doesn't care what your proximity to the throne is, he will eat you all the same."

"Your idle threats grow stale. You promised our king results, and all you have so far is—what," she scoffed, tossing her hair, "a book that burns you when you touch it and a human who spits on not just your orders but the commands of her king. Her refusal to submit is high treason."

"She isn't to be touched." Syrelle slammed his hand on the desk, making the water in the bowl jump.

Coretha paused by the door, twisting a braid around one finger. "You've made that clear," she deadpanned, "but I was talking about a more imaginative way to inspire pain."

Apprehension stippled Lore's arms with goosebumps, but she

tried to push the feeling down. Lore refused to show Coretha that she was making her nervous. The creature was a predator, she salivated at the smell of fear. Whatever this sadist suggested . . . Lore could handle it. She'd been in pain before. She wouldn't bow to it.

"I don't wish to know the twisted things you've conjured in that head of yours. This discussion is over," Syrelle said, his voice quiet, lethal.

Coretha blinked slowly as if perplexed. "Syrelle, why else did you drag that halfling barkeep along with us? Surely you plan to use him in more creative ways than keeping them apart?"

The world tilted on its axis. Terror flooded Lore, icy and suffocating.

"Leave Finndryl out of this!" Lore snarled at Coretha, the sound raw and desperate. She ripped the grimoire off the desk and surged to her feet. Her hands exploded with *Source*, magic crackling around her like lightning. "You hurt him, and I swear, I'll unleash everything I've got. This room, this whole damned ship, won't hold to the tempest I'll summon."

For the first time since Lore met her, Coretha dropped her pompous attitude as trepidation flitted across her features, her eyes dipping between the grimoire in Lore's hands and the fury on her face. Wide-eyed, Coretha glanced at Syrelle, who stood by the window, his arms crossed over his broad chest. Coretha's voice trembled with unbridled fury. "Syrelle, get control of your pet!"

She dared not take her eyes off Coretha to gauge his reaction. If Syrelle wanted to, he could stop Lore in her tracks. She was still not powerful enough to best him.

A drip of sweat slid down Lore's back. Syrelle made no move to take the grimoire from Lore, nor to intervene.

Coretha, seeing this, addressed Lore once more. "If you would just do as you're told, you wouldn't have to worry about your friend."

"You are foolish in your privilege." Lore took a step closer to Coretha, where she stood by the door. "I'm sure you've never had to worry for anyone's safety, not even your own." Lore cocked her head to the side. "You aren't in charge of me, and neither is your despicable king. I will not sit idly by while you threaten those dear to me. One more word from you about hurting me—or him—and it will be your last, Coretha." Lore raised one ink-stained hand, making sure that Coretha saw the strands of silvery light threading through her fingers. "That is a promise."

"Syrelle, aren't you going to punish her for threatening me?"

Syrelle raised an eyebrow. "Why should I? You've been told enough times not to threaten Lore with violence."

Coretha sputtered momentarily. "What? I didn't! It was her friend that I—"

"How Lore reacts to that is her own prerogative. You should have grasped that hurting Finndryl was not a part of my plan." Syrelle examined his cuticles before leveling a cold stare at his cousin. "*My plan.* Not yours. You were sent here to watch, not to interfere."

Hurting Finn was not in Syrelle's plans. Neither was hurting her. Lore had to wonder, why then, had he brought Finndryl along?

"I can't believe this. I'll be writing a letter to the king, alerting him that you let her threaten me!"

"Please do, so Lore and I can get back to work. Dawn is approaching."

Coretha screeched momentarily before she left through the door, slamming it behind her.

Petty imp.

※

Thadrik, Syrelle's appointed second-in-command, replaced Coretha the moment she departed. He took up his usual position behind Lore–his unwavering gaze upon her back sent chills of unease.

"Lore, please place the grimoire on the table so we can continue."

Her fingers, which trembled from Coretha's threats, clenched tighter around the binding. This was the first time she'd held *Deeping Lune* since she'd awoken on the ship. The warmth it exuded, the power in her chest, her belly, filling her entire body—it thrilled. Every muscle screamed at her that she should not be the one required to relinquish it. A wild thought flashed through her mind. *What if she didn't need to keep up this ruse anymore?* What if this was her chance to fight back? To rescue Finndryl? She could locate the other grimoire on her own. Eventually.

"Lore," Syrelle growled, "do not force me to use *Source* on you. Whatever you are thinking, it won't work."

Lore detested that he was right.

Loathed that Syrelle seemed to have an endless well of *Source*— that she was not yet strong enough to defeat him. Another reason why she needed *Auroradel*. Another reason why she had to find it first.

Using his resources was the best way to make that happen.

Her defiance deflated. She placed the grimoire on the table and sat back down in the chair.

"Thank you. Now, back to work, dawn is approaching," Syrelle said as he took his seat across from her.

"Promise me that you won't hurt Finndryl," Lore whispered. She couldn't bear the thought of him being hurt because she'd been stupid enough to get herself into this predicament. She couldn't bear the thought of him being hurt, period.

"You have my word."

His word amounted to shit. But she would have to believe him for now, or she would go mad.

Lore bit her lip, something gnawing at her from the conversation before she'd blown up. "What in gods' name is a 'Takuma'?"

Syrelle rubbed his eyes in a frustrated motion. "If I appease your curiosity, will you scry without any more delay?"

She nodded.

"Takuma is a mythical sea beast. It's said to be larger than the span of three ships but more cunning than a sea snake."

"And this 'Dread Abyss' business?" Lore pointed below them, toward the water, the ocean. "This is where it dwells?"

Syrelle's lips thinned even as he avoided looking at her. He didn't like to look at her, she'd noticed. Whereas Asher had always sought out her face . . . for understanding, to make sure she was all right, or just to share a secret, intimate glance.

The male before her hadn't properly looked at her since that first interaction on the ship. Was he ashamed of his betrayal? Or was the change because he'd ceased pretending to care for her? She wished he would look at her properly, if only to feel the fury in her gaze.

"Don't fret about the moniker. Our ships have crossed the Dread Abyss many times before, and only the most sea-addled sailors admit to seeing anything even resembling the beast. It is widely known that Takuma is simply a legend." He waved his hand through the air in a dismissive manner. "Scholars chalk it up to too much booze, lack of citrus, mold growing in their food storage, or the like." He pushed the bowl toward her, his movements agitated, and some of the water spilled over the shallow lip of the bowl to puddle on his desk. "Now, quit worrying about mythical sea monsters and focus."

Lore placed her hands beside the spill, ignoring the bowl of water, continuing to study Syrelle. She could tell that her gaze made him feel uncomfortable. She liked that. He deserved to feel uncomfortable for the rest of his days.

"Oh, I'm not vexed by a sea monster, mythical or otherwise. The only monsters that concern me are on this ship."

Syrelle's jaw began to twitch. "Scry, Lore."

Lore was about to comply when her hand accidentally brushed the open grimoire, and her head was jerked backward, the sharp edge of a knife pressed to the delicate skin of her throat.

"Don't even think about it, you little horror."

Lore clenched her teeth, wanting to jerk away from vile Thadrik's grip. Syrelle's second-in-command reminded Lore of a boy she'd grown up with who loved to sprinkle precious salt onto slugs just to watch them bubble up, writhing in agony until their eventual death.

"If you so much as brush one of those pages with your foul fingers, it will be your blood that gives them color, not witch ink," he said, his foul breath wafting over her, making her want to gag, though she didn't dare even swallow with his knife poised so close to her artery.

Witch.

It's what the guards and sailors had begun to call her. That or *abomination.*

Desecration.

Evil.

They knew she was a human with magic, something that, in their opinions, shouldn't exist. It was just another fallacious reason for the fae to despise her, not for her deeds but for *what* she was.

To them, she wasn't just a lowly human, but a criminal. One who had committed the most heinous of crimes: discovered a way to pull herself above her "station" by pilfering magic, a resource that should only belong to, well, anyone else, they didn't care who, as long as it wasn't her kind that benefited from it.

The guard was everything bad about the Alytherians compiled into one hideous package. She couldn't see his face, but she knew his thin lips would be pulled into a sneer at just the thought of being allowed the pleasure of killing her. The male itched to do more than that. He made it clear any time he escorted her from her rooms to Syrelle's quarters, describing in horrible detail how much he would love to carve her up and feed her to the fishes.

He was sadistic.

And Syrelle had no qualms about him threatening Lore with violence.

"Stand down, Thadrik. She won't touch the grimoire again." Syrelle sounded bored.

At the word of his overlord, Thadrik lowered the blade and backed up a single step. He may be a creep, but he appeared to be loyal to Syrelle, despite Syrelle's insistence that all the guards aboard the *Lavender Lark* had been appointed by the king.

Thadrik backing up one step was not enough. Lore wished he would back up another step. Or five. Hundred. He could just keep walking until he dropped off the ship, and then he would still not be far enough.

There was a time when Asher would have sent Thadrik out of Lore's presence simply because the male made her anxious. Asher would make sure Lore never had to suffer Thadrik's threats. But this wasn't Asher. This was Syrelle. He neither noticed nor cared that Thadrik's very presence made her skin crawl.

Syrelle had only one thing on his mind.

Auroradel.

Lore pressed her fingers to her throat and rubbed where the sensation of the blade lingered. Thadrik was practiced with his knives and hadn't broken skin—because he hadn't wanted to—but still she felt the presence of the knife as though he had. Lore gritted out between clenched teeth, "Maybe if you let me hold my grimoire, then my scrying would work."

Syrelle's expression remained impassive. Lore knew it must be a mask. He wore his apathy like armor.

"I've seen you do magic with the book concealed in your pack—farther away than it is now. You can do it."

"I can't! That was a matter of life or dea—"

"This is a matter of life or death!" Syrelle shouted, his apathetic mask cracking as he slammed his palm onto the desk. Lore flinched. "What do you think will happen to Duskmere if Coretha has her way and convinces the king to crown her as heir? Finding *Auroradel* for me is the best chance your people have."

Lore sucked her teeth. "Perfect. My people being in your hands makes me feel *so* much better."

Lore was tired of resisting. It always came to this point, anyway. Syrelle gave commands. She defied his orders for most of the night, but she always relented. She couldn't resist the pull of doing magic for long.

She picked the bowl up off the desk and gingerly rested it upon her lap. Whoever oversaw filling the wooden bowl had overfilled it today.

Lore cleared her thoughts of all that was wrong with this situation (everything) and concentrated on finding the one thing they both wanted: *Auroradel*.

She harnessed her magic, focusing on the warmth coiled within her. That delightful gathering of *Source* had become so familiar to her that in the morning when *Deeping Lune*'s power banked, or when she was locked in her room and *Deeping Lune* was with Syrelle under lock and key . . . she felt lacking, deficient, wrong. She yoked the magic, *her* magic, let it pool within her, though it was harder to come, weaker than when she held the grimoire in her grasp and held an image of what she thought the other grimoire might look like, feel like, be like.

Within her mind's eye she saw dreamlike glimpses of loving hands sewing the bindings of two books with silken thread infused with *Source*. Scarred hands pressed to pages, their fingers appearing to be dipped in ink, mirrors of Lore's own. But these were not Lore's hands. Not her *Source* flowing into the pages.

She immediately recognized one of the books, her grimoire, *Deeping Lune*. Its binding was already completed, the stitching of flowers and moons gleaming in the light from some nearby window just out of sight, brand new. The other, thicker tome was *Auroradel*.

Made by the same alchemist. Infused with the same *Source* that was even now stirring within her chest, flowing through her veins, making her magic shimmer and glow.

Lore held the vision within her mind, freezing it like a painting, arresting this moment from another time, and compelled it toward the water in the wooden bowl. Willing the shimmering pool to still. The surface to become a mirror. No, a window, a vessel to look through, to the other side.

Show her not where the book had been, but where it was now.

Lore's mouth went dry as she looked through the surface, through the window, and saw . . . nothing.

There was nothing there, it was as though the book only existed in the past.

She'd seen this before when she'd tried to look and had given up. But Syrelle was right, if Coretha became heir and reigned over the people of Duskmere, things would be worse.

So she looked back at the nothingness, trying to push it aside, move through it maybe . . . and that was when she realized, it was not that there was nothing there . . . there was something.

Darkness.

Lore thought she'd known darkness.

When the moon was new, the fires banked, and the earth shrouded in night. But this darkness was unknown to her. An absolute dark so deep it seemed this place had never known the concept of light.

She pushed further into it.

Cold.

It was cold here. Despite it being insubstantial, as if it were happening within her memory, goosebumps erupted on her flesh, her physical body reacting to this other place as if she were truly there.

She swallowed, trying to moisten her dry mouth, tasting metallic rock upon her tongue. She smelled something damp and rotting. Mold maybe? Ancient. She tilted her head at a sound. There was a scratching beneath her. Little claws from a darkling creature skittering over rock. She heard the sound of water—was that outside the ship or here with her on this other, dark plane?

But the moment she focused on the smell, the taste—it dissipated, slipping through her fingers like sand beneath a strong river current.

A bead of sweat dripped into the bowl, breaking the spell.

She glanced up at Syrelle where he sat with his head in his hands, his shoulders hunched.

Lore would catch him sometimes raising his hand to tap on antlers that weren't there. Reaching for fluffed curls to pull into a bun.

As if he himself forgot who he was at times.

"It's almost dawn. We will try again in the evening. Thadrik, have Cecil escort Lore back to her cabin."

"Yes, Commander."

Cecil. Lore might be able to see the sunrise from the deck today, then.

Cecil, a guard with floppy rabbit ears, was Lore's least hated guard. The quiet female didn't have much to say, and despite being mostly kind, to Lore's chagrin, she wouldn't take Lore to see Finndryl, or tell her where he was or how he was doing, but she did bring Lore topside some days. Mostly, unlike the others, she didn't call her "witch," and Lore appreciated her for that.

Lore followed the guard, who was short by fae standards—only a few inches taller than she—down the corridor. Cecil may be short, but she more than made up for it with muscle honed from years of practicing with the intimidating sword hanging from her hip. The two arrived at the fork—turn this way for Lore's cabin and a locked door, or continue straight, toward the sunrise. Lore hesitated. Cecil turned to look, her eyes scanning Lore's face.

Pity for the hated human girl shone in her overly large eyes, though Cecil tried to conceal it.

"Would you like to go up on the deck today?"

"That would be lovely." Lore tried to sound calm, and not at all desperate, though she was. *Desperate*, that is.

Lore's childhood had been spent exploring the thicket of woods within the borders of Duskmere. Catching frogs on the lake's edge.

Rolling down the grassy hill until her skirts were green, her hair filled with leaves and twigs and petals. She wasn't meant to be locked in a room all day, only brought out at night to stare into a bowl of water.

Then again, she didn't think anyone was made for this life. It was unnatural. Terrible.

Please take her above. Let her feel the sun on her face, the breeze in her hair.

"All right, but if the crew starts to grumble, back to your quarters right away; I don't want to cause any trouble."

"Won't be any trouble; right back down as soon as you say the word."

The guard nodded more to herself than to Lore and absently adjusted the belt on her waist.

Lore sighed with relief when Cecil turned away from the room with the lock and toward the stairs leading to the rising sun.

The sound of flapping sails met Lore on deck, and her breath caught in her throat. Stepping onto the deck . . . she didn't see how she could ever get used to it. It set her heart racing, her fingertips tingling. Falling off the ship, she'd realized . . . well, the fright of it would kill her before she drowned.

Lore surveyed the deck, pushing her fear *down, down, down* so that she could enjoy this time outdoors. Mist surrounded the ship as dawn broke across the horizon. Damp, languid air played with Lore's curls listlessly.

Two sailors were cleaning the deck with seawater, but when Lore passed them, they both halted their mops mid-swab to glower, their eyes shooting hateful daggers at her. Even the watch, a lanky male at the top of the foremast with a wide jaw and thick, chin-length locs, took his eyes off the horizon to watch her, his body language sending signals of revulsion from his great height.

Lore avoided looking too long at them because, as she'd discovered, a single glance from her would have them muttering prayers and hurriedly making signs to their preferred gods to ward against evil, corruption, or whatever they thought a look from her would do to them.

And that would alarm Cecil, who would make her turn around and return to that locked door.

So, Lore passed by them, trying to make herself small, and pretended not to see their glares.

Lore squeezed in between barrels tied down to the deck, stepped over coiled ropes and carefully stowed netting, and braced her elbows upon the thick railing. She leaned over the rail, still amazed by how elevated from the water they really were. This ship was massive and artfully designed. It required a crew she guessed of at least twenty-five or thirty, but she hadn't had a chance to count, what with not being able to look directly at the sailors.

Lore eyed the water.

This stretch of sea was rightly called the Dread Abyss. The water, no longer the cerulean she'd grown used to, resembled a wine so dark it appeared almost black. A sea of bloodred glass, the only ripples created by the ship itself as the prow cut through the sea.

The water was as red as Queen Riella's poisoned wine.

Lore shivered, averting her gaze.

She chose to look at one puffy cloud instead. At least then, she could pretend she was lying on her back in Duskmere, the familiar press of trees surrounding her. Though they had come to be a prison as she'd gotten older, the trees were all she'd known, and as a child, they were a comfort.

Here she was exposed for miles and miles to emptiness.

And if she were back in Duskmere, there wouldn't possibly be a sea beast called Takuma swimming beneath her, waiting to swallow the ship whole.

Lore could hear the crew growing restless.

It was only a matter of moments before Cecil would heed the sailors' grumbling, the whispers of *witch* that circled Lore like a flock of vultures trailing an injured animal belowdecks.

She dropped her eyes back down from the too-big sky. It made her feet tingle in fright. It was so big that she felt she was going to tumble off the ship, but instead of landing in the water, she would fall up toward the sky, and it would swallow her whole. She closed her eyes to its vastness and tried to ignore the hateful whispers of the sailors, pretending to be anywhere but here.

She felt Cecil's presence behind her.

Lore opened her eyes. Plucking damp curls from her cheeks, she pushed them behind her ears.

It would rain soon.

Lore wished the dawn had brought with it burnished orange and apple pink. But it had turned now into a gray morning, and even with the rising sun, it wasn't likely to allow much color.

Lore pushed back from the ship's railing and walked back toward the entrance belowdecks before Cecil gave the order.

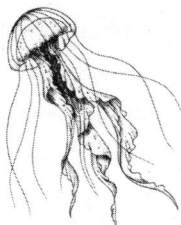

CHAPTER 3

For all of Cecil's kindness, the guard still slammed the door to Lore's chambers and latched the lock to her nautical prison with a decisive click.

Loneliness rolled over Lore, an oppressive pang that crammed itself into the hole her magic left behind.

She'd been away from home for too long. Her loneliness was palpable. She'd never felt this isolated in her life. As a child, Mama was always a few steps away. When she was older, and Mama and Baba were gone, Grey was there. And if not Grey, then any of the kiddos at the shelter, Aunty Eshe, or Uncle Salim. When she turned twenty and moved out of the shelter and into the attic above the apothecary, she may have had a few hours between obligations where she was alone . . . but then, she'd never felt loneliness.

Lore's entire life . . . being alone was a prize, rarely tasted.

Now, she would do anything to be surrounded by loved ones, even the young ones fighting and screaming. Or . . . gods, even just being near someone who wasn't using her or actively wishing she were dead.

The washbasin had been cleaned and replaced while Lore was with Syrelle. She splashed cool water onto swollen, bloodshot eyes before pressing her face into a fluffy towel that smelled of lavender and rosehips.

A tray of food and drink was set out on the table. She drank the cider in one go. Immediately, the effects of the cider warmed her belly and dulled the unsettled impression lingering from the wine-red sea of the Dread Abyss.

Lore wondered what Aunty Eshe, Uncle Salim, and the kiddos were doing in this moment, though it hurt to think of them. Hopefully, the babies were letting everyone sleep, as the day had barely begun.

Lore chewed on a slice of dried apricot and forced it down, wishing she had more cider. Her appetite fled the moment she'd awoken on the *Lavender Lark*, along with her ability to sleep, and more cider would probably remedy at least one of those problems.

Maybe she could ask Cecil for another cup; she was likely posted on the other side of the door, keeping watch. *Eh*, she couldn't be bothered. Begging a favor through a locked door was humiliating.

Lore lay back on the bed, fists clasping the quilt.

A few months ago, Lore risked everything by entering the cursed library in order to rebuild a devastated, shattered Duskmere. Now, rebuilding was the last thing she would do. When Lore led her people from their prison, she would light a fire and burn that slum and all the horrible memories to the ground.

They would settle far away from any fae—and if the walls they built weren't enough to keep them out, she would spend her life setting wards and spells that would do it. The humans of Duskmere would never be plagued by the fae again.

She turned on her side, pulling her knees up to her chest. Restless, she turned again onto her back, biting her lip. She hated this feeling of helplessness. Of not being in control.

Maybe tonight, when she was brought to Syrelle's office and forced to scry, she would pick up her grimoire again. Only this time, she wouldn't hesitate; she would utter a single word and eviscerate Syrelle with moonlight.

Then what, Thadrik would stab her in the throat?

Or worse, make good on his threats and take his time carving her up before tossing chunks of her into the sea? And anyway, if she killed Syrelle, what would happen to Finndryl? Thadrik would probably kill Finn in front of her before setting in on her.

But what if she killed Thadrik too?

Lore raised her hands up, palms facing the ceiling, and wiggled her fingers.

Her fingertips were still stained black with ink or magic, or whatever it was that had gotten inside her when she'd made the deal with the grimoire. Free the grimoire from Wyndlin Castle and be gifted with magic. The grimoire had made good on its bargain; it had given her the ability to harness the power of moonlight, the knowledge to craft potions and cast spells. But that magic had left its mark on her, staining her fingertips a deep black, which now had bled like ink covering her palm and the backs of her hands, stretching up her wrists. Lore didn't mind it so much; in fact, it was growing on her.

Let the power stain her hands, her arms, her face; what did she care, if she could only wield it?

She imagined calling on her power now. Remembering how it had felt that first time she had used this gift to drown those guards in moonlight. To direct it into them, down their throats while they clawed at their skin with bloodied fingernails. She could do that again. All she would need to do was touch the grimoire.

But no.

Lore snapped her hands into fists.

She would be more likely to blast a hole in the ship than to direct the power where she wanted it to go. And then she would have to search the entire ship for Finndryl. And if she didn't find him in time? Finndryl would drown. And then, so would she.

Of course, even if she managed to locate him, how could she repair the ship—after vanquishing guards and crew?

It wasn't like the two of them could flee or swim to safety. They were in the middle of the ocean. There were a few rowboats secured to the side of the ship, but . . . what had Syrelle said? Takuma would eat them, rowboat and all. With her luck, she couldn't trust that the monster was truly a myth.

Regardless, she didn't know where they were. She peered through the window at the endless wine-stained sea.

A glimmer of silver flashed in the water.

A curious whale? She'd seen one two days ago, heard its mournful cry even through the walls of the ship. In another life, Lore might have marveled at the splendor of a being so vast choosing to share its song with her. But in this life, she didn't have it in her. To marvel.

No, she would have to think of another tactic to find Finn.

Then maybe she would be able to sleep again.

She slid the curtains closed, the thick fabric blocking out the light completely. Syrelle must have requested the curtains specifically because he knew they would be awake every night, only sleeping during the days. Lore had not lit the oil lamp, nor the candles. She closed her eyes to the darkness. Her body longed for sleep, yet her mind was a millstone incessantly turning anxious, fretful thoughts, grinding serenity to a fine dust.

Her bed was clean and comfortable. Almost *too* comfortable; she'd never slept in a bed filled with down feathers before. She was used to straw shoved into a cloth sack, changed out a few times a year before it got moldy, if she was lucky.

Syrelle must have given her one of the best suites on the ship, but the sentiment was empty.

What was Finndryl's room like? Was his bed also too comfortable? Or did they have him chained somewhere in the belly of the ship? Had he, too, been able to see the sunrise?

Lore flicked the curtain open to let in a bit of light and pushed off the bed.

She couldn't sleep.

She might as well continue plotting how to reach Finndryl.

Especially with Coretha threatening him today. Lore had lost it when Coretha had considered hurting Finn to get to her. She'd actually held the grimoire! She'd been so upset, so irate, she hadn't realized in time what that meant. She'd wasted an opportunity— maybe she could've kept ahold of it, continued to threaten them, make them bring her to Finn. But she hadn't been thinking clearly, obviously, and when Coretha had ceased threatening him and left . . . Lore had been so relieved, she'd just placed *Deeping Lune* back on Syrelle's oversize monstrosity of a desk.

And Syrelle hadn't even threatened her! She'd just placed it down like it was a plate and she'd eaten all the tasty food off it!

Lore heaved a frustrated huff through her nose and began to pace, following a path in the rug she'd worn in days ago.

She was beginning to think she'd had a spell cast on her when she'd left Duskmere, skewing her reality. Or maybe it was when she'd entered the library. Or was it when she'd made the bargain? Had that been the true price she had to pay, for power? The alteration of her sanity? Because when she really stopped to think of every fucked-up thing about her current circumstances and that it was all because of him . . . Syrelle . . . she couldn't fathom how she'd let herself fall for Asher.

She must have imagined everything with him . . .

The market that first time, when he'd introduced her to his favorite food. She remembered the taste of those dumplings. He'd enjoyed sharing his food with her, so much so that he had given her his portion. The kind way he spoke to Tarun and Libb. The swing. Laughing over godsdamned lemon tarts. That time in the woods when he taught her to use a dagger. His hand on her hip.

A traitorous tear slid down her cheek. She brushed it away with a harsh motion.

"No, choose anger, Lore," she whispered to herself, clenching her fist against her mouth to stifle a sob.

She would not cry for Asher—for Syrelle. She would not mourn his death. For that's what it felt like. Like her friend was dead. And in his place was a shape-shifting demon from the old tales.

Had she been so desperate to be liked and accepted by one of the fae that she'd imagined the warmth in his smile? His lips against hers? The way it felt to be pressed against him, his weight pushing against her so hard—like he'd needed to feel her. Be close to her.

That last night in the Exile. His mouth on her, tasting, devouring, making her feel better than she ever had in her life. *A work of art*, he'd called her.

And then . . . that last lingering kiss by the tower. He'd clung to her, as if her lips were a source of life itself.

Lore heaved a cry. It escaped out of her, bypassing the fist pressed to her lips to stifle her sobs.

She'd really believed him. It had been a lie. Worse than a lie . . . deception, a cruel, abysmal trick. She'd been so stupid. Naive. Desperate.

And yet . . . yet it had felt so right. His lips on hers—him being on her side.

She would give anything to go back there, to the time before she learned the truth about him.

Before she ever saw Asher in his garden.

CHAPTER 4

Lore despised the salt-kissed trails on her cheeks. Another day, drowned in sorrow until exhaustion finally pulled her under, though her dreams were haunted by the echo of her own sobs. She was almost glad when, like clockwork, the staccato knock came at her door, jolting her awake.

Moonrise. Time to return to Syrelle's quarters and scry for *Auroradel*.

Cecil brought with her a slight smile tinged with sadness, coffee with too much milk, and a dragonberry tart for Lore to eat on the way.

Cook was wasted in the galley of her enemies' ship; the flaky, buttery pastry of the tart had the perfect amount of dragonberry jam baked into it. The tiny, jewellike berries tended to be too sweet, but Lore could taste lemon juice, which added the perfect balance. The tart was dusted with lemon zest and sugar so soft it puffed like powdered snow.

Lore only wished she had an appetite.

She downed the coffee as she entered Syrelle's quarters and dropped the tart, unfinished, into the rubbish bin.

Syrelle's office was bright today. The moon had been slowly waxing, and now, it swelled in the sky, full and brilliant, casting its light into the room with pride. Lore's magic was strongest when the moon was full. Syrelle knew that. His face wore that apathetic mask she'd come to hate, but the impatient tap of his polished boot showed that he was eager to put that strength to the test.

The grimoire sat open before her.

Syrelle had removed the bandages from his fingers, the burns having healed since last night. Too bad. Maybe Lore could trick him into burning himself again. Just so he could feel a little of the pain he'd inflicted on her.

The scrying bowl sat before her with fresh water, and beside it was a portable apothecary chest filled with herbs. Anything that Lore needed to help her find *Auroradel*.

"Take me to Finn," Lore said as she dropped into the chair.

"Don't start. Not tonight."

"Yes, tonight. Where are you keeping him?"

"As I've said before, he's comfortable. In a room just as nice as yours."

"He's well-fed and healthy enough to have put one of my guards in the infirmary just this morning trying to leave his room to find you," Thadrik the Despicable volunteered from his usual position behind Lore.

"Hush," Syrelle snapped at Thadrik. His mask faltered, and he grimaced, clearly not liking that his second had given something away.

Had he? Given something away?

Doubt clouded Lore's mind. She questioned everything now. She couldn't help but worry that she'd imagined it all with Finndryl too.

These dark thoughts that had swirled within her since Asher's betrayal were inescapable.

But Thadrik had said that Finndryl was fighting to see her. Relief glazed her trepidations. This was proof that she hadn't imagined it. He cared for her. Just because she had been hurt didn't mean that Finndryl would hurt her too.

She wouldn't let Syrelle's darkness taint her friendship with Finn . . .

"This won't do. We are running out of time, Lore." Syrelle was annoyed.

"You say that like there is a *we*. There is no longer a *we* or an *us*." She relented for now. "Pass me the bowl."

Syrelle's eyes flicked away from the point on the wall he preferred to stare at when he spoke to her, and begrudgingly met her own. Lore had to withhold a gasp. He hadn't properly looked at her since that first day on the ship, and now, in the light of the full moon, she realized why.

His eyes were the same as Asher's.

Looking at them, within them, she could almost believe that it was Asher peering back at her right now.

Doubt once again filled her mind, her heart.

Was Syrelle's apathetic mask the lie?

Was he pretending to be aloof and uncaring for the sake of Coretha, the spy? His deal with the king? She imagined that Syrelle would have been endangered by the king because of his feelings for her. For what had bloomed between them over the months they'd spent with each other.

But even if that was the case, even if knowledge of their bond, the depth to it, had been discovered and the king threatened Syrelle with death for caring for a human, that was no excuse.

He should *never* have kissed her.

Never pretended to be there for her if he was going to turn on her all along. Lock her in a prison—more lovely than the one she'd grown up in—but a prison all the same.

Even if . . . she reminded herself . . . even if his feelings for her had grown despite his true nature . . .

Syrelle had used Lore from the start.

From the first moment he had seen her in the apothecary, he had manipulated her. Perhaps that alone she could have forgiven.

But since the day he had chosen to appear as Asher, to lie to her, betray her—how genuine could those feelings truly be, when they had bloomed from the rot of his own greed? Any affection he had shown her, any feelings he may have felt, were forever coated with the bitter tang of his own selfish desires.

Lore, despite the reality of her situation, wanted to believe that the Syrelle version of himself was the lie. That he was treating her with indifference so that Coretha couldn't use it against him; after all, that would only further hurt his desire to beat her out as heir.

Lore wanted more than anything for Asher to be his true self—the joyful, teasing male who cared for his friends and knew what it was to be trod upon by those born to privilege. But that version of him could not coexist with the one that plucked a human from her home and thrust her into jeopardy all for his own gain, not caring if it consumed her in the process.

Anger seethed within Lore, swirling, smoking, choking her from the inside out. She didn't want to feel this anymore. She had to stop thinking of *why* Syrelle had done what he did.

It would drive her to madness.

She could no more comprehend the cruelty of his mind than the fledgling bird when the cat killed it for sport.

She needed to focus on what she *could* change.

Getting to Finn, finishing the path she'd started, and acquiring the second book before Syrelle. Those she could do, because she had no other choice. Failure was not an option.

She didn't know how she would manage it, but she knew with certainty that she could not let an Alytherian bond to *Auroradel* and harness its might.

She blocked out the sight of Syrelle's ticking jaw, his familiar gaze, and Thadrik's heavy, irritating breathing in the corner behind her, where she knew he stood across from his commander, itching to use his knife on her.

She focused on memories of Finndryl.

On his rare, crooked smile. His graceful hands as he chopped ginger, placing a piece on his tongue to savor while he worked. The sway of his locs with each practiced movement of the knife. How he looked in the dappled light of his favorite place, the Wilds, behind his house. The way Finndryl's face softened, *almost* vulnerable, as he dozed with his head propped on his crossed arms while Lore foraged close by for herbs and mushrooms.

Always close by, Finndryl wouldn't let her stray far—worried about her, though he'd never confess to it.

The sensation of his muscled shoulder pressed to hers.

His low, rumbling voice weaving stories while she burned with fever, freeing her from the poisons' nightmares.

Good girl. Her abdomen clenched as she remembered his praise in the woods.

The scrying magic took hold, and Lore was no longer gazing at a bowl of water in her hands, nor at a mirror or more accurately, a window. Her magic, kindled by the feeling of being close to Finn, protected by Finn . . . Lore tumbled into the bowl itself, her consciousness separating from her body entirely, moving through the water as if she were spectral, a ghost.

Separated from her physical self, she cast her awareness throughout the ship; surprise flicked through her as she felt the presence of many people. A few gathered in the galley for dinner; more lounged on hammocks in what she assumed was either the barracks for the guards or the lodgings of the sailors, she couldn't be sure—they were strangers to her, and their forms were obscure, unclear, as if she could see their shadows but not who cast them.

She moved on, pushing past the sleeping forms, moving through a few storage rooms, the armory, and then she felt a tug of something familiar.

She sniffed. Smelling spice, the hint of something smoky like whiskey or aged bourbon. She pulled on that thread and grasped hold of it with her mind, this thread that she and Finn had built fiber by fiber as they'd laughed and worked in the tavern, weaving themselves together. Round and round the loom the thread looped, until, when they fought, united in the tower, it had tied itself into a knot, binding them.

She followed the thread down yet another level. It seemed as though Yissa, the trickster god, had designed this ship, with its twisting corridors and seemingly endless levels. Until finally—*there!*

His form was not shadowy or hazy; he blazed with a sunlike brightness that astonished Lore—warming her from the inside out. Finally, she saw him, clear as day.

Lore could cry.

Finn was safe. Whole.

Here.

CHAPTER 5

Sweat glistened on Finndryl's bare shoulders and back, contouring each corded and flexing muscle, illuminating the power in their every ripple, a testament to the raw strength he wielded with each deliberate movement. Finndryl held on to one of the wooden beams slatted across the low ceiling of his room, suspending in the air with just the grip of his hands for leverage as he pulled himself up again and again.

Lore's gaze swept over him hungrily, greedy to see that he was alive and really, truly, here on this ship with her. The vision of him was sharp, vibrant, as though she were standing in the room with him.

His ankles were crossed, and his black pants, woven from thin cloth, did nothing to conceal the outline of his muscular thighs.

Lore had never done a pull-up in her life, not successfully, anyway. Finndryl was lifting himself, then dropping low, slow, controlled, and then drawing himself up again with ease as if he weren't a ridiculously tall, *heavy* fae male.

Finn, Lore said. But not out loud. Her lips, which felt far away and insubstantial, did not move.

She spoke directly into his mind.

Finndryl tensed, every muscle in his body freezing for an instant before he loosened his grip on the wooden rafter and—graceful as a panther—dropped to the floor.

He turned around and—his face, gods, his face was the *same*. The familiar face that she remembered, lovely lips drawn into a frown, brows furrowed, eyes clever and haunted—twin lakes of ink so black they threatened to drown her.

Relief flooded through her, washing away the tension that had been a constant, gnawing companion for days, even clinging to her in this ethereal state.

But his eyes did not meet her own—he cast his gaze around the room, searching. He couldn't see her.

He was barefoot. Lore had never seen him barefoot before, and something about it was so . . . intimate. More intimate than seeing him without a shirt for the first time.

If she had been in her body, she would have blushed.

"Lore? What is this?" he said aloud. His eyes narrowed in suspicion. He was probably wondering if this was a cruel trick.

It's me. I am scrying, like we used to practice in the Wilds.

"How is this possible?" Finndryl took a hesitant step forward, still searching the room, the walls, as if she were hiding behind them.

It's a new trick I've learned. Like it?

"Depends on how long you've been spying on me." His lips quirked upward into a smirk. "It's not very fair, I should like to see you too."

I haven't been spying on you! Not for very long . . . *Besides, I don't have time to spy on you even if I was inclined to do so. I don't have long as it is; I am scrying for . . . him. Looking for the twin book to my grimoire,* Auroradel. She thought of something. *I think if you think what you should like to say back to me, I might be able to hear it.*

Finndryl looked dubious, but his eyebrows drew together in concentration, and then she heard him. *Are you safe? Has he hurt you?* The last question came through as a growl somehow, even though it was in Lore's head. *I'll kill him if he has.* That was not a threat; it was a promise.

I'm safe. No, he hasn't hurt me. She added bitterly, *Well, unless you count my pride . . . How are you? I didn't believe them when they told me you were unharmed. I'm glad to see he wasn't lying about this, at least. Are you okay?*

Finndryl dropped onto the bench at the foot of his bed, flicking his locs behind him. Lore tore her gaze away from his abdominal muscles, studying the room. Finn's room was smaller than hers, or maybe that was his immense size making it look so. Furnished nicely, it felt comfortable. As comfortable as a prison could be. He had no windows, but he had plenty of candles to see by.

Don't worry about me. I'm golden.

Lore pressed insubstantial palms to her eyes as relief swept through her body at just hearing that he was doing well. *I'm so glad to hear that . . . and also incredibly sorry that I got you entangled in this mess.*

Finndryl sat forward, his expression stern. *Don't apologize. None if this is your fault.*

Lore clasped her hands together. *I mean, I don't feel right not taking any responsibility. You were only in that garden because—*

—because I chose to be. You are not to blame. The only one responsible for this is him. He clenched his jaw for a moment, the anger within him flaring in his eyes. *Blame Asher.*

Lore nodded, though Finn couldn't see her. *I wish Asher were real, so I could blame him.*

Right. I wonder what my sister will say when she learns the truth about her closest "friend."

I wouldn't want to be on the other side of Isla's wrath. Lore imagined it would be every bit as potent as her joy.

Syrelle is in for a surprise, I think . . . So, this is what magic feels like? Conversing from within one's own mind?

Well, this is new for me but . . . yes. Lore cocked her head to the side. *Didn't you go to school for alchemy? Can't you . . . do magic?*

She thought back to their time at the tavern. Gryph, his father, had definitely possessed simple earthen magic. He used it in so many inconsequential ways, as the fae did. But neither Finn nor Isla had ever used magic in front of her, not even when Finndryl was battling in the tower or in the aftermath, in the garden when Asher had morphed into Syrelle and overpowered them. Lore had wondered about this, back in the Exile, but it seemed rude to pry . . . back then. Finn was such a private person, and she hadn't had a chance to ask Isla before she left. Something had changed, though; maybe it was that they both had the shock of their lives together in the garden, maybe it was their time in the tower, battling together . . . or maybe it was just that he was Finn . . . and she felt comfortable now, asking him.

Finn shook his head. *Actually, Isla and I had our magic taken from us before we were born, the consequence of a blood curse placed on my grandfather. None born of his line will ever wield power.*

Oh gods. A blood curse . . . Lore hadn't realized that was something that could even happen. It sounded awful. Violent. *I am so sorry that you and Isla had this happen to you. I wish I had known . . . I feel terrible for even asking.*

No need to be sorry. How could you have known, when I don't talk about it? I wasted years of my life searching for ways to break the curse. It's why I broke into the Edgemoor Academy library . . . When I was caught, my true lineage was discovered, and I was kicked out of the university.

Sounds like another reason to find Auroradel. *I wonder if it could break the curse,* Lore wondered.

Hmm. Maybe. Finn didn't sound like he thought it would. Then again, maybe he'd given up hope long ago to stop himself from being disappointed when nothing worked. Lore knew what it was like to live in a world where most had magic, and to be without it. She felt for him. For Isla. She wanted to ask why their family had been cursed, but now wasn't the time.

I can't stay long, but I'll be back around moonrise tomorrow. Lore peeked at him through her lashes, suddenly shy even though he couldn't see her. *If you want me to, that is.*

Of course I do. Finndryl's eyes glimmered with mirth as he waved a hand across his bare chest. *I'll make sure to be wearing clothes.*

She wanted to say: Please don't.

Lore wasn't quite ready to leave yet . . . even though she needed to scry for *Auroradel. I'm surprised you don't hate me,* Lore confessed, the words coming out quick and breathless, even though they were spoken from her mind.

Do you want me to hate you? He arched an eyebrow.

No, I just . . . I know you told me it's not my fault you are trapped on this ship . . . but I can't help but feel like you are full of shit. It is my fault. I've brought nothing but bad luck since I met you.

Don't worry, Alemeyu. If I didn't choose to be here, I wouldn't be. He leaned back onto his bed, resting his head on his arms crossed at the nape of his neck. *I'm just biding my time until we dock next. I have a plan to free us, just waiting on one more piece to fall into place.*

What piece?

Cecil, the female guard, has a kind heart—

Lore leaned forward. *Cecil, she's my favorite guard. Makes you wonder how she ended up on this ship with the rest of these degenerates.*

I wonder that too; the rest of the guards seemed to be handpicked for their depravity. Finn smirked. *I'm hoping that with just a little more time, she will see reason—or at the very least, maybe I can convince her to leave my door unlocked . . .*

No, don't do anything! I've got a plan. Sort of. I need to stay on the ship until we find the book he's searching for.

I just hope you aren't looking for Auroradel *on my account. The only reason I'm still here is because it will be easier for us to escape once we've reached land.*

No, trust me. I need the book for more nefarious reasons than rescuing you. She felt her lips frown, though her physical body was far away still. Just because *she* needed to stay on the ship didn't mean that he must. Though she hated the idea of him leaving her here. Gods, was she really such a selfish person that it pained her to even think of being trapped here alone? Of course, she wanted him to be free from here . . . but the thought of being without him also terrified her at the same time.

Lore heaved a sigh. She had to tell him that he need not feel beholden to her. If he could convince Cecil to free him . . . then who was she to keep him here? *Finn . . . don't stay on my account, though . . . if you have the opportunity, you should absolutely—*

Finn slashed his hand through the air, cutting her off. *Hush, Alemeyu. I'm not leaving you.* There was the hint of his crooked smile. For the first time in weeks, she felt a glimmer of warmth. *If you want us to stay . . . we stay. Enlighten me on your plan, please.*

Far away, Lore could feel Syrelle stirring in his office. *I will, I promise. Just . . . be safe. And no more putting guards into the infirmary.*

Finndryl dropped his jaw in surprise. *You heard about that, did you?*

Yes.

Finndryl shrugged. *He called you a witch, so I broke his jaw.* Finndryl absently rubbed a hand over his knuckles. They were visibly bruised, and a few fresh scabs littered his knuckles.

I've been called worse. Don't let it bother you. I have to go.

Finndryl looked unnerved for a moment. *Lore, check in with me tomorrow.*

I will, if I can . . .

Lore severed the connection and compelled her awareness back toward her physical body. She passed by the faceless forms of strangers, of enemies. Until she saw one form she recognized. *Syrelle.* She wished that she couldn't see him. That he was a stranger to her, a faceless, insignificant form, but there he was. As clear to her as Finndryl had been. He sat at his desk, perusing through what looked to be an old journal, marking something in the margins. He kept glancing up at her, gnawing on his lip in worry, more emotion showing on his face than he'd let her see in weeks.

Lore saw herself, where she sat in front of him. Her hands on the bowl, her eyes squeezed tight, her brows pulled together, strain in her shoulders.

Lore walked toward her body and tapped her own shoulder.

A second later, she was back in her own familiar body. She didn't open her eyes, but she flexed her fingers against the wood of the bowl, feeling the scented oil used to polish it smooth, the few drops of water that had spilled over the lip when she'd pulled it onto her lap, which still coated her fingertips. She concentrated on the sounds in the room with her, focused on her breathing to ground herself to the here, the now.

The physical plane.

Finndryl was here. Finndryl was safe.

Now she could get to work.

She thought of Duskmere. Aunty Eshe, Uncle Salim. Milo, Katu . . . She focused on the love of her people, the strength it gave her, and used it to help her focus on the bowl clenched between her palms. Her eyes were still closed. She couldn't see when the scrying took hold, when the water morphed into a mirror, then a window, but she *felt* it, as the magic poured from within her toward the scrying bowl.

Where are you? You're the last piece to this puzzle. With you I can break the chains holding us back. I can forge a new path for us. Let me find you, please.

She left her body behind once more.

Please, Auroradel. *Show me where you are. I will bind myself to you as I have your sister book.* Lore threw her plea out into the expansive world. Spreading her magic wide. She could feel it breach the hull of the ship, dispersing out across the water, her magic a web of coiling, shimmering threads, spreading, hunting.

Lore cast herself farther out—widening her web until it was more akin to a fishing net.

She lost sight of herself completely, floating above the ship, which looked so small, surrounded by the stretch of moonlit ocean. With reckless abandon, she pushed farther than she ever had before, feeling her breath grow thin. She tasted copper in her mouth, felt the swell of blood in her nose. She urged the threads of her magic to stretch and lengthen. She was pushing herself too far, but she couldn't care about that now.

A trickle of blood slid down past her lips and her chin, dripping into the bowl of water.

I haven't much to give you, but I will give it all, she promised. *Where are you?* she called out.

She sank into the silvery, watery existence of this plane, this other place, until the world around her lost all color.

That same black swath that had consumed the scrying bowl now surrounded her; the pressure of something she did not understand enclosed her mind, pressing into her. Alarmed, she looked around.

There was nothing—just unfathomable darkness.

Lore's spectral form startled, cringing back at the infiltration within her mind. Something was speaking, though, and it was not in a language she knew. She focused on it, fighting the urge to shove it away, out of her head, and claw herself free of this intrusion. But then, the voice changed. She still could not understand what it said, but the cadence changed.

She knew this voice.

It was Mama telling stories of the gods, humming little snippets of a song she'd created as she shucked peas for dinner . . . No, wait. Had she been wrong? Now this cadence . . . this rhythm . . . it was Finndryl reading from an alchemical text, his words a soft purr. Or was it Grey when he told a story, laughing through his fingers, barely able to push the words past his mirth? Now, Uncle Salim was teaching Lore her numbers in that soft-yet-firm voice of his as he slipped hand-carved beads from one side of an abacus to the other. It sounded like Aunty Eshe singing a lullaby to the littles as they burrowed into their blankets, their eyes heavy with sleep.

She relaxed the knot in her shoulders and breathed. She let the words drift through her mind, not straining to understand, just making space for them.

They changed, once more, into her language.

The human language. The one the Alytherians did not like them to speak, and yet it had been the language Lore had heard in the womb. The first tongue she'd understood, the first she'd learned to form in her own mouth.

Where griffin cries pierce the sky, and shadows strike the mountain's heart, here I lie, an earthen hold, in slumber deep, a hidden spark awaits one who dares to seek.

Was this the grimoire or something else, something wicked, answering her call? If she could feel her body, she imagined the hair would be standing up on her arms.

The voice continued.

Where griffin cries pierce the sky, and shadows strike the mountain's heart, here I lie, an earthen hold, in slumber deep, a hidden spark awaits one who dares to seek.

Please do not give me riddles. I am just a person who has not explored much of this world. Can't you show *me where you are?*

A picture formed inside her mind. Or the absence of one, for she was cloaked in utter darkness. She'd seen glimpses of this while scrying when the water in the wooden bowl would turn black as pitch. Blacker than pitch.

But this was different. The vision was pressing into her mind.

Lore flinched backward—or tried to, as she did not have a body to make it happen.

She stirred sluggishly here, too slowly. She was cloaked in darkness, a shock wave of realization as it dawned on her that she could not find her way out.

This darkness was a web. It pressed on her, smothering in its obduracy.

Please stop, I can't bear it.

She tried to protest within her mind, but the darkness leached coherent thought like a fungus.

A parasite.

Lore gasped for breath, phantom chest heaving, but there wasn't enough air to satiate.

Where griffin cries pierce the sky, and shadows strike the mountain's heart, here I lie . . .

The voice continued, repeating the riddle over and over until it grew discordant and deafening. Now the voice had the piercing edge of panic. It was afraid that Lore would not find it, that it would be trapped in this tomb forever.

The impenetrable darkness became tainted with the taste of damp, dank earth. Creatures with hundreds of legs skittered across her skin. She tried to jerk away and brush them off, but her arms wouldn't work; she couldn't do anything at all.

Putrid darkness pressed itself on Lore's tongue. Shoved itself down her throat. Filling her lungs.

She tried to thrash, to brush the creatures from her skin.

This was all in her mind.

Lore could not feel her body, she could not feel her body at all.

What body?

Had she ever had a body?

This was all she knew, this darkness, this was all she'd ever known, these swarming, creeping creatures her only companions. This was all there was, all there had ever been, all there would ever be.

No one was coming to save her . . .

She opened her mouth to scream, not caring if the creatures invaded her. Let them eat her from the inside out, let them end this misery, let them . . .

CHAPTER 6

"**R**eturn to me, Lore."

Lore came to, shaken back to awareness by a pair of elegant hands gripping her shoulders.

Lore screamed, the sound bursting out in a torrent.

She coughed, heaving, gasping, filling her lungs with sweet, fresh air. She breathed in again and again, gulping it down. The more she inhaled, the more her terror subsided, the more aware she became of her current circumstances.

Syrelle's grip was tight on her shoulders, where he'd been shaking her. His eyes were wide, scared. Magic poured out of him in waves, reaching for her, surrounding her. Heat from his fingers burned through the linen of her dress.

This was the first time he'd touched her since *before*.

"Don't touch me." Lore lurched out of his grip.

It wasn't hard. The moment she'd spoken, he'd jerked back himself as if she were her grimoire and had burned him for daring to place his hands upon her.

Lore wished she *had*. Burned him.

She craved seeing him in pain.

She wanted to pull him from his body and send him to that place where she had just been. That dark, horrid place. Lore raised her fingers to her lips. Used the back of her hand to swipe the blood on her face.

She could still taste damp and rot and corrosion on her tongue. She worried she would retch.

"You've been scrying for hours. Your heartbeat slowed; your blood moved sluggishly within your veins. I didn't realize . . . maybe we should find another—"

"No. It's fine!" Lore croaked, as she regarded the room.

The scrying bowl lay turned over across the room as if it had been ripped from her hands and thrown aside. The water seeped into the decorative rug.

"I'm fine." Her voice was raspy, her throat dry. As if she'd been trapped within a desert deprived of water. Or like she'd been shrieking.

Syrelle's hand closed into a fist. "This is too dangerous. You will not scry again, Lore. We will find another way."

She'd had tangible communication with *Auroradel*. It had worked. Syrelle had been right, scrying was her best way to find *Auroradel*.

"I almost had it," she lied.

In truth, it, whatever *it* was, had almost had *her*.

She shivered, thinking of the tales of Brokyr the elders told, the wrathful god who many believed to blame for the humans' exile to this world. He was a devourer, that god. Of hopes. He would eat one's wishes if he heard them before Rahada, his partner, the wish granter, did. As a child, she'd felt entirely composed of dreams and fought her way through many a nightmare with him at the center, always intent on devouring her whole.

This had felt like those dreams—something was trying to consume all that she was.

Syrelle dropped onto his desk and wrapped one arm across his chest, gripping the opposite shoulder. It was almost . . . vulnerable. *Almost.*

"You don't know what you looked like. You were barely *breathing.*

Your body looked empty, like a shell. As if you had traveled so far from yourself, there was a chance you wouldn't—or couldn't—return."

"I *was* far away. Isn't this what you wanted? For me to find 'your' grimoire?"

A muscle twitched in his jaw. "Yes, but not at risk to your life."

Lore huffed. "You pretend to care about my life, why?" She hated herself for asking this, for giving him an opportunity to hurt her with his answer, but she had to know. And then, a thought struck her. Her stomach heaved, and once again she feared she would be sick right here in Syrelle's quarters.

If she died . . . if something happened to her, either while scrying or searching for the book, or . . . wouldn't that mean Syrelle would be able to create a bond with the grimoire himself?

Wasn't she *really* just an obstacle?

His original plan was to take *Deeping Lune* the moment she retrieved it from the library, and yet . . . he had let her keep it. He knew she had found the book he was looking for . . . and he had let her take what she'd thought was a journal to her room. She'd had it for weeks before she'd known the magnitude of what *Deeping Lune* even was. And he'd said . . . he had said back in the garden that he'd *felt* it. The moment *Deeping Lune*, unknowingly hidden beneath her cloak, breached the doors of the library. He'd *known*.

Then, when she'd learned the truth and fled with the book, he'd *met* her in the garden. Led her through the woods. Orchestrated a safe, isolated spot for her . . . encouraged her to build upon her bond with it.

So that she could take from the book exactly what *he'd* wanted.

Its power.

Something wasn't adding up. Why keep her alive at all, when Syrelle bonding with the book would give him what he wanted?

Lore studied the male above her. He looked grim, tired, anxious. The usually brown knuckles of his fingers, where they gripped his arm, were pale with tension. He had really been frightened *for* her.

She wanted to voice these questions out loud. To demand answers. Lore pressed her lips into a thin line, refusing to let these thoughts leap unbidden from her lips.

If Syrelle was anything, he was a liar. She doubted he would relinquish any truths.

And either way, reminding him that her *death* might solve his problems could possibly go exceedingly terribly for her.

Lore looked around the office. Something was different. "Where is Thadrik?"

Syrelle released his death grip on his arm and rubbed his hands over his face roughly. "I sent him on an errand."

"You didn't want him to know that you were worried about me." Lore's words came out as a whisper. What did this mean?

Nothing.

The bare minimum someone should feel for another person is *not wanting them to die.* Unless . . . that person was an egotistical prick of fae nobility whose own ends always outweighed his capacity for empathy.

Lore could get lost in that loop of uncertainty if she let herself.

Syrelle was quiet. He neither confirmed nor denied. Lore didn't need him to; his nonanswer was answer enough.

And more importantly, it changed nothing.

Syrelle extended a hand toward hers, where they clutched the edge of his desk. She must have reached for it when she awoke, needing something solid to ground her. The joints of her fingers protested when she opened them. Releasing the desk, she pulled away and folded her hands into her lap.

Her message was clear. *Don't touch me.*

"Let me bid Cecil to take you to your room. You need to eat something. Rest."

"I don't need a watchdog. I'm not going to run away or escape." Lore stood up, too fast. All the blood rushed from her head, disorienting her. Her vision grew tunneled, dark. She staggered, stumbling backward, and bumped into the chair. It toppled over, landing on the ground behind her with a clatter.

Lore shook her head, trying to clear it.

Her legs felt shaky, and she realized that she was freezing cold; her teeth started to chatter.

"No, *don't*," she said sharply. Or tried to. Her voice came out weak. Her throat was still raw, and her voice rasped out as if through gravel. "I'm fine. Really."

She needed to pull herself together, or he would resume the discussion about whether or not it was safe to scry again. She bent down and lifted the chair, setting it to rights before he had a chance. If he started down that road again . . . then any chance of obtaining the other grimoire before Syrelle managed to . . . would be lost.

And she wouldn't be able to meet with Finndryl.

"I think I just need some air." She clenched her teeth together to stop them from chattering and squared her shoulders, though her head still felt woozy, and her body felt off.

Foreign.

She hadn't realized scrying could be dangerous. She'd done it just fine back in the Wilds with Finndryl. Then again, she hadn't left her body before. She'd just looked at the bowl of water like it was a mirror.

What would have happened if Syrelle hadn't shaken her out of her trance? Could she have been *lost* to the darkness? Had she detached, separated, her body and mind so thoroughly that she truly risked being forever trapped in that demonic place?

A shiver rose up her spine at the thought, and she had to clench her teeth even harder together to stop the shivering.

Her head began to pound.

"I'm sending for Cecil, either way. You have a guard for your protection, not because I think you have anywhere to run to. We are on a ship in the middle of the Dread."

Lore blinked.

The walls began to pulse, contract. Like they were closing in. Terror made her stomach heave. Lore swallowed bile.

"Take me to get some air yourself."

It was the least he could do after she'd almost been devoured by a dark entity of some kind trying to find *his* book. And was apparently still suffering the adverse effects of it. Lore fixed her vision on the gleaming doorknob and avoided looking at the walls, though they continued to pulse just on the edge of her vision.

"It's best if we aren't seen together outside of our work."

Lore edged forward on wobbling legs toward the door handle. "Our work? Seems like I'm the one doing everything."

"You aren't doing enough," he bit out.

Lore turned back to him sharply and opened her mouth to respond, even though her hands were beginning to tremble, but all she managed to do was sigh instead of reply. She was genuinely too drained to quarrel with him.

Syrelle held up one hand, palm forward as if to motion for peace. He closed his eyes and pinched the bridge of his nose with the other. "Wait. Pretend I didn't say that. I didn't even mean it. It's just that we are running out of time, and now my concern is that this route might be . . . too perilous to continue."

Shit. He was bringing up the dangers of scrying again. She racked her brain for something to distract him, though now she was focusing on the gleaming golden cuff link that stood out so vividly against the black of his shirt, focusing on that and not the pulsating walls, the way her stomach was still in knots . . . when Syrelle did the job for her.

"What did you find?" His tone wasn't demanding but rather tentative and curious. "This time was different; I think you found something."

"I found a clue."

His eyes flashed with excitement. "Tell me, and I'll bring you up to the deck."

Lore wanted to slap him. Again.

But she hadn't the energy, nor total control of her limbs. Truly, if she tried to slap him right now, she would probably end up on the floor. Besides, she had to be clever about this. She couldn't tell him anything that would lead him to the book before she'd discovered more and properly designed a plan of action. Though, the thought of willingly heading toward that putrid darkness . . . it seemed ludicrous.

"I tasted something. Dirt. Earth. It was . . . ancient. Undisturbed for a long time. I think it means the book may be buried underground."

"Dirt? That's it? Dirt has you so out of sorts, even now?" He pushed away from the desk, straightening his posture, and took a deliberate step toward her. "Lore, I know you. I can tell that you are frightened. And that it was something you *saw* or experienced that frightened you." He eyed her, searching her face.

She returned his gaze warily. *Please, let it go for now.*

His face softened. "We will discuss this further tomorrow. For now, let's go above and get some air."

Gods. Lore must look a wreck for him to let this go so easily.

Syrelle plucked a cloak from a stand and handed it to her on the way out the door. The cloak was long; if she were barefoot, it would drag on the floor, though even wearing boots, it would just barely miss it. The fabric was dyed the pale green of lichen, spun with golden thread and adorned with golden motifs in a twirling arrangement that mimicked creeping vines. Two buttons carved from bone in the shape of moon moths decorated either side of the collar and could be secured with a golden ribbon that appeared to be spun from a bar of gold.

"This arrived by post this morning. I had it made for you."

Lore didn't want anything from him.

But it would be cold on the deck; it was winter, after all, and she was already shivering in this room. It was as though the frigid air had seeped into her very bones and formed its home within them—despite the fire crackling cheerfully in the hearth.

Lore took the offered cloak and slipped it over her shoulders. Her fingers shook as she coiled the shimmering golden loop around the bone moth buttons. The fabric of the cloak slid over her shoulders, contouring to them like water. And it must have been spelled, because the material inside the cloak was *warm* against her skin, as if it had been hung by the fire in Syrelle's hearth and not dangling on a hook across the room by the door.

The warmth instantly loosened the knots in her shoulders. Her frozen fingers uncurled and the tremors racking her body stilled.

"Post? How can a messenger find us in the middle of the ocean?" Now that she was warm, her voice was less raspy, her throat less raw, and she felt like that lingering taste on her tongue was beginning to dissipate.

"Our messengers can fly, Lore, and our course is charted and logged with our military."

"Oh, yeah. *Wings*," Lore said as she followed his enormous wings out the door and down the corridor.

Syrelle led the way onto the deck and promptly pretended to leave her to her own devices. He busied himself by walking the length of the deck, talking with Thadrik in low, hushed whispers. Scheming the top-ten best ways to betray your friends and loved ones, probably, before he sat next to the first mate, who was busy mending nets despite the darkness.

She supposed the elderly male had been mending nets so long that he didn't need light to see by.

The first mate was wind-blasted and sun-damaged, with a patchy white beard and yellowing gray hair that he kept tied in a knot at the base of his wrinkled neck and covered with a ratty old knitted cap. She'd heard the others call him Old Salt, which Lore couldn't be sure that, at birth, despite him being a fresh baby, wasn't the name his mother had given him, because he *embodied* it. Old Salt was straight out of a pirate adventure novel. Lore didn't know how to explain it, but the old fae male looked like he was born on a ship and would die on a ship, and he wouldn't want to live life any other way.

He was the only sailor who offered her a smile and tipped his hat at her in greeting when they crossed paths. As he did just now.

Lore returned his smile, but hers was cautious, wary.

Gods, she was desperate for a friend.

Syrelle, who looked entirely too . . . noble to be sitting on a salt-stained oak barrel beside Old Salt, picked up a needle, extracted a net from the pile at the old sailor's feet, and began the task of repairing it himself. The two seemed like old friends. Syrelle laughed and joked with the old man, his fingers skimming across the latticed material, searching for rips and tears, all while keeping one eye on her.

If he had been Asher, it would have made sense. Asher was low-born like her, like Old Salt no doubt was. But Syrelle was a different creature than Lore or Old Salt. He carried himself differently . . . He was wearing a tailored coat and boots that were shined so fine they positively glowed in the dark.

Lore's cloak was undoubtedly more expensive than anything she or Old Salt had ever owned combined, and because of that it fit her, strangely. Not *strangely* because it fit her perfectly, but . . . she wasn't used to such luxury. She wasn't born to this, and it showed.

Syrelle, however, wore his wealth naturally. And yet, he sat on that barrel and picked up seaweed-laden netting like it was nothing. Then again, there had been a reason Lore had taken to Asher so well. He played the lowborn convincingly.

Old Salt began to sing a shanty about a crew of sailors and their losing battle with three siren sisters. He'd sung this one before, it must be one of his favorites. She tapped her boot to the fast rhythm of the shanty, which felt at odds with the ballad's tragic ending, and turned toward the rising sun, ignoring Syrelle's watchful gaze, heavy upon her back.

If she could find the sun book, she would never be powerless again. It wouldn't matter whether the sun was up; possession of *Auroradel* would mean that she would always have access to power.

How was she going to get to it before him?

She really must have been in a trance for hours, because it had seemed like only a quarter bell had passed since she'd walked into Syrelle's office that evening, and yet, here was the sun. It broke across the horizon in all its glory, casting its light for all to see, announcing with pride that today would be a glorious one.

She let the wind whip across her face, tear her hair from its ribbon, and disperse the lingering sensation of creatures swarming over her skin. The smell of the dark. The damp.

She closed her eyes and soaked in the sun's rays.

The only good thing about being on a ship was that no trees could shade her from the sun's light. She'd spent many a winter's day wishing she could just feel the sun on her face without fighting the thick canopy above her for a little sunshine.

As long as she had this, the sun on her face, then she had hope.

Lore could do this. She could solve the riddle herself. Gods, why was there a riddle at all? Couldn't the book have given her directions? Sail to this port, turn at the haberdashery, and find me in the cave with the three-headed pine tree outside the entrance.

No matter. She would solve the riddle, free Finndryl, and bring back immeasurable power to her people.

Syrelle's designs and small hopes for being the lesser of two evils to rule over her people wouldn't work for her. Wouldn't work for *them*. She would take them back to Shahassa, the motherland. Or, if she still couldn't locate it by the end of this, she would settle for as far away from the Alytherian fae as possible. So great a distance that even those with wings couldn't find them.

They would build walls. Set traps. She would spend her life weaving a thousand spells so that they would be free of the fae forever.

On the way back to her rooms, she made a request of Syrelle. "You owe me. For putting my life in danger, and for . . . a thousand other wrongs."

"What is it that you need?" His curiosity was piqued; he was being patient by not demanding she tell him everything she discovered on her scrying trip right this moment, but he knew that whatever she asked of him would lead him to the book eventually, and so he was humoring her.

This encouraged her. "Have maps of Ma Serach sent to my room. I know you have a few." She thought for a moment. "And the next time the post comes, I'll need you to put in an order for me; I'll need all the books on the ecology and geography of all continents. As many books as they can carry."

CHAPTER 7

It would be several days before the tomes arrived, but the maps were waiting for Lore when she awoke from a brief nap. She'd been so exhausted she hadn't stirred when someone had slipped in and deposited a mountainous pile of maps onto the table. The thought of someone entering the room while she'd been sleeping sent a shiver down her spine, and she made a mental note to lodge a chair under the door handle the next time she rested.

With a resigned sigh, she piled her hair atop her head and bound it with ribbon until it resembled something akin to a pineapple, cleaned her teeth, and splashed water on her face. It was time to get to work.

Usually, this would be the time she'd munch a quick bite of food and attempt to sleep. Since she and Syrelle kept a nocturnal schedule, daylight felt a muted imitation of life. The absence of her grimoire gnawed at her, an insatiable hunger for the power it liberated within her. But with the arrival of the maps, now that she had a riddle, a real clue . . . she felt possessed by a restless energy.

She combed the maps, keys, and cartographer logs, letting the task consume her.

When Cecil arrived that evening to escort Lore to Syrelle's office, she slipped out the door the moment Cecil slid the lock free.

Lore's steps were hurried and she practically raced Cecil down the hall.

Syrelle was busy perusing a stack of ledgers, and his only acknowledgment of Lore's presence was to tell her to shut the door behind her. Lore complied, before sitting down in her usual chair, picking up the scrying bowl, and picturing Finndryl.

It didn't take long to navigate her way to his room. Tonight, Finndryl was dozing on the armchair beside his bed, a novel haphazardly splayed on his knee.

Should I let you sleep?

His eyes shot open, and he sat up, one hand flying to his face to wipe away any evidence of sleep left behind. The book almost fell from atop his knee, but his reflexes didn't miss; he scooped it from the air and snapped it shut in one fluid motion. *Please don't. The amount of sleep I've been getting recently would rival a house cat's.*

Good, because I wasn't going to let you, anyway.

I would expect nothing less. Gods, it feels strange speaking to you inside my head and not being able to see you . . . You can't . . . hear my thoughts, can you?

Lore laughed. *No, I can only hear what you purposefully project toward me. Why, what are you thinking right now?*

Finndryl smirked, easing back into the chair and splaying his long legs out before him. *Oh, nothing much, just planning my world domination.*

Diabolical. I would expect nothing less from you.

Speaking of world domination, are you any closer to finding the other grimoire?

Lore couldn't wait to tell him. *I have a lead. Sort of. It's a riddle. I think it's from* Auroradel *itself.*

You think?

Yes, I think. I haven't been able to confirm it, yet . . .

Have you let this . . . entity into your mind?

We have linked—sort of like how we are talking now. She didn't mention that she had been almost lost to the dark; there was no point in worrying him when there was nothing he could do from his own locked room.

There are some who can infiltrate one's mind, sift through one's thoughts, and even deposit their own. Please be careful. In fact, you might need to practice protecting yourself before you reach out to it again, just in case.

Lore grimaced. She had been thinking the same thing. She wasn't ready yet to connect with *Auroradel*. After last time. Too afraid to be trapped again.

Finndryl continued, *Tell me about this riddle.*

Lore recited it to him and then told him about her plan to use the maps and ecological books to pinpoint the grimoire's location. When she finished her explanation, she asked him, *What do you know of griffins? Of a place called Ma Serach?*

Unfortunately, being from the southern half of a continent an ocean away from Ma Serach, I don't know much about the empire. He shifted in his seat. *Griffins are rare beasts, large and territorial. As far as I know, they don't migrate. They nest in the location of their birth and protect that land until their death, the cycle continuing for generations. Wherever griffins are found should be well chronicled as the fae tend to avoid those places—nobody wants to fight a flock of griffins over territory, they will lose.*

Lore bit her lip. *Rare is good, it might not be difficult to locate the correct location then.* When the books arrived, she would scour the volumes, cross-referencing nesting grounds with mountains or cave systems on the maps.

What happens when you solve the riddle and find the book? Any ideas on how you will bond with Auroradel *before Syrelle?*

Lore was relieved that he said *when* she solved the riddle and finds the book and not *if. Not yet, but I'll cross that bridge when I come to it.*

He nodded. *Just make sure I'm with you.*

If I have my way, you will be.

After saying their goodbyes, Lore returned to the suffocating silence of Syrelle's office and set aside the scrying bowl. He was keeping things from her, and it was time he came clean. "Where exactly are we sailing to, Syrelle?" Lore had to stop herself from wincing; she hadn't meant to sound quite so loud, but her voice had been jarring.

Luckily, Thadrik, their silent observer, hadn't been disturbed by her question and still dozed in the corner. Coretha hadn't bothered them again; now that it was made clear she couldn't torture Lore or Finndryl, she left it to Thadrik the Despicable to monitor their sessions.

At her sharpened tone, Syrelle's quill slowed on the parchment before him, and lines formed between his brows, a flicker of hesitation shading his eyes for a brief moment. But then, a silent acknowledgment passed between them.

It was time.

He owed her answers, and she was done playing his game.

Syrelle laid his quill down and closed the book he'd been marking in before he plucked the ink-pot lid off the desk. He took his sweet time pressing the corked lid into the pot's mouth. "My grandfather Matleus," he began, his voice low and measured, "was a powerful shapeshifter and an even stronger alchemist. He had a fondness for travel and spent decades searching for answers to Alytheria's budding fertility problems. He eventually returned, hope in his wake, with a new power unlike anything our people had known." His voice trailed off, a hint of sorrow in his eyes. "But he had changed. He became a hermit. Secretive. Paranoid. And our people still suffered."

Lore listened intently, her heart pounding in her chest. The pieces were falling into place, but the picture they painted was still shrouded in shadows.

"I do not know why he cursed the library . . . or what prompted him to hide *Deeping Lune* within its walls. The night he placed the spell on the library," Syrelle continued, "he left, claiming he was going to hide *Auroradel* within the Ma Serach Empire with instructions for my grandmother to tell only his descendants that we would be unaffected by the curse. I don't think either of them suspected that would be the last time he would be seen alive."

Lore's eyes widened. "Is it known that he died? I know the fae's lifetimes are vastly longer than humans' . . . a thousand years is too long, but what if his magic sustained him somehow?" A chilling thought crept into her mind: What if his grandfather was still alive, still in possession of *Auroradel*? She would never be able to take such a powerful alchemist's own grimoire from him. Nor did she think she had the constitution to try.

"Oh, he's long dead," Syrelle said, his voice flat. "Fifteen years after he journeyed to Ma Serach, an owl flew to my grandmother's window with a bag filled with his ashes. They were confirmed by a priestess to be his. It became clear that her children and their children would never find the grimoires, that he had stolen their legacy from them."

Lore's mind raced. "Who sent Matleus's ashes to your grandmother?"

Syrelle shrugged. "The owl did not have a note attached to it. Just another of my grandfather's twisted games, I think."

A new thought occurred to Lore. "Ma Serach Empire. Will they just let you, an outsider, scour their lands for the grimoire?"

"My uncle has made it clear *no one* outside of his closest advisors are to know what we search for. If we are questioned, we will tell them that we are on a leisure trip. Coretha has visited Ma Serach many times before . . . many Alytherians travel there. Coretha actually spent some of her childhood as a ward of the empress—that's another reason why she's come along. Though her unfortunate presence is little more than a thinly veiled cover, and she's truly just here to be the eyes and ears of the king."

Lore's frown deepened. She'd seen Ma Serach on the maps. It was a vast empire, five times the size of Alytheria. "What happens if the empire discovers it isn't a leisure trip and that you are plotting to remove an impossibly powerful magical object from *their* lands? One that they would surely want for themselves?"

Syrelle shrugged, as if this had occurred to him but did not worry him. "The empress would go to war with Alytheria before she let an artifact as powerful as *Auroradel* leave her shores. Nobody knows it's even on that continent outside of my family. And if it had come into her possession, she would have boasted to the world about her new weapon. It would secure her empire's protection from any and everyone who would ever consider invading her."

"Well, Creepy Thadrik knows about it."

Syrelle laughed. "Technically, he is family—he's a second cousin of mine."

"I see. So, being a scummy person runs in your family, then?"

"I like to think that I am set apart from them. Though, from your perspective, I can see how my lies would make it seem like I fit right in."

"From my perspective, you're worse than all of them." All of them save Coretha and Syrelle's uncle, the king. And perhaps his grandfather who had chosen to ban everyone from a library for a thousand years because he didn't want anyone to find his book. Which he could have hidden anywhere! But she wouldn't give him the grace of saying that to his face.

All humor dropped from his expression as his eyes flicked to Thadrik, who snored softly in the corner. His voice dipped low. "It pains me that you feel that way. You wouldn't if you knew the truth."

The words pierced Lore's heart, but she refused to show weakness. "How else am I supposed to feel?" she retorted, her voice barely a whisper. "Your single apology when I woke up was supposed to be enough? I was supposed to . . . what? Just absolve you of your deceptions? Of all the lies, the memories that are now tainted forever?" She swallowed, the bitterness rising in her throat. "You broke my fucking heart, and now I question everything . . . *everything*."

She shrugged off her emotions and pushed them down until all she felt was numbness toward him. "Besides," she said, her voice hollow, "you seem to be allergic to the truth."

Syrelle's gaze locked onto hers, his eyes burning with an intensity that sent a wave of shivers up her spine. "One day, Lore," he rasped, his voice thick with emotion, "I will lay myself bare before you. I will reveal every harsh truth, every revolting action I've been forced to take to mend the destruction my great-uncle's unnaturally long reign has wrought upon Alytheria. You will understand that my hands have been tied, bound by duty." He closed his eyes for a moment as if steeling himself against the weight of his words. When he opened them again, his midnight-black irises seemed to pierce her soul. "And you will see," he uttered, "that when it comes to you, I am engulfed in a constant battle to stay the course, to continue what I have worked toward for a *decade*." His voice dropped to a whisper. "When it comes to you, Lore, I am utterly lost."

Lore opened her mouth to respond, though she had no idea what she would, *could* say to that admission, but Syrelle straightened his posture and broke away, molding his face into that apathetic mask as though he were putty. Cutting the tension between them as if with a sword, he stood up from his desk and walked toward the hearth, the broad expanse of his back to her. He placed a hand on the mantel and spoke, his voice smooth, unbothered, as though they hadn't just had maybe the first substantial conversation since *before*.

"It grows late. That is enough for now; I'll ring for Cecil."

Lore said nothing as they waited for Cecil to arrive. She chewed on her lip, her thoughts churning through her mind too fast to keep hold of one for long.

Finally, the guard arrived, and Lore scrambled out of her chair. Her footsteps were hurried as she raced toward the door. She didn't think it possible, but she actually longed for the seclusion of her room.

Just before she cleared Syrelle's quarters to the safety of the hallway, he spoke up. "I'm glad that you are no longer fighting me. It's nice to be on the same team once more. It will only lead us to our prize that much sooner."

Lore hesitated, looking over her shoulder at this stranger, where he stood by the fireplace, oranges and reds flickering across his face.

This was good. She gave a soft smile.

How wrong he was to think that she was on his team, that he had fooled her into siding with him. If anything, she was more determined than ever to take command of *Auroradel* before him.

She would take everything from him. She would be his utter ruination. And then, she would set his entire beloved kingdom on fire.

CHAPTER 8

Lore had been asleep only a few hours when a knock came at the door.

She was surprised that the knock had come so early; midday meal usually arrived at dusk, so she had time to eat before the nightly meeting with Syrelle.

She opened the door, her jaw dropping momentarily. It was not Cecil on the other side holding a tray of food, but Syrelle himself.

The male wore a sienna-colored, tight-fitting linen shirt, the collar buttoned up to his throat. His sleeves were cuffed on his shapely forearms, the tight fabric showing off his biceps. Black, formfitting breeches hugged his muscled legs and were decorated with a stenciled brown belt, two short swords slung low on either hip. His brown boots had gleaming golden buckles. Syrelle's wings were on display today, and the feathers cresting the tips of each brushed against the ceiling of the corridor.

Held beneath one muscular arm was a large box the color of lilacs.

"Oh. It's you." Lore craned her neck, looking around the hallway, even though she could clearly see that he was alone. Odd. She thought they were forbidden to be alone. "Are you to escort me to your office? We have hours yet until darkness."

"We are trying something different today. I've brought you new garments; please dress quickly."

He held the box out to Lore, and she thought about not taking it, leaving his offering suspended in the air just to make him feel awkward, just to spite him. But being difficult just for the sake of it was exhausting. And anyway . . . this was a welcome change in routine.

She'd exhausted the maps and still waited for the books to arrive—she truly didn't want to spend another day trapped in her cabin.

She took the box and shoved the door with her hip, slamming it in his face.

She laid the package on her bed and lifted the lid. Inside was shimmering paper so thin and delicately folded that she was afraid it would tear just by untying the ribbon. She untied the bow with diligent care—it seemed as though some law would be broken if she ruined this lovely paper—and spread the thin sheets, revealing a dress.

Lore pulled out the frock and gently laid it across the quilt.

The outer layer was a see-through gossamer fabric adorned with delicate flowers that appeared real as she rubbed a petal lightly between thumb and finger. The fresh scent of the flowers reached her nose. The cream color of their petals was bright against the gray-blue of the fabric. *Real flowers pressed into the fabric of a dress?* If she moved wrong, they would bruise, wouldn't they?

Then she laughed as she remembered that there was magic, and they were likely spelled to resist damage and aging.

The inner fabric was a shade darker blue and had quite a low cut on the bodice. The sleeves were puffed and short; they would end right at her shoulders. The dress was picturesque, clearly costly. She withdrew a new pair of thick woolen stockings and reached for a rectangular box tucked into the corner.

Lore opened it to find a pair of ankle boots with a raised heel.

They were made of buttery-smooth leather, the warm brown color of chestnuts. The laces were quite impractical, as the strings were a latticed lace the same color as the flower petals. If these were Lore's only boots or if she had to run for a long distance in them, the laces would surely fray.

Beside the shoebox was a slim velvet pouch. Lore withdrew a golden chain with a round pendant. The pendant was glass with a small moon moth embedded in the center, its tails so delicate Lore could see through them. Surrounding the moth, studded in the deep blue fabric right above it, was a circular diamond.

A reminder from Syrelle of *Deeping Lune*, the thing she craved . . . but could not have?

The necklace was beautiful, but Lore did not want to wear it if it came from him. She fisted her hand around the cold metal and squeezed, wishing she could break it. Wanting the glass covering the moth to shatter and cut into her hand. If she were bleeding from a physical wound, then maybe the gaping wound inside her would not hurt as badly.

But the necklace was well-made, and the glass did not break. She slipped the necklace back inside the velvet pouch and put it away in the drawer of the bedside table.

When she escaped, she could sell it and feed the kiddos for a year.

Lore washed her face; refreshed her curls with water, drops of almond oil, and cream; and assembled her hair into a bun on the crown of her head, leaving a few curls to frame her face, before slipping into the stockings and gown. The boots, though brand-new, were easy to pull over her stockinged feet, and when she took a few tentative steps, they did not pinch at all, nor feel stiff like fresh boots usually did.

Lore regarded herself in the mirror.

The dress's neckline was cut low, and the bodice pushed her breasts up in a lovely way. The puffed sleeves slipped off her shoulders. The dress was beautiful and skillfully made. It fit her like a glove, showing off her thin waist and curvy hips.

The change in her was startling, and weariness settled over her like a storm cloud. Lore knew that stress was taking its toll, but apparently it had been a while since she'd studied her reflection in daylight. The nocturnal lifestyle had lightened the warm brown of her skin more than she was used to, and her freckles, which were usually unremarkable, were prominent. Dark shadows smudged beneath her eyes, looking as though she'd smeared charcoal on her face and rubbed it in. Her cheekbones were sharp, and her usually full cheeks looked hollow. She traced her fingers along jutting collarbones that a few weeks ago had been less evident.

She wanted to rip this dress off and go back to bed, sleep until the sun swallowed the earth and she crumbled to dust.

She raised her chin instead. She might be weary and stressed, but despite it, she looked beautiful.

Syrelle waited in the hall, leaning against the wall. He had one leg bent, a boot pressed to the wall behind him, his head thrown back, his eyes closed. He swallowed, and Lore followed the bob of his throat.

For a moment, memories of Asher waiting for her outside the library flashed through her mind, superimposing the visage upon Syrelle.

Syrelle, then Asher, then Syrelle once more.

Lore swallowed, trying to dislodge the thickness in her throat. Her chest ached, missing a person who didn't exist. He stood the same, but that was where the similarities ended.

Lore cleared her throat, and Syrelle opened his eyes, heavy-lidded as they swept over her, taking in her form.

Lore told her body to settle; she wanted to hate the raw desire visible in his eyes as he perused her from curls to boots, lingering on the swell of her breasts. She told herself he was not admiring them, only checking to see if she had chosen to accept the gift of the necklace by wearing it. The necklace could only have been designed with her in mind, a token of . . . something . . . she wasn't willing to consider. She knew that her choosing to wear it would send a message to him, one she would *never* send.

But her body did not settle. Not surprisingly—when had it ever done what it was supposed to? Her cheeks flushed as warmth pooled within her, reacting to his dark desire, completely against her will.

"I knew that color would look lovely on you," Syrelle said, his voice a purr.

"What is all this for, then?" Lore asked, gesturing to the dress.

Syrelle closed the distance between them and his hands were around her waist before she could protest. "You aren't eating enough; I'll have the cook double your provisions."

Her eyes fluttered, overwhelmed by his closeness, as her heart stuttered in her chest. "I haven't been hungry."

"Don't make me *order* you to eat, because I will, if I must," he growled. "I'll visit your room for every meal, just to make sure you finish them."

The *last* thing she needed was for Syrelle to be in her room during meals or otherwise, not with the way the weight of his hands warmed her entire body through the fabric of her dress.

"You cannot order me around. Just because I *chose* to wear the clothes you picked out today, you think I your puppet?"

His hands were still around her waist. They tightened for a moment, his thumb pressing into her hips.

Her legs went weak.

Gods—Lore knew she should, but she couldn't muster up the strength to push them away.

Push *him* away.

Lore's lips parted against her will as Syrelle's hungry gaze dipped low to them.

"Stop fighting me, Lore. Together, we can be the two most

powerful alchemists on the continent." His breath brushed over her face.

Blackberries and honey.

He smelled the same.

That ache within her intensified. She missed Asher so damned much. Syrelle's face softened and tilted a fraction toward hers.

Their breaths mingled as they inhaled the same air. She heard his breath hitch and knew his own heart must be stuttering like hers, because he was now gliding one hand up her waist. His knuckles grazed the fabric near her breast before slipping over her shoulder, his thumb brushing her collarbone. His touch was maddeningly light. Goosebumps erupted across her arms when he cupped her cheek.

Lore wanted to melt into him, to close the last bit of distance between them, to see if he kissed and tasted the same.

She was not in control, right now. In fact, this exchange was wildly outside of her control. Her emotions were once again dictating her actions, and gods, her body was being downright mutinous.

"I'll be the sun to your moon," he murmured, his dark eyes searching hers. "I can't think of anything I want more than to rule with you at my side."

She jerked backward, out of his grasp, slamming herself into the wall.

The . . . sun . . . Her eyes flashed, anger superseding any lasting lust. It was one thing to fool him into thinking she was not just cooperating but on his side . . . It was another entirely to listen to whispered promises, to let him kiss her.

For the first time in days, she didn't bank her rage, she coaxed it to life, feeding the writhing fury within her. He was the enemy; this was simply a game, and she would not lose to him. She siphoned the lingering heat from his touch until every last cinder inflamed nothing but her rage.

"Why settle, when I can be both sun *and* the moon?" Her voice was a blaze.

Syrelle's face, which had been soft and hungry a moment ago, shuttered. His head tilted to the side as he regarded her with eyes like hoarfrost. He straightened up, brushing a nonexistent wrinkle from his pressed shirt.

Lore was trying to catch her breath, her head spinning. She might have given too much of her intentions away just now, but she was desperate to gain back some control. Had she *really* almost kissed him just now? She despised him. She wanted him out of her life.

Not in her bed.

She held her anger close, caressed it. Anger was righteous. Anger would save her.

He took a step away from her.

One step, but the distance between them was a chasm that neither could cross.

Syrelle opened his mouth to respond, but two guards rounded the corner just then.

His mouth snapped shut and he cleared his throat. "I thought we would try something different today." He repeated his earlier declaration. Whatever he'd been planning on saying, he clearly didn't trust the guards to hear it.

Lore sighed. She didn't want to know what his response would have been, anyway. Let them get this over with so she could be rid of him once more. She unclenched her jaw. Relaxed her brow, her clasped fists.

"New, how?" she asked, trying to settle the pounding of her heart. She walked in step beside Syrelle but kept her distance. She tried to ignore the two guards who fell in behind them. One was Thadrik, the other was a wolfish guard with disdain in his eyes. Both made her uneasy.

"You'll see," he said as he shoved the door to the deck wide.

It was easier to ignore the guards, as practiced as she was when it came to ignoring Thadrik, but the sailors on the deck were in a mood.

Lore slipped her cloak over her shoulders against the biting wind. Winter was in full swing today. She was just clasping the cord over the bone moth buttons when she heard shushed whispers on the wind.

The witch . . .

. . . fault.

. . . murdered.

Murdered? Was someone dead?

A wave of unease washed over her, settling as a tight ache between her shoulder blades, but then, the wind changed, and she heard a shrill whisper:

The only one of us who showed any kindness to her, and she killed him in cold blood.

"What's going on with the sailors?" Lore asked Syrelle out of the side of her mouth as they made their way toward the rowboats hooked to the side of the ship.

"One of them perished last night," he said, his voice grave.

"Who?"

"The first mate. The one they called Old Salt."

Lore stumbled, then halted, closing her eyes.

Old Salt, the sailor who'd smiled at her. He'd seemed straight from the pages of a book. She'd longed to sit with him over an ale and listen to his stories; she had no doubt he had a thousand good ones. She would've collected them like jewels.

She'd wished she could've enjoyed his raspy, bawdy sea chanteys without the presence of everyone else's contempt for her. Fear of her. It always soured her mood, and his songs.

She didn't say any of this to Syrelle.

"He seemed healthy. Was it fever?"

"Something happened with his head. Doc said he came in complaining of pain. He was just about to examine him when Old Salt gave a shout, clutching his skull. A moment later, he'd passed on."

Unexpected deaths were the hardest. Lore opened her eyes, nodded. Then she glanced around, observed the sailors.

A pall of mourning filled the atmosphere. Somber faces, groups huddled together, a few leaked tears. It didn't take a seasoned sailor to see that the mariners respected the late first mate more than their own captain. But their anguish and the suddenness of his death clearly left them wanting someone to blame.

It looked like they'd chosen to pin it on *the witch*.

Never mind that Lore *wouldn't* do that. And didn't even know *how* to kill a person without at least being in the same room as them.

But there was no point in telling them this.

They would rather blame her for their sorrow than accept that something had gone wrong inside Old Salt.

That it had just been his time.

Their enmity chafed, nettling her skin. Lore lowered her gaze away from them, wondering why Syrelle had brought her out here at all, when she looked past the ship toward the horizon and spied mountains jutting out of the sea.

Land.

And not just land—there was a village in the distance.

CHAPTER 9

The ship was too large to dock at the anchorage inside the crescent-shape harbor, so it moored well outside. Syrelle stepped into a rowboat hooked onto the ship's side and offered his hand to Lore. She brushed his hand aside and climbed into the boat without his help, though the skirts of her dress made it difficult. The two guards that had shadowed them from Lore's room climbed in behind her. A slight nod from Syrelle, and sailors began the process of lowering the dinghy.

The sailors' eyes were daggers trained on her as the rowboat made its descent; Lore was half convinced that if Syrelle himself hadn't been in the boat with her, they would have let the ropes slip from their hands to let her tumble into the sea, boat and all.

Lore averted her gaze and pulled the hood of her cloak forward until her face was swathed in shadow. Stilling her hands in her lap to stop from fidgeting with the fabric of her cloak, she turned her back on them, gazing outward toward the village.

Which was remarkable.

Houses and buildings were carved directly into the sheer cliff face that erupted from the ocean, and Lore's eyes, mesmerized, followed gleaming pathways that wound back and forth across the mountains like stitching in a quilt. Though many houses and buildings dotted the cliffs, most people seemed to live on the water. Docks built from various types of wood and debris and stitched together with little more than hopes and dreams, speared out in every direction from the short rocky beach.

Slanted houses built one on top of the other sagged from rot caused by constant exposure to the water and the thick, salty air. The entire village looked like the smallest storm should've blown every house out to sea, and yet it was a marvel, a testament to resilience.

As their rowboat drew closer to the docks, Lore heard the cries of fae children as they ran down the docks, their bare feet slapping against the wet planks. Some pushed themselves on rafts from one dock to another, their small arms using poles to traverse the slim channels teeming with watercrafts with expertise that surprised Lore. A few boats with tapered edges, these ones better built than the rafts, were filled with brightly colored fruits in knit bags, nuts and spices in woven baskets, and buckets of what looked like salted fish. Others had netting, fishing poles, and fabric piled high as their sun- and salt-weathered owners pushed their boats through the floating village, calling out prices and wares.

One guard steered the dinghy farther into the village, keeping to the outskirts, where the hustle and bustle of the water city was calmer. Their boat was designed to simply transport those from the ship to land; it was not made to traverse the inner channels. It was much too wide and lacked finesse.

"Where are we?" Lore asked, breaking the silence on the boat.

Syrelle smiled, falsely taking her question as a sign that she maybe hated him less since he'd been oh-so-benevolent to let her free from her prison for an afternoon. Truthfully, she would've asked the guards, but one guard was looking slightly panicked as he tried to steer the boat, and the other, Thadrik, gave her the creeps.

No matter. Syrelle was quick to give her a reply. "Galjien, as you can see, is unaffected by the blight that the Alytherians suffer from. Their children are numerous and live carefree lives here in the shallows. Some don't step foot on land until school age. The water is all they know; all they wish to know."

Peals of laughter carried on the wind. It rang with the joys of freedom.

"It seems a sort of paradise."

"You aren't the first to say this; my grandfather felt the same and spent a few summers here."

"Ah, I see. Your grandfather must have brought *Auroradel* here."

"He did. I am hoping that you might catch a signature of it. Maybe if you can feel where the book has been, then it will aid you in our search."

The dinghy bumped into the dock, jarring Lore a little. She gripped the railing tightly as Thadrik hopped out to tie the boat to a hook jammed into the dock. When the boat was secure, Thadrik tossed a coin to an eager youth with storm-cloud eyes waiting on the dock, to watch the boat while the small group headed into the village.

Lore wasn't sure she trusted these docks. They rose and fell with the pulse of the ocean, and these ones on the outskirts weren't as frequented and, therefore, were slick with algae.

She was glad she'd put on the new boots; despite their beauty, the soles had a surprising grip to them. If she had worn her slippers, she would have already slid off the dock, and no doubt cut herself to shreds on the barnacles that had made homes for themselves on every surface they could. Including the sea turtle that lay sunning itself on an abandoned raft.

Lore had never seen such a large turtle before. The ones at home in ponds and rivers had shells no larger than the palm of her hand. Yet here was this gentle sea beast, calmly sleeping, its shell alone larger than the wheel of a six-person carriage.

As she followed Syrelle's broad shoulders farther down the docks, Lore wondered what would happen if she pushed him off the edge.

No doubt her effort would be wasted. She doubted she could successfully push him, but what if he did manage to stumble and fall? It would be quite satisfying to see his surprised look when his face broke the surface of the water and he pulled himself back onto the deck, his clothes soaking wet. But what good would that do? It would be better to wait until they were on the edge of a cliff.

Lore remembered when they sat side by side on the edge of his cave, their feet dangling hundreds of feet above the raging ocean and jagged, deadly rocks. She could have taken the fish he'd offered her and given him a shove in exchange, but back then, she hadn't known that he was an imposter.

But then again, the bastard had *wings*. Lore resisted the urge to push him and followed him, Thadrik, and the other guard into the village.

Lore was surprised when a pair of antlered children broke away from a gaggle of kiddos and ran toward them.

"Uncle Syrelle! You're back!"

Uncle Syrelle? *What?*

"Inesca, Iither! Come here!"

The children were a blur of curls and rosy cheeks as they raced into Syrelle's arms; he bent to their level and picked them both up to give them a fierce hug. Lore's mind was reeling from the sight before her. Syrelle had a niece and nephew? There was no way she could've predicted that this would be on her list of things to witness today.

"What have you brought for us?"

"Hush, Iither! It's impolite to ask him that before we've even asked him how he is!" the girl admonished her brother, who only shushed her in reply.

"I'm doing just fine, thank you, Inesca; it's good to see that someone remembers her manners." Syrelle grinned. "Though Iither knows I've never visited without bringing *something*." He placed the children down and patted the pockets on his coat.

Syrelle gave an exaggerated frown as he continued to pat every pocket on his person. "Oh no, it seems I forgot them."

Inesca shrieked a giggle and abandoned any manners she possessed in her small body and dug into his coat pockets herself, giving a joyful shout when she pulled out two small packages wrapped with familiar paper and tied with a bow.

"I knew you wouldn't forget to bring us something, Uncle Syrelle!"

She handed one to her brother, who promptly ripped into his package. Inesca unwrapped hers with more care, carefully folding the paper and bow and slipping them into the bag hanging from her shoulder before examining her gift.

Just as Lore had this morning.

Their gifts were the same. One didn't have to be a parent to know that twins needed two of any gifts, lest one covet the other's more than their own. The twins proudly held up a . . .

"What is this, Uncle?" asked Inesca, his chubby fingers turning the object over and over in his hands.

Lore was glad he asked, because she wanted to know too.

"They're a new invention, straight from the university in Viba. Adventurers use compasses to establish which direction they face."

"Why not just use the stars?" the girl, Inesca, asked, her eyes wide as she turned the compass over and over in small, chubby fingers.

Of course, a child raised on the sea would be so familiar with the stars that navigating by them would seem effortless.

"Because 'Nes, this device is much more accurate than having the stars guide you. Soon every ship in the world will have at least one of these on them, I guarantee it."

Syrelle plucked the metal item from Inesca's hands.

He turned it round until he located a latch. He pressed it, and the lid sprang open on tiny hinges, revealing an intricate map painted beneath the glass. "But your finder is special because not only does it have a pointer to reveal one's direction . . ." He turned it, and the black needle turned with him, pointing to the *S* on the bottom of the map. A red needle stayed pointing in the same direction despite his rotation of the device. "Your compasses were intended to be two halves of a whole. They will lead to the other. Your compasses will always point the way to their twin."

"Wonderful," Inesca and Iither said in unison. Inesca grabbed her compass back and turned it around as Iither wrestled with the latch on his.

"Is your mom home?"

"Yes, she should be!"

"Thank you, Uncle Syrelle!" both children exclaimed, giving him a quick hug before running back to their friends, waving their gifts high.

"You have a nephew and niece?"

"Technically, they're my cousins. Their mom is my aunt, my mother's sister."

His aunt, it seemed, didn't live far from where the children were playing.

It was a small, single-story house that floated on the water and was tied between two docks. It was in no better shape than any of the others around it. This one appeared to once have been painted a lovely shade, but had since faded to an unappealing chartreuse. One of its shutters hung at an angle, held up by a lonely, crooked nail, the other was missing entirely, no doubt blown off by a storm long ago. The roof had green and red algae concealing its shingles, and a seabird had made the roof its home. Its piercing cry was mournful; the sound plucked the strings of Lore's own sorrow.

Lore had never seen a house that was also a boat before. She didn't even know one could build a house on the water.

Syrelle's knock on the door was answered immediately by a female wearing trousers and a billowing, tucked-in shirt. Her cheeks were flushed, her skin was a beautiful shade of brown, and her hair, which was cut short, encircled her head like a crown. Her feet were bare, and she had smudges of yellow, blue, and shades of purple smeared on her pants, cheek, and fingertips.

The smile on her face from ear to ear and her genuine warmth were almost as startling as the antlers sprouting from her head.

His aunt had antlers. His cousins had antlers. Something wasn't adding up here.

Syrelle's aunt, who looked no older than him, pulled him into a tight hug and ushered them inside. Lore was glad to see the guards remained outside, taking up a post by the door.

His aunt's house was small, and none of the furniture was new or even appeared to have been crafted by the same carpenter, but the atmosphere was comfy and warm. A family lived here, and you could tell that this was a home filled with love.

"I didn't expect you back for at least another year or so, Syr."

"I can leave and come back then if you like," Syrelle said with a joking grin.

"Oh, hush." She addressed Lore. "Come in, love. Mind you take your shoes off, please." Lore complied immediately. She squished her stockinged toes into the plush rug that covered the floor.

"Maple, this is my friend, Lore Alemeyu."

Friend? No.

Prisoner? Yes.

Lore bit her lip and refrained from correcting him. Instead, she mumbled, "Nice to meet you." She shook Maple's hand, glad to see the smears of paint on her fingertips were dry and did not transfer onto Lore's own.

"You as well. I'm Maple Gylthrae."

"Gylthrae?" Lore asked, startled, and looked at Syrelle. That was *Asher's* last name. His *fake* last name.

"Why, yes," Maple said, her expression bemused at Lore's reaction.

Syrelle rubbed the back of his neck. "Gylthrae is a family name. My mother's last name, and mine as well, before my father insisted that my brother and I change our names to Jibrann to match his," Syrelle supplied, his expression unreadable.

"Please sit down." Maple fluttered a hand toward her couch as she headed into the kitchen. "Would you two like tea to warm you up?"

"She'll take coffee, Maple, if you have any."

"Coffee it is!"

Lore almost forgot to hate him when, a few minutes later, Maple pushed a chipped clay mug into her hand. She blew on the hot liquid before taking a sip. "Is that . . . cinnamon? And butter?"

"Yes! You have a sharp palate! I make a cinnamon roll spread that tastes good on—or *in*—just about everything." Maple took a sip of her own cup of coffee and gave a happy, contented sigh as she settled her plump self into an oversize armchair.

The coffee table, Lore noticed, was laden with clay pots, an unrolled canvas sack with slots filled with brushes of various shapes and sizes, and a few different canvases covered in various stages of artwork.

"Are you a painter?"

"I am! It doesn't pay for everything we need, but it helps supplement during the slow season."

"Slow season?"

"My husband, like most around here, is a fisher. Soon, the water will be too cold, and the fish too deep. My art sales pick up at this time, when everyone is home and wanting portraits done or something bright to adorn their walls."

Lore surveyed the living room. Portraits and paintings covered almost every inch of wall space. Most of the landscapes were clearly painted from here, with lots of blues and shades of gray from the seaside and cliffs.

"They're lovely."

"Thank you! I know artists aren't supposed to be their own bard, but I am quite proud of my work."

"As you should be," Syrelle said. "I'll have to buy another from you before we go; I would love to see what you have for sale."

"No need to pay, as long as you brought me more of those paints from—"

"Of course. I know these colors are hard to come by, what with Galjien being so remote." He dug into an inside pocket and withdrew a woven bag filled with what Lore could only assume were jars of pigmented powder that Maple could mix with water or oil to paint with. With much the same enthusiasm as her twins, Maple grabbed the bag and rummaged through it, delightedly remarking on the different tints, when Lore saw . . .

"Is that—sorry to interrupt, Syrelle, is that *you*?"

Lore extracted herself from the cushioned couch, which was so comfortable that she was half convinced it was sentient and had been slowly trying to eat her, to get a closer look.

Nestled among an array of landscapes was a painting of a family.

Two small boys smiling wide; a female, presumably their mother, stood behind them, beaming as well, her hands on both of the boys' shoulders. If not for the height difference, Syrelle and his brother could have been twins. They both looked like younger versions of Syrelle: brown skin and sharp, intelligent eyes, though his cheekbones, hollowed cheeks, and sharp jaw were beveled at the edges, filled in, softened by childhood . . . but the smile on the younger version was so *unlike* Syrelle. They were only paint, but their brightness and unfettered joy were so vivid they leaped off the canvas in such a way that Lore had to stop herself from returning their smiles with one of her own.

It was hard to imagine that Syrelle had ever smiled like that. She glanced away, up toward their mother.

Goosebumps rose on her arms. She, like the boys, looked familiar, but not because of their resemblance to the older Syrelle.

"She looks just like . . ." Lore whispered, her voice strangled by a surge of emotion.

His mother was the female version of Asher. Two proud antlers parted brown, curly hair the color of ancient, well-loved, leather-bound books. Sharp cheekbones, midnight-black eyes that shone with more wisdom than Asher's had but with that same mischievous gleam, same full lips, the bottom a little pouty . . . and her smile shone with the light of a thousand candles.

A wave of dizziness surged through Lore. She felt like she'd stepped into an alternate reality. If Asher had stayed Asher and the world hadn't been trying to kill her, she imagined that this could have been their future. He could have brought Lore to meet his family, to see the seaside village his mother hailed from, the family he was so evidently close to.

"Sounds like you have some explaining to do, Syrelle," his aunt said before withdrawing from the living room to busy herself in the kitchen.

Syrelle sighed and placed his mug of tea down, untouched, before stepping up beside Lore, his frame towering beside hers.

He spent long moments studying the portrait before finally answering. "My mother is from here. Unlike my aunt, who delighted in their childhood home, my mother abhorred it. She detested the smell of fish, the cold, severe winters, and the thought of spending her life either out at sea fishing or being married to one always away, working a perilous trade. This place stole her joy. So, the moment she was of age, she packed her belongings and moved to Alytheria.

"She had no connections on the mainland, but she was quick-witted, knew how to follow orders, and was no stranger to hard work. She impressed the master cook and secured a position in the kitchens of Wyndlin Castle, and, for a time, her life seemed perfect. That is, until my father, a royal and youngest brother to the king himself, fell for her." Syrelle grimaced, his eyes darkening, losing the wistful look he had when he'd begun his mother's tale. "It's not like the storybooks; Javad Jibrann didn't buck his station when he won my mother's affection. He didn't exchange her food-stained uniform for exquisite ball gowns, her servant's quarters for any of his many estates, or ask for the young scullery maid's hand in marriage . . . not even when she swelled with my brother." His voice was thick with fury. "Falling for my mother was his *great shame.*

"My father comes from generations of wealth. His wings are a testament to that—eons of breeding a carefully cultivated royal line. But his royal upbringing and pride in his caste didn't stop him from siring two children on her. Ashamed, he let us spend our childhoods with her. We were loved and happy. The story I told you about my brother and me playing in the castle as children and stumbling upon the garden? All true. But our wings drew questioning looks. We didn't fit in with our peers, especially because Olivyre and I closely resembled our father. My mother used to say that we were painted with the same brush as him. I hated that. My father, often cruel, was despised by the servants."

He huffed a laugh devoid of humor. "My brother and I were both naturals when it came to glamour—it didn't take us long to master the art of changing our face. We chose to mimic our mother's features, to hide our wings. As children, we would have done anything not to see our father when we looked in the mirror.

"Until it became clear that he and his wife, highborn and suitable for a royal, were never going to have children of their own. One day, as adolescents, he sent for us. We were forced to leave the castle. Move to his estate. Change our surnames. Gylthrae to Jibrann. Lie about our upbringing. He would have us beaten if we even mentioned our real mother. He despised that we were his only children, bastards born from the disgrace of loving my mother. His wife, who was almost crueler than him, despised where we came from, *who* we came from, but she loved to remind us of our 'shameful' origins."

"We didn't see Syrelle or Olivyre for many years," Maple said as she walked back in from the kitchen, her voice filled with grief.

"My father wouldn't let us visit our mother or the island. Not even when our mother died were we allowed to mourn her. Not publicly, anyway." His voice was far away, tinged with bitter, painful memories. "When Javad and his wife died, I finally had the freedom to reinitiate my relationship with this side of my family. I skipped his funeral to come straight here."

Maple placed a paint-stained hand on Syrelle's arm, giving it an affectionate squeeze. "We will always be thankful that you made it back to us. We just wish your brother could have, as well, before he passed."

"I know Olivyre would have loved to. He talked about it all the time. He was older, so he had more memories of here than I. Of course, my mother was a maid, she couldn't afford to come visit often."

"So, 'Asher' is . . ." Lore started.

". . . who I could have been in another life . . . a better one," Syrelle finished.

Lore didn't know how this revelation was supposed to make her feel. That Asher wasn't all a lie. He was a dream, a wish, of a child. Shedding his true face, his father's face, would have been a balm to ease the years he spent with him. Choosing the life of a lowly guard named Asher and carving out that path for himself . . . It would have been a difficult choice to reject his titles, even if only temporarily, as she was sure the king would not let him completely discard his duties . . . but for Syrelle, maybe it would have been the only choice that made sense to him. And one that honored his mother in what way he could.

Turmoil churned within her. She understood as much as she could . . . and yet. Syrelle's gaze was heavy on her own. His eyes were filled with the emotion of his story: sorrow, anger, loss, shame, and regret. His eyes searched her own, uncertain. He wanted something from her. Forgiveness? Understanding? She could give him that, but forgiveness? No.

Her gaze shifted away from Syrelle's face, his father's face, and looked back toward the painting.

Lore opened her mouth three times; nothing she had to say felt right . . . She finally landed on: "Your mother was beautiful."

"Yes, she was."

Maple's gaze flitted between the two of them, her lips drawn into a frown. She probably didn't understand the history between them, how Syrelle's admission had the *potential* to change . . . things . . . maybe. But Maple could surely feel the tension in the air, for it was palpable, drawn between them, a braided sailor's rope, thick as the anchor line. But there was no way that Maple could grasp just how pertinent that line was. How it was pulled taut as though there were really an anchor embedded within the both of them and it was protruding from their chests. No matter how much Lore tried to wrench free, the flukes held fast. Where once that cord between them had been a lifeline, it now felt to Lore like a chain, locking her to him, Syrelle's decisions coating the cordage like algae.

The grave mood was broken by the door bursting open and two tittering children raced inside.

"Ay, yi!" Maple exclaimed. "Shoes off, you rascals!"

The children skidded to a stop and hurled their boots somewhere close to, but not quite within, the vicinity of the door.

Syrelle chased them around the house, their socks making them slip and slide on the hardwood floors before they grew tired of that game and begged him to play hide-then-seek with them using their new compasses. While they played, Lore surveyed more of Maple's art. She was truly prolific, and her brushstrokes were sure, steady, and cleverly placed, but it was the emotion she conveyed that made Lore fall in love.

She wished she had the coin to purchase the one of the sea turtle. Maple had painted him in the same spot where Lore had seen him earlier; it must be a favorite place to sunbathe for him. She wished she could buy it so she could bring it home and show the kiddos at the shelter. They would never believe a turtle could grow so large without proof.

After the twins had been found multiple times in their hiding places, Syrelle hugged them goodbye, and she and Syrelle set out to search the town, the rocky beach. Lore wanted to slow her journey just for the simple fact that the earth was, for the first time in weeks, not moving beneath her. She couldn't believe how long it had been since she'd touched solid ground. She missed it. Sea life was decidedly not for her. They spent hours looking for any traces of the *Auroradel*, but Lore found none.

Syrelle had errands to run up on the cliffs and left to find the stables to lease a horse.

Unfortunately for Lore, though she longed to explore the cliffs, she was ordered back to the ship with Thadrik.

CHAPTER 10

The sun was setting as the dinghy rose steadily into the air. When the smaller boat was level with the deck, two sailors hooked it and pulled it flush before securing it with ropes as thick as Lore's arms. Lore clambered over the *Lavender Lark*'s railing and landed ungracefully on the deck.

Cecil, the rabbit-eared guard, was waiting for her there. Lore wasn't ready to go belowdecks. This was the most time she'd spent in the open air in weeks, and the thought of being locked into the room set her heart hammering in her chest. She wasn't ready to be shut away again; she needed just a few more moments with the breeze and fresh air. Lore stepped backward, away from Cecil's sympathetic face, but yelped when her back hit something hard behind her. She whirled around, only to see that she had collided with Thadrik. The guard towered above her, and his grin . . . the smile was a sick smear across his face.

Goosebumps erupted on Lore's arms, and suddenly, she wanted nothing more than to be belowdecks, locked in her room.

"You can press up against me all you want, abomination; you won't tempt me with your demon powers." His voice was low and cruel, his words at odds with his eyes that lingered on her cleavage.

Lore crossed her arms over her chest, taking another step back. His gaze made her skin crawl.

"I would tempt a hog before temping *you* with anything."

He took a menacing step toward her. "You think we don't know what you are? A demon sent from the depths of whatever demented void your lot hails from."

Lore sputtered. "A demon? You think—"

"You cast a spell on our commander, and if you are left to your own devices, you'll cast one over the rest of us."

Lore squared her shoulders against his accusations. "I understand that you're too senseless to comprehend that just because I'm different from you, it doesn't mean I'm bad or evil, but I would appreciate it if you kept your thoughts to yourself."

"You would appreciate it, huh?"

"Thadrik, stop it. You know our orders; we aren't to engage with the prisoner," Cecil said from beside Lore.

"Shut it, Cecil. She's got you under her spell too; it's clear to anyone with eyes. You're soft on her, letting her out on the deck to see the sunrise, putting extra food on her plate when we shouldn't be feeding her kind at all. And don't get me started on how you pant over the clanless fae down there, wishing he would let you into his bed. But he never will, because he's under her spell too."

Cecil's face turned bright red, but not with embarrassment—anger. "Shut your narrow-minded mouth, Thadrik!" Cecil tensed muscled shoulders, fisting her hands until veins stood out on her forearms. "You overstep. Distant relation to the king or no, you'd best not insult me or the human again."

Lore prepared to smirk. Thadrik may tower over Cecil as well, but the guard wasn't timid—Lore would cast her bet on Cecil against the creep any day.

But Thadrik had dismissed Cecil already, his eyes trained on Lore. "It's clear you need to be taught a lesson." He raised his voice, projecting it now. "We don't take kindly to a demon whore making a fool of our commander."

Lore's gaze swiveled around the deck. Every sailor had stopped mid task to watch the scene. Fear slithered up Lore's spine as realization dawned on her that not one of them looked on sympathetically. In fact, they seemed to be nodding along—supporting Thadrik's twisted thoughts.

"The witch shouldn't even be on our ship! We're just asking for something to happen and drag us down to her dark depths," said a sailor sporting a row of rusted rings through one pointed ear, before spitting on the deck and making a sign against evil.

"—'Tis not safe. I told the captain myself just this morning, either she goes, or I do—"

"—I've got a family to get home to, I'm not going to be murdered like Old Salt by the likes of *her*—"

"—She's going to cast her power over us next. I saw her in my dreams last night, trying to lure me into temptation. Only it wasn't a dream. It was a vision that she put into my head—"

"—The same thing happened to me last night! She must be pushing her evil magic on us all!" someone else shouted, voice awash with terror, before being lost to a fray of other baseless accusations.

"Quiet!" Cecil tried to order, but her shout was strangled by the din of turbulent sailors.

Thadrik's perverse smile grew, splitting his face in two. "I knew I wasn't alone. See how many recognize you as an abomination? A sickness. What if your ilk spreads to the other humans? You are rotten fruit waiting to corrupt the rest."

"None of this is true!" Lore called out. She understood they were grieving Old Salt, but blaming her was nonsensical. "Cecil, take me to my quarters." Lore's voice was shrill from fear. She was surrounded now by jeering sailors.

"Thadrik—back off. I have orders to escort the girl to her room upon her return from Galjien."

"Cecil, you are under her spell. Go below; let the clanless prisoner cheer you up." He rubbed his hands together. "Just leave the witch to us."

Cecil shoved her way between Lore and Thadrik; her hand now gripped the hilt of her sword. She was prepared to draw it. Tears pricked Lore's eyes at the sight of the guard defending her, even if Cecil was her captor. "Back off, Thadrik. You're way out of line. When I inform Commander Syrelle what lies you are spreading to the sailors, he'll have your head for mutiny."

"You won't be saying a thing to him, Cecil, because if you do, you'll meet the same fate as the witch."

Coretha appeared from behind a gaggle of sailors, her expression ambivalent.

Lore urged, "Coretha, order them to let us pass!"

Coretha did no such thing, only tilting her head a fraction, crossing her arms. Waiting. Waiting for what? For someone else to step in? Waiting to see how far Thadrik would take this?

"Coretha, make them see reason!" Lore shouted. "I am innocent!" How long would Coretha let this continue? If she ordered them to stop, they would. She outranked them all in class, in proximity to the throne. She had more sense than this—yet she stood back, watching this exchange with impassive stolidity.

"Enough," Cecil roared, finally making herself heard. She let go of the hilt of her sword, reaching out to clasp Lore's hand and take her to safety. But Thadrik, a blur of movement, shoved Cecil forcefully away before enclosing his hand on Lore's arm, and she froze in fear.

And to Lore's horror, as she gaped, she realized that Cecil's hesitation was her downfall. The guard should have already had sword in hand, because two sailors leaped forward and gripped her arms, pinning them at her sides. A third sailor swept in, his arm slashing, the movement so quick, Lore didn't see the knife cut Cecil's sword belt in two; she only saw the belt come apart, heard the sword and scabbard as it clattered to the deck.

Without a weapon, Cecil couldn't fight them off her.

Lore felt numb. She watched the sequence of events as if she were a bystander, an onlooker; this wasn't really happening to her . . . because of her. Thadrik dug sharp nails into the flesh of Lore's bicep. Lore jolted, snapping out of it. "Take your hands off me!" Lore cried, trying to wrench free from Thadrik's vise-like grip.

He ignored her plea and clenched his fingers, his grip harsh, painful, his nails piercing further. She didn't have to look to know that her arm would be purpling with bruises.

"Throw me some rope!" Thadrik called to a sailor. Before Lore could process it, her arms were jerked behind her, and her wrists were tied, scratchy rope biting into the soft skin.

Thadrik pushed her, and she stumbled forward, her legs not wanting to work. Her mouth twisted in confusion as she realized she wasn't being herded toward the stairs to be tied up—maybe held in the brig. She looked around wildly—what did they have planned?

If these assholes even had a plan.

Lore's wrists burned. Fear ricocheted through her body like a darting dragonfly.

She thrashed wildly, her eyes bouncing from jeering sailor to sailor trying to find Coretha. Lore would beg her if she had to—this chaotic heinousness had to be stopped.

Finally, Lore spotted her. She opened her mouth to plead, but Coretha turned away, a smirk on her face. Lore watched her braids sway as she stepped through the door, slipping belowdecks.

Lore's breath left her lungs in a whoosh. Coretha wasn't going to stop this.

She really wasn't going to stop this.

The taunts of the sailors, the pushing and prodding of them all, muddled together, and time seemed to slow down. The mob's energy crackled through the air, polluting everyone on deck.

Lore swallowed. She began to plead with them; she just had to assuage their fears, get it through to them that she meant them no harm, *that this was a mistake.* It was only when their voices melded together into one single chant that she realized they *did* have a plan for her, that she comprehended what it was they intended to do.

Her heart dropped, and Lore swayed, her vision going hazy momentarily.

Her legs would have given out beneath her, and she would have fallen had she not been held aloft by the surging mob pushing forward, their long, dirty fingernails pinching and scratching. They tore her cloak from her shoulders, her beautiful cloak; it was quickly trampled under their feet. But that did not matter now, not the cloak, nor the pinching, nor the unceasing torrent of abhorrence that propelled her along like a wisp caught in a gusting wind . . . because the mutinous sailors were chanting, their breath and hearts and mind as one:

Drown
the
witch.

CHAPTER 11

Salted wind tore Lore's hair free from the ribbon she'd tied that morning. Her boots slipped on the thin railing of the *Lavender Lark* as she fought to keep her balance.

It didn't help that her hands, bound at the wrists behind her back, ached with a numbing cold that had little to do with the frigid wind that penetrated the torn fabric of her dress, and everything to do with the lack of blood in her fingertips.

Whatever shit-wit, inbred sailor had tied these knots had been heartless.

There seemed to be no blood flow to her wrists at all, and she thought—wildly—that it must all have collected in her head, which pulsated with a relentless throbbing, the pounding so strong that her brain itself thumped in tempo with the frantic thrashing of her pulse.

Thadrik's grip on the rope was the only thing keeping her from tumbling forward into the sea.

Lore's gaze skittered away from the choppy water just below her.

He was yelling something at the sailors. She couldn't make out the words over the pounding of her pulse. It didn't matter what lies he was spewing; she had pleaded with them to let her go, begged them, and all it had gotten her was a fierce slap across the face, a dirty, stinking rag shoved into her mouth, and the ropes around her wrists tightened.

And here she was, bleeding from a cut on her cheek, gagged and tied, barely balancing on the decorative edge of the ship's railing, less than a mile, but still a mile too far, from shore.

The docks of Galjien were lined with lanterns that twinkled cheerfully into the night. Welcoming, even. Her fingers, devoid of sensation, twitched in a futile attempt to break free.

If only her hands were untied. She could've *possibly* swum to the docks. It was dark, but those lanterns could light her way to safety. She could find Syrelle or Maple, and they would keep her safe until the sailors were punished for their mutiny.

But the facts were: Her hands *were* tied (and *numb*), and the temperature of the water was glacial—if the cold didn't stop her heart in moments, there was the other glaring problem. Lore was *not* a strong swimmer.

There was virtually no chance she could kick all the way to shore without slipping under too many times.

And then, the last shred of hope of reaching land was ripped from her numb grasp as someone sloshed a bucket of something over the railing. At first, she didn't realize what it was. Her mind foolishly thought . . . *red paint?* But then, as bloody scales flashed in the light of sailors' outstretched lanterns . . . she realized what it was.

Chum.

Bloodied decapitated fish heads and entrails and everything that sea monsters loved to eat.

Within seconds of the *plop plop plop* of fish guts, large jaws with rows and rows of pointed teeth snapped them up, red eyes glowing in the moonlight, their thick bodies slipping and sliding over one another in a frenzy as they fought over every morsel.

"Slice her up before we toss her in, so the razorfins know that whore-witch is what's fer dinner," a voice bellowed from the other side of the deck.

Cries of support rose up from behind her. Lore watched as the razorfins consumed the last vestiges of her hope.

Lore struggled against her bonds, panic engulfing her mind, before she remembered—if she tore free from Thadrik's grip on her bonds, she would slip off the railing and into the water below.

That creepy fucking cousin of Syrelle's grip on the rope was the only thing between her and a bloody, violent end.

Salty tears mingling with ocean spray burned the cut on her cheek as she prayed to the gods for Syrelle or the captain or anyone with a fucking brain to show up and put a stop to this. For Finndryl to hear the commotion from where he was locked away so he could break free. Save her.

Finndryl could cut through every sailor and guard in a matter of moments, before slicing through the rope on her wrists, commandeering the dinghy—rowing to safety.

But Finndryl sat three decks below, and if he was aware of what was happening, he would've gotten out to save her by now.

Nobody was coming to save her.

Lore needed her grimoire. She needed her grimoire to make sure she wouldn't slip—she wouldn't fall.

"*Deeping Lu*—" She called to it by name, though the muffled sound barely carried past the vile, stinking gag shoved into her mouth, her call morphing into a scream as someone took a dull knife to her flesh.

Immediately, blood began to stream down her arm to drip onto the railing.

"Again!"

Another cut delivered with a sinister laugh doubled the blood flow, and it dripped from the railing into the ocean. The sea beasts went into a frenzy again, frantically searching for the source of blood.

The razorfins began to bump against the side of the ship.

Lore lost all reason.

She tossed her head back and forth, shrieking through the gag. She couldn't escape, she was trapped on this railing, held by her captors, suspended in wretched agony. What right had they to cut into her flesh?

To let her precious blood?

Someone gripped her other arm, cruel fingers bruising her flesh. A third cut bloomed.

Lore screamed again as the scorching pain of dull, rusted metal ripped her skin apart; rage lanced her gut, tearing through her body and mind.

She would kill them all.

She would blind them with the light of the moon that came only when *she* called it.

She would transform that light into diamonds, cleave them with it, flay their skin from their bodies, and feed them to the razorfins.

In her mind, she called to the grimoire, which sat locked in Syrelle's chest on this very ship.

She demanded it come to her.

She couldn't fall. Gods, she couldn't fall.

She beseeched, she raged, she cried to her *Deeping Lune.*

Let me save myself and have revenge on these sailors.

But the grimoire did not come.

CHAPTER 12

Another slash, this time on her calf. Again, a gash, her ribs. They came faster now, the sailors using any sharp object they could find.

Lore blinked tears from her eyes and searched the sea for *Source*, for there was hardly any on this cursed ship, and finally—there!

The razorfins. The beasts themselves writhing below, gnashing their jaws, awaiting another taste of her blood . . . just waiting for her to fall.

She could see it.

Living, glowing *Source* inside each razorfin.

Lore, desperate, gnashed her teeth against the rag in her mouth, fisted her hands, and called to the *Source* forty feet below her.

When she had *Deeping Lune*, she commanded more *Source* than this.

Let her command it now.

And to her surprise, it *came*.

It rose from the sea, siphoned from within the bodies of the razorfins, and swirled around her, funneling into her chest and filling her body with strength.

Lore stilled her frantic movements, her screams.

The only movements from her were her billowing skirts on the wind, her wild curls, and the steady drip drip drip of her blood onto the railing.

Thadrik wouldn't have been able to see the *Source* flowing into Lore, but he must have sensed a change in her. Or maybe it was at that moment that the grotesque fuck grasped that if they kept at this, he wouldn't have his way. Lore would bleed out before she ever hit the water. Where was the fun in that? "That's enough!" he shouted at the clamoring sailors. "Commander Syrelle will be on his way back by now." Thadrik pressed into Lore, stroking her bloodied wrist with a thumb, almost gentle, almost caressing, as he savored this moment. "Time to drown, Witch," he whispered, victorious.

He released his hold on her bonds.

She should have slipped and tumbled forward.

She should be falling to a hideous death.

But Lore remained poised on the railing.

She would not fall.

She would not fall.

Not even when Thadrik uttered a curse under his breath and shoved at her back with all his fae strength, would she fall.

She could *feel* him attempt to retreat a single step despite the rabid sailors at his back clambering ever closer. Fervent and vicious snarls imploring him to *push*.

Be done with this witch.

Rage coursed through her as the ropes on her wrists loosened and dropped.

She tore the disgusting rag from her mouth, letting the wind rip the cloth from her still-numb fingers. Surprise rushed through her as she gazed at her hands. The black, inklike stains on her fingers were wavering, shifting like candle smoke. Was this how she was commanding the *Source*? Was it *Deeping Lune*'s ink that stained her hands? Magic imprinted within her very skin, a connection to the grimoire?

Lore's blood-spattered boots lifted off the railing as she elevated into the air, her body revolving gradually until her back was to the sea, her face toward the ship.

She looked for Cecil, who had tried to save her. But she must have been dragged belowdecks, for her kind face was nowhere to be seen.

The sailors' and guards' shouts morphed into terror-filled screams as they changed course. Their gleeful cries of misplaced rage had only ever been fueled by terror and Lore was supposed to fall. It took this one thing to tip their minds over the edge.

Lore gazed down upon the sailors, this incurable, writhing sea of beings.

If they were the tide, then she was the moon.

Rush forward to hurt her.

Recede to run from her.

It was all because of her.

She lowered herself until her boots met the deck of the *Lavender Lark* and walked forward a single step. They tripped over each other in their haste to run, no different from the razorfins' frenzy. Lore felt what they had felt, as if their former glee had been transferred to her. She was enjoying this.

The sailors and guards alike backed away, some already pressed against the opposite railing, but they dared not move too fast. They looked at her as if she was the predator, and they her prey. With nowhere to flee, besides a churning sea of razorfins, they stilled. She could almost see their desperate thoughts as they froze, one by one.

If they stayed still, maybe she wouldn't see them, and they would be spared.

If they were to accuse her of it anyway, terrorize her for it, end her life for it, then she would embody it.

Let her be their monster, their demon, the witch from their nightmares.

Lore unclenched her fists and felt her power unleash.

She struck Thadrik first.

The guard hissed, stumbling backward, covering his face with hands red with *her* blood, trying to block the light that emitted from her palms. Two sailors who stood just behind him were next. They must have been among the ones who cut her because they each dropped a small, glistening, red-edged dagger to the deck, their hands flying to cover their eyes.

It wasn't long before every one of the murderous sailors was cowering on the deck, their screams rising in crescendo as Lore broadened her arms, amplifying the light.

She shouted her wrath, her scream mingling with theirs, as she shifted the light, compressed it with her mind into diamonds. Small slivers of jagged light began to cut the sailors' hands and arms where they covered their faces.

She craved more.

She drew more *Source* from the creatures in the sea. She pushed, urging the crystalline light to not just hurt; she wanted it to maim.

She would make them feel her fear. She would make them *drown* in it. And when she was done, when they gasped their last breath, she would find Finndryl, and her grimoire, and they would be free.

Not long now. Lore almost smiled. Some of the sailors were starting to quiet, as their strength bled out of them. How fitting this was. For them to be the ones to die by a thousand cuts.

Relief coursed through her. She would have her revenge. And soon, this would be behind her.

Lore pushed her power outward, willing the fractal moonlight to finish the job and shred them to pieces, when a shroud of dark power enveloped her, dampening her magic. Lore struggled against the force, looking around wildly through a haze of shadows.

Syrelle.

The male was climbing over the railing of the ship, a thick, writhing vine clenched in his hands wrapped around the railing.

Now he appears?

Not in time to save her from being murdered by his guards and sailors! No, just in time to stop her from having her revenge. Fucking typical.

"Lore, end this!" Syrelle boomed from across the deck.

Lore growled in rage, urging her light to shred him, too, but he was shielded from her power. Her light reflected harmlessly off his shield and scattered like moonlight on water.

He retracted the vine and dropped onto the deck. He moved toward her, pushing through the sailors and guards scattered around him, his gaze trained on her as plumes of dark magic billowed out of his open palms, protecting him from her light. His magic shot outward like shadowed vines, writhing across the deck toward her.

"Get those away from me, Syrelle!"

"You are killing them! Stop this now. You will be forever stained with their slayings." His voice carried over the winds, magicked to sound as if he were already standing right in front of her and not across the deck.

"They tried to kill me first!" she cried out, her voice ragged, haunted, even to her own ears.

"I know," he crooned softly. "I see the blood on you."

"Stop where you are," she commanded. He was too close, gods. She needed to keep him away from her. She wouldn't be . . . couldn't be held by his magic again, robbed of her will. He was closer now. Her light was doing nothing to stop him; it barely slowed him down.

"It doesn't have to be this way."

Lore looked around frantically for something to hurt him with. She'd been trapped for too long, powerless, but in that moment, the power she'd siphoned from the sea beasts wavered, waned, and flickered out.

She did not have to see them to know that she had used up all their *Source*. She had probably drained the creatures of not just their intrinsic magic, but their very lives in her efforts to save herself.

"No, no, no." Lore shook her hands, trying to cast her magic again, but it was no use, the ink stains on her hands had ceased their movement, no longer reacting to the *Source*.

Lore looked to the edge of the ship and back to the door leading to Finndryl and the grimoire. If she tried to race below and find them, Syrelle would stop her.

If she leapt over the edge, there was a possibility she could disappear and hide from him in Galjien until she could devise a plan to retrieve them. Lore turned and ran for the railing, but it was no use. Syrelle and his black vines were abruptly *there*. A blur. From behind, he clamped his arms around her and pressed her to his chest. "I've got you. It's over." She bucked against him, trying to dislodge his hold, but it was as though he were honed from granite; she couldn't free herself from his grip.

"No!" Lore shook her head, writhing. But his magic pushed into her mind, and she felt her struggles weaken and her muscles relax—no matter how hard she fought, she could not combat him without her grimoire or *Source* of her own.

He wrapped her in vines, too tight to move, not so tight that they hurt. He was careful that none of them touched her wounds. Once Syrelle was sure that she was secure and wasn't going to try to jump over the railing or rush him from behind, he turned around to survey the scene.

Sailors and guards alike were helping one another to stand. The deck was slick with their blood, and they were weak from blood loss, pain, and terror.

"We are saved!" someone called out.

A few cheers rose up in response, but mostly everyone looked weary. A few were crying, heaving sobs, as they tried to stop the bleeding on themselves or crewmates.

Lore had done this. With light. She'd managed to stop them from killing her, without her grimoire.

She watched them, her gaze unflinching. She was not sorry for their pain. She did not have it in her; she still burned with rage, and if given the choice, she would do it again, only this time, she would find a way to bleed them until the life drained from their eyes.

"Silence." One quiet word from him and all quieted. There wasn't a rustle of movement nor a whispered word.

"You disobeyed my orders, and you think I came back to 'save' you?"

"—We were trying to protect you from the witch, my Lord—"

"—She's a demon, my Lord—"

"—She murdered Old Salt—"

"The next to speak had better choose wisely, it might be the last thing they ever say," the captain bellowed between pants from the doorway. The captain was flushed and sweat streamed down his face despite the cold. "I'm sorry, Commander Syrelle, I didn't know."

Syrelle ignored the captain as his gaze swept over the sailors and guards until they landed on Thadrik.

"When the king appointed you as my second, I knew that you would cause problems for me—but I didn't realize you were this stupid."

"Syrelle," Thadrik sputtered. "Cousin, I—"

"Your ignorance and hatred have condemned you and those under your command to death."

Thadrik pulled himself to a standing position. He was weak and in pain and nearly blinded, Lore thought, from the way he was squinting toward Syrelle, but he wasn't going to let that stop him from pleading for his life. "I'm innocent! It was their idea!" he whined, trying to shift the blame. "You wouldn't kill your own cousin—I'm protected by—by—" Stupid indeed. He couldn't even think of what could possibly protect him from Syrelle's fury.

"You can lead your mob in one last thing." A vine extended from Syrelle's hand, its tip a hardened, pointed casing. It coiled in the air for a moment, writhing like a snake before Syrelle whipped his hand forward. "Death." The vine shot out and pierced straight through Thadrik's right eye.

An uproar of gasps and screams.

Syrelle turned to look at Lore, his voice severe. Lore wanted to shrink from the wrath that seared in his eyes as he regarded her. "They will be punished for their crimes against you, Lore Alemeyu. But their deaths will be on my hands, not yours."

Calamity ensued as sailors and guards scrambled away from their lord.

Those nearest the railing attempted to throw themselves overboard, anything to escape Syrelle, but he was fast—it wasn't the first time Lore had seen him use the earthen powers that she usually attributed to Asher, but it was clear now that he had dampened his power, another layer to his facade, because the one vine split and multiplied until every single one of the mob who had tried to kill Lore lay dead. The last of them hadn't even ceased the jerking spasm of death before Syrelle recalled the vines back into himself. They slithered across the deck through pools of blood before disappearing into his palms, which dripped with blood.

CHAPTER 13

Surrounded by the dead, Syrelle released the vines that encircled her form, calling them back into himself.

Lore wrapped a hand around the deepest cut on her arm and watched him wearily.

Seconds. It had taken him seconds to end their lives.

"Get down below," he seethed.

Lore skirted past the captain on her way belowdecks. She avoided looking at the tears streaming down his face. His crew had mutinied, a crime punishable by death. But she wondered if the captain did not think a "witch," in his eyes, was a worthy cause for so many fae deaths.

Syrelle spoke to the captain, his words too quiet for her to hear, but his tone was vicious.

Lore did not stick around to find out what Syrelle had to say to him.

Since the captain would have been in command while Syrelle was away from the ship, she wondered if he would be punished for his failure to keep order. Or was the execution of almost everyone on his crew punishment enough?

Lore didn't make it far before Syrelle's long legs ate up the distance, and he was by her side.

Lore slowed her steps for a moment when Coretha poked her

head out of a door. The female's face was wan, pale, and Lore sneered when she saw the embarrassed expression on her face. Not guilt for not helping Lore; no, it would be because Syrelle would know that she hadn't helped. The despicable female opened her mouth to say something, when a warning sound rumbled in Syrelle's chest.

"I'll deal with you later," Syrelle spat out. His tone was coated in deadly venom. Coretha slammed her mouth shut and closed her door, locking it.

Lore hoped he fed Coretha to the razorfins.

When they arrived at her room, Syrelle followed her in and slammed the door behind them.

Lore was shocked that it didn't explode off its hinges.

Syrelle was furious; his hands were visibly shaking. He pressed on the wall, and a secret compartment—hidden in the wall this whole time—popped open. Lore would've cursed—what else was hidden in this room that she could've used to escape?—if she wasn't so fucking terrified of this raging male who had just systematically ended the lives of nearly thirty souls. Who was rifling through the compartment with way more intensity than felt necessary until he found what he was searching for.

A large leather bag.

Syrelle gripped the bag in his fist like he was going to strangle it as he stomped toward her. Lore shrank away from him, but he grabbed her arm, and . . . oh, okay, the leather bag was a medical kit. Like one her aunt brought with her on house calls. Only way more stocked and sophisticated. He found a bottle of something vile with vapors that assaulted Lore's nose the moment he yanked the cork out with his teeth; gods, he was unhinged. He spat the cork across the room, not even watching as it bounced off seemingly every piece of furniture before disappearing behind the wardrobe.

Lore pursed her lips. It would be him on his hands and knees later to locate the cork—she wasn't going to find the damned—

"Ow, that burns!"

"I have to make sure you aren't infected; sailors are notorious for neglecting their weapons," he gritted out through clenched teeth. He made to set the bottle down before thinking better of it and doused her still-bleeding cuts with *more* of the liquid fire in a bottle.

"Okay, that's enough! Whatever this stuff is, there is no way any impurity can flourish now."

Syrelle growled.

Lore hissed.

No way she was letting him pour more of that on her without putting up a fight.

He cut his eyes at her before shaking the bottle and setting it on the bedside table. "No more left, anyway." Then, with alarming quickness, he scooped a clear goop out of a small, squat jar, and before Lore could ask, *What the hell is that stuff?* he slathered it on her arm and calf.

Lore sniffed at her arm warily and relaxed a smidge.

She recognized this one by its earthy smell. She'd made a similar salve for her aunt countless times, and at least her wounds had immediately stopped burning from the first medicinal concoction he'd subjected her to.

With another growl, Syrelle ripped a length of cloth from the bag and wrapped the pieces around her arms, tying each of them tight, though his fingers, she noticed, were still shaking.

He finished tying off the one on her calf before tending to her cheek.

"Stay still. This one isn't deep, but still needs to be cleaned," he ordered as he gripped her chin. She couldn't help it, she'd flinched away the moment he'd procured *another* bottle of that blasted burning liquid from the bag and came near her face with it . . . This stuff was torture.

"I am staying still," she said through a sharp intake of breath. Gods, it *stung*. She felt like her face was on *fire*.

"As still as the puppy I had as a kid."

"Must have been a very calm and collected dog . . ."

"No, he was wild and rambunctious and only stopped moving when he would finally wear himself out and sleep."

"Are you finished yet?" His attempt at a distraction wasn't working.

"Just about." And then he doused her again.

"Fucker! It burns!"

"I know. I know. I'm sorry."

He slathered her cheek with the earthy-smelling salve. The familiar aroma calmed her still-racing heart a little.

He clenched the little bottle in his hand. Lore was afraid the glass would burst and cut him, and then she would have to help clean him up . . . only she wouldn't.

She still hated him.

"Feel better?"

"No."

"No, I don't suppose you would after what they tried to . . ." He dropped the bottle of salve back into the leather bag and placed it on the bed.

"They were going to feed me to the razorfins." Lore cackled. The sound bubbling out of her was not so much a laugh as . . . hysteria. "And then . . . and then they were going to all watch whatever was left of me *drown*."

She felt a little shocked saying it out loud like that. She was almost murdered. She was almost eaten alive.

She thought . . . maybe . . . too much had happened in the last few bells, and she might not be taking it at all *well*.

Especially with the way Syrelle was regarding her. As if she were going to break into pieces right before him. She needed to change the subject quickly before she emitted another terrifying, hysterical laugh. "Remember that time you cleaned and wrapped that cut on my thigh?"

Syrelle's nostrils flared, and his eyes flashed. "In the cave. How could I forget?"

"Your hands were so . . . gentle . . . and we didn't have any of these fancy supplies. You chewed a *leaf.*"

"That leaf tasted terrible. Worst thirty seconds of my life."

Lore hiccupped. Shit. Was she laughing or crying? "It made me feel better, though."

"Yeah. That was the point."

"I hate to think about those times . . . before . . . because it hurts."

"I can't stop thinking about them. They're the only thing getting me through . . . this mess I've made." He grunted, running his hands over his scalp.

"Does that help you? Thinking about before?"

"No." His voice was a hoarse whisper. "It's *devastating.* And yet I can't stop playing the memories again and again, despite the pain . . . I should've told you the truth. I never should have lied." His eyes shimmered, as they bore into her own. "I can't believe I had you, and I lost you . . . I'll never stop hating myself."

Lore didn't know if it was the excitement of the last bell or the fact that Syrelle had just killed the entire crew for her, but she couldn't help but ask, "Why didn't you?"

"It got to the point where I wanted to believe the lie. I wanted to just be a guard, whose only task was keeping you safe . . ." He laughed, the sound strangled with emotion. "And to stop you from thieving."

"You weren't very good at either of those." Lore raised her chin in defiance—of Syrelle, yes, but she also was determined to fortify herself against the emotions battling within her. "After all. It was you, Syrelle, who hurt me the most."

"That it was," he said with a nod. "Not to mention, despite my watchful eye, you stole my heart." He gave a soft, sad smile. "Ever the thief."

Lore shook her head. "Don't do this, I can't—"

"It's true, Lore. You've had my heart since you trusted me enough to sit upon the swing in the garden. I'd tried to fight it . . . Gods, I tried to ignore your irresistible charm, gorgeous freckles, and wild, unyielding spirit . . . but every wall I built crumbled when I saw you swinging there in my favorite place in the entire world, the moonlight kissing your hair . . . I wanted to kiss you so badly it terrified me."

Lore's eyes welled up again. "I hate you."

"I deserve your hate . . ." His tone turned bitter. "And I still can't keep you safe. I leave you alone for a single bell, and it's my own people who try to kill you. I thought this was safest, getting you away from my uncle, but you're in danger no matter what I do."

His voice broke off, and he pulled her into his arms.

Lore stiffened for a second before she melted into him.

She'd gone through too godsdamned much today to resist anymore. As much as the disinfectant had, it hurt to be embraced by Syrelle—it hurt because it was also a balm, like that soothing, healing salve, because when she closed her eyes, he *felt* like Asher. His arms tightened around her as she pressed her face into his chest, inhaling his blackberry and honeyed scent, and pretending for just a moment that he hadn't ruined everything.

The instant she allowed herself to relent, to give in . . . she was crying, heaving sobs into his bloodstained shirt.

He planted kisses in her hair. He tightened his grip, rubbing soothing circles on her back. He whispered, "The only way to keep you safe is to become so powerful that no one would dare hurt you. Help me find the book, Lore. Together, we can make it so no one will hurt you or anyone you love ever again."

Lore felt like someone had tossed a frigid bucket of snowmelt on her. She drew back so she could see his face and searched his eyes.

"Was all that about my stealing your heart just another ploy to inspire me to find the grimoire for you?" Her voice was rough, hoarse, barely above a whisper. "Despite the fact that *Auroradel* is so dangerous, it almost separated my mind from my body from *hundreds* of miles away while I scried at your behest. Even though *your* soldiers and chartered sailors tried to *drown me*." Her shoulders were shaking as sobs morphed into laughter. She pushed him away, using all her strength. "Doubling down on your plan to make the stupid human fall for you, so I would do your bidding, like the pawn your kind love to pretend *using* is all we're good for."

She clenched her fists, her nails sharp daggers in the soft flesh of her palms.

"You would become so powerful that you could 'protect me'?" She inhaled, stopping the next manic bout of laughter threatening to erupt from her. She wiped her tears with bloodied palms. "I've got a better idea." She leaned in closer to him. "I'll find *Auroradel* for *me*. Then I'll become so powerful I can protect myself and everyone that I love from *you*."

The raw fury in Lore's voice echoed through the room, each syllable a jagged shard of ice. Her hands, slick with blood and tears, shoved against his chest, a desperate attempt to push away not just him, but the torrent of emotions threatening to drown her.

Syrelle clenched his jaw. A vein began to throb on his forehead. "No," he said vehemently. "You mustn't." He gripped her shoulders. "Look at me, Lore. It is important that you hear this." He shook her, his grip painful. "What matters more than my feelings, more than how you feel about me, is that no matter how much magic you acquire, even if you find *Auroradel*, it won't be enough; my uncle's source of magic is too powerful." His voice cracked. "Promise me, Lore. Promise me that no matter what happens, you will never confront him."

Lore made no such promise. Of course he would do or say whatever he had to dissuade her from taking power from him. She seethed with fury.

He loosened his grip on her. "Just know, I would *never* use my feelings for you as a ploy, a trick. You may not believe me, but deep down, you must know it to be true." He swallowed thickly. "I can live with you not believing me for a while longer. Soon, I will prove it to you."

His grasp on her shoulders felt like shackles. She was confined.

A prisoner. This was torture, and he, her tormentor. Lore shivered. Her chest felt constricted; she couldn't pull in breath. It was as though a fist were strangling her heart and it was about to burst.

"Leave!" she screamed, the word a guttural sob tearing from her throat. "Get out! I can't breathe with you here." Her eyes blazed with a cold fire, reflecting the wreckage of their affection. "I need you out."

The weight of her words hung heavy in the air, erecting a tangible barrier between them.

In that moment, they were ships passing in a typhoon, each locked in their own tempestuous voyage. His heart was an unknowable vessel, one without a flag or standard; no insight to articulate, with certainty, the veracity of where he stood.

Her own heart ached for the storm to subside, for safe harbor.

But the storm raged on, the waves of his betrayal colliding against her ability to ever trust him again.

If this persisted, it would kill her.

Syrelle stood there, a silent witness to the chaos within her, his own emotions seeming a tangled mess that mirrored her own. Lore needed him to honor her request for space, this desperate push for solitude to navigate the treacherous waters of her pain, even though he honored nothing else when it came to her.

More than at any other time in the last two weeks, she yearned for Finndryl's presence.

Finndryl was a lighthouse in her storm, a beacon of hope guiding her through a darkness that was close to swallowing her whole.

"Keep the medicinal case. I'll send Cecil with hot water to wash with. When you're done, change your dressings . . ."

"I know how to fucking heal myself when the fae cut me, Syrelle." She closed her eyes against the sight of him. "Go."

The sound of the lock sliding into place behind him was louder than the thundering in her ears.

CHAPTER 14

L ore slept for three days, only waking to change her bandages, eat, and use the chamber pot.

This room had become her prison and her sanctuary.

All she could do was watch out her window as the *Lavender Lark*, manned by a skeleton crew, headed farther away from Duskmere. She whipped the curtain closed. She was sick of the endless ocean. Galjien was long gone. Alytheria was two weeks behind them. Ma Serach was one week's sail away, and Lore wasn't any closer to finding out where the book was on the continent.

Lore knew she should scry again. Not for the book—right now, she couldn't bring herself to comb through that sentient darkness. Not so soon after the razorfins. No, she *should* scry so that she could see Finn. There wasn't anything she wanted to do more than to see him. But she couldn't bear the thought of only "seeing" him in that way. She didn't want to be a ghost to him.

Invisible.

She had no doubt that, just from the sound of her voice, he would know that something had happened to her. She wouldn't be able to hide it. And when he learned what had almost been done to her, she wanted to be *with* him. Really with him. To reassure him that she had made it out . . . alive.

Not whole. But not fractured either. *Transformed.*

Lore trailed a fingernail along the deepest gash on her arm that, thanks to the salve, was already healing into a jagged, lumpy scar. She did not wish the scars away. They were proof that she had overcome an entire boatload of fae intent on killing her.

And more importantly, she didn't need the grimoire within reach to channel power.

She just needed *Source.*

Like her godsdamned grimoire. Deeping Lune was honed from *Source* itself. And Lore could access it. As long as it was nighttime . . . especially if the moon was full. And it seemed to have an amplifying quality.

She rolled onto her back, imagining how much stronger she would be with access to *Auroradel.* She didn't believe Syrelle. About her finding *Auroradel* being futile. If she had control of both books, she *would* defeat anyone who came between her people and freedom. And if that meant the king, then it meant the king.

There was a reason the king wanted the books, wasn't there? Maybe his power was waning.

Either way, his time had come.

Lore let her eyes flutter closed, imagining that she held both books. That her people were leaving Duskmere behind for good. She would find a better place. Build walls. A fortress if she had to. She would devise a spell that would incinerate the fae on the spot— crossing the threshold into their village would be their instant, painful death.

She frowned. Obviously, not all fae were malevolent. Maybe she could call up a permanent fog instead—any fae with ill intentions toward the humans would vanish in the fog forever. If their intentions were honorable, they would be allowed to locate the gate . . . but none could enter. It would be a completely fae-free town.

SCREEEEEECH

Every muscle in Lore's body locked up, petrified by a horrific symphony of sound that ripped through the room. No, the entire ship. Heart hammering against her ribs, a trapped bird desperate for escape, she sat up, looking around wildly.

It wasn't the usual creak and groan of weathered wood; she'd grown used to that. Nor the sound of the wind inflating the sails, which sometimes echoed through the ship. No, this was a bone-jarring grind, the sound of beams being crunched.

SCREECH

Again the sound tore through the room, only this time it was accompanied by a tremor that rattled her teeth. The floor beneath her tilted violently, throwing her against the wall like a discarded rag doll.

The ship stood frozen, a captive in an unseen grip. Terror choked her, a viper coiling in her gut, which was shouting at her that this wasn't a rogue tempest or an anchor caught on an uncharted reef.

This was something ancient, primal, a leviathan awoken from nightmares in the ocean's deepest trenches.

Gods, was it Takuma?

Shivers spread down Lore's spine that felt like the icy caress of death.

Lore clambered to her feet and rushed to the door, trying the handle. Locked, as she knew it would be. She made her hands into fists and pounded on the door. "Hello? What's happening out there?" She waited, listening for a reply, pressing her ear to the door when one didn't immediately come. "Cecil? Are you there?"

What had the power to halt a ship this size? In such a way that she would be thrown against the wall?

Lore tried not to imagine tentacles, thick as a mast, rising from the abyss, dripping venom that hissed as it burned its way through each deck of the *Lavender Lark*. An obscene mass of barbed claws, scraping across the hull to pull the ship into its gaping maw.

She raced to the window and thrust the curtain wide, terrified she would see a single, enormous eye, like a burning ember, breaking the surface of the sea, but there was nothing there but endless wine-red water of the Dread Abyss.

She rapped harder on the door, ignoring the sharp sting in her knuckles. She needed her grimoire.

She needed Finndryl.

"Cecil, let me out! If the ship goes down, and I'm locked in here, I won't even have a chance."

Lore heard the thud of something heavy hitting the level above. Someone, a guard or one of the few sailors left, screamed, a blood-curdling sound that ended abruptly. People shouted to each other, their cries echoing down the corridor, pitched with horror. The sound of boots running to and fro above her—and louder footsteps out in the hall—and then—

She felt the ship lurch again, a sickening tilt, then a dead stop. Her stomach heaved as the floorboards trembled beneath her boots.

Lore hammered harder on the door, her hands bruising. "Let me out!"

But no one came. She felt utterly alone, adrift in the deafening silence punctuated only by an occasional shudder or thump.

She rested her forehead against the hardwood. Goddess, she *wasn't* going to die in here.

Maybe she could open the door by dislodging the handle?

Lore studied her room. Then shoved the washbasin off the small table, not caring when the porcelain shattered on the floor. She picked up the table and, with a shout, heaved it over her head directly into the doorknob.

The wood table was dented, and a corner broke off, clattering to the floor.

But the doorknob stayed firmly in place.

The room began darkening with shadows. Something was obstructing the window. People. They climbed the ropes like ants on a stem, their bodies briefly blocking the light, cursed shadows.

Thistle and sage. This wasn't an attack by a sea beast . . . people were boarding the ship.

The ship stuttered again, groaning under the pressure of whatever was holding the vessel immobile in the water.

Agitation shot through her as a whispered "Lore" warbled through the keyhole.

Hope and fear twisted within Lore's trembling frame. It was a lifeline, yet the familiar voice held an edge of desperation. What was happening on the other side? *Should* the door be opened?

"I'm here! Is it safe to come out?" Lore hissed back. She picked up the nearest candlestick, plucked the tapered beeswax free from the sconce, and held her weapon high, edging closer to the locked door.

"The lock is stuck, hold—" Cecil's voice choked off, and the handle stopped jiggling. Lore heard the sounds of a muffled scuffle followed by a soft thud.

Footsteps.

"Cecil?" Lore tried the knob. It didn't budge. She knelt and looked through the keyhole, but a key blocked her view.

With a silent cry, Lore scrambled backward away from the door. Blood pooled beneath, running in rivulets along the floor, blooming like constellations on the rug.

Cecil's blood?

Lore stilled. Whoever had wounded Cecil was still outside, and the key was now in the lock. A moment ago, she'd desired nothing more than to escape this room, and now the last thing she wanted was for that door to open.

Lore's fingers were beginning to ache for how hard she was clenching the candlestick. Cecil was a trained guard who possessed a sharp sword, and she'd been wounded. By the amount of blood slipping under the door, most likely the wound was lethal.

She watched the door, pulse thundering in her ears as she waited for the knob to turn.

But the hall was silent; the muffled battle sounds were far away, up on the deck, and still, she waited for the knob to twist. It felt like an eternity, but whoever had hurt Cecil appeared to have moved on.

What about the window?

She glanced at it. The attackers had climbed up the sides of the ship, and—there was a thick rope butting against the window in the wind.

She'd looked for weaknesses in and around the windows before but never outright attempted to break the glass. She could break the window and grab the rope, using it to climb up to the deck. She would figure out where to go from there.

However, smashing the window would be so fucking *loud*.

Lore cast a quick glance at the door, candlestick poised in the air, before stilling, flesh pebbling with shivers. There was something *off* about the blood.

It should still be darkening into a stain and yet . . . the blood that had soaked through the bottom of the door was no longer red, thick. Streams of it were still leaking through, the color now weak, muted.

Lore stepped down from the bed, crossed the room, and bent down to see.

The sharp smell of iron reached her nose, but it was tainted with another smell. Something much worse.

Salt.

Salt water.

The ship was sinking.

And Finndryl was on a deck beneath hers.

Raw terror flooded her senses. Lore raced to the window. Hurled the candlestick at the glass. Picked it up and pounded again and again.

What should have shattered easily refused to break. There was not even a crack in the glass to show for her effort.

It was spelled or something. Reinforced to prevent her escape.

This room had been her prison for weeks, and now it would become her tomb.

Lore waded through water that was up to her knees now. Her skirt absorbed the water, slowing her down. She tried not to think of Cecil's blood. If she went down, her layers would restrict her movement. With shaking fingers, Lore untied the strings of her simple cloth corset. She stripped until she stood in just her dress. The water was rising at an alarming rate. The table she'd broken to pieces floated around her.

Lore climbed up on the bed and examined the window for a weakness in the wooden sill. She'd never found a weakness before, but goddess, if she could find a weak spot, she could pry it up. Lore heaved a frustrated shout, slamming her hand onto the wall. This fuck-ass ship seemed to be honed from a single tree. Fucking fae and their ridiculous craftsmanship.

Was this how she died?

Imprisoned by the male she'd once loved?

Drowned in bloodied water?

No. She wouldn't fucking *have* it.

By now the voices above had gone quiet. The ship groaned. It was not going to sink to the bottom of the ocean without its cries of outrage. Lore, angry, roared with it. She cried out to the gods and goddesses who had never done anything to protect her. Who had begot life but offered nothing but suffering.

She dug her fingers into the quilt and cursed them for it.

And then she heard the key being slid sideways, the locking mechanism detach, and the wretched doorknob begin to turn.

Please be Finndryl, free from below, come to save her.

Lore held her breath as a shadowy figure shoved at the door.

Would it be Syrelle who came to let her out of his prison?

Inch by agonizing inch, the gap widened, revealing slivers of darkness beyond. A flicker of reflected light caught her eye—an iridescent sheen dancing along the shadows that seeped in from the arching door.

Lore's heart hammered against her ribs, a frantic drumbeat in the suffocating silence.

Then, with a swish, the door swung wide, revealing a nightmare encased in the doorframe.

Scales, like polished gemstones, shimmered under the dim light filtering through the window. Each one a kaleidoscope of emerald and sapphire, reflecting the terror in Lore's wide eyes. But it was the maw that stole her breath, gleaming with predatory hunger— a row of sharp teeth with tapered canines, made for ripping flesh from bone, sawing through muscle and sinew. Fingers, too long and slender, tipped with webbing that stretched between each bonelike digit, reached for her.

Lore's hands tightened on the bedpost, a quiet plea escaping her lips before she could stop it. "No," she whispered, the word stifled with dawning horror.

The creature's head tilted, unblinking eyes like liquid emeralds fixing on her.

And then, from the depths of that horrifying mouth, a melodic note resonated through the room, cold and seductive, a guarantee of oblivion.

Lore wished that the key had not been found. That the door had not been opened. One word clanged through Lore's mind before it no longer belonged to her, but to the creature itself.

Siren.

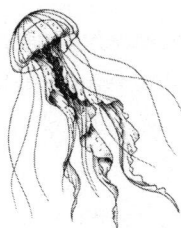

CHAPTER 15

"Are you what all this fuss is about?" The siren's voice was dulcet and curious. Lore relaxed her grip on the bedpost, the tightness in her jaw; the candlestick in her other hand fell from limp fingers.

She shrugged the terror from her body like a shawl.

But . . . *Wait*, her mind pleaded, *wait*.

Shouldn't she be afraid? Her pulse picked up its frenetic drumbeat once more. This was one of the creatures that attacked the ship. This ship may have been her prison for weeks, but . . .

It's better the demon you know, right?

The creature waded through the water on scale-covered legs; the siren wore a shimmering purple, scaled armored vest cinched tightly over a gossamer gown of vermillion and chartreuse, the color of an algae bloom swaying in the water. The siren's eyes were large and gleamed like a forest reflected on water, and Lore could not look away from them. She couldn't tear her gaze from the striking face at all. The creature was predatory, beautiful, terrifying. Shoulder-length brown tresses floated around the siren's deep-brown face like they weren't sure what they were supposed to do when not underwater.

"Are you my savior, my captor, or my end?" Lore asked.

The siren blinked. "Maybe I am none of those."

Lore frowned. "What else could there be?"

"What if I were a friend?"

"My friends are lost to me. I am alone."

The creature was standing in front of her now. "You need not be alone anymore."

Lore could smell the fathomless depths of the sea on them. It was intoxicating. Enthralling. Dangerous. No human should know what the bottom of the ocean smells like.

"What are you called?" asked the siren.

Lore should lie, like she did with Queen Riella. She shouldn't give up her name. Her mother had told her, long ago, that when a demon asked your name, you should never tell them.

"Lore Alemeyu." *Fuck.* There was magic at work here; she could not lie to this creature.

"I heard you called something else. A hateful word whispered on the wind."

"They call me witch. I do not mind. To be hated for being something new. Unknown. To be feared for it . . . It is better than being pitied." Lore frowned. She hadn't known she felt this way, but it was the truth. She would rather be called "witch" by the fae than any of the other words she'd had pitched at her.

The water was rising. Icy tendrils kissed her waist.

If Lore did not escape this sinking ship soon it would not matter what they whispered about her on the wind or otherwise. She would not hear it. This ship would be her grave; she would be dead.

"Come with us; we siren, too, know something about being feared."

Lore shook her head with vigor. "There is a male on this ship, I cannot leave him."

The siren's lips quirked into a smile, though it was not one of kindness, but mischief. Lore imagined this was the face Yissa, the trickster god, wore when he banished the humans to this existence of misery.

"Tall, dark, and handsome with locs that flutter in the water? Stubborn?"

"Yes!" Lore gasped.

"I see you have similar motivations. He wouldn't leave the ship either, without the promise that we would find you."

This creature had spoken to Finndryl already?

"Have you freed him from his room as well . . . ?" Lore asked, wanting to know if going with the siren would lead to "freedom."

The siren blinked. Its lashes were otherworldly long, captivating. "He only complied when we told him the truth of why we are here."

"And what is the truth?"

"We have been searching for something new. Something . . . unknown." The siren blinked emerald eyes before narrowing their gaze upon her. "Something new, like you."

Lore was the reason the ship was attacked. That Cecil was most likely lying dead in the corridor?

"Is he safe?"

"As safe as a lander can be in the ocean."

"If I come with you, will he be whole, unharmed?"

"I swear it."

"But wait, there is something else I need. It's in the commander's quarters."

"We do not have much time before the ship sinks. Your kind will not last long below water without our ritual."

"I must have it. Please—let me try."

The creature cocked their head to one side, calculating, before giving a slight nod.

The hall was dark, but Lore could see where Cecil floated face down in the water. She sidestepped the guard, wishing she had a moment to turn her over, close her eyes if they were not closed, and say something in her honor. She may have been her captor, but there was no denying that she was kind, unsuited for the position of jailer. Her end had been violent and tragic.

And Cecil wasn't alone.

The farther they went, the more dead guards they saw, yet not a single dead siren. They had had the benefit of surprise, and it seemed that they were in their element.

Syrelle's quarters were the floor above Lore's, and the water had not reached it yet.

She ran with the siren down the hall, the creature following her like an apparition. A ghost. Seawater mixed with blood dripped from their clothes and stained the ornate carpet. Lore stepped over bodies, wishing she could stop and check to see if any were alive. If she knew them.

If one was Syrelle.

She did not know what she would feel if she found him cut down. She knew she *should* feel relieved that he would no longer have power over her.

And yet, she knew that *relief* would *not* be what she felt.

Though, if she should come upon Coretha floating in the water—it would be a welcome sight.

Finally, she and the siren reached Syrelle's quarters. The door hung broken, suspended from one hinge. The locked chest Syrelle kept the grimoire in lay on its side, empty. The room had been ransacked.

Lore stepped over a toppled candle sconce and began to rifle through already opened drawers and cabinets. Maybe Syrelle had moved it. "Where are you?" she called to it, now searching through Syrelle's well-stocked closet and dresser, but it was clear that the grimoire was no longer here. Despite the daylight, Lore's tether to *Deeping Lune* would lead her right to it, even if it was hidden. Even if the cabinet was spelled.

"Where is it?" she whispered to herself, frantically tearing open the last of Syrelle's cabinets, throwing aside silk shirts, cashmere sweaters.

"Is the item you seek not here?"

"No. Someone must have taken it." Did Syrelle have it? Did he take the book and leave Lore to drown in her room? That would solve his problem, anyway, wouldn't it? Either way, Syrelle was not here, and neither was the book. "I have to find it, maybe it's—"

Lore's boots splashed with each step. Icy water lapped at her skirts once again. Another floor of the ship was lost to the sea.

The siren clamped a long-fingered hand on Lore's arm and began to pull her toward the door. Lore shuddered. The creature's skin was an odd texture. Smooth on the palm, despite the scales that peppered the top of either hand and wrist. "We are out of time."

The ship would sink; it did not care for Lore's plans. Tears of frustration burned in the backs of Lore's eyes.

Without the grimoire, Lore was nothing.

Worse than nothing. She was someone who had tasted power and now did not think that she could live without it.

Lore tried to pull her arm out of the siren's grip. "I can't leave without it. You don't understand." She pulled against the siren's grip again, but the siren's hand on her arm wouldn't relent.

"I had hoped you would come with us willingly, but I see I will have to resort to other means."

Dread filled Lore's belly. "Let me go!" She yanked harder. "I just need more time, there is another place it could—"

Then, the siren opened their mouth. A sound erupted, not song, but a raw, primal force that slammed into Lore like a tidal wave.

Lore's world dissolved into waves of melody; each note a barbed hook ensnaring her thoughts. Alarm flared within her, urging her to flee, to fight. But the song, so rich and warm, promised sanctuary and quickly smothered any spark of defiance. It flowed through her veins, quieting all resistance with a sweet caress. Lore squeezed her eyes shut, desperately clinging to the scent of blackberries in Syrelle's quarters.

But it quickly became clear that the siren had permitted Lore to block the effects of the song earlier while in her room—luring her into a false sense of control. Lore tried to pull away, but her arm, heavy and numb, drifted *toward* the siren as if drawn by an invisible current.

Lore's voice, a ragged breath lost in the symphony, croaked a final, broken *no* . . . before the world narrowed to the song, its meaning an inconceivable, enthralling, enigmatic mystery that conveyed belonging, oblivion.

What did she need with power?

Lore had this song, the melody so honeyed that it filled her up. She need not feel fearful anymore; she was no longer alone. She didn't need air or food; this song was sustenance enough.

PART TWO

THE SUNKEN
GARDEN

CHAPTER 16

Lore awoke drowning.

Pressure was crushing her from every side. Lungs, arms, skull, ears battered by colossal weight.

She was in agony.

Lore pressed her palms flat against a sandy floor and heaved herself to a kneeling position. Deprived of sight by darkness, she clawed at the sand, desperate for an anchor against a suffocating tide of water. She flung an arm wide, trying to feel anything in this pitch-black hellscape. All she felt were the currents of ice-cold water that threatened to freeze the blood in her veins.

This was becoming a pattern for her. This wasn't a new dance—someone claiming her mind, plunging her into oblivion, she'd been here before. Only now there was no air to breathe, she was underwater, and she was being crushed to death.

A flicker in her peripheral vision, then a blessed blaze!

Lights, ethereal and strange, bathed the chamber in a hazy glow. It wasn't fire, not a lantern, but something alien, casting an underwater visual of distorted shapes and shadows.

The glow illuminated a door, the handle just above her. She reached up to it and tried to turn the knob, but it was locked.

Of course it was locked. Lore was doomed to always be hindered by others' lock and key. She searched the room desperately, her eyes barely able to see through the watery haze, but she noticed—gods, she wasn't alone!

In the corner, a figure writhed, a silent symphony of agony echoing through the water.

Why would they take the time to drag her beneath . . . deposit her and this stranger in a room . . . just to drown them?

Drown. Gods, she was drowning.

No. She couldn't panic. Goddess. She needed air. *No, no!* Panicking *ensured* death. If she panicked, she would pull water into her lungs and she would die.

She focused on the figure on the other side of the room. There was someone in here with her, bent over at the waist as if in pain too. She was about to drag herself over to them when one of the unfamiliar glowing lights on the wall caught her eye.

It wasn't a light like she was used to, not an oil lamp, a candle, a torch; nor was it a glowing crystal like they used in Queen Riella's mansion. This was round and flat, in the shape of a seashell.

That glowed and pulsed with *Source*.

Lore placed her fingers on it and pulled what little *Source* the shell possessed within its casing. The *Source* did not help her to breathe, but it quelled her panic for a moment, her need for breath, and some of the weight crushing her was alleviated. If she had *Source*, it would sustain her for a moment longer.

The shell winked out, and there was no more magic within it.

She waved her arms and maneuvered herself toward the person in the middle of the room. She hurried, as much as she could, her bare feet slipping on the sandy ground, growing weaker with every second without air. The only remaining lights in the room were positioned above the drowning figure. A chandelier, a beacon, drawing her as a moth to a flame, flickered out as she was cast into darkness.

But then the lights flickered back to life, steadied.

She squinted her eyes, which burned. She was almost to them.

Her heart dropped to the sand-covered floor.

Black shirt, black trousers. Locs that spread around him, moving to and fro in what little current Lore was creating as she swam toward him.

Finndryl, she tried to shout, but she had no air to speak, and opening her mouth did nothing but let out precious air bubbles.

He glanced up from where he stood, bent at the waist, his hands on his throat. For a moment, his eyes widened, and he looked agonized to see her as realization hit. If she was here, then she was in danger too. He shook his head side to side—no, looking around the room frantically, as if he had given up on saving himself, but seeing her here, in danger, was too much for him.

The room had not changed; neither a way out nor a glass orb filled with sweet air appeared, and so, his shoulders slumped, defeated, and he mouthed her name. She did not have to hear it to feel his anguish. It only took a moment for him to drop his hands from his throat and pull her to him. As if he did not need air, he only needed to feel her here with him in these last moments.

Lore's bare feet lifted off the sand. She was weightless in his arms, in this underwater tomb, and she folded herself into his chest. Finndryl, at last.

She was dying, but at least she got to see him one last time.

But no, if she was dying, then so was he. He was dying.

Finndryl would die!

Lore extricated herself from his arms and pressed her hands on either side of his face, caressing his cheekbones with her thumbs for the briefest of moments before pushing down on his shoulders. The momentum propelled her up toward the chandelier of glowing shells. She closed one hand upon an arm of the chandelier, the rough coral making her shiver, and pulled the *Source* from one of the shells.

She did not take the magic for herself, though. Instead, she reached out her hand. Finndryl pushed off the ground himself and clasped her extended hand, threading his fingers through hers.

She funneled the *Source* from the shell lights into him.

His face was twisted into a pained grimace. Not just from the pain of being crushed under the weight of the ocean—she knew his lungs must be like hers, aching for air—but from sorrow, sorrow that they were out of their element here.

She pushed the magic from the chandelier into him, and his eyes widened in shock, his pained features softening a fraction. She would give them as much time as she could. Though whatever magic flowed through this chandelier was weak to begin with, the light emitted from the shells barely enough to see by. The first shell winked out, and she pulled from another, giving more magic to Finn.

His dark, intelligent eyes roamed over the shells, counting—ten shells in total. They had eight shells left to share between the two of them. As she started to push the third shell's *Source* into him, he shook his head fiercely, and pointed to her chest.

You, he mouthed.

Lore nodded, taking this shell for herself.

He reached up and gripped one arm of the chandelier, and slid his arm around her waist with the other. She glided through the water as he closed the distance between them. His waist-length locs floated in the water around them, curling around Lore's shoulders as if they, too, wanted to be close. The dim light illuminated his face. His eyes roamed over her as if he would take in every inch of her, commit it to memory.

Sorrow reverberated within her.

She would lose him before she'd ever really had him, and she had nobody to blame but herself. There he had been in Tal Boro every day helping her with her grimoire, and all she would have had to do was reach out to him. Close the distance between them, like he had done now.

But she had been a coward.

And it had cost her everything.

And when he'd wanted to escape Syrelle's ship with her, she'd said, *Not yet* . . . not yet, and now . . .

Finndryl leaned toward her, pressing his forehead to hers as two more shells winked out above them. The room was almost dark again, and Lore closed her eyes. She pressed her free hand to his cheek, running her thumb across his lower lip. She wasn't going to die without feeling them, at least once. She leaned forward and closed that last bit of distance between them just as the last of the lights winked out.

His lips met hers, and fire ignited where they touched. They released the rungs of the chandelier in sync. Floating there, shrouded in darkness, Finndryl gripping her waist with one arm, pressing her to him, and sliding his fingers through her hair before gripping the back of her neck, she parted her lips, ignoring the water and deepening the kiss.

If the world hadn't been dark from lack of light, she knew that it would be darkening regardless from her losing consciousness. She wondered who would find them in this room, intertwined.

Would they know that they had murdered two people before giving them a chance to know what love really was?

Lore was losing consciousness; her head drifted back, and Finn pulled her to him as they slowly sank to the sandy floor.

They were reunited at last, only for their final moments to be so brief.

CHAPTER 17

Acidic burning pain in Lore's arm jolted her from the brink of death.

An agonized cry ripped from her chest as her back arched with torment, every single muscle in her body constricting and convulsing. Her skin was being flayed from her arm, the flesh bubbling and dissolving into pieces, as whatever was devouring her consumed her flesh down to the bone.

Her body jerked and shook. Beside her, through her suffering, she could feel Finndryl convulsing as well.

She screamed again, reaching out for him, wishing for this to stop, to make their agony end. She pleaded, begged the gods to let them go quietly as before, let this torture end. She would gladly choose death over this.

It took a moment to realize that the unintelligible babbling, the shrieks of pain she was emitting, were audible, and she was not pleading with the deity of death in her mind, but out loud. This shocked her so much that she opened her eyes from clenching them tightly against the pain.

Gone was the haze from being underwater where her eyes were not designed to see clearly. The aching, biting cold from the frigid depths no longer bit into her muscles, and the weight from being in the deep ocean dissipated in sweet relief.

Lore stilled on the sandy bottom, her limbs light, as she took in a massive breath. The water around her was altered; it felt no different from air.

She looked at her arm and shrieked.

A mottled mauve-and-rose-colored jellyfish had stuck itself to her wrist, its poisonous tendrils wrapping around her forearm and reaching up to her shoulder. She scrabbled backward and began to pull at the jellyfish's round body. The jellyfish complied, its tendrils releasing the hold on her arm all at once before it fluttered smoothly upward with the current.

It was peaceful, gentle, and somehow adorable despite the agony it had just inflicted on her. The jellyfish gave a little twirl in front of her face before undulating its body and floating toward the door.

The door where there was a creature standing, waiting to enclose the jellyfish in something that, oddly enough, resembled a birdcage.

Finndryl was on the ground, his eyes shut tight, the veins in his neck standing out against the strain as he fought against the venomous acid of a jellyfish himself. Lore couldn't believe that he wasn't screaming. She hastened to him and tugged on the jellyfish, this one a twin to the one that had just assaulted her. When she pulled on its slimy, jellied body, it released his arm and floated away, following the other jellyfish to its cage.

The moment it released him, Finndryl sat up, inhaling a ragged breath. Upon seeing her, he pulled her into his arms, though she knew one must still be burning. "Lore, you're alive! How are you alive?" He whispered the words against her cheek as his hands roamed along her back and shoulders, her throat, lightly dancing along her skin, as if checking that it was really her. That she was really warm and alive in his arms.

"*We* are alive," she whispered to him, her voice rough from screaming.

Lore pulled away from him and gripped one of his hands, turning it palm up. Where the jellyfish had entwined around them were matching, glowing, purple burns—perfect imprints of the jellyfish, twirling around their arms, up to their shoulders.

With every beat of their racing hearts the imprint pulsed, glowing with *Source*.

"You poor creatures. I apologize on behalf of our queen for the close call you both just experienced."

Lore jumped, her head turning toward the owner of the dulcet voice heading toward them. Lore stiffened. The siren from her room. Who, when Lore had not complied fast enough, had mesmerized her with siren song.

They had changed out of their bloodied gown and now wore an elegant vest. Adorning the lithe creature were two bangles on each wrist, shimmering with emerald stones that matched their eyes, and a formfitting leather apparatus that wrapped around defined biceps, securing a thin weapon with a sharp blade fastened to the wooden staff. The weapon was long and extended above a sympathetic face that was mostly hidden by their wild, shoulder-length hair. Lore's eyes roamed the length of the creature, trying to come to terms with the fact that where the siren had previously sported legs on the ship, now sprouted a long fish tail.

Though the tail didn't resemble a fish, not truly.

The tail was tapered, agile, and a sleek, glittering black. It was peppered with elegantly shimmering fins, here and there, that no doubt helped the siren to reach incredible speeds. "My song usually lasts much longer. You both should still be sleeping peace-fully before the song's spell abated, requiring the Puallas Kiss to breathe. As our most welcome guests, we would never have purposefully . . ."

Lore blinked.

The siren continued swimming toward them; their apologetic voice thrummed and hummed, reaching Lore's ears as if they were speaking through air and not in a room filled with water.

The moment the siren was within reach, Finndryl gently but firmly moved Lore aside, stood, and pulled the siren's spear-like weapon from its sheath. In surprise, the siren dropped the jellyfish cage, which floated gently to rest on the sandy bottom.

"You call that a 'close call'?" Finndryl seethed, the blade's sharp edge pressed to the siren's side, where Lore imagined a beating heart would be. "You almost killed her."

The siren swallowed, managing to hold almost perfectly still, the only movement their tail that fluttered at the finned end just enough to keep them afloat in the water. The siren squeaked, clearly surprised that a land creature had commandeered their weapon and was now threatening them with it.

Lore bet they wished they hadn't removed their armor before coming in here.

"I apologize. It was a grave mistake that we do not take lightly. Please, if you let me . . ."

"You are lucky I let you keep your head attached to your body, you piece of—"

"There has been a misunderstanding," pleaded the siren. "Please—let me go so I can explain!"

"Quiet!" Finndryl, who somehow managed to resemble a lethal and deadly wolf, despite being *underwater*, bared his teeth in warning. "I don't trust you to speak just yet, in case you decide to sing."

That was a good sign, though. The siren had had time to sing them into compliance, to force Finndryl to let them go—and instead they had chosen to reason with them.

Finndryl's eyes narrowed, as though he was mulling over the same thing, but he didn't remove the blade poised at the siren's ribs; in fact, from the look on their face, it appeared Finn had increased the pressure. "Tell us who you are and why you have brought us here." The siren gave a squeak as Finn pressed the blade deeper; any more pressure and it would pierce their skin, their heart. Finn growled. "If you start to sing, I'll slip this knife between your ribs before your song can incapacitate me."

The siren placed two fingers on their chin, just below their lips, in a sort of salute. Finndryl pulled the weapon away a smidge, just enough to ease their discomfort. The siren sighed with relief.

"Thank you." They glanced between Finndryl and Lore, their face grave. "I assure you, you will not hear our song while you remain here. My name is Cuan Merilani. I am a palace aide." They dipped their head slightly in greeting. "I have been assigned to your detail during your stay here. I assure you, I only used my song as a last resort to bring you safely to our empire, Lapis Deep." They gestured toward the jellyfish, floating gently in the cage, bumping listlessly against the bars as though bumbling and harmless, as if they couldn't cause more pain than Lore had ever experienced in her life. "The jellyfish that bestow the lifesaving kiss, Puallas Kiss, are deep-sea creatures. The Puallas jellies cannot be brought to the surface without injury from the pressure difference. My song allows your kind to survive the trip below, until the kiss can be bestowed. I apologize for the pain my mistake caused you."

"And what of the answer to our question on *why* we are here?" Lore asked.

The siren beckoned toward the open door. "If you both will follow me, I'll take you to the queen. She will answer your questions." Cuan raised an eyebrow, pointedly looking at the blade Finn still hadn't pulled away from them. "The rest of your party is already at the palace."

The rest of their party? Who? Syrelle, Lore's captor? Any surviving sailors and guards who would lock them up the moment they had the chance? If so, why had they been woken first? Why had they been separated? A hundred more questions flitted through Lore's mind, but she voiced none of them.

Finndryl looked to Lore. Lore gave a slight nod.

They might as well follow the siren to the queen.

It was clear they were out of their element, and there was no telling how long the *Source* from the jellyfish sting . . . or the *Puallas Kiss* as Cuan had called it . . . would provide them with the ability to breathe, see, and not be crushed by the weight of the tons of water above them.

Finndryl released the siren aide but kept the weapon firmly clasped in his grip. In a flash, the siren grabbed the Puallas jellies' cage and dashed toward the door, only needing one powerful flutter of their tail. For a split second, Lore's breath hitched, afraid they would close the door and lock them both in here once more, but the siren simply pulled the door open wider and waited for them to follow.

Finndryl entwined his fingers with Lore's, their shared pulse a rhythmic counterpoint to the thrumming ocean. Together, they stepped through the doorway onto a path bathed in ethereal luminescence. The intoxicating scent of crisp, fresh salt enveloped Lore as she craned her neck, eyes widening in awe.

Above them stretched a liquid sapphire sky shimmering with ineffable depths.

"It's a wonder we weren't crushed by the pressure before waking," Lore murmured as she took in the seemingly infinite expanse of water above them.

"That room is spelled to withstand pressure. That's why the door was locked."

Lore swallowed.

"If you had left the room, the spell would have been rendered useless. Without immediate access to the Puallas jellies, the two of you would have imploded within minutes, your bodies unable to withstand the weight." The first thing she'd done was try to open the door. There was no denying it. She was completely out of her element. One wrong move here, and it would not just be her death sentence, but Finndryl's as well. "Even your bones would have been pulverized," Cuan explained to Lore, their voice cheerful now that there wasn't a spear poised to pierce their heart.

Apparently, Finndryl's death threats hadn't dimmed their spirit.

Lore and Finndryl followed Cuan through a mercantile district of a city. The shops were rounded, made from clay, stone, and coral. They looked abandoned. She stepped over what looked like a child's toy that sat half-buried in a once-manicured public garden that was now filled with decaying plants. Small fish the size of Lore's pinkie darted in and out of the planters, searching for food.

There was no one around, save them, and the darkness was eerie.

She moved closer to Finn, and he squeezed her hand. He was here with her, every step of the way. Lore glanced at him as he walked, head high, his eyes constantly scanning the abandoned city.

He didn't have to say it, Lore felt it too. Reunited at last, nothing and no one would separate them again.

Walking underwater with the ease of walking on land was a peculiar sensation. Her skirt fluttered around her as if caught in a breeze, but otherwise, she could move as though she were on solid ground. The magic surrounding the Puallas Kiss was magnificent.

They pushed on until their surroundings took on more of a domestic feel. Rows and rows of homes, all abandoned. Caught in the current, a strip of torn fabric floated from an alley and snagged on Lore's ankle. She stepped over an open satchel that had been discarded in the road.

At length, they met the border of the city in the form of a drop-off, a glistening ramp, the same width as the road, that led down and down. Glowing shells, the same ones that Lore had siphoned *Source* from, adorned the fringe.

They paused at the pinnacle of the ramp. At its base, beneath the expanse of a seemingly endless sea, where even sunlight surrendered to the twilight depths, stood a palace.

A mosaic of coral, pearl, and crystal, the palace appeared sculpted by the currents themselves. The walls, a living colossus of coral, burst with sea life. Lore's eyes alighted on countless spires, twirling and elegant, stretching toward the surface like the yearning arms of drowned lovers. Each spire was adorned with luminous shells, their soft glow illuminating the palace grounds.

The palace was so lovely, all radiant and shining, Lore almost didn't notice the entire siren platoon posted at the gates—and the well-armed and armored soldiers weren't just guarding the palace; it seemed that they were there to watch over every inhabitant in the kingdom. Families were set up all along the palace grounds, amid colorful steepled tents throughout the expanse like a strange, shimmering mirage born of a dream.

Laughter, music, and the low murmur of conversation drifted through the watery twilight, a patchwork of sounds that stitched a portrait of a kingdom under siege. Something had happened here . . . something requiring the inhabitants to abandon their homes and shops to lodge in the very shadow of their palace.

Lore's skin prickled. How did she and Finndryl fit into all this?

An echo of Lore's own unspoken questions, Finndryl's eyes settled on the army before them, fixed in a probing gaze. The last few hours' unpredictability seemed to weigh on him. He was unprepared for whatever would happen next, and it appeared that didn't sit well with him.

There was a shallow trench carved in the sand at their feet, positioned between the city and the downward ramp to the palace. Lore tracked the indentation. The line extended in either direction, curving in a wide arc, a circle around the palace.

Finndryl made to take a step over the line, and Lore tugged on his hand.

"What is this line here?" Lore didn't bother to suppress her suspicion. The line was perfectly formed; the water, kelp, or various fish should have marred the perfect arc.

Magic was at play here.

"You will not be harmed; the mark of Puallas Kiss grants you both safe passage through our shield," answered Cuan with a polite dip of their head.

"All right, it grants us safe passage in, but how about *out*?" Finndryl's question rumbled between them and the siren poised on the other side of the line.

"In or out, the shield will not harm you unless the Kiss is removed," Cuan answered.

If the Puallas Kiss were removed, that would mean instant death for them, regardless; the shield would not have to do a thing.

Lore shivered at the thought. She looked around at the abandoned city and up toward the sky. Without her book to act as a *Source*, they were trapped in the deep regardless. Only with permission from the queen would they ever reach the surface again.

It made her uneasy to know that the only indication of the shield was a shallow line in the sand; otherwise it was completely invisible. If the two of them hadn't had the mark, they could have unknowingly walked right into the shield. Then again, if they hadn't had the mark, they wouldn't have been alive to collide with the shield.

Still, she wondered at the magic behind it. When she had her grimoire back, she would see if this was a spell she could master. Having a protective shield around her people and her home would be invaluable.

And she would find great satisfaction in knowing that it was invisible to unwelcome intruders.

"Please, come, my queen is waiting."

She had no choice but to trust the palace aide.

As she lifted a boot to cross the last of the distance to the shield, a stricken expression came across Cuan's face as they peered at something behind them. "Please, hurry into the shield!" Cuan shouted, motioning with their hands, their movements frantic.

Lore and Finndryl spun on their heels.

Three beasts raced toward them, lithe bodies carving through the water at a frightening speed, their chests glowing with *Source* in the dim light, so bright and quick that their serpentine grace made them seem less like creatures and more like living streaks of light.

They must have been stalking them for some time, to sneak up on them.

The one in the center, the largest one, opened its gigantic mouth to reveal rows of jagged teeth. But its vicious teeth and mouth, large enough to fit a Finndryl-sized fae into it whole, weren't the worst of it. Horror overtook Lore as ropelike tentacles unfurled from its mouth, writhing from its maw like a knot of snakes.

Her mind shuddered. The middle monster's snake-horror tentacles were aiming straight for her waist. She wouldn't even have time to scream before they enclosed her and pulled her into its mouth.

But it was Finndryl—whose reflexes were, blessedly, infinitely faster than hers—who encircled a corded arm around her waist and vaulted forward, propelling them both through the shield. Lore felt a shocking pulse—a rush of *Source* and light and energy. She barely had time to register the one-word thought of *safe* before the three monsters' tentacles punched into the invisible shield with such force they flattened against it. And then the creatures were screeching, writhing in pain as they retracted their tentacles back into their jaws, and raced upward and away.

Finndryl and Lore stood panting, the protective shield humming around them. They watched until the monstrous forms faded into the darkness of the abandoned siren city.

"That was close," Lore said, her voice barely a whisper.

"Too close," Finndryl agreed, his gaze locked with hers. A shared moment of relief passed between them. They were safe. Free. Rescued. And finally, together.

Lore truly saw him, for the first time in weeks not through a scrying spell or, today, through the murky depths of the ocean.

He was imposing, his locs drifting around him like dark ribbons.

She opened her mouth to speak, but her hair billowed into her face. With a laugh, she tried to push it back, only for it to immediately flutter forward again.

With a chuckle, Finndryl gently brushed her hair aside. "What are we going to do about our hair?"

"I don't know," Lore replied. "It feels as though it has a life of its own!" Standing on tiptoe, she reached up, past his broad shoulders, and began to gather his locs together. She split them into two sections and tied them in a loose knot behind his head. "There. Now I need to find something to—"

A smirk played on Finndryl's lips as he produced a simple piece of twine from his pocket. "Turn around."

Lore did as he asked. Finndryl's large hands expertly gathered her unruly hair, twisting it into a neat bun and securing it with the twine.

"Thank you," Lore said, turning to face him again.

"Of course. It should hold for a while."

"I wonder how long we'll be here . . ."

I suppose there is only one way to find out," he said, casting his gaze across the expanse of sand toward the waiting palace.

They walked past hundreds of families on their way to the palace.

Siren leaned on each other's shoulders as their siblings or children played with delight, racing through the water, small bodies flipping, tails undulating—playing as only children could, despite a clear crisis happening.

All of their families' possessions were piled on boards secured to sea animals or wagons. It was clear to Lore that the families camping here were ready to leave or flee at a moment's notice. She could see why they hadn't left, if beyond the shield were creatures like those tentacled beasts.

The palace doors were not closed and guarded but thrown open, and more displaced people were inside the palace. They were everywhere: camping out on grand staircases, sleeping against the pillars, all in the flickering, wavering light of the shells.

They had to pause as they maneuvered through the space when the lights flickered and went out. The palace was thrown into complete darkness, just like what she had awoken to inside the holding room.

Lore braced herself against Finndryl, gripping his muscular forearm, suddenly brought back to that darkness *Auroradel* had shown her. Her breaths came shallow, too quickly, as she dug her nails into Finndryl's arm. She expected a cry to rise from the children.

But the darkness only lasted for a few breaths. Lore sagged with relief.

When the lights flared back to life, the children remained playing as they were, unfazed by the dark.

Or used to it.

CHAPTER 18

Though the palace served as shelter to the siren community and appeared open to all, from peasant and merchant class to nobility, the queen's wing and private parlor remained strictly off-limits and, as such, were guarded by royal soldiers. The guards wore ornate armor of polished chest plates carved from shimmering abalone shells; pauldrons shaped like cresting waves adorned their shoulders, and decorative wrist guards resembling river currents gleamed on their forearms.

Cuan paused outside the throne room, fixing their piercing gaze on Finndryl. "Would you mind surrendering my spear? We would prefer if you were unarmed when in the presence of Queen Naia and Prince Consort Jaladri. Once you have left their presence, we will provide you with a weapon of your choice."

Finndryl leveled his gaze at them. "I would prefer to keep a weapon when in the presence of those who abducted us."

Cuan drew their lips into a thin line.

Lore tensed.

They needed to find out why they were brought here. So far, the siren had been respectful . . . Lore placed a hand on Finndryl's shoulder. Finndryl studied her expression before releasing the spear to Cuan.

"We will return it once you are no longer with the queen," they said and opened the double doors to the queen's parlor.

Lore had only ever met one queen and, if you had asked her that morning, she genuinely hoped to never meet another. If Lore was asked to describe Queen Riella in one word, she would have chosen, without hesitation: *petrifying*.

What would the siren queen be like?

Lore and Finndryl followed Cuan into the sea queen's opulent quarters. The walls were adorned with pearls and jewels in every hue. The floor was covered with stunning carpet woven from shimmering plant fibers and threaded with various colors, creating an elaborate pattern. They traversed a large room, passing gorgeously embossed columns that stretched toward an amethyst ceiling casting a lilac haze over the space. The entrance room tapered until they passed through an arch that led to the queen's receiving room.

Lore raised her chin, squaring her shoulders.

But as they reached the dais holding two impeccably fashioned thrones, Lore found them empty. Confusion twisted her mouth as she glanced around.

"I've always hated those thrones; it never suited me to sit elevated above everyone else. Lording over everyone in your presence doesn't make for decent conversation, and I enjoy nothing more than stimulating confab," said a siren sitting at a round table to the right of the thrones, her posture straight as the columns lining the room. Her silvery hair was plaited into an elaborate braid that fell over one bony shoulder. A delicate crown fashioned from laced coral, studded with pearls, was clenched in wrinkled hands as though she feared her crown would be ripped from her at any moment. Lore swept her gaze up from the crown to a lined face. Queen Naia wore her age with pride, and Lore couldn't be sure, but she had the strangest feeling that the queen's map of exquisite age lines had been impressed lovingly into her warm brown complexion by years of laughter.

She couldn't say *why* she thought that, though, as the queen was not smiling now.

Maybe it was in her eyes. They danced with mirth, though it was dimmed, no doubt due to the hundreds of displaced subjects living in and around her palace.

Her prince consort sat beside her, a protective arm resting on the back of her chair. He was ancient too, his curling hair silver with age. The queen's wrinkles might possibly have come from laughter, but his mouth was drawn into a frown, and his guarded, cunning eyes were overshadowed by thick, wild, silvery eyebrows.

Lore would never have guessed that these two elders were royalty if not for Cuan's deep bow to them.

Unfortunately, sitting on the other side of the queen was a figure Lore would recognize even if her sight were still blurred by the water. Syrelle sat stiffly, didn't move a muscle besides his eyes, which roamed over Lore as though checking for injuries or signs of trauma. His expression, though, was void of all emotion. Ah, that apathetic mask. Lore had almost grown used to it. Syrelle was adorned in the finest leathers. Not one hair out of place, he looked beautiful, as always, with his wings spread out behind him, the black-and-gray feathers shifting in the water.

His dreaded cousin, Coretha, perched beside him on the edge of her seat. Lore was glad to see that at least she looked the worse for wear. A bandage on her cheek and escaped hair from her usually perfect braids were proof that there had been a battle on the ship before they'd found themselves under the sea.

Lore bared her teeth at them.

She had thought that with the battle and the ship sinking, she might never have to see him again. She knew it unlikely that Syrelle would have been killed in the chaos, but she hoped that maybe she would be free of him.

"Queen Naia, Crown Prince Jaladri, may I introduce you to

Lore Alemeyu and Finndryl Hwraeth," Cuan announced, rising from their bow.

Finndryl's bow was graceful, and his murmured "Your Majesty" elegant. You would never know he learned to walk amid a rowdy tavern crowd. Lore, however, hoped nobody noticed the wobble in her curtsy. How Finndryl and Syrelle existed in the water as if on land was a mystery to Lore.

Queen Naia guffawed and made a motion with her hands, brushing their formalities away.

"Please sit with us. Though you may want to stop eyeing Cuan's spear, son. You won't need it here." She turned an elegant head toward her aide. "Cuan, please can you bring those refreshments to us? I'm sure our guests could use something to eat and drink."

"Right away." Cuan gave a slight bow of their head and fluttered out a side door, their shimmering tail flickering behind them. Lore wanted to ask how they had been standing on two feet on the ship, and now had a tail, though she supposed it wasn't much different from Syrelle and Coretha's wings materializing and vanishing at will.

Lore chose the chair as far from Syrelle as she could manage without turning and doing an awkward swim-run and not stopping until she was out of the palace and a thousand miles from him. Once Lore was seated, Finndryl sat in the chair next to her, across from the prince consort, glaring down the table at Syrelle, as if daring the male to say something to Lore so he would have a reason to wrap his hands around his throat.

"I appreciate your kindness, Your Highness, but I must confess, I am wondering why we are here," Finndryl said, not taking his eyes off Syrelle, who returned his gaze with his own vehemence burning through his stoic mask.

"Well, I suppose it comes down to this." The queen placed her crown atop her head before lifting a see-through chest honed from a lattice of bone and seaweed and placing it on the table before her.

Finndryl made a sound of surprise beside her, and Lore, startled, exclaimed, "My grimoire!" She reached out to grab the chest, but the prince consort, who so far hadn't said a word, shot out a surprisingly agile withered hand, and stopped her with a light touch.

Of course there would be a catch before they gave it to her. *If* they planned on giving it back at all.

"You won't want to touch that. It's been spelled. If you attempt to open it, the mark on all four of your arms will be reversed."

Lore and Finn shared a glance.

Coretha huffed, muttering quietly, "It's outrageous, my fate being tied to *theirs*."

Lore stared the queen down. "I see. Do you intend to explain what you are doing with my grimoire and what we are doing down here, or will I have to guess and hope I can correctly divine the whims of a queen?" Lore spat out.

Lore could feel the grimoire from here; it was power, a beating heart, calling to her. She craved it.

A thrill shot through her chest—she could *feel* the book. That meant it was night. And despite being far from the moon's light, it still had power here. Then again, wasn't it the moon that controlled the tides?

Prince Consort Jaladri had already removed his hand from hers, placing it back upon the table. She could use her power to pull the book from the chest. She could use the book to sustain her and Finndryl until they reached the surface.

Maybe.

Possibly.

Or it could all go terribly wrong; her power could not be enough to keep them alive, and they could die a crushing, painful death.

Not to mention, could she really be responsible for Syrelle's death? She'd thought about it plenty. Fantasized about it, even. When she was forced to sit across from him and scry. When his every feature reminded her again and again that he had lied to her. Betrayed her.

And yet, if it came down to it, she didn't think she could kill him, even if the act was an inadvertent consequence.

"*Your* grimoire? Why does the Alytherian lord here say that the grimoire belongs to him?" asked the queen with a silvery eyebrow raised.

"Everything that comes out of his vile mouth is a lie. The book belongs to me."

The queen laughed at her outburst, a laugh as carefree as the way she had plopped the grimoire upon the table. Abruptly, the queen sobered up. "Child, you *will* refrain from any attempts at taking the grimoire by force."

Lore clenched her teeth. What right had the queen to withhold her grimoire? She studied *Deeping Lune*. It appeared to be doing fine despite the water, the pressure of the deep.

The queen startled Lore with another laugh; she tore her gaze from the book.

"You young ones have not lived long enough to learn patience yet, I see."

"I feel as though I have *been* patient," Lore said stiffly before adding as an afterthought, "Your Highness."

"I was hoping to have our refreshments first. If you are anything like my Jaladri, business is best discussed with a full stomach."

"If you wish us to needlessly wait to 'discuss business,' then why show us *Lore's* grimoire before the refreshments have arrived?" asked Finndryl, his voice cold.

Lore warmed. She loved that he took up for her.

"Jaladri, this one reminds me of you at that age." The queen grinned fondly at her partner. "Abrupt, irreverent to his elders, and quite striking."

Lore had to admit the queen wasn't wrong. That was Finndryl

to the letter. It was clear, even in their old age, that the queen and her prince consort had both been striking in their day—and time had not diminished their beauty at all, only transformed it.

The queen continued, addressing them all, "Now, I showed this alarmingly powerful object to assuage any worries you might have that it was lost to the deep. To know it was located, safe."

"It will be safest in my hands," Lore said through clenched teeth.

"Ah, so it doesn't burn you when you touch it?"

"Of course not."

"I only wish my scout who recovered it could say the same; she's been badly burned."

"I can make a poultice for her. It works on both humans and fae, so I imagine it would help siren." Lore frowned. "Though it will have to be oil-based to withstand the water, and I worry putting oil on a burn will only insulate the heat of the injury and might actually *hinder* the healing properties of the salve. I suppose it would depend on how long ago the bu—"

"Child, let me interrupt you, though I can see you feel quite impassioned about healing. We may be siren, but we deal with burns quite often. You won't be surprised, but living atop an active volcano creates the ideal environment for burns."

Lore widened her eyes. Did she just say an *active* volcano?

"Are you saying we are, right now, as we speak, sitting on top of a volcano?" Coretha cried out. She glanced down as though she expected lava to erupt through the rug at any moment.

The queen cut her eyes at Coretha. "How do you think we cook our food, girl?"

"I hadn't thought ab—"

The queen dismissed Coretha with a look, turning back to Lore. "Our healers expect her to make a full recovery. Our kind heal very quickly— Oh there are our refreshments, thank you, Cuan, dear, I was beginning to think you'd gotten lost."

Lore eyed the tray set before them. Sautéed oysters drenched in garlic and butter and returned to their shells sat on a bed of seagrass. Slices of grilled fish rolled in seaweed with strips of an unknown root or tuber were drizzled in a peach-colored sauce. Six clear orbs made of artfully blown sea glass were placed on the table next, with an odd, short bit fixed to the top of each.

The queen picked up the round glass and held it out to Lore. "If you drink the fresh water through here"—she pointed at the opening—"the water will flow. Simply stop, and it will remain in the glass, safe from seawater."

"Let me, Lore." Finndryl plucked the glass from the queen's outstretched hand before Lore had the chance. He sipped from the straw mechanism and swished the water in his mouth for a moment before Lore could protest.

"It's fine," Finndryl announced as he moved to place the glass down in front of her, but Lore, suddenly realizing just how parched she was, snatched it up before it even had the chance to touch the table and took a long pull.

The queen raised a thin eyebrow. "Boy, if I were going to poison you, why would I go through the trouble of keeping you alive?"

"I've heard there are other ways your kind can persuade; I know it's not just from your songs. I was testing for a serum," Finndryl replied to the queen, his gaze steady, brazen, before pulling deeply from his own glass.

Meanwhile, Lore would have been poisoned, persuaded, she didn't care, as long as she could drink the contents down. *Thistle and sage*, she had been thirsty. She was pretty sure the salt water they were in, despite the magical properties of the . . . jellyfish's kiss . . . was actively leaching all hydration from her body.

She noticed midswallow and quite against her will that Syrelle refused to drink any water at all, despite Coretha gulping hers down beside him, not any more or less frantic than Lore probably looked. Was his lordship too arrogant to drink a life-giving substance? Asher, if he were still Asher, would have gulped the water with her. Oh, well. She wished dehydration on him and a migraine from the depths of hell.

Satisfied, Lore pulled the straw from her lips and twirled the glass in her hands, inspecting it. Despite the removed water, no seawater filled the empty space. And even when she tipped it upside down, the straw pointing at the table, the fresh water that remained at the bottom within did not escape. This was rather ingenious; she would have to find out how this was done.

The queen laughed again, not unkindly; she was just . . . joyful, Lore observed. "If I could add a serum to the water supply to guarantee I achieve my every desire, I would be the queen of more than this section of the sea, dear." She picked up her own glass and took a sip. "Indubitably, you've heard gossip spread by the many clans who distrust siren. Yes, we can influence others with our song." She waved her hand at Cuan, who floated behind the queen. "But only those possessing great power can usurp the mind of another. And it is only through our sacred song that we can do this."

Queen Naia placed her glass on the table, turning it idly between her hands, as she took a moment to look at each of the four guests—hostages—at her table.

Lore had to force herself not to lower her eyes from her discerning gaze.

"We can also do *good* with our song, you know. We can call a pod of whales who have beached themselves back to the waters before they die, crushed by the weight of their own bodies. We can soothe our children's nightmares with a single note or comfort those who return from war with demons they cannot shake. But do any landers ask for our help?" She speared an oyster and pulled the meat out of the shell before popping it into her mouth and chewing with gusto. "Never."

Her tapered canines were needle sharp.

That may be true, but Cuan had corrupted Lore's mind

completely. Whittled her like wood into a puppet and drew her into the deep where she came inches from death.

"Now that I have provided you with food and drink—"

"—and breath and relief from Great Water's weight," Prince Jaladri huffed through a mouthful of fish.

"Yes, dear. Those are a given, though, as our guests would be dead without them."

"Well, go long enough without fresh water and food, and they would be dead without those too."

"I suppose you have me there, dear." Queen Naia cleared her throat, patting his hand, before turning back to the four of them. "As I have provided you with food, drink, and, as my lover so unnecessarily pointed out, breath and relief from the pressures of Great Water, I can finally tell you why I have gathered you here with me and hopefully answer any pressing questions you may have."

"They are the ones who need to be answering *your* questions, my pearl," Prince Jaladri grumbled, butting in again.

"Yes, dear, I'm hoping they will. I am also hoping to do a sort of trade with them, you see. I'll answer some of theirs, and they, hopefully, will feel inclined to answer some of mine." She smiled at him, affection and warning swirling in her eyes.

"They'll answer them, all right." The old siren prince consort squinted across the table at Lore and Finndryl, his lips pulling into a threatening grimace. Lore fought the urge to lean backward.

The queen gave his arm a light slap. "You old squid, don't start with the demands. I know how you get."

Prince Jaladri opened his mouth to retort, when Cuan cleared their throat. "Perhaps we can start with *why* we have brought them here, Your Highness."

"Now, Cuan, don't *you* start with me, I was going to get to that before my husband butted in—"

"—I have never 'butted' anywhere in my life—"

Lore bit her lip, holding back a smile. Despite the current circumstances, the royals' bickering was just . . . so typical of an old married couple. Apparently, it didn't matter if one was raised on land or beneath water, if a couple had been together long enough, they were bound by the very laws of nature to squabble.

Cuan's brown face turned a bright shade of red at the admonishment from their queen, and they closed their mouth with a snap. They had obviously been trying to steer the monarchs in the right direction, but it had backfired immensely.

"Cuan, might you procure more water for Lore? She needs to keep herself hydrated."

Lore lifted her brows at Finndryl, surprised by his request. Cuan, who seemed eager to escape the cutting words of Queen Naia, nodded eagerly and escaped through the door.

Queen Naia yelled something unintelligible at her prince, picked up a snail, and hurled it at her husband, who, surprising everyone at the table, caught it before it could splat on his shirt.

Lore pressed her hands to her mouth to stop herself from laughing. The royal couple continued to bicker, completely ignoring their four guests at this point.

A few moments later, Finndryl held out a fresh glass of water to her. "Here you are," Finndryl murmured as he placed the glass gently in her hands.

Lore clutched the water tightly, her cheeks warming, as she placed the mouth of the straw between her lips. Finndryl had surmised correctly that she was still thirsty. She drew a mouthful of water before tipping the glass back to him to share. His original glass was empty too.

"That's all for you. Drink it down," Finndryl ordered.

Why was it so . . . attractive that he wanted her to be hydrated?

She consented, taking another large pull through the straw. Had fresh water ever tasted this wonderful to her before? She couldn't imagine when it would have.

A moment later, she placed the empty glass next to her other one. "Good girl," Finndryl purred in her ear, his voice like velvet. Lore's stomach did a flip at his words, and her core immediately melted at the praise.

Good girl.

He'd said that to her when they had been in the woods and Lore had held up her dagger, ready to fight. She hadn't remembered it being so . . . delicious.

Finndryl reached across the distance between their chairs and squeezed Lore's thigh under the table. "Do you want more, or are you satisfied?"

Lore peeked at Finndryl beneath her lashes.

What had the queen said about him? That he was striking?

Striking, indeed.

His gorgeous face was stoic, but desire sparkled in his onyx eyes unabashedly, pointedly right there for her to see, and Lore had to look away from him.

Finndryl's hand was still on Lore's thigh, and it burned through her dress. She had never been so hyperaware of any one hand or its placement in her entire life. Just above her knee, and yet, she could feel the presence of his touch all the way up past her stomach, which was doing little flips and trills, to her rapidly beating heart.

His hand felt so *right* there; it belonged on her, always.

She wished she could wish everyone away. She wanted to shift her dress so his touch would be on her bare thigh. She wanted his hand more places than her thigh; *gods*, she needed to pay attention and stop thinking about his fingers . . . but . . . ah, he slid his thumb across; the barest of movements, one he seemed to do without even thinking, and even though he wasn't even touching her skin, it was sending the wildest sensations through her core and up to her breasts. Stars, her nipples had hardened against the fabric of her dress, and the slight move of the fabric in the water against her breasts combined with his thumb, which was now, idly, doing a little swirly thing . . .

And now she was thinking about a better, more private place she would rather he stroke with his thumb. All you had to do was take one look at him and know that the grouchy barkeep from Tal Boro knew his way around a lady's body. He could probably play her like a fiddle, have her singing his name—

But she shouldn't be thinking like this.

If recent events had taught her anything, it was that her judgment couldn't be trusted. She shouldn't be wishing Finndryl do any of these things to her.

Lore needed to find out what it was the queen wanted from them, obtain her grimoire, and get them *home*.

To their *separate* homes.

She could not let herself be distracted by these feelings. Besides, if she let him do any of the things she'd imagined him doing to her, it would only make it that much harder when she ultimately got what she wanted. Which was to free her people from Duskmere and move them as far from all fae as possible.

Having these feelings for Finndryl only distracted her from her purpose. She was obviously unequipped to make any decisions based on affection or desire. No matter how right or wonderful his touch felt, she could not allow him any closer to her.

Look what she'd already done to him.

Pulled him from his life, had him imprisoned on a ship, for gods' sakes. Because of *her*. Because she trusted someone who had also given her feelings of safety and love and desire.

And look where it landed all of them.

Trapped in the ocean, sat before a bickering queen, who hadn't even gotten around to giving them any hope that they would be escaping this place with their lives. Finndryl was, once again, put in a dreadful position because of *her*.

Just an hour ago, he had been heartbeats from death, and there had been *nothing* Lore could have done to save him. Despite trying, she had failed him. He had been *dying* in her arms.

And it was all her fault.

If she had never trusted the dimpled guard. If she had never let Gryph, a male entirely too good for this earth, put his family and livelihood in harm's way by harboring her, a human. A fugitive. If she hadn't let Finndryl or Isla risk their lives for *her* cause, Finndryl would be safe right now, in the Dragon's Exile. Making drinks or studying alchemy, trying to break his grandfather's blood curse.

Regardless of what he would have been doing, he would be living his life on *his* terms.

And instead, she had . . . kissed him? She had. She had kissed him. Because she thought she was dying, and she couldn't handle leaving this world without knowing what it was like to kiss Finndryl at least once. And that one single kiss had set her entire body aflame. It had scorched away the hurt and the panic and terror of drowning, and it had burned so fucking sweet.

And even now, she was losing it over the simple fact that his hand was *resting* on her thigh.

She wanted nothing more than to shove this table away, banish everyone else from this room, so she could straddle Finndryl right where he sat. So she could taste his lips again. She could rip his clothes off and then hers until there was nothing between them, nothing at all to separate him from her.

And, she had to admit to herself, she didn't want them to get any closer, not just because she was so obviously not just terrible for him, an actual *literal* danger to his life, but because the more he touched her, the closer they got, the more she wanted to give herself to him. Not just physically, but she wanted to hand him her heart and beg him to keep it safe. She wanted to give him everything. In every way she could. Every glance from him, every time he looked out for her, put himself between her and danger, did something as small as making sure she had enough to drink, she wanted to tell him that she was his. That she belonged to him. Had belonged to him since he'd found her in the Wilds and told her that she was magic.

But right now, nothing made sense. She didn't know why they were here.

Not to mention, what could be done about the traitor sitting three and a half feet from her, burning a hole into the side of her head.

The very *reason* that her heart was damaged, shattered.

And she could not give Finndryl something that didn't even fully belong to her yet.

Lore gently pushed Finndryl's hand from her thigh. He pulled it into his lap, clenching his fingers into a fist. Lips drawn in concern, he checked on her out of the corner of his eye, but she avoided his glance.

She didn't want to worry him, or hurt him, but she knew that any contact between them would only make things harder in the long run. She wouldn't lead him on. She wouldn't let him touch her, kiss her, she wouldn't do any of the things she wanted to do, because she was disastrous for him.

The queen smoothed wisps of silvery hair away from her face, though they floated right back, and gave one of those long-suffering sighs that only a married woman has mastered.

The queen stood up, and the rest of the table followed suit. Lore was about to ask what she'd missed when the queen announced, "I have decided against telling you all here in my sitting room. This will be most effective if I just *show* you."

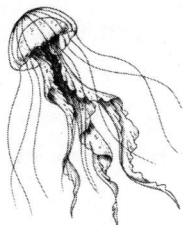

CHAPTER 19

Beyond the palace walls, the party descended a winding coral staircase that spiraled downward until they reached a network of underwater caverns where a sunken garden bloomed. Bioluminescent algae clinging to the cave glowed an eerie green, illuminating walls adorned with vibrant anemones and swaying kelp forests. Small purple and blue mushrooms grew out of the caverns' walls, homes for tiny, quicksilver fish.

The queen and prince consort, flanked by their advisors and guards, led the way. Lore and Finn followed closely behind, Finndryl holding the spear, which as a show of trust the queen had bid be returned to him, while Syrelle and Coretha brought up the rear. The twisting, labyrinthine curves of the path and the muffled silence of the underwater world amplified Lore's unease.

From the shadows, a touch sent a jolt through her, making her jump.

She whirled around, eyes narrowed. "What?"

"Lore," Syrelle began, his voice barely a whisper above the gentle current, "I need to talk to you."

"Take your hand off me, Syr—"

Before she could finish, Finndryl's spear was poised with its sharp tip mere inches from Syrelle's throat. Syrelle's eyes tightened, but he raised his hands in a gesture of surrender. "Call off your guard dog, Lore," he said, no hint of amusement in his voice. "We must speak."

Lore laughed, though it was devoid of mirth. "Finndryl is his own person. He can do what he likes, and if he wishes to run you through with that spear he commandeered, who am I to stop him?"

"He can try all he likes. We all know that without magic of his own, he would never manage to successfully hurt me."

Lore wasn't worried. Finndryl was deadly without magic.

Finndryl looked bored. "I don't require magic to end your miserable life."

"I would like to see you try, *clanless*," Coretha hissed from where she stood behind Syrelle.

"Call him that word again, viper, and I'll carve your tongue from your head," Lore said, fury raging in her chest.

Lore had been trying her best to pretend that Syrelle's dreadful cousin wasn't along on this escapade with them, but Coretha loved to open her mouth and let drivel escape, depriving Lore of her fantasy.

Syrelle rubbed a hand over his face. "Gods, Coretha, can you be any more abysmal? Why are you even here? None of this concerns you."

"Syr, all of this concerns me. You act like I am not just as trapped down here as you!" she whined.

"Just go on ahead; you're making things worse," said Syrelle through gritted teeth.

"Fine, but you'd better be coming up with a fucking plan to get us out of here." Coretha stalked down the path after the queen.

"Spit it out, Syrelle; I have half a mind to go on ahead with Coretha if it means I won't have to talk to you." Lore's gaze bore into his, her chin raised, defiant. "I've nothing to say to you. I'll never have anything to say to you again."

"Don't say anything, then. Just listen. Something is very wrong here. I visited a siren kingdom in my youth with the king, and it was *nothing* like this. I'm not sure what happened here, but you aren't safe. You need to attain the grimoire as soon as possible." With a sharp movement he pulled up his sleeve and gestured to the Puallas Kiss on his arm. "I don't trust these marks." Lore despised that his marks were perfect replicas of hers and Finndryl's, as if they had all decided to get matching tattoos. "I can't guarantee my power will be enough to keep you safe. We need to devise a plan to acquire *Deeping Lune*. Now. I think—"

Lore held up her hands, cutting him off. "Keep me 'safe'? The last thing I want is to find myself once more in your twisted version of 'protection,'" Lore scoffed. "And do you think I haven't noticed the throngs of displaced siren? Or that I'm just impervious to reason? It's obvious that something isn't right here. And I imagine if you would stop slowing us down and let us see what it is, all will become clear."

"Fine, *safe* was a poor word choice, but I have done everything in my power to keep you alive, you *know* that."

"When it comes to you, Syrelle, I don't *know* a damned thing. Now if you would kindly fuck off, I don't want, nor need, your opinion on anything. Stay away from me." She glanced at Finndryl, who stood scowling at her side. He looked as if he were carved from stone. "And for gods' sakes, keep your bratty cousin away from the both of us."

"The both of you, huh?" Syrelle's eyes darkened. "So, it's the two of you against everyone else, is it? You wouldn't even know him if it weren't for *me*."

"What's that have to do with anything?"

"All I'm saying is, you don't know everything about him; there is a reason that he doesn't have magic of his own—"

"Gods, you still think that what you say holds any weight with me, don't you? You lost that privilege when you imprisoned the both of us on a ship, Syrelle."

"I did what I had to, in order to keep you safe from my uncle! Which is what I am *still* trying to do!"

Lore exhaled a frustrated groan.

But it was Finndryl who cut in. "Nothing you have ever done

has been to keep her safe. Not when, for your entire life, you ignored Duskmere's plight, though you knew what your king inflicted upon her people." He held up his hand. "No, don't deny it. You may not have been the one causing her or the humans' pain, but your silence and refusal to act makes you complicit." He stepped forward, using his superior height and weight to glare down at Syrelle. "Were you keeping her safe when you pulled her from everything she's known and asked her to enter a library with a deadly curse in order to use her to further your own ends? Certainly not when you left her in Tal Boro, recovering from your guard's poison." Finndryl smiled, though it was a fearsome, terrifying thing. "You let her be captured by siren and almost killed only hours ago."

"I was there, just like you, helping to free the women and children from Steward Vinelake!" Syrelle glanced at his cousin's retreating form and lowered his voice. "Every move I've made since I came of age has been to remove my uncle from his throne. My dream is to improve things for not just my own people but those in Duskmere as well! When I am king, my first order will be to withdraw all sentries from Duskmere and bring down the wards that surround it."

Lore ground her teeth, stepping up beside Finndryl. "You still don't get it. And why would you? You've never been in the position of an outsider. Your 'dream,' Syrelle, is the dream of my enemy." Lore pushed a stubborn coil of curls out of her face. "It isn't enough to *remove* the sentries and take down the spells that have imprisoned us for centuries! Your monarchy and your leaders need to be tried for their crimes and sentenced to death." He opened his mouth to retort. "No, let me speak. The king, his culpable wife, your superiors, every single sentry, no matter if they are retired from old age and eating their food through a toothless smile, and every one of the king's advisors, all. But don't worry, Syrelle. When *I* have my grimoire back, I will be the one who brings them to justice."

"I—"

"You are weak, Syrelle. You've always *been* weak. You would make a pathetic king, and honestly, I will do everything in my power to make sure that never happens." Lore took hold of Finndryl's hand and spun on her heel. She didn't bother to look back to see if Syrelle was following or was lost to the twists and turns of the sunken garden.

Finndryl and Lore ventured farther into the labyrinth.

By now the queen's party was so far down the path, she couldn't see them. Their only company was a siren guard who swam above them, never taking their eyes off the pair.

"What do you think is waiting for us at the center?" Finndryl asked, breaking the silence, his voice hushed.

Lore's eyes widened as a spectral form floated past them, its gauzy white robes billowing like a ghostly shroud. Spilling out from the veiled hood of their cloak, the blindfolded siren's mournful song rang a haunting melody that echoed off the cavern walls, sending echoing chills down Lore's spine. How could they see if their face was covered? "At this point, I'm expecting an entire host of ghosts with plans to consume our souls for dinner."

If she didn't know Finn better, she would almost think his chuckle had a nervous edge to it. "I was thinking the same thing. That, or a colossal version of one of those tentacled horrors that tried to nibble on us earlier. What if those monsters were the sirens' true leaders, and they actually plan to sacrifice us all?"

Lore shuddered. "If that's the case, my only goal is to ensure Coretha is eaten first. No way am I letting her watch me be devoured by a mouth with ten arms."

Finn's mouth spread into a mischievous grin. "You're right; that would be so embarrassing for you."

"I would honestly die from the shame of it before the monster had a chance to even swallow me."

"Don't worry, I'll help toss her in first to spare you the humiliation. But only if you scream like a banshee to distract the beasts while I make my escape."

Lore playfully shoved him. "I would expect nothing less."

In truth, Lore couldn't even fathom what would be waiting for them at the center. But they passed three more blindfolded sirens, shrouded all in white, softy singing prayers—each one crooning a song eerier than the last.

"Our clerics follow this path in prayer so often they need not use their eyes to know when there will be a curve in the bend," Cuan murmured as they materialized from the shadows. Lore jumped; she could've sworn Cuan had swum ahead with the queen.

"Oh. I see." Lore smiled sheepishly, trying to pretend she hadn't just startled so obviously. "Is that why they wear the hoods?"

"Darkness during prayer is one way our clerics honor our goddess. For them to weave through the labyrinth without error is believed to convey their devotions right to her ear."

Darkness may be what the apostles sought, but Lore hated the dark and was glad that the labyrinth had seemed to lighten up the last few turns. The farther they moved into the sunken garden, the more vivid the algae became. Eventually, Lore began to see glimpses of something very bright; its shimmery light filtered through the twists and turns.

Finally, the path opened to a massive amphitheater surrounded by towering columns. It, like the path, was studded with decorative seashells and stones, but unlike the caverns, a luscious, carefully cultivated garden bloomed. Benches were placed for people to sit in contemplation or prayer. Marble statues stood guard throughout the space.

But the beauty of the garden was understated compared to what stood proudly in its center.

CHAPTER 20

Lore had seen pearls before. She had found a few freshwater ones in the river at home—shades of black and gray, lumpy and misshapen, but lovely still. She threaded them onto cord, gifting one to Aunty Eshe and another to Grey's mother.

This, however, was the opposite of those freshwater pearls. It made the ones from Duskmere look like rocks. The pearls she'd pulled from the river could be rolled between thumb and finger. This was massive, taller than Lore herself. Its spherical silhouette was so flawless that it was impossible for this to have come about naturally. Nothing in the natural world could be this pristine, could it?

The shimmering light emanating from within captivated her. The pearl's beauty was undeniable, but what truly fascinated Lore was the glow of *Source* radiating from its core. It pulsed outward in waves as though the pearl did not only possess *Source*, but was *made* of it. Lore circled the pearl, careful to keep her distance from the twelve siren draped in identical flowing vestments circling the pearl overhead, their haunting voices raised in rhapsodic worship.

Queen Naia floated onto a bench with a sigh, rubbing her back. Her magnificent tail swished absently, carving patterns in the sand.

She looked at the pearl, her lips trembling, devoid of the humor she'd displayed in the parlor.

"This is our Mother Pearl," Queen Naia began. "A gift from Anuya, Mother of all Gods, the Goddess of Vitality, Giver of Life and Home. Before Mother Pearl, siren were doomed to live in darkness."

"If you could call it living," huffed Prince Jaladri, positioning himself behind his queen.

"Rightly so." Queen Naia continued, "We had no community, no language, no spirituality or home. Anuya saw the plight of her children, and it filled her with sorrow. One day, she asked her lover to crack open her chest and remove her beating heart from her body. He only complied because seeing his true love in such torment pained him.

"When he held her still-beating heart in his hands, she bid him rip it into thirteen pieces. Twelve to carve into pearls, gifts for her siren children, light to guide her children into a better life. One to place back in her chest, so she could continue to live and watch over us.

"Once she had shaped her heart into pearls, she flew into the sky and cast them all around the world. One for every great siren kingdom. Eight of them in the depths of the oceans. Two in the deepest lakes. One, long dead, its grave now a desert in Ma Serach, the ocean that once was its home long since dried up. And one is in an underwater cave system in the heart of the bottommost continent, Ethuella.

"Our ancestors, drawn by the light, moved to the pearls and rejoiced. Basking in their light, they could now see the beauty in each other, warm their children, build houses, and even cultivate food, for the sunlight that fuels your landers' food does not reach down here. Without our Mother Pearl, we cannot grow food.

"Soon, we learned that we could use its power for more than the basics. It could power our shields and protect us from the demonic Nikoryxia and the Pasvils that hunted us in the dark. Our empires thrive as long as we each have our pearl . . ." The queen's voice broke, a sob escaping her lips.

Prince Jaladri's arm encircled her frail shoulders. They exchanged a glance, and she drew strength from her love before continuing. "You might have noticed that my city is empty. Our gardens, save for this one, are barren. Our Mother Pearl is—"

The pearl behind Lore flickered and went out.

The world was cast into darkness.

The clerics raised their prayer in a fervor, the unnerving sound filling the void. Terror shot through Lore, and she instinctively reached out, clasping Finn's arm. He was there, beside her, a comforting presence as he leaned into her. Something he'd been doing since they'd studied in the Exile.

"—failing. As you can see." Queen Naia's voice trembled.

"Do not be frightened." Jaladri's voice was calm, though thick with grief. "Mother Pearl will gift us with light in a few moments. Ah, see, here it is."

The pearl flickered back to life, its glorious, powerful glow whirring through the garden, and Lore realized that the palace towers, visible over the walls of the amphitheater, also flickered into sight, as though also coming back to life. That must have been what happened when she'd woken up—a momentary darkness caused by the pearl's failure. And again, when they entered the palace for the first time.

"But it's not just the sporadic darkness that is a problem; its very power is dwindling. Our shield, which once encircled all of Lapis Deep, is barely strong enough to cover the palace grounds, and only remains in place during the dark times because our alchemists are selflessly channeling all their power to it.

"Half of my population have absconded and, as we speak, make the perilous trek to our closest neighboring empires. Families have been torn apart and hunted by the Nikoryxia, who have been attacking in droves, picking off the old, frail, and young and draining their magic. Those who have chosen to stay have had to abandon their homes and move onto the palace grounds, but every day the shield weakens, the darkness increases.

"Soon we will all have to make the same choice: be lost to the dark or leave my kingdom to die. Our nearest allies, Black Diamond and Silver Waves, have offered us sanctuary, but we will be foreigners there. Refugees. And my crown will be forfeited."

Lore blinked back hot tears. She knew what it was to live under the thumb of another, the land not your own. She wouldn't wish this plight on anyone.

"That is where you come in." The queen rose off the bench, gliding toward Lore, and clasped Lore's hands between her own. Her fingers were wrinkled, the skin thin, sliding over brittle bones beneath. A grandmother's hands. They felt soft and fragile. "We heard the whisper of you on the wind. Something powerful. Something new. And then, three days ago, we felt that power, even down here. We thought we might have found the answer to our problem. And your grimoire, this book, like you, gives off the same essence as our Mother Pearl."

The queen gripped Lore's hands in her own; though they shook with a tremor, her grasp was strong. "We hope, we pray, that with your help our Pearl will be restored to its original splendor. Our kingdom will thrive once more." The queen let go of one hand and placed a palm on Lore's cheek. "It seems wrong for one so old to ask you to be our savior, but we have much to give. Jewels, gold, a ship full of fish, whatever you wish; help us and it will be yours."

"I can try. I will try. But I do not know that I can. What will happen if I fail?"

"Puallas jellies are one of the few creatures who, like us, rely on the pearl for their spring of life. When its power wanes for good, so will the mark of their sacred kiss. We will return you landers to the surface before I cast aside my crown and my people lose their home."

"How long until . . . it gets to that point?"

"The failures have been more frequent every day, and at the rate that the shield is shrinking, we think a week, no more."

"A week? That's all?"

"I'm afraid so." Queen Naia swam a distance and made a clicking sound, and Cuan swam forward and placed the latticed chest containing the grimoire in her hands.

"We watched you for a few days; some of my kind can turn themselves into seabirds, which is very convenient when you wish to spy on landers and remain unseen. My spies have deduced that being in possession of this book, the power within, will grant you the chance to take yourselves to the surface and leave us to our plight, if you wish to." The queen's hands clenched around the bones of the cage, and she raised her chin. "We are strangers to you. I have no doubt there is somewhere you would much rather be, with people who are not strangers. So I will return your book to you in the hopes that you will not abandon us without at least trying to help." Naia shifted the cage to one hand and waved her free one in front of it. Where there had not been a visible opening before, the water shifted around the bones, pulling and rearranging them until there was an opening just big enough for Lore to pull the book free.

Lore reached her hands inside with some trepidation, perhaps an unfounded fear that the siren queen would readjust the bones to trap her hands in the cage. But she shoved the thought from her mind, pushed her hands into the cage, and pulled her tome free.

Power soared into her hands, vibrating up her arms, and settled warmly into her chest. She had been incomplete without her grimoire, and Lore thrilled at the feel of the binding. The weight of it was lighter than she was used to, due to being in the water, but familiar all the same.

Now that she had it, she would never let it go again.

"Queen Naia," Lore began, clutching *Deeping Lune* to her chest and meeting the queen's gaze. "I have one question before I decide. You have the power to sing your sacred song and force me to help. You could make it so my mind was not my own, and I would do your bidding regardless of my choice. Why, then, did you not just do that?"

"Some on my council rallied for that path," the queen admitted. "They reasoned that the welfare of our people far outweighed our laws. But I forbade anyone from using the song on you."

Lore glanced to Cuan, where they stood behind their queen. The queen noticed her look. "Well, I forbade it *unless* it became a matter of your own safety. It was imperative that Cuan bring you here unharmed, so we granted them permission for the sole purpose of keeping you all alive and bringing you here in one piece. Despite the mythos surrounding our kind, we believe that to use our sacred song for evil—to force control or obedience or to rob someone of their will—is to defile our goddess Anuya and pervert our gift. Those who sin are punished most severely."

"We melt their tongues with lava," Prince Jaladri piped in from where he sat on the bench. "It's long been a most effectual deterrent."

Lore winced at the thought and ran her tongue against the back of her teeth, just to remind herself that she still had it.

"This is neither the time nor the place to be gruesome, Jaladri! Can't you see she's unsettled enough?"

"I thought it would put the girl at ease! To know that she didn't have to worry about anyone using their song on her while she's here," Jaladri said in protest.

The queen guffawed. "Look at her! The thought alone made her turn green around the gills."

"She doesn't have any gills."

"Oh, for kelp's sake, you *knew* what I meant, you manatee! Now hush, let the girl answer."

All eyes returned to Lore, making her want to squirm from the attention.

She gnawed on her lip, thinking of how this would delay her return home to Duskmere. She'd already been gone far too long. But she couldn't abandon these people to be displaced, left at the mercy of the tides, and preyed upon by demonic sea beasts with tentacles in their mouths.

"I'm not sure how much you know about humans, Queen Naia, but we as a species know something about being banished from one's homeland. We know what it is to be forced to leave all that you know and bend to someone else's will, customs, and way of life. And even if my people didn't know firsthand, *I* do."

The queen wrung her hands together, waiting for her verdict. Lore met Finndryl's gaze. She asked him silently, *Do you mind if we stay here a little longer?*

He nodded, his eyes telling her that the choice was hers to make, he would support whatever she decided.

She looked back to the queen. Lore didn't want to leave the queen waiting, but she had to be clear about her misgivings. "I make no guarantees. You are right, I *am* new. And that also means un-tested. I am neither proficient nor particularly skilled with being what they call me: a witch. But I vow to do everything in my power to help. To restore your empire to glory."

The queen and even her prince consort smiled.

"Thank you. What do you need to begin?"

Lore gazed upon the pearl, studying it, watching as it pulsed with *Source*, steady as a heartbeat.

She didn't know if this power had truly been born from a god-dess's love for her people, but she did know that within every story was a seed of truth, and truth was usually the answer.

She did not know what to ask for when she did not know what she needed to fix the problem. She would start with the one thing that could steer her in the right direction when she was floundering.

"Your Majesty, do you perchance have a library?"

The queen grinned and turned to her life partner. "Jaladri, will you take them to your greatest pride?" She looked at Lore, then said in a mock whisper, "His greatest pride after *me*, of course." Queen Naia winked.

CHAPTER 21

Having grown up on land, Lore struggled to comprehend the concept of an underwater library. Coretha, complaining of a headache, had been led away with Syrelle to another part of the palace. The moment they were out of sight, Lore relaxed.

As Prince Jaladri guided her and Finndryl to his "pride and joy," Lore wondered what on earth it would look like. The books she was used to would disintegrate underwater. She held the grimoire to her gifted dress—a yellow gown Cuan had pressed into her hands upon reentering the palace—relieved that the grimoire, created from *Source* itself, could withstand the sea.

What could the books in the library be made of? Her grimoire was rare, possibly one of two on the entire earth. Jaladri's library couldn't be filled with others like it. She couldn't imagine what she would find. And when the prince consort pushed open the doors, allowing her and Finn to step inside, they gasped in unison.

Finndryl whistled as he surveyed the library. "I could spend decades in here and never grow tired of it."

"I was just thinking the same thing," Lore murmured as she twirled in place, trying to take in everything all at once.

The library resembled something out of a dream, unlike any

she imagined could exist on land. It dawned on her all at once that this underwater kingdom was truly something foreign to her, and it was hard to wrap her mind around it. For one, the shelves weren't straight. They curved and warped in such a way they gave the impression the architect had never seen anything perfectly straight in their life and, therefore, could not conceive of it.

Each shelf was a different size, some short and squiggly, and others reaching up toward the glass ceiling far above. Ladders were unnecessary here; if one needed a book from the top shelf, one simply had to swim to acquire it.

"I'm glad you appreciate it," Prince Jaladri huffed, pride in the beautiful space that he'd built betraying his gruff facade.

Lore couldn't put the grimoire down, of course. There was absolutely no way in a demon's hallowed hall that she would relinquish hold of it now, so she tucked the book into her skirts and set to work.

First, the religious texts. She would start at their origins to understand the problem.

Lore was supplied with wax paper and a stylus with a fine tip for notes and the like. She wrote down a few ideas of what might help her and handed Prince Jaladri the list. The library was so large that it employed three librarians and a host of scribes. Before Lore could say, *Please let me explore, I might be in heaven*, the librarians began to bring volumes of religious texts, philosophy books by long dead siren scholars, and histories of the twelve great siren kingdoms.

Most of the books were made with water-resistant paper derived from a hardy marine plant; a few books from land were clearly spelled not to turn to mush and disintegrate; and some were made from wax paper, the words simply pressed into it like the paper Lore had been supplied with.

Finndryl ran an elegant finger over an intricately adorned spine of a book, a smirk playing on his features. Lore tried not to follow the dip and glide of his fingers as if every movement he made wasn't art in motion.

Gorgeous, *stimulating* art. Really, could anyone blame her? The male looked gorgeous perusing a library.

His resonant voice cut through her transfixed stare, and she glanced away from his hands as if she'd been caught spying on something naughty. "If only my old professors could see me now . . . the things they would do to trade places with their least favorite student."

Lore laughed as she accepted another book from one of the librarians, grateful for the diversion. She was supposed to be reading the titles, just in case any of these books could help her with the sirens' problem . . . not watching Finndryl read the titles. "Serves them right for withholding knowledge from you. I still can't move past your banishment from your university for simply wanting to *read*."

Lore shifted her arms. This stack was starting to get a little big. The librarians were very thorough.

"It's true, I was just an innocent youth on a quest for knowledge . . . never mind that I stole the key from the Master of Scholars himself and broke into the library." Finndryl's hands brushed hers as he scooped the stack of books from her arms to carry them to one of the many tables scattered around the library.

"Finn . . . I didn't know you were the type to carry a lady's books for her."

Finn grinned, the cheeky thing, before his face twisted in mock offense. "Should I be insulted that you thought I was the type to *not* carry a beautiful woman's books?"

Lore's cheeks heated, and she pulled a random book off the closest shelf just to have something to do with her hands. But then she couldn't stop herself from adding, "I didn't realize you thought I was beautiful."

Finndryl side-eyed her as they rounded the corner. "You need to have your mind tested for parasites if my thinking you're beautiful is *news* to you."

"I just . . ."

"You're beautiful, Lore. Even when I didn't particularly enjoy your company . . . I would never have denied how beautiful you are."

Lore almost fell over.

"Wait, so now you enjoy my company too?"

"Don't twist my words, Alemeyu. I haven't admitted to that yet."

"All right, I was worried for a moment that you were the one with parasites. The barkeep I knew would never admit to something as pleasant as *enjoying* my company . . . *tolerating* maybe . . ."

Finn paused beside the table, his gaze heavy on her own. His voice lowered, dropping the jovial tone. "The bartender you knew had a lot of time to think when he was locked away on a ship."

Lore swallowed. She'd had a lot of time to think as well. And it was often spent devising ways to see him again.

"Maybe the reason I kept scrying . . . wasn't only so that I could find the other grimoire . . . but was that it was also my only way to see you."

Finndryl's lips turned up into a smile.

"Don't think I didn't notice how often you 'visited' during my strength training."

Lore sputtered. "That was not on purpose—you're, for some reason, always training!"

"How else am I supposed to carry your books and make it look this easy?" He flexed, his muscles straining the seam of his cuffed sleeves.

Lore rolled her eyes. "Finn . . . anyone can carry a stack of books underwater."

"Yeah, yeah, yeah . . . but not everyone can make it look this good," he said as he set the books gently onto their chosen table. It was in the coziest spot, nestled between a bookshelf and a heater vent.

"All right, Alemeyu, stop flirting with me and put me to work," Finndryl said, sitting down at the table.

Lore smiled sweetly and pushed the stack of books toward him. "Look through these while I grab another stack. Don't worry, I should manage to carry this one on my own." She twirled around. That would teach him to be cheeky. She called over her shoulder, eyeing him where he sat, lounged in his chair, watching her walk away, "And mark any instances of another magical drought that might have happened and been thwarted."

"By the stars above, your will is done," he said, cracking open the tome on top of the stack, *The Coral Codex: A Sacred Study on Ethical Teachings of the Siren Faith.*

"I thought my fingers would have pruned by now," Finndryl said in hushed tones as he eased himself onto a cot beside Lore. They had thumbed their way through countless books until one of the scribes had finally ushered them to a hallway filled with cots splayed out in various places, all but two filled with unhoused siren families who were already sleeping.

They pulled theirs to a small alcove as far away from the sleeping families as they could.

Lore gazed at her own fingertips, swirling them through the water. There wasn't a bit of wrinkled skin on her fingertips. "It is odd, isn't it? Too long in the bath, and my fingers look like my gran's . . . This Kiss has powerful magic. I honestly feel like I'm sitting in *air*. Thick, heavy air, but air. I can even smell you. Which doesn't make sense if you think about it. How can I *smell* underwater?"

Finndryl raised an eyebrow, his lips twitching upward into a smirk. "You can smell me? What do I smell like?"

Lore's cheeks warmed. *Spiced whiskey, ginger, and something else delectable that she couldn't quite name.* "A stinky male."

He breathed a laugh and settled into his cot, placing his arms beneath his pillow and staring at the ceiling in the distance. "I'm sure that's not it. Should I come closer so you can sniff me again? That cot looks big enough for both of us."

"No need; you're pungent enough from over there."

Finndryl's nostrils flared, and he flicked his gaze over her body, taking his time to admire her from head to toe. Lore's cheeks warmed when she saw his onyx eyes brimming with heat. "I can smell you, too, you know. I can always smell you."

"Oh gods, what I smell like right now is none of your business. I probably smell like seaweed and despair."

Finndryl screwed his expression into mock surprise. "Exactly like that."

Lore faced him, flipping onto her side, propping her head on her hand. "Well, now I'm curious."

"Comforting. The faint scent of parchment. Fresh, like dew in the morning. Though sweet." He licked his lips, his sharp canines flashing in the low light. "Edible, like freshly plucked marigold."

"Marigold? Are you saying you want to *eat* me, Finndryl?"

"Something like that," he murmured, his voice a husky whisper as his eyes, dark with longing, locked onto hers, revealing the depths of his desire.

Lore's heart skipped a beat. His cot was close enough, she need only lean forward just a bit . . . No! This was exactly what she was trying to avoid.

If Finndryl put his delicious mouth on her, she would lose herself to him completely. Something she couldn't afford to do when the problems of this fucked-up world were crushing her. When she needed to be focusing on getting away from the fae, not *under* one of them.

She looked away, collapsing onto her back. "Go to sleep, smelly. We have a queendom to save in the morning."

"You got it, Alemeyu."

In the morning, Lore and Finndryl found themselves alone in the library. The librarians and scribes had taken the morning off for a religious service, and they barred other visitors from the library so as not to disturb them. Even Prince Consort Jaladri left them to their research, closing the doors behind him after letting them know where he would be should they need assistance with anything.

"Have you ever heard of a 'radiance swell'?" Lore asked Finndryl as she placed a massive tome on the table.

He frowned and placed a fingertip on the page in front of him to keep his spot. "Never. What is it?"

"It says here, *radiance swells appear seemingly at random, though one can sometimes find them by following the Nikoryxia, for they, due to an ecological factor, are able to locate them*." She tapped a finger on the passage, leaning toward Finndryl, her eyes alight with discovery. "Apparently, the Nikoryxia only lay their eggs within radiance swells—the essence of the swell, coupled with the natural warmth one emits, is the only thing that allows their eggs to hatch. If a swell wanes too quickly, the eggs die off and the creatures must go another year or more, sometimes as long as a decade, before another comes along and they can lay their clutches."

"I've never heard of an animal that relies on magic to reproduce."

"Me neither."

"But a radiance swell sounds similar to what we call ley lines."

"What's a ley line?"

"They're natural paths of a sort that crisscross the earth. *Source* is abundant along those paths, especially at the junctions where the ley lines intersect."

Lore tapped her chin, thinking. "You know, when I was rescuing Grey, I think I felt a ley line. I noticed that the land on which Queen

Riella's mansion was built was positively brimming with *Source*. I wondered at the time if she built her mansion there because of the *Source* or if the *Source* had accumulated there because of the queen."

"They're extremely rare, very hard to pinpoint, and can cause magic to act strangely . . . but it makes sense that the queen would do something as mad as build her house on top of one. She would want to keep it for herself."

"Right, but these radiance swells appear to move. And you make it seem like ley lines are fixed."

"They are."

"So, could these essentially be ley lines that move?"

"Possibly, but how would someone find one of these moving magic spots?"

"I suppose one would have to have the ability to see *Source*, now, wouldn't they?" Lore pushed back from the table and began to pace, her boots making no sound on the sandy floor. "And if that person could see *Source*, they could harness it. Even channel it."

Finndryl marked his spot with a stylus and placed his book down before standing up to follow Lore as she left the table area to enter the stacks. "Maybe the Nikoryxia can see *Source*, too, and that's how they know where to lay their eggs. Maybe the pearl was originally on a ley line, and it's faltering . . . dissipating." She chattered excitedly, turning a corner and heading into the ecology section. "Finn. If *I* could find a radiance swell, I could funnel the *Source* into the pearl; the magic might power the ley line itself." She stilled for a moment, the book she'd chosen halfway off the shelf. "Or maybe it's the pearl that powers the ley line. But no matter what, it seems like we must find one of these radiance swells."

Finndryl's arms crossed, the black fabric of his shirt straining against his muscled frame. "You're suggesting leaving the safety of the shield and venturing into the unknown, aren't you?"

Lore paused, tilting to face him. "I—yes, I might be suggesting that." She placed a hand on her hip. She didn't appreciate that he wore an expression of wry amusement plain on his face like that. "It's not like I can send a scouting party out there and *not* go myself. They can't see *Source* like I can." She searched his eyes, seeing more than amusement there. Worry. He was worried. "Finn . . . It has to be me."

A low, gravelly sound rumbled in his chest. "*Us,*" he said, his voice dropping all indication of amusement as it morphed into a growl.

"What?" Lore crooked her head, confusion clouding her features.

"It 'has to be' *us*, Lore. You won't be going alone."

The memory of the Exile resurfaced—Lore and Grey's reckless vow to free the human captives of Wyndlin Castle, Isla and Finn's selfless offer to help. Lore had been shocked, honored. But look at what it cost him . . . Finndryl had been forced to kill. He'd been taken captive. Separated from his twin.

He still hadn't been able to return home.

She pushed the poised book back onto the shelf and turned fully toward him. "Once again, I would never assume or ask you to—"

Finndryl closed the distance between them. He was so damned tall that Lore was forced to crane her neck to meet his gaze.

"Once again," he retorted, taking another step closer, "I am telling you that I'm not letting you go alone. I'll never stop you from diving headfirst into danger." He placed a hand on the shelf beside her, his grip tight, and leaned forward until their faces were mere inches apart. "As long as I'm there to dive with you."

Lore's breath hitched. Her heart hammered in her chest. Gods, his smoky, spiced scent was intoxicating.

She shook her head, opening her mouth to protest, but Finndryl silenced her with a kiss. His lips brushed against hers, featherlight, yet the fleeting touch sent a jolt through her, scattering her protests in the current as heat rushed through her.

His mouth brushed over hers again, and stars shone behind her closed lids. "As long as you'll have me by your side, there's no place I would rather be," he whispered against her lips.

He pulled back and watched her with heavy-lidded eyes that swirled with craving.

The sudden loss of his warmth, his touch, was a sharp, painful thing.

Her hands ached to grab him, to pull him down until their lips crashed. To never, ever, come up for breath. But she looked at him, really looked at him, and knew that if she let that happen, it would be devastating for both of them. So she resisted the urge and said instead, "I'm poison, Finn. You don't want this. You can't want . . . this. I'm broken. I come from something so broken, and all I can promise is confusion and pain. Uncertainty." The words felt heavy, and her voice was shaky. But she had to say it; she had to warn him . . . She could never make him happy, because she was being tugged in so many different directions, she felt like she'd been splintered. Fractured.

Save her people, provide a home for them. Her want to live her own life, to love without fear or uncertainty. Her desire for him . . . for Syrelle . . . She could never give herself to him while she did not belong to herself. She belonged to the humans of Duskmere. He would be better off far away from her. Her mistakes weighed heavy on her like a boulder. She felt trapped.

She told him this.

Finndryl listened to her, his face resigned, patient, as he waited for her to finish.

Silence. Lore bit her lip, glancing upward to stop the tears from escaping. She'd ruined the whole of everything between them. Just like she knew she would. "I understand your fear," he began, his voice low and steady. He reached out, brushing a stray curl away from her face, his touch a lightning bolt. "You think you are too messy, your circumstances too . . . much. You think I want a butterfly flitting from flower to flower in the sunshine without a care in the world?"

He paused, his eyes searching hers with an intensity that made her breath catch. "You are more moth than butterfly," he continued, his voice dropping to a near whisper, as he cupped her chin, tilting her face up. "I'm not afraid of the darkness that follows you . . . that tries, even now, to bury you. Instead of being lost to it, you thrived."

His thumb traced the curve of her cheek, delicious heat spreading through her at the contact. "The dark means stars and moonlight . . . You shine *golden* in the moonlight; you thrive under the glow of the stars, Lore. You are worthy of adoration. Unveil your mosaic wings for me. Let me adore you."

His words suspended in the space between them, thick with emotion. He knew how messy her life was, and he didn't care; he'd never shied away.

Her eyes dipped down to his full lips. They were perfect, pillow soft, in the shape of a bow. And she was hungry for the taste of them.

That brief kiss hadn't been enough.

The whispered words he'd spoken against her mouth lingered. He would be by her side. If she would have him.

And gods, did she want to have him.

She knew that the list of reasons why she shouldn't give in to what she wanted and kiss him, touch him, taste him, which she'd been repeating for days now, should be stopping her. But in truth, she couldn't think of a single one of those reasons that he hadn't already heard, and decided it didn't matter right now when he was this close, and he'd just kissed her.

"Gods, you're so beautiful," he murmured, his hand cupping her cheek, his calluses rough, his thumb tracing her lower lip, maddeningly soft, as his eyes devoured her face, hungry.

"Kiss me again, Finn. Please."

He expressed a sharp exhale of breath at her request and claimed her as his with the hot brand of his mouth. He peppered her jaw and throat with kisses, and she tilted her head, welcoming them, her eyes fluttering closed. Goosebumps rippled over her arms, and before she could talk herself out of it, she dug her fingers into his locs and angled his jaw so that his mouth covered hers.

The world stopped.

For a moment, everything halted: all her worries, her fears, her stupid fucking ideas that this shouldn't be happening, that they should ever be doing anything other than *this* marvelous act.

She pressed her fingers just beneath the elegant curve of his jaw and felt his pulse thrumming beneath them.

She was what was making his heart race. A thrill shot through Lore, and she parted her lips, inviting him to explore, and he did, his tongue flicking over her lip, savoring her, as a shudder of pleasure wicked through her.

Lore nibbled on his bottom lip, delight sending a pulse straight to her core as Finndryl growled and pushed her back against the bookshelf, his large hands protecting her head and back from the stone edge.

He kissed her with a dizzying fervor; his hand roamed over her body, skimming along the curves of her hips, settling on her ass. Finndryl lifted Lore, and she wrapped her legs around his waist as he pinned her to the bookshelf. She moaned into his mouth and moved against him. Pressed between them, Lore could feel the impressive length of him straining at the waistband of his trousers, and she needed to feel him *there*, at that pulsing, throbbing spot between her thighs.

Finn hissed at the movement and deepened the kiss, his mouth moving faster across hers, exploring her with his tongue. He gripped her ass tighter and ground into her, eliciting another moan from her, as his length brushed against her center.

"You feel so good, so warm and soft, and I'm not even inside you," he said, as he scraped his teeth along the sensitive skin of her jaw.

His words made her shiver with heat; just the thought of him being inside her was enough to make her abandon all reason. She pressed into his hardness, rhythmic now, and trailed her own kisses up his throat. His dark skin was so damned smooth and soft; she could smell the oil he'd massaged into it that morning, taste that bourbon scent that had driven her mad for months, the taste sharp and bright on her tongue.

His hands found their way beneath the pleated fabric of her skirt, his fingers flitting along the laced edge of her panties. She wriggled, wanting him to—

"Touch me," she stammered.

"These are in the way."

"Take them off."

With a growl, he pulled her tightly against him and dropped, lowering them both until he was pinning her to the ground.

She was flat on her back, the soft sand forming to her instantly, and he was kissing her still, expertly managing to lift her skirt and slide her panties down without parting his lips from hers.

She twisted to help him slip her underthings from her ankle, and when he parted her legs, he broke the kiss and leaned back on his knees so he could gaze upon her, unhindered.

For a moment, she felt shy.

Finndryl was so nonchalant and reserved, and Lore remembered, when she first met him, how he intimidated her. Regarding her from behind the bar; a predator.

But in the here and now, he breathed out, "My gods, you are so lovely," and his words danced across her skin like a balm, smoothing away any anxiety wrestling beneath it.

She remembered that he was no longer that irritable fae from the tavern but simply Finn, her Finn, and he thought she was lovely.

His hand brushed over the downy curls at the apex of her thighs, and his thumb slipped past them, finding her bud with ease. Lore gasped at that slight brush of friction, and Finndryl's eyes flashed with fascination blended with a liquid, molten desire. "Is this what you've been wanting from me, Lore?" He slid his thumb over the taut bud, in slow, deliberate circles, coaxing a whimper from her. She bucked her hips against his hand, craving more than he was giving.

He leaned over her and kissed her lightly on the mouth, at odds with the quick, maddening strokes he was unleashing on her.

His swirling fingers made her clench her thighs around his hand as it dawned on her that she was empty. "Yes, that's what I want," she said, shifting against him, seeking that feeling.

"Tell me what else you want." His voice dipped low, demanding, his mouth pressed against her ear. He was going to keep teasing her like this until she gave in.

"Inside . . . me," she managed to pant out. "I need . . . your fingers . . . inside me. Please."

"Mmm, *please* sounds delicious coming from your sweet mouth," he said, his lips parting into a smile against her own. He complied, pressing one finger inside her, and when he met no resistance, her body—how it ached for his touch—he slid in another.

She accepted him eagerly, her core slick, and he growled against her lips, sounding every bit the hunter. He drew his fingers out and then slowly pushed them in again before hooking them and finding that sweet spot inside her. He moved his fingers back and forth now, rhythmically, and pressed his face into her throat, breathing her in as if her scent were life-giving nectar.

Lore bucked her hips, the sensation of Finndryl's fingers inside her driving her mad; she pushed the fabric of his shirt up and slid her hands over the taught muscles on his abdomen, then up to feel the contoured pecs on his chest. His skin was on fire. Or maybe she was on fire as heat was conveyed from him to her and her to him. She would have checked, but she'd thrown her head back into the sand, her eyes shut tight, at the feel of him.

Finndryl, gifting her sweet pleasure.

If just his fingers felt this delicious, she could only imagine what his hard length would feel like, thrust inside her, as deep as he could go. But she couldn't imagine it now, because his fingers felt good, so good. She moved with him, as he stroked her from inside, his fingers hitting the right spot every damned time.

So close, gods, she was so close.

She grabbed his wrist with both hands, holding it firm between her thighs, panicked that for some unknown reason, she would be deprived of his perfect fingers, of this indulgence.

"That's it, ride my hand, Lore, you're doing so good," he praised, his breath coming out in pants.

At his approval, the current that had been building inside her, that precipice she'd been suspended from, released all at once, and she cried out; stars exploded behind her lids as ecstasy enveloped her entire being.

Her body twitched with wave after wave of elation as he coaxed them from her with assured strokes. Before the sound of her cry could make it past the stacks, Finndryl captured it in his mouth, kissing her through her honeyed release.

"My gods, Lore, you make the most exquisite sound when you climax." He slid his fingers out of her and placed them into his mouth, tasting them. The side of his mouth quirked up. "I was right; you taste like marigolds, Alemeyu."

Lore should have felt satiated, but the sight of him licking *her* release off *his* fingers, fingers that were just inside her, made her core pulse all the harder.

The view of him kneeling above her, his eyes heavy, glassy with desire, his beautiful dark skin glowing with lust as his locs floated in the water around him—he was the most beautiful thing she'd ever seen. She was sure of it.

She wanted more of him. Needed *more* of him.

All of him.

He stood up and reached out a hand for her to grab, intending to pull her to her feet. But Lore was starved for the taste of him.

She ignored his outstretched hand and sat up a bit until she was propped on her elbows, the sand soft and gentle beneath her, and gazed at his breeches. Like everything he wore, they were black and formfitting, and they were tied shut with a string. She eyed the ridged outline of him, proof of his desire, and she realized that she might actually die if he didn't let her see it. It was only fair, after all; she wanted to know what sounds he made when he climaxed.

In one swift movement, she was on her knees before him, with the soft fabric of the strings to his pants poised between thumb and finger as she looked up at him. *Is this okay?* He nodded once in answer to her silent question, his throat bobbing as he swallowed.

She untied the strings and had barely tugged his trousers down, when his length sprang free, jutting up, proud and eager. She had felt that he was large, had suspected it when he pressed her up against the bookshelves, but *damn*.

She fisted his length tightly, marveling at the silken, hard feel of him. His burning gaze lit up with heat, and he hissed when she began to slide her hand up and down his length.

The sight of his pleasure worn so openly on his face made her own desire sing in response.

She dipped her head down to place him in her mouth. She'd never done this before. Had never wanted to give anyone pleasure with her mouth before; but right now, there was nothing more in the world that she desired.

He was so large she had to stretch her mouth to fit all of him, but she did so eagerly. Encouraged by his groan of pleasure, she teased him, like he had her, circling the tip of him with featherlight licks. He gasped and shifted his hips forward. She loved that. She opened her mouth wider for him, and Finndryl groaned, fisting his hands in her hair as he slowly eased his hips forward, gently sliding along her tongue until the head of him pressed against the back of her throat. Lore moaned in encouragement when he began to rock himself back and forth.

Her core pulsed in response to his barely controlled movements inside her mouth.

She wasn't aware that giving pleasure could elicit her own, but she was having to stop herself from reaching down to circle her own bundle of nerves, to assuage the throbbing, so she worked his shaft instead.

She glanced up at him, expecting to see his eyes closed, but his gaze was fixed on her, watching her take the entire length of him as if she were the most beautiful thing in the world and he couldn't look away if he tried.

She began to suck on his length, and he let out a groan, which, Lore decided, was the greatest sound she'd ever heard, and she craved more. She bobbed her head faster and faster, finding her rhythm, sucking his length with enthusiasm as her hand pumped his shaft. "Godsdamned, Lore," he grunted. "You're perfect. A fucking treasure."

She was down on her knees in the sand before Finndryl, and she'd never felt so beautiful, so powerful, as his erection pulsed in her mouth from the pleasure she was gifting him.

She sucked harder, twisting and squeezing his base. One of his hands fisted tighter in her hair, and the other flew out to grab onto a bookshelf to keep upright as his eyes closed. "Fuck, Lore, Lore, love, I'm close," he warned, giving her a chance to pull off him now, but she craved the taste of him. She continued her rhythm until he grunted, his thighs tensing, as warmth surged into her mouth, hitting the back of her throat. She moaned as she swallowed each spurt; gods, she couldn't get enough of him.

Finndryl hissed, sliding himself out of her mouth, and lifted her up to him, wrapping his arms around her waist to lift her up and press his lips to hers, kissing her slowly, his lips soft and sweet.

As she basked in this kiss, Lore thought, this was it; this must be bliss.

"You're a fucking goddess," he murmured as he set her down

gently on her feet. "What I wouldn't do to squirrel you away in a room right now. I ache to keep you all to myself."

Lore bit her lip. It felt swollen from kissing Finndryl; she squirmed with desire. "I wonder if we could find one?" she asked as she stepped back into her underthings.

"At this point, I'm considering banishing the queen from her own rooms."

Finndryl fastened the strings on his trousers before he pulled her toward him and placed a crooked finger under her chin, tipping her face upward. He kissed her softly, slowly, instilling the promise of what would come if only they had more time alone, together.

Lore wished more than anything that they were not here, but somewhere just the two of them. She wanted to explore every inch of him, learn every contour and sharp angle of his lithe body.

The glowing lights of the library that bobbed and wove above them flickered and went out.

"The pearl failed," Lore gasped and opened her eyes wider in the complete and utter darkness. They were cloaked in pitch-black water—water that she could not feel a moment ago, but now, robbed of sight, felt oppressive.

Lore broke away from Finndryl, crouched down, scooped up her grimoire, and gripped it tightly to her chest. It was daytime, and the tome would not help her create magic, but she felt better with the book in her possession, even if she couldn't see.

"Do you remember the way back to the library's entrance?" she asked Finndryl. Her words felt trapped behind a knot in her throat.

She was starting to loathe the dark.

He gripped her hand tightly, and the knot in her throat eased slightly.

"I don't, but I'm confident that I can—"

Whatever Finndryl had been about to say was lost in an explosion, a shattering of something massive—it sounded like the library's glass ceiling.

CHAPTER 22

With a growl, Finndryl enclosed Lore beneath him, wrapping his arms around her, protecting her body with his own, but not before a jagged shard of glass sliced her cheek.

As the lights around them flickered back to life, Lore peeked through splayed fingers that burned in the salt water from tiny cuts.

Most of the glass floated harmlessly around them; but a few unluckily angled slivers managed to pierce Finndryl's leathers. He winced as he straightened to a standing position, but his expression remained stoic. Lore shook with fear as she began to search his clothes, pulling out larger chunks of glass, looking for signs of blood. "Are you hurt?"

"I'm fine. I'm more concerned with what caused the glass to break."

Lore wondered that too.

Some of the pieces of glass scattered around them, piercing through books and scrolls on the shelves and stuck firmly in the sand, were so large . . . Lore swallowed hard. If they had been on land, the larger pieces of the glass ceiling would have pierced through them before they had a chance to realize what was happening.

She opened her mouth to remark just that, but her words were drowned out by an earsplitting screech. A purple-hued sea monster was slithering toward them from the shattered ceiling, its circular mouth wide open, tentacles stretching toward them, intent on encircling them and drawing them both into its giant maw.

Finndryl picked up his spear and swiped it through the water, cutting off the closest tentacle with a sickening squelch. Blood sprayed from the tentacle like an ink cloud. The creature screeched in pain, retracting its tentacles back into its mouth, and it flipped around, slithering away, taking a moment to gather its bearings.

"Gods, why didn't I bring a weapon as well?" Lore whispered, crouched low, her voice trembling.

"You aren't supposed to need a weapon in a library, Alemeyu," Finndryl growled. He stood in front of her, his eyes never leaving the quivering sea creature. It zoomed toward them once more, its red eyes hungry. This time, the creature prepared for the swipe of his spear, dodging it, its serpentine body agile in the water though it bumped into one of the shelves. It ignored the books raining down on its back; a mere nuisance when its scales were thick enough to be armor.

Lore screamed. Another sea monster had snuck in from the stacks behind them. A writhing tentacle wrapped around her grimoire. She gripped the book, her knuckles going pale with the strain. Trying with every fiber of her being to hold on—to keep the one item that encapsulated all her hopes and dreams.

"Let. Go!" She kicked out with her foot, but all her boot managed to do was slip right off the tentacle and make her lose her balance. She twisted her body so she fell onto the book, not caring that now she was being dragged toward the creature's mouth. She would rather die than lose the grimoire again.

Finndryl, with a roar, grabbed hold of the tentacle and severed the writhing thing in two. The creature shrieked and shot straight up, until it was out of sight.

Lore cursed as she lay heaving on the ground, *Deeping Lune* clasped in her arms as she ripped the disembodied suckers off her book one by one. "Finndryl," Lore exhaled as she gazed into the water above them. Three creatures now soared, circling the shelves that towered over their heads. Lore felt so small as their shadows flickered across her vision.

The monsters chattered to each other as if planning their next assault.

Finndryl crouched low, his sharp gaze flitting over them. Preparing for their next attack. Lore hastily tucked her book into the bodice of her dress, though she realized the thin fabric would do nothing to stop the creatures from taking it from her.

"Are these the Nikoryxia? Can they sense the *Source* in the book?" Finndryl asked, as he hauled her to a standing position. He kept his sights above, but his hand was clamped firmly on her shoulder.

"I think so," Lore replied, her voice quavering with dread.

"When they attack next, you will run as fast as you can toward the door."

"I won't make it," Lore protested.

"You will. If you don't look back."

Lore shook her head, trying to ignore the taste of coppery fear on her tongue. "If I run, then what is your plan?"

"I'll hack them to pieces while you focus on making it safely out of here."

"Absolutely not. Their teeth are six inches long and razor sharp. They will shred you to ribbons."

"They can try," Finndryl said, his voice grim but determined.

"They—" Lore started to argue, but Finndryl cut her off.

"No time! *RUN!*" he shouted, pushing her toward the door.

But it was too late. In perfect sync, as though they were of one mind, the Nikoryxia dove, their bodies cutting through the water like spears.

Lore plucked a book off the shelf, one with a jagged piece of glass sticking out of its spine, and held it aloft.

"We survive together, or not at all," she said through gritted teeth as she crouched low. She would stab at least one of these beasts before she was devoured.

"Together, then," he responded as he pushed off the sand, jumping in front of her.

Finndryl, with a practiced thrust, drove his spear deep into the yielding flesh of a Nikoryxia's underbelly. A twisting yank released the weapon, leaving behind a gaping wound spilling iridescent entrails. Lore, meanwhile, brandished the book as a makeshift weapon, aiming for the nearest creature's eyes. She hacked at its face as she tried to avoid its teeth and tentacles. Yet the beast's slimy, suction-cupped tentacles proved too agile, deflecting her blows and encircling her wrists with an iron grip.

A cry of despair and rage escaped her lips as the monstrous maw, reeking of decay, loomed closer, rows and rows of jagged teeth gnashing mere inches from her face. She was going to fucking be eaten alive—and gods, its mouth was so vast. She gagged as the smell of rotting fish and seaweed slammed into her; she almost fainted at the sight of the sharp, churning teeth, so close to her face.

She dug her heels into the sand, trying to resist being pulled by the beast as she worked to twist out of its grip, but when another tentacle extended from inside its mouth and shot out to wrap around her ankles, she lost her footing and fell, her knees digging into the sand. The Nikoryxia, bleeding from a wounded eye, chittered in triumph and began to drag her across the sharp, glass-strewn sand. Lore yelled as sharp, jagged pieces of glass bit into her knees and thighs. This was not merely predation; this was a sadistic beast that planned on playing with its food.

She flipped onto her back and managed to turn; her desperate gaze found Finndryl, and a fresh wave of horror washed over her.

Suspended in the water, his face contorted in agony as he fought against the relentless pull of *two* Nikoryxia, their tentacles wrapped around his wrists like living ropes. His spear, embedded in the bone of one creature's jaw, was lost to him. Without his weapon, the two Nikoryxia had managed to capture his wrists, and the vicious things were swimming in opposite directions.

He was going to be torn in two.

Lore screamed his name, an anguished plea. *Not him, gods, don't let him die.*

Suddenly, a spear flashed through the murky water, severing all three tentacles that held Finndryl's left arm. With a scream, the Nikoryxia, three tentacles down, began to convulse. With one arm free, Finn didn't hesitate; he twisted, his legs wrapping around the remaining beast's body. He wrenched his spear free from its jaw and plunged it into a bloodred eye, driving it deep into the creature's brain.

With a shudder, the beast went limp.

But Lore's relief was short-lived.

Because streaming down from above like harbingers of death were more Nikoryxia.

So many more.

Darkness engulfed her as a tentacle coiled around her face, covering her eyes and mouth.

She was submerged in terror as she fought with everything she had, but there was nothing to be done. There were too many of them, and Finndryl was so very far away. She had been dragged too far; no matter how fast he was, no matter how perfect his aim if he threw the spear, there wouldn't be enough time to save her.

Another tentacle coiled around her arms, pressing them to her sides. Lore didn't even have enough breath to whimper. This was it.

This was the end.

Then an eerie, harrowing melody echoed through the library, bouncing off the shelves and swirling around Lore.

The Nikoryxia about to devour her screeched, its undulating body twisting and turning. Its tentacles spasmed, releasing its hold on her all at once.

Too in shock to move, Lore watched the Nikoryxia retract its feelers and turn to flee. But the beast was cornered by the shelves and mad with terror. It thrashed against the bookshelf, writhing, its eyes rolling into the back of its head as the song swelled louder.

Finndryl, his face etched with terror and relief, gathered Lore into his arms, scooped her up, and turned to run past a host of siren guards, their spears flashing in the filtered light.

Lore swallowed bile as she clung to Finndryl, pressing her face into his chest, trying and failing to stop herself from trembling.

Haunting death shrieks echoed down from above as the water ran black with the creatures' blood.

CHAPTER 23

Finndryl pressed a kiss to Lore's temple.

"It's over," he reassured her. "They've finished them off and are now scouting for any stragglers from the pod."

Lore unclenched her eyes. They were still surrounded by siren guards.

She looked around, relieved to see that the haze of blood had already begun to clear, thanks to the library's unique filtration system. Designed by the prince consort himself; Jaladri boasted of its efficiency. Devised to prevent algae from forming on the books and shelves, it utilized well-placed, hollowed-out whale bones and the sea's natural current streams. She doubted he had imagined that his invention might one day double as a purification method on the off chance copious amounts of monster blood were introduced into the library.

The guards surrounding them parted, heads bowed, to reveal a handsome siren in the doorway. His sleeveless vest, encrusted with radiant rubies, gleamed in the shell lights. A slim crown of driftwood, adorned with polished lapis and translucent moonstone, rested atop his unruly black hair. His pointed chin and proud forehead were adorned with intricate, swirling spirals and lines that had been artfully inked into tawny skin. The tattoos glowed, blue-white bioluminescence in the dim library. Delicately arched, manicured brows sat above storm-cloud eyes.

His prominent, clear voice rang through the stacks. "We aren't being very suitable hosts, are we? Please don't hold this against us—I swear, we usually try to keep our guests' near-death experiences limited to just one."

Lore squirmed, and Finndryl released his grip on her just enough that she slid out of his arms to stand on her own, though he kept her firmly pressed to him, which made Lore's curtsy even more awkward than her curtsy to the queen. Oh well, let her curtsy be awkward; nothing could tear her away from Finndryl's side right now, not even royalty.

"Prince Hazen, you have returned," a guard with pale skin, green eyes, and a tight bun of copper hair said, rising from a deep bow. "Welcome home, my Liege."

Prince Hazen dipped his head respectfully to the guard. "Echosmith Jade, excellently spun songwork." He looked around the library with a grimace. "I see things are worse. Two breaches from the Nikoryxia in as many days?"

"Yes, Prince," Jade, the echosmith, replied, her voice grave.

"And you two"—he addressed Lore and Finn—"I hope you are not injured. Shall we call for the royal physician?"

Did Lore need a physician? Her mind was still reeling as she assessed her physical well-being. Her fingers trembled where they clung to Finndryl's arm. She swallowed, suppressing a gag as she tasted monster blood. It coated her tongue, and she could feel it between her fingers . . . suspected it was in her hair. Her dress was ripped, her knees and thighs scraped raw from where she'd been dragged across the glass-littered sand, and her throat was badly bruised. She ached all over.

Lore had almost been devoured whole.

She'd almost seen Finndryl torn in two. "Nothing a waterspout and fresh clothes can't fix." She assessed Finndryl's face. Blood leaked into the water from a cut lip. "Finndryl?"

"I'm unharmed. I would like to remove Lore from the library until we can be sure the shield is back in place."

"Of course. I am relieved to hear that. I was just on my way to introduce myself and invite you, at the behest of my grandmother, to sup with us in her quarters when I heard the alarm." He leaned in toward Finndryl's spear, which had flecks of Nikoryxia still stuck to it. "You managed to fight them off with just the one spear?" His eyebrow rose a fraction as he eyed Finndryl's weapon.

Finndryl grunted. "Not for long. If it hadn't been for a well-aimed spear from one of your soldiers, I wouldn't be standing here right now." Finn cleared his throat. "I prefer a sword."

Prince Hazen studied Finn, his expression admiring. "Not many trained siren would have held out against three bonded Nikoryxia males for as long as you managed—and with barely any wounds deeper than a scratch on either of you to show for it." Prince Hazen grinned. "What do you say we get you cleaned up and fed, then visit the armory after our meal and see if we can find you a suitable sword?"

Finndryl nodded. "Sounds like a plan."

"It's settled," the prince said, leading the way toward the exit, the guards flowing around the three of them in formation. "Lore, I'm eager to hear if you've managed to find anything of worth despite the tedium of my grandfather's library. But I understand if you wish to rest before—"

Lore clenched her fingers involuntarily, tightening around Findryl's arm. *Tedium?* Imagine growing up in a palace with your very own library and referring to it as tedium.

"Don't call a library tedious around this one," Finndryl said as he gently pried her viselike grip from his arm. Lore winced; gods, his arms were probably bruised where the Nikoryxia's tentacles had been. He didn't let her go far, though, as he tucked her into his side.

"She'll have no qualms about smacking you with a book, high treason against the crown or not." Finndryl huffed a laugh, the sound settling over Lore like a poultice, relaxing her tense muscles almost instantly. "Actually, better not tempt her while we are still in the library; she somehow managed to turn a book into a weapon just now."

"I can't take credit for the glass-shard-lodged-in-a-book. It was just the closest book to me on the shelf." She bumped his hip with her own, smiling. "Besides, I was going to let that one go, having just met the prince and all . . ."

Hazen's eyes crinkled at the corners as he stood aside, letting his guests exit the library first. "Noted, no slander against libraries. Though with my grandfather joining us, I don't know if I'll be able to stomach two bookfish at the table at once."

Finndryl smirked. "Oh, you should have seen the two of them when he gave us a tour of the library. It was difficult to watch. I didn't know two people could be so enamored by—"

Lore shoved Finndryl's arm. "You act like you don't have an entire wall of books and scrolls at home in your room."

"That's a secret, you'll blow my cover."

***

Later, alone in the bathing chamber, Lore sank onto the floor, clutching the skirt of her dress to her chest. She buried her face in the soft fabric—fabric that should feel soggy and wet, but didn't—and cried. Heaving sobs that tore at her throat, burning her chest as her shoulders shook with release.

What was this life she was living, that she had had the most pleasure she'd ever known and the most terror she'd ever experienced in the same morning—and then could be teasing Finndryl right after? When this was all over—when she'd acquired the book and created a sovereign nation for humanity—would a quiet life be enough for her?

She hadn't let herself think that far ahead because it was hard for her to imagine what came after, when things in the new village were settled and she wasn't needed anymore. What would happen when she'd built her wall, cast her spells?

When she was alone at night.

Would she be bored?

Would she miss this?

Lore hiccupped into the dress. Nobody would miss almost being eaten . . . but there was one thing she knew for certain . . . she would miss *him*.

She would miss him as though a part of her had been carved out. Hacked off. She had told him how she felt earlier . . . how she was unworthy of his love . . . afraid that she would only bring him more pain.

But she hadn't the courage to tell him the entire truth. That she was planning on building a wall, and he would be left on the other side.

She couldn't conceive of a way to keep her people safe without keeping the fae out. And how could she weave spells that would allow for one to visit? How could she keep them safe and still allow him in?

It couldn't be done.

She would have to tell him.

She would have to tell him that they couldn't be together again, not because she didn't crave his touch—even now, she was aching with need just at the thought of the heated brush of his fingers. Her heart keened to be given to him, a lament that Lore should hold it captive within her rib cage instead of allowing him to cherish and protect it. But once she told him that they didn't have long together . . . that one day, she was going to leave and shut the world out, and no one would be allowed in, not even him . . .

There would come a time . . . whether it be next week, next month, or a year from now . . . when she would close the gate, turn the key, and disappear the new village from anyone who dared to hurt them . . . anyone . . . and that meant everyone.

CHAPTER 24

Lore still had to cleanse the Nikoryxia blood and gore from her knotted curls and skin.

She peeled the bloodied, ripped, and tattered fabric of the dress she'd donned only a few hours ago from her body. With heaving breaths, she crumpled what was left of the dress into a ball and shoved it into the rubbish bin.

When she was sure there weren't any remaining slivers of glass spearing her skin, she picked up her sponge and scrubbed. And scrubbed. And scrubbed. Until her skin was puckered and red. An hour ago, she thought she would never wash Finndryl's kisses away. And now, here she was, wishing she could have new skin. Replacement skin. She could still feel the slippery, suction-y, clinging sensation of the Nikoryxia's tentacles on her face, her throat, her arms.

The soap paste the sirens used smelled like rain; it was pleasant. She scrubbed her entire body again before she felt the essence of the soap and sponge more than suction cups.

Then, she went to work on her hair. At this point, her curls resembled locs. She parted her hair into four segments, and then again, into even smaller sections, hacking with the bone comb, too rattled to take care with her curls, hardly differentiating between knot and coil, until every tangle disappeared. Satisfied, she stepped into the jetting stream.

The powerful current had long since whisked away all blood, sand, and glass . . . yet Lore couldn't bring herself to step out of the hot streams. Not when the heat felt this good on her aching and sore muscles. Not when, out there, were more Nikoryxia. More responsibility. And a conversation to be had with Finn.

A knock sounded from the door on the other side of the curtain.

"I have fresh clothes for you," a palace attendant called.

"Thank you. I'll be out soon."

"Take your time; they are just out here."

With an exhale, Lore twisted the handle, closing off the stream of hot water.

She wanted nothing more than to towel off, put on *dry* clothes, crawl into her bed in her little attic room above the apothecary, and sleep for days. But that wasn't possible—and wouldn't ever be possible again, considering her bed might still be underneath a pile of brick and stone from the earthshake.

It was a struggle putting the clothes on. She was thankful it wasn't another dress—they just didn't work down here, not with the current. She slowly pulled the pants up over her legs, bit by bit, then hopped up and down until the waist was high enough to clasp the buckle and she felt almost normal. Lore was glad she was alone; she shouldn't be breathing this heavily just from donning clothes.

At least the Puallas Kiss had a certain bit of magic that made it so once the clothes were fully donned, they didn't feel so . . . wet.

She glanced at the bench. Beside knitted socks and boots, there was another piece of clothing. A vest of some kind. A note was pinned to it.

Lore,

I am deeply apologetic that my realm continues such an onslaught on your well-being. Please accept this armor as a token of my sincerest remorse. It was forged from the very scales of the Nikoryxia that sought to harm you. I hope it may serve as a symbol of your strength and a testament to your resilience.

With profound respect and affection,

Queen Naia

Whoa. The queen's tailors worked fast. Lore had only been in the bathing chamber for one bell. With a smile, Lore collected the vest from the bench. A supple marine leather was fitted with cascading rows of iridescent Nikoryxia scales in hues ranging from amethyst to cerulean. Lore brushed her fingertips over the frigid scales, admiring their unyielding construction. The pattern was reminiscent of the scales along the Nikoryxia spines, which acted as armor, protecting them from predators above. What could possibly desire to attack one of them from above, though? Lore shuddered to think—and hoped to never find out. She hugged the vest to her chest.

These scales were nearly impenetrable; this would be superb protection.

She donned the vest over a simple linen shirt and studied her reflection in the looking glass. The vest fit her perfectly, and it would protect her most vital organs. Efficient. Stunning. But then her gaze fell upon the wild tangle of her hair, each strand seemingly determined to intertwine. She'd just untangled it! With a frown, she seized her hair and tugged the stubborn curls forward.

A single braid, though effective on land, felt too tame for the continuous currents. Two plaits wouldn't fare much better, unless she braided them tightly against her scalp. Which was a skill she'd never quite mastered. Spend sixteen days transcribing a novel letter by letter? No matter that her eyes would ache, her hand would cramp, and her nails would be stained black for weeks afterward. No problem, Lore adored it. A quarter bell of time wrestling her hair into tightly woven plaits? There wasn't a reason to. Not when her mother and then her aunt were such talented weavers, their nimble fingers coaxing her hair into submission with ease.

Lore had never had to learn, when they were so willing. When the act of having her hair done by them was love in its most simple form.

A knock came at the door, accompanied by a gruff voice. "Lore, are you clothed?"

Finn.

She cleared her throat, making sure she didn't sound as though she was having a pity party for herself in here. "Yes! Come in."

Finndryl somehow made the massive bathing chamber feel small. Thoughts of their hurried, stolen pleasure flashed through Lore's mind. She blushed.

"I thought I might offer my services." His smile was cautious despite his casual stance. Squared shoulders, hands in pockets.

Intrigued, Lore inquired, "Services, how?"

"When we were little, the tavern was so hectic, my mother was often too busy or tired to braid Isla's hair, so I taught myself to do it. If you want . . . I can braid yours as well."

"You want to . . . braid my hair?"

"Only if you wish."

"I do wish."

"Excellent." Finndryl swung a satchel off his shoulder. "Because I had Cuan procure bands and oil."

Lore laughed. "All right, let's see those skills."

Finndryl lowered himself onto the bench. Lore knelt on the floor below him, leaning against his knees.

"Are you tender-headed?" he asked as he applied oil to her hair. Lore closed her eyes, suppressing a moan of pleasure as he massaged it into her scalp.

"Yes, I'm convinced I was cursed as a baby. Mama's beautiful hair—but with a tender scalp to accompany it."

"Isla is, too, so I'm used to it."

But Lore needn't have worried.

His touch was impossibly light as he parted her hair. It was more than just braiding; it was a nuanced cadence of his fingers. Lore could feel his care for her in every twist, lace, and twine—a warmth that spread from his dancing fingertips down through her chest to settle into her spirit. Lore leaned into his caress, a sigh escaping her lips as she closed her eyes. All other sounds faded away save the rhythmic whispering of his fingers against her crown. She would savor this moment—carve it into her memory as if it were stone so that she could always return to this time with him.

"Your hair is so mischievous." He chuckled, a mini-current from his breath tickling her ear. "Like the first curling vines of spring."

As he wove the final strands into place, Lore almost wished she had more hair for him to braid. She didn't want this to be over. She opened her eyes, turning to meet Finndryl's gaze.

Finndryl smiled, twisting a braid that lay over her shoulder between thumb and finger. "Let me know what you think."

She stood up and once again gazed into the looking glass. Only this time, she saw that he had woven her hair into a masterpiece—a macramé of hair and cowry shells—eight-stitch braids tightly woven in horizontal rows to fall down her back in exquisite ropes. Turning side to side to see it better, Lore grinned—her hair had no chance to escape.

Finndryl came up behind her, his hands resting on her shoulders, his fingers tracing the line of her collarbone.

"Thank you," she whispered, locking her eyes with his in the mirror, her throat tight with emotion. "It's beautiful."

Finndryl leaned forward, his lips brushing against her shoulder in a fleeting kiss. "As are you," he murmured, his tone resonant, an echo of his favorite wildwood.

CHAPTER 25

One three-hour strategy meeting masquerading as the midday meal in the council chamber and a fitful night's sleep later, Lore found herself miles from the Lapis Deep Palace, searching for a volcano.

Searching for a *volcano*.

She'd heard stories about volcanoes, of course, and had generally thought that one should avoid them when at all possible.

Many people chose to do the opposite . . . but she never understood why. Why build your house at the base of something that could erupt without notice, swallowing you and everything and everyone you hold dear in ash and smoke and debris, only to eventually end the spectacle with blazing *molten* rock?

Especially when this particular volcano was a slumbering god?

Lore knew all about gods—and she was thankful that none of the ones she was raised with chose the shape of a volcano. They had spiders and stars and even one odd one that preferred the shape of a stunted, barren pear tree . . . but she could only imagine what kind of havoc a volcano deity would inflict upon the humans. Instead of exiled and stranded in this hostile world, her ancestors would probably have been suctioned into the volcano deity's mouth. She whispered a silent prayer that the sirens' volcanic deity was one of the rare benevolent ones . . .

Lore wasn't quite sure how it had come to this.

And she still couldn't fathom how Syrelle had wrestled his way onto this expedition. Despite Lore's protests during the midday meal, he'd somehow convinced Queen Naia that he wasn't a conniving, lying, imprisoning villain. She'd insisted Syrelle accompany them to protect Prince Hazen.

Lore then tried to dissuade Prince Hazen from coming at all, but he'd been adamant about protecting *her*, given the risks she was taking for his empire.

Still trembling from her near-consumption by the Nikoryxia, Lore couldn't think of a way to further oppose the queen and prince without resorting to whining or crying or, gods forbid, *both*, so she'd relented before fleeing the council chamber, desperate for her cot and sleep.

And now here she was, surrounded by her enemy, a prince, a barkeep she couldn't keep her hands off of, a palace aide, and (in her opinion) far too few siren guards.

Lore stumbled over a boulder hidden in the sand and flapped her arms against the current to keep upright. She was, once again, ambling in the dark. Always in the damned dark. Lore made a promise to herself, as soon as she returned to the palace, she would seek out a spell in the grimoire that would allow her eyes to see in the dark.

If such a thing existed.

Though it wasn't so bad this time as she followed the attractive outline of Finndryl's expansive shoulders, which were cast in relief by the orb clasped in his hands. Lore was thankful that he had volunteered to hold the lantern—she didn't think she could stomach the view of the slimy slugs that writhed inside the glass. Their slime was nauseating but useful, as it glowed blue and cast off *almost* enough light to see by.

Behind her she could hear the quiet *swish swish* of Syrelle's footsteps.

Cuan, Prince Hazen, and six siren guards swam above and around them. Lore could neither see nor hear them as their finely evolved forms cut through the water, silent as spirits. But still, knowing they were there . . . it was comforting.

The only guard she recognized was Jade, who, Lore had learned yesterday, was of the highly admirable echosmith class—who was there not to help with the mission to the volcano, Mount Vatraol, Great Hearth, to restore life and magic to Lapis Deep, but was there to ensure Prince Hazen's safety, and only that. She'd made it very clear, multiple times, that nothing mattered to her except her prince's well-being.

The prince was something special to inspire such loyalty in his subjects. And not just Jade, but all of them.

All the royalty Lore had ever heard of were generally awful, synonymous with tyranny and cruelty. It was a revelation, refreshing—and somewhat healing—to discover that there existed royalty who truly cherished their empires and subjects, fostering a reciprocal love and loyalty within their realm.

The farther they ventured toward the volcano, the more Lore's human eyes allowed her to see.

The water was gradually warming, not too hot for Lore's skin. Not yet, anyway. She imagined that had to do with the Puallas Kiss. It protected her from the cold. From the heat. She pressed a hand to her forearm, thankful for the life-giving magic that now swirled on her skin. She hoped the kiss of the jellyfish never faded; the purple swirls looked beautiful. Lore had never had the guts to get a tattoo herself with permanent ink—not just because the process was painful, but because in Duskmere, one tried to avoid all things that could lead to infection and death.

But she had one now and wanted to keep it forever.

Now that she could see, she noted the gradual changes in the landscape around them. The closer they got to the volcano, the more evidence of its immense power shaping the earth. There was no coral here, no curious fish nipping at Lore's fingertips when they paused for a rest or to hydrate. Nothing could survive here, evidence that their god may have a temper. The earth changed too often for life to form.

Here the ground was barren, uneven. The magma had hardened into hexagonal shapes of varying size, thickness, and height. Swimming above it wouldn't be an issue, but Lore, Finn, and Syrelle were forced to navigate the jagged terrain on foot.

Another two hours passed, and pockets of glowing, molten rock began to appear underfoot. The heat of the water was becoming oppressive, and the tattoo on Lore's arm began to glow lavender as the power of the Puallas Kiss worked overtime to combat the warming water.

Though Lore knew: One wrong step, and no magic could protect her from instant, searing pain.

Lore turned her head to the left, squinting her eyes. In the distance a Nikoryxia's undulating, shifting body could just be seen. This one had been following them for some time, but it stayed on the outskirts of Lore's vision, appearing and disappearing in intervals but never gone for long.

Drawn to Lore's magic, hungry for it no doubt, it did not dare come here, where the volcano could decide to erupt at any moment. Agitation twisted Lore's insides.

Stay away, Nikoryxia, please. She didn't want to be within a hundred feet of one again. Not ever. Not for the rest of her life.

The glowing pockets were becoming more numerous, and Lore feared that at any moment, the hardened shelf of lava beneath her feet could crumble, give way, and she could slip through. She could not feel it, as she was underwater, but she knew that she had begun to sweat—from both the oppressive heat and the fear that was slowly eating at her resolve. People needed her help, she reminded herself. She couldn't turn back.

"There's a new one," Syrelle stated from behind Lore.

"Where?" She whipped her head around.

"Just there, behind that spout." Syrelle pointed.

Lore squinted her eyes in the dim, reddish glow of lava. Indeed, behind a tall rock formation pumping out swirling clouds of steam was another Nikoryxia, larger than the original one that had been following them.

"Great. If we manage to get to the *Source* without being burned alive, we will surely have a horde of them waiting to eat us when we are done," Cuan said from somewhere above Lore.

Gods, she wished she had a tail. It would be much easier to evade their wriggling tentacles.

"We won't have to worry about them soon, my grimoire will awaken any moment. We timed this perfectly; night is upon us." Lore tugged a ribbon from her pocket and pulled at her hair, twisting and pushing the braids into something that almost resembled a bun. "And if . . ." She bit her lip and wrapped the ribbon around three times before double knotting it. "If our plan works . . ." On second thought . . . she might as well . . . She twisted the strings of the ribbon and pulled them tightly once more. Maybe three knots would hold. "The *Source* waiting to be harnessed in the radiance swell . . ." She could worry about extricating the knots and her braids from the ribbon later, when she survived. ". . . will be more than enough to protect us."

"Right, of course," Cuan said. They did not sound convinced. Lore tried to ignore their apprehension; she had her own dread to contend with.

Magic, which had been skittering on the outskirts of her vision like the Nikoryxia trailing them, began to swirl, as if alerted to Lore's presence. *Deeping Lune* began to vibrate as it woke from slumber.

Excitement broiled in Lore's chest, warring with her anxiety.

She patted *Deeping Lune* where it lay strapped in and secure under her scaled vest. The straps were awkward and not designed for a book, and they were beginning to chafe in the spots her undershirt didn't cover. Still, she was thankful she had something to tie her book to, more secure than a pack that could slip off her shoulders if things became messy.

The vest itself was incredible. Lore was thankful for the gift . . . However, she had something else she wanted to ask the queen for when this was over. The idea had come to her when she'd seen a map of the siren kingdom in the council chamber, and the idea had been nagging at her ever since. Something far more useful and precious than a vest.

Every one of them cursed when a shrill, hissing sound erupted from their left.

A dormant stack of rock had morphed into one of the many hydrothermal vents of Mount Vatraol. A reminder that molten lava swirled, eddied, and bubbled, just layers beneath them. This was the reason no sea life thrived here. Why, despite the warmth, and *Source*, the Nikoryxia refused to enter this area to nest, to live, to hunt, because it was ever-changing. Unsafe. Great Hearth did not care that life walked above it. It was a life force. A deity. The reason that land existed at all. It would explode, covering, devouring everything, and then, in time, life would be rebirthed atop the grave. The cycle of life, death, rebirth. Kill, to live.

"Lore, we are close to Great Hearth. Can you see the magic?" Prince Hazen asked, swimming down to float beside her.

"It's just over there." Lore pointed to a glowing, swirling field of *Source*.

They couldn't see it, of course, but Lore could, and it was magnificent. It looked like starlight. It shone like the sun and the moon. The *Source* twirled and danced in the water as though it were alive.

They were close, indeed.

"Another one!" called Jade.

"Another what?" Lore almost didn't want to broach the question, but she was hoping it would be something harmless, like a particularly juicy clump of clayberry or a bunch of sweet kelpi shrooms—which Cuan had been overjoyed to find earlier, as apparently the fungi only grew beneath one specific strain of kelp, and only when that kelp forest was home to a specific type of crab.

Jade didn't need to answer, because Lore spied it just as the question left her lips.

Six. Six Nikoryxia. Their scales, which were naturally a greenish blue, sometimes purple, glowed an absolutely horrifying red—reflecting the light of the volcano. Lore shuddered at the sight of them.

"We can't worry about them just now, please," Hazen said, his voice a sharp hiss as he lunged sideways, barely avoiding a spout of steam.

"Maybe don't swim directly over the burning vents, Your Majesty," said Cuan, their voice shrill.

"Nikoryxia aren't known to hunt so near Great Hearth—and yes, Cuan, I am trying to avoid doing just that."

Jade piped in as she swam closer to her prince. "As we siren are not the only creatures affected by the disruption of magic—the Nikoryxia are desperate and may make a move at any moment. Stay vigilant."

Stay vigilant? Lore felt she'd never been more vigilant in her life—or more aware of all the things that could currently end her life . . . Nikoryxia, spouts of scalding steam, lava . . . she yelped a curse as her foot slipped through a crack between the hexagonal rocks she was scaling. Finndryl, so fast Lore hadn't even had a chance to finish spitting her curse word, turned and gripped Lore's arm before she twisted her ankle.

He held her upright as she slowly, carefully, extracted her foot from the crack.

So much for staying vigilant. "Thank you."

"Would you like to climb on my back? I can carry you the rest of the way."

"You are serious, aren't you?" Lore asked, her lips cracking a smile as she sighed in relief now that both feet were firmly on one rock and not between two.

Finn eyed her, his face stoic. "Of course."

"That won't be necessary. I'll be more careful."

"The offer stands, if you change your mind." He squeezed her hip, his hand lingering. A thrill shot through Lore. She would never, could never, be used to his small moments of affection. They electrified her.

"Be sure that you do; a lot is riding on you, Lore," Cuan called down. "Though, speaking of riding . . . if you won't ride on his back, I might take you up on that." Cuan swam in a circle above them, waggling their eyebrows.

"Cuan, let's trade. I'll take your much more efficient tail, and you can ride on Finndryl's back."

"Sweetie, I would make that trade with you right now if I could."

Finndryl crossed his arms, his eyes crinkling at the corners with amusement. "This doesn't seem fair. If we are handing out tails, I should like one as well."

"Can everyone focus? It's getting so hot, I'm about to combust," Jade snapped, her voice brittle with the heat.

"I can feel the magic," Syrelle intoned, breaking his silence. "I cannot see it, but Lore is correct, we are close." His words hung heavy in the air, a reminder of the powerful alchemist he was.

Lore whirled around, her eyes flashing with defiance. "I don't need you to corroborate what I've already said. And do us a favor," she spat, "don't siphon the magic for yourself, Syrelle. Do you think you can handle that?"

A flicker of amusement danced in Syrelle's eyes. "I hadn't thought of it, but that's a good idea."

Lore's voice was a hiss of venom. "Don't even joke about that."

"You started it!"

"I wasn't joking."

Syrelle uttered a low growl. "I know."

Lore turned her back on him. She had been blindsided by him before, but she reminded herself that would never happen again. She was once again making her own decisions, with *Deeping Lune* back in her possession where it belonged. Syrelle, despite his power, could not take it from her again.

Goddess, the heat was relentless; Lore's boots were beginning to stick to the rocks. Their very soles were melting.

Lore bit her lip before squaring her shoulders and addressing the others. She raised her voice, urging it to sound more confident than she felt. "Why don't you all wait here while I venture on alone? It's not much farther."

"Please don't argue with me when I tell you that I will be by your side." Finndryl's jaw was set.

"I won't argue with you, Finn, but I will point out that something could go wrong—or very right. The power could be too much; what if I can't control it right away, or at all? I believe that *Deeping Lune* won't let anything hurt me, I have faith, but that doesn't mean someone standing right beside me won't get hurt."

"I'll take my chances."

"I'm coming too," said Syrelle.

"If you so much as take a step toward her, or the book, or even look like you are planning to siphon some of the *Source*, I'll put this dagger through your heart." Finndryl's voice was cool as ice.

"I can't just take magic like her; no other creature in the world can, so there's no point in worrying about that."

"The vile Nikoryxia can, so maybe you can too," said Finndryl.

"Technically, the Nikoryxia don't take magic, they eat it," Prince Hazen remarked.

"Isn't that what he does? He's insatiable. There will never be enough power to appease him, he will always want more. No matter the cost," Finndryl replied, his eyes trained on Syrelle.

Lore stepped in, her voice calm but firm. "It's fine, Finn. He can come. I doubt he would let anything happen to me, because, I imagine, he still believes that I am his only hope of finding *Auroradel*."

Syrelle wisely remained quiet. If he had tried to protest this, Lore would have just called him a liar, and it might have made her so mad that she would've had to expend more energy arguing with him until he stayed behind.

"Call if the Nikoryxia try to eat you. I don't know what we can do from back here, but at least we can witness your sacrifice," Cuan said from where they floated beside Jade.

"Cuan, you're just the sweetest."

"I try." They grinned for a moment before their expression turned solemn. "Seriously, good luck. The Nikoryxia shouldn't bother you over there. As you can see, they are keeping their distance. Just worry about funneling the magic without disturbing Great Hearth. If that happens . . . well, I think we all know what would become of us."

"I crave a death by burning magma just as little as you. I'll be careful."

"I think what my grandmother's favored aide is attempting to say, Lore Alemeyu, is that Mother Pearl's radiance undeniably falls upon you. Your life, risked for strangers, for beings apart from your own, shines brighter than even our royal jewels. We, who witness your valor, stand in your debt."

Prince Hazen was so eloquent. She could see why Queen Naia picked him out of all her grandchildren to be heir.

Hazen extended his arm to Lore, their hands meeting in a firm clasp. What could she say that would compare? Nothing as fine as his speech, nor as positive. She feared the sirens' confidence in her was misplaced. That she would let them all down. That Finndryl would be hurt. She opted for truth. "I will try my hardest to measure up to your kind words, Prince Hazen."

"Lore, when this is over, I'll be thanking you for more than saving my empire—you see, it's not often that a prince has a chance for adventure, and if it weren't my empire at stake, I would find this all quite thrilling."

"I wish I shared your enthusiasm, Prince." Lore returned the prince's smile, though hers lacked his confidence and felt rather shaky. Right now, a quiet, uneventful life sounded superior to this one. She would give anything to trade her circumstances for another version of life, one where she and her loved ones were safe, one without a volcano and Nikoryxia, betrayals, and despicable kings. *Adventure* was beginning to sound like a bad word. "Let's discuss your adventure-seeking later, once this current one is accomplished."

"Let my optimism embolden you." The prince grinned, his eyes shimmering. "And it's a deal; I have much to discuss with you when it comes to future escapades; I should not like to be excluded in the future," Prince Hazen said before turning and clasping Finndryl's and then Syrelle's hands, to thank them.

Lore couldn't believe that Syrelle was even here, and despite their complicated history, he was risking his life to protect her. And while his motives might be self-serving, the results would be the same—his actions would ultimately benefit the siren people.

Lore turned away from the prince, Cuan, Jade, and the other guards, her gaze fixed on the boiling sea.

CHAPTER 26

Incalescent water shimmered before Lore's eyes, streaming rivulets wavered like heat ascending from clay bricks baking in the midsummer sun. It was an ethereal, once-in-a-lifetime view. The only problem was that she was submerged within it and felt moments away from being boiled alive.

As the three of them approached the gaping mouth of the volcano, *Source* emerged in a torrent from Lore's hands, shimmering silver as it flowed from her fingertips to coat her entire body. Trails of it wove in rivers from her to Finndryl, coating him as well.

Syrelle did not need Lore to protect him from the heat; he used his own magic, shaping it like black marble to protect himself.

Despite the protection of magic, Lore felt feverish and flushed; pain was beginning to flare up, not just on her feet but on her cheeks, her arms, and her shoulders. She gritted her teeth and pressed on. The ground here was no longer hexagonal rock formations but smooth rivulets. The rock was hard, but the ground here changed a lot more quickly than the surrounding area, and the ground looked like a riverbed, though not formed from centuries of water flowing, but from fast-cooling magma.

She prayed to her gods that the volcano did not decide that now was a good time to unleash its lava. Their bones would surely melt into the ground where they stood. Then she prayed to Anuya, the sirens' goddess, just in case. And then to Great Hearth himself.

This was it; this was what they had been preparing for.

Above the cavernous, hungry maw of Mount Vatraol, Great Hearth, *Source* danced and twirled among the blooms of steam. It was as though the volcano itself was the source of all magic on earth. And maybe it was. No scholar alive knew where magic came from, and it was impossible to create something from nothing. Maybe the volcano was the source, or maybe the magic came from deep within the core of the earth, and the volcano was simply one of many vectors for its liberation into the world.

It made sense that some of the creatures here had found their very lives, their mating and birth cycles, so entwined with magic, if their habitat was so close to this . . .

This sublime sight before her.

Lore halted when she could not stand to move any closer. When another step risked her magical shield failing. The Puallas Kiss would boil off along with her skin, and the grimoire's magic would not be able to keep it intact, even here. She could feel the warning from the book—not in words, for it did not speak to her in words anymore, but in a feeling of caution.

This is as far as we go.

Lore heeded the warning, for *Deeping Lune* wanted to protect her as much as she wanted to protect it.

They were as one, just as it had promised back in Wyndlin Castle.

Lore gritted her teeth against the searing pain in her skin.

This magic was like scrying, though instead of using a bowl of water to cast herself away from her body, she was immersed within the bowl itself. There was water all around her, magic swirling in eddies above her, and all she had to do was reach out her hand and take it.

So she did just that. She reached up and thrust her hand into one of the rivers of *Source* and opened herself to it.

The *Source*, as if alive, as if it wanted a place to go, a purpose, as if it craved life itself, jumped at the chance. Here, there was no life; it would float around above the volcano until, maybe, eventually, it would wither and die; water *gave* life, but it was *not* life, and Lore was.

She was eager for it, too, so when she raised her hand, palm forward, fingers splayed wide, open, inviting, magic erupted from the volcano.

It flowed into her, bright hot.

In a single breath it soaked into her palm, and she was filled with magic, to the brim, she thought, but there was no stopping it. It pushed into her, without care.

Lore gasped, clenching her jaw as the magic ignited her every nerve ending.

It felt like she was struck by lightning, on fire, boiling. It felt like she was being frozen, crushed, ripped apart. Lore cried out, though no sound escaped her lips. Nothing could escape this onslaught of power.

Lore's body went rigid, her back arched; she floated off the ocean floor as more and more magic entered her body, her being. It was filling her up in such a way that there wasn't going to be any room left for her.

It was overpowering her very self.

Her life force.

Lore felt herself unraveling.

Everything that made her *her*. Her skin and organs—the very particles in her body that kept it all together, that made it work. Too much. It was too much. She tried to expel the magic, to close herself off to the unending force. She was going to rupture; she was going to come undone completely.

Her lungs seized up; her heart stuttered.

Lore's mind exploded.

Or, it would have if Finndryl hadn't gripped her hand, the one thrust up into the river of *Source*, and if Syrelle hadn't taken her other hand.

The magic leaped out from her to them, eagerly using Lore as a vessel to seek out more life. Her pain lessened for a fraction of a second, and she felt Finn and Syrelle stiffen beside her as agony overtook them. She knew what they were feeling, though it might be worse because, unlike her, they couldn't feel the intention of this raw, powerful magic that invaded their bodies. They couldn't know that it was not trying to do harm—magic was neither good nor evil, it just *was*.

Still, that fraction of a second of relief, and the fact that it was now shared between the three of them, gave her the barest breath of reprieve, and Lore remembered her goal. She remembered why she was willingly letting her body be inundated by *Source*. She was here to repair the path to the pearl, which was made to harness this power. She was here to save an entire kingdom.

She had somewhere for the magic to go.

And there was one other thing she'd planned to do, though she had kept this to herself.

Lore used her second sight to tunnel down into the volcanic rock and find a dried-up lava tunnel, one honed eons ago by some unknowable force. Was it the love of a goddess, or chance? She did not know. But this path, this tunnel, was wrecked. Fragmented. Smashed. Something had altered the ground here, and the magic had grown stagnant, listless. It had nowhere to go but up into the water to float languidly without purpose.

The broken path to the pearl. It didn't take long for her to find it. Underground there were many pathways, and all had caved in. Only the barest trickle of *Source* still made it through the collapsed rock to follow the path.

She followed the tunnels, urging her body to hold on just a little longer. She pushed her intentions onto the *Source*. She wasn't its only path to life. She wasn't its only path. *See here*, she urged the volcano, *see these other routes. This way leads to a pearl that will be your home; let it be a beacon, race toward it, and light it up. It will gladly give you a home.*

See here another path. This way leads to cave systems filled with eggs that need Source *to hatch, to live, to create more eggs, and more and more; they are eager for a taste.*

She used her magic to push rock aside, carving new pathways where she could not fix broken ones. She found more, hundreds more, that once teemed with torrents of *Source* and had long since dried up, been blocked.

She ushered the magic forward, nipping at its heels, a sheepdog guiding its flock.

The magic flowing into her, floating above the volcano, began to wane, and just before she lost it entirely, she pushed the last flood into Finndryl.

She felt Finndryl stiffen beside her.

Where, moments ago, he'd gripped her hand willingly, sharing the burden, he now jerked as he tried to rip his hand free from her. She held on, using *Source* to strengthen her grip. She opened her eyes for a moment and saw his head thrown back as a silent scream of agony tried to rip free from his vein-lined throat.

Lore closed her eyes against the sight of him in pain.

She hated that she was the cause of his pain. She wanted to tell him that this wouldn't hurt forever, but her mouth didn't work, and anyway, she was busy keeping the magic in line. It was happily doing her bidding, but magic, she had learned, was a mischievous thing.

At her command, the *Source* sought out the curse lurking within his blood since before he was even born; it was there, a fungal blight within his body. She urged it to find every lingering piece of the wretched curse that had taken his grandfather from him too soon. That had been the reason his mother had never had magic. Why he had been exiled from his university for the simple fact that his grandfather was a hero, wrongfully punished—resulting in generations of pain. Missing an integral part of themselves.

With a determined cry, she forced her intention, her feelings, and her care for him into the *Source* and urged it to wage a battle against the curse.

She urged Finndryl, with her mind, to endure.

She repeated her intention again and again; it felt like an eternity. *Break it apart, burn it away—cleanse his body until the curse is eradicated completely.*

The magic did so eagerly.

When the last of the curse was gone and Finndryl was himself, without a hint of that wretched curse inside him, she closed all three of them off to any of the magic still lingering around the volcano.

She opened her eyes, gasping at the onslaught they had endured.

Finndryl was free, and he glowed with *Source*.

He was more powerful than Lore could have imagined.

But he was still, obviously, in pain.

Lore wished she could take the hurt from him, but she knew Finndryl, and she knew that his discomfort must also be sweet. Because even now, she could feel his magic blooming inside him. This magic would be different, unlike how Lore had been bombarded with magic from the outside—it was a part of him that had been cloaked, shadowed, locked away so he couldn't reach it. Something that should have been a most beautiful part of him had been taken from him, and now it had returned.

And it was as much a part of him as his soul. Only it had been missing from him his whole life. Dampened, rotting away.

What that must have felt like, Lore did not know. All she knew was what a gift magic felt like when shared with her from *Deeping Lune.*

The pain of it being taken from her.

The joy of wielding it.

She imagined he must feel at peace. Whole, maybe.

She *hoped* that was what he was feeling.

"You broke the curse," Syrelle choked out from beside Lore. Lore glanced at him. He massaged his hand, the one that had held Lore's. It was red, raw. Syrelle's expression was one of awe.

Suddenly, Finndryl doubled over, clutching his chest, then swayed and collapsed onto the ground, despite the volcano's molten heat. His body was racked with tremors as he struggled to contain the immense power coursing through him. Gritting his teeth, he squeezed his eyes shut, pressing his hands to his face, a low groan escaping his lips. Every few seconds, his shoulders jerked as if lingering ripples of pain shot through his body.

Lore knelt beside him and reached for his arms, fear coating her words. "Finndryl, stand up, you're going to be burned."

She gripped his arms, planning to pull him up to where it was a tad cooler, but promptly dropped them with a shout.

He was burning up; he felt as hot as the molten earth beneath them.

It was a wonder his clothes hadn't melted to his skin.

With wild eyes, Lore implored Syrelle. "Syrelle, he's scorching hot."

Without hesitation, Syrelle knelt beside Finndryl and gingerly reached out toward him. Finndryl's eyes were still closed, his jaw clenched tight against the pain, against whatever was happening inside him. At Syrelle's touch, his eyes flickered open for a moment.

They were glazed, shimmering with fever, before they rolled into the back of his head.

"Oh gods, what if his body doesn't recognize the magic and

rejects it or something? What if I've endangered him?" Lore shouted, terror coursing through her.

Syrelle's voice was even and gentle. "Lore, he will be fine. He just needs time to control his power. Most of us with significant power don't have it unleashed on us all at once. It awakens in us gradually. And when we are old enough, we study under alchemists who teach us how to control it and, when we are ready, to wield it."

Finndryl groaned in pain and reached out instinctively until he gripped Lore's arm. His hands felt like a searing, fiery poker straight from the fire, but Lore's own magic flowed to where his hands gripped her, acting as a shield, protecting her skin from blistering and soothing most of the sensation.

Most, but not all. His grip *hurt*. But what was a little pain, when he was clearly in agony?

"I've got you, Finndryl, I'm right here. I'm not going anywhere," Lore murmured, smoothing his locs back from his face. His full mouth was pinched tight with pain, his expression twisted into a grimace. He gave another groan before losing consciousness.

Lore pulled him to her. Ignoring her pain, she wrapped her arms around him, pressing his face to her chest. She raised her eyes to the heavens. "Oh gods, I should've never done this to him! I fucked up."

She murmured, as she stroked his cheek, her eyes stinging at the unbearable temperature, "Wake up, love, please."

Lore caught Syrelle's gaze, begging him with her eyes to help, to do something, to fix this.

Syrelle nodded, determined. "This will pass, and I promise, when he wakes up and has the chance to wield this *gift* you have given him, he will thank you." Syrelle cloaked himself in darkness, infusing his own, innate power as protection, and with a heave, extracted him from Lore's arms, lifting Finndryl onto his back. "Let's get him back to the palace, quickly."

CHAPTER 27

Lore was sitting in a chair next to a sleeping Finndryl in a massive room just off the queen's quarters.

It was obviously reserved for royalty and had, until a few bells ago, been used as temporary lodging for a noble family that had had to flee their home when the shields began to fail.

By the time the team had returned to the castle—Syrelle carrying Finndryl—the palace had been emptied out; all refugees had packed up and returned to their homes. The palace servants had been buzzing around putting the palace and extensive grounds to rights, and the queen had made sure that each of them had a room prepared upon their return. Lore was relieved, because Finndryl still hadn't woken yet, and she was delirious with exhaustion.

Though when they returned, Finndryl was still so hot that they'd had to push the rugs aside and lay him on the sandy floor at first because he would've melted the netting of the seagrass-filled mattress.

The royal family's personal physician had been sent for. He'd examined him, given him a draught, and declared to no one in particular that his body had had quite a shock and that Finndryl just needed to sleep it off. When he awoke he would be fine, and any hint of his fever should be gone.

Once the draught took hold and Finn's body temperature lowered, Syrelle and the doctor lifted him onto the bed to rest. The moment Finndryl's head lay upon the pillow, the physician practically flipped over himself getting to the door to make a swift exit. He'd kept staring at Lore's legs and feet, which were bare beneath the loose, flowing dress she'd donned upon her return, with barely concealed horror.

Lore had sat down in a chair, tucking her offending legs and toesies beneath her.

Lore didn't think the physician felt comfortable around landers. Though as a healer you would think he would be more comfortable than most around others' bodies.

She hadn't moved from the chair, though dawn had long since come and gone.

Finndryl's broad, well-muscled chest rose and fell at regular intervals. His brow was smooth, unfurrowed. His flawless mahogany skin positively gleamed in the low lights cast by the glowshells on the ceiling.

Not one of his hairs was out of place, the beauty of artfully coiled locs—no flyaway curls or bad hair days. He permanently looked ethereal, immaculate. Lore couldn't help but lean over him, sweeping aside a phantom strand. In truth, Lore brushed her knuckles across his cheek because she just wanted to assure herself that he was still here. That he was no longer scorching hot to the touch.

He is fine, she repeated silently. More than fine; his breaths were soft. He was sleeping.

Serenely, even.

She hadn't killed him with her wild idea to save a kingdom and, at the same time, surprise one of the most important people in her life by breaking a generational blood curse that, oh, turned out to be . . . yes, possible to accomplish, but maybe was a *shock to the system*, quite *dangerous*, and extremely, if his groans of agony were any tell, fucking *excruciating*.

She brushed his cheek again with her knuckles.

He *was* fine. Just fine.

He would wake soon, and maybe they could laugh about this. If not, she would let him be as grumpy as his big, secretly bleeding heart desired.

She couldn't believe that she'd thought him selfish when she first met him. Callous, even. Finndryl always put others before himself. He just did it in an understated, subtle way. Usually. Unless he was cutting down fae guards in a tower in order to free women and children from a maniac's clutches. Or risking his life to restore a kingdom of sirens. Or grabbing her hand without a single ounce of hesitation when magic threatened to tear her apart. Then . . . Finn was the opposite of understated. He was just . . . him. A natural-born fucking hero.

And she almost fucking broiled him alive from the inside with his own magic.

Once again, Lore was losing faith in her decision-making skills. She just so often made the wrong ones, and it endangered everyone she loved—again and again, on repeat.

Goddess, what if he didn't wake up? What if she'd jeopardized him to the point where he slept forever and died?

A sharp knock at the door startled Lore out of her spiraling thoughts. It slid open before she had a chance to inquire who was there.

Syrelle had changed clothes, which had all but melted from carrying a scorching Finn on his back for hours. He looked striking in formfitting checkered trousers, black boots, and a dark-blue button-up shirt. Because of course he did. What about the fae made them constantly look like they had seventeen hours of sleep and dined on the gods' diet?

Finndryl would hate for him to be in here. She should ask him to leave, tell him to leave, or order him out.

Out of the room. Out of the palace. Out of their lives.

But Syrelle had carried an unconscious Finndryl. Lore could actually see the heat radiating from Finn; it would have burned like hell, no matter how powerful Syrelle's magic was, and still, he'd carried Finndryl all that way to Lapis Deep.

Over uneven volcanic rock, safely skirting spouts of steam. Across miles of ocean floor. Through kelp forests, up and down valleys, around venomous anemones.

And Lore had no doubt that if the Nikoryxia, who had been trailing them all the way to the volcano, hadn't fled the moment the magic was set free, Syrelle would've protected Finndryl with his life.

Despite their mutual dislike.

Everything Syrelle said was continuously at odds with his actions.

"I still can't believe you managed to break the curse. We all thought it impossible," Syrelle said, walking into the room.

Lore wrung her hands together before dropping them into her lap and twisting the fabric of her dress. "I try to live my life as if nothing is impossible. I've been thinking about this for days. I just needed a super-powerful, practically infinite flood of *Source* to achieve it." Lore's determination broke, and she swallowed back a sob. "Maybe I shouldn't have. When it put him at such risk. It's not like he asked me to. I just thought . . ." Her sob escaped her clutches, and she spoke through tears that she wiped away purely out of habit because tears were indiscernible in salt water. "I just thought that it would make him happy. Not almost . . ." Lore hiccupped, trying desperately not to wail. "Not almost kill him!"

Syrelle's gaze alighted on her face. "I wonder what form his magic will take."

"Wh . . . what?" Lore asked, once again wiping her cheeks. She could feel tears squeezing out of her ducts, but the salt water surrounding them just accepted her tears as its own and whisked them away.

"His magic. I wonder how it will present. His grandfather—

you've heard of him, I'm sure, his namesake? Finndryl Hwraeth the first had the power to manipulate the weather. He could call a typhoon while sipping his morning tea. Or so the legends say."

"I couldn't imagine containing magic of that magnitude."

"Most can't. It's extremely rare. To this day, some call Finndryl's grandfather an abomination." Syrelle settled onto the arm of the chair opposite the one Lore perched on, his eyes on Finndryl, but his gaze far away.

"An abomination?" Lore could relate. "That seems cruel."

"Some do, not all . . . The people of Freya Isle have always, and will always, call him 'savior.'"

Lore sniffed back tears and took the bait, thankful for the distraction from her cyclonal thoughts. "Finndryl never told me the story about his grandfather. He mentioned him a few times and told me about the curse but . . ."

"I've heard the story of the Savior of Freya Isle more times than I can count. He's even got a few songs dedicated to him that are so popular they're sung in every tavern on the continent. There isn't a bard out there who doesn't croon his saga and sing it loudly." Something flashed across Syrelle's face. Lore could've sworn, if he was anyone else, it was diffidence, but Syrelle wasn't shy. No, she realized that Syrelle must be shaping the story within his mind, making sure he told it well. Because Finndryl was here in this room, and Isla was Syrelle's friend, and Syrelle wanted to do their grandfather justice.

As Asher would have. Lore waited patiently for him to begin.

"Despite him being regaled as a hero to most—his own queen didn't care that he saved his home, an *entire* island, from a devastating hurricane," Syrelle began, his voice weaving a tale of injustice. "Freya Isle had cried out for aid, begged their queen for ships, enough to evacuate them from the island. Of course the wealthy fled at the first sign of the storm. But tens of thousands remained, their pleas ignored by Queen Riella.

"Freya Isle was a small island, colonized by Riella's mother, Queen Jharaka. Riella viewed its inhabitants as incidental, their land neither fertile nor beautiful, their economy barely beginning to recover from the decades-long war. That they were a joyful people with a rich, vibrant history, a history her own mother had tried to erase, was irrelevant to the queen.

"So when they called for aid from their sovereign, Riella ignored them. Sending ships, harboring them during and potentially after the storm? She chose to leave them to their fate; the problem, as she so callously put it, would 'take care of itself.'"

Lore massaged her bruised hands, a grim echo of her recent ordeal. "I detested Queen Riella before, but my feelings can, it seems, intensify. How did his grandfather save them?"

Syrelle's voice grew softer, drawing Lore into the heart of the tale. "Hwraeth was born on Freya, but intent on carving out a better life for himself, he left as a young man. By then, he was living on the mainland with his wife. When he heard of the storm, he gave his wife a kiss and sought out a fisherman to take him home. Every fisherman refused, of course, the storm too fierce."

"Wait, how did he get to Freya, then?"

"Hwraeth spent his life savings purchasing a boat. He took a fishing vessel meant for a crew, alone. He made it home just as the seas began to rise. He tied the ship to a dock, knowing it wouldn't last, and began to climb."

"Climb? Climb what?"

"The highest cliff. He broke his wrist and three fingers in the ascent. No ropes, just sheer determination. And he made it in time. He stood at the highest point of the isle and, for eleven hours, single-handedly shielded the isle from the largest storm in the Sea of Jewels' recorded history."

"Goddess," Lore breathed, captivated.

"Indeed. Hwraeth managed to save thousands of homes and businesses from being swept out to sea or blown to bits by the high winds. Saved even more from drowning. When the storm abated, he collapsed from exhaustion. The people of Freya found him, heart barely beating. They set his broken bones and brought him home to his frantic wife who, it's said, almost broke his other wrist when she heard what he'd done. She didn't stay mad for long, of course."

Lore smiled, imagining his wife's reaction. "So, what happened then? How did he lose his magic to such a vicious curse?"

"When Freya wasn't wiped off the map, Queen Riella inquired. She heard of Hwraeth. A nobody, one of Freya's own, who risked everything to save them all. His ordeal was straight out of a legend. He was a hero. The queen invited him and his wife, who was with child, to her palace. A golden invitation, a carriage sent to fetch them in style."

"Oh gods, it was a trap, wasn't it?"

"She was terrified of him. And probably more jealous than she was scared. So yes, she set a trap. At a banquet in his honor, they were seized and dragged before the throne. She falsely accused them of treason and cursed them, a blood curse so foul it took six of her most powerful alchemists to enact it."

"As thanks for saving her subjects, she stripped him of his power and cursed his bloodline," Lore said, aghast.

Syrelle hummed his confirmation. "And not only that, as further punishment, she imprisoned him and his pregnant wife in cages hanging from the rafters in her ballroom as decoration until they perished from starvation."

"Wait, perished? Something isn't adding up."

"Word got out, no doubt a Freyan maid or cook leaked the news. The tale of Hwraeth's heroism spread like wildfire, and thousands showed up in protest. The queen learned that day that she may be petty, heartless, and cruel, but she could not kill a legend just because she *felt* like it. She freed them but never removed the curse."

"She'd taken what she'd coveted," Lore said bitterly. "His magic."

"Right. Hwraeth was no longer a threat, not that he ever was, but evil like she is sees threats everywhere. He mourned his magic and the fact that his children and entire bloodline would never know magic as he had, but he made the most of it. Lived the best life he could."

Lore's brow furrowed. "Whatever happened to the fishing boat? Did it survive the storm?"

Syrelle looked at her, surprised. "Well, I don't know. Why would you ask that?"

Lore frowned, her voice tinged with sadness. "He spent his life savings on it. And then to have a curse put on him, be almost starved to death by his own queen, and come out on the other side not only with no possessions left, but . . . now . . . he was . . ." Lore could feel her eyes welling up again. She wasn't sure why this, out of all the horrible parts of the story, was affecting her the most. "Completely *coinless*?"

A tired, gruff voice broke in. "Turns out, my grandfather had saved the fisherman's brother, who lived on Freya. Despite the boat being damaged, the fisherman returned every coin down to the last copper." Finndryl rubbed his hands across his face and tied his locs back with a ribbon before shifting, stretching out, and placing his hands behind the pillow in a completely unconcerned attitude.

Finn was awake!

Minutes before, Lore's thoughts had been spiraling into darkness. He was in a magically induced deathlike slumber. He would never wake up, and she would lose him before she ever really got him, and it was all her fault. She had murdered him even though all she wanted to do was be near him and make him smile and see him laugh and unleash his cursed magic so that he could be his whole self, in all its glory; but she had actually been so damned foolish endangering him, which had resulted in him being in agonizing, terrifying pain before falling unconscious, and oh gods, *she was spiraling again.*

How was he so nonchalant?

"Actually, the fisherman ended up repairing the boat and setting it up as a tourist attraction. For decades, he convinced wealthy people to pay an exorbitant sum to tour the boat. Pay double, and he would take the 'daring adventurer' on the very route that the Great Finndryl Hwraeth sailed to save Freya Isle," Finndryl continued, unaware that Lore was gripping the seat to stop herself from launching across the room and swimming toward him to squeeze him until he popped.

"That's pretty ingenious," said Syrelle, who also sounded quite calm.

"Right? Can't fault someone for acquiring that coin." Finndryl sat up, punched his pillows a few times—seagrass pillows were quite uncomfortable—and pushed them up against the headboard before leaning back, now in a sitting position, his long legs crossed at the ankles before him. "On a whim, when we were kids visiting our mom on the coast, Isla and I tried to go once. We cleaned a prominent merchant's house every day for a month to collect the coin, but the boat had apparently hit a rogue rock and sunk a few years before."

"That would've been so cool to see. If I had known about it, I would've gone myself."

"I imagine it was a good time. Especially because I was a kid, I was a little bit obnoxious about my grandfather's legacy back then; I wouldn't have shut up about who I was and how he was my relation to every single passenger on that boat."

Syrelle raised an eyebrow, his lips quirking up into a smile. "Obnoxious back then? You are *now*. I'm shocked you've managed to know Lore this long without recounting the tale multiple times."

Finndryl huffed a laugh. "Honestly, I would have loved to, but someone locked us in separate prisons on his ship."

"*Prison* feels like too strong of a word for how nice those rooms were! And anyway, that wasn't my ship. It belonged to the crown."

"If a room has locks on the *outside*, it's a prison."

"Fair enough, but I'm trying to make up for that."

"You have a long way to go."

"I know I do." Syrelle slid from the armrest into the seat of his chair before propping his feet on the ottoman. "So, tell me, what did you and Isla do with the money you had saved up from cleaning that merchant's house? I imagine Isla convinced you to spend it all on sweets."

Finndryl groaned through a smile. "Of course she did. We bought a mountain of sweets and ate them all in one sitting. I was sick for two days, and my mother didn't even take pity on me, saying it was a lesson to be learned or some such nonsense."

"I knew it. Isla never did grow out of that sweet tooth."

Lore's mouth hung open as the two of them conversed as if they didn't hate each other with every fiber of their beings. As if . . . almost as if they had really been friends once. Back in the day.

She'd waited long enough; the only reason she'd contained herself this long was that she was shocked the two of them were even chatting, let alone doing it in a joking manner.

"Finn, how are you feeling?" she asked, trying to keep her voice light.

"I feel a bit as though I was dropped into a cauldron, and then when I got to temp, I was slowly devoured by a Nikoryxia."

"That's about how you look," Syrelle said with a straight face.

Finndryl laughed then, actually laughed. "I don't doubt it."

"No, honestly, you look damned good; it's a little upsetting. For having gone through the change all at once like that, you should at least have a black eye or something."

Finndryl rubbed the back of his neck and feigned bashfulness. "We can't all look this good; it wouldn't be fair. Besides, you'll grow into the size of your head one day, I'm sure of it."

"I pray every night for that to happen."

Lore blinked. Finndryl was laughing, and *so was Syrelle.*

Lore's jaw was on the floor. She snapped it closed lest a small fish try to make a home in it.

What was going on? Was this all it took for the male species? They save a kingdom together; one passes out and almost burns the other's flesh off while the other carries them on their back, and then they're suddenly friends?

Lore leaned forward and placed her hand on Finn's forehead.

"Something on my head?"

Ass. "I was just making sure you weren't burning up with fever again, is all."

"Honestly, I'm a little sore, and my pride is a bit bruised, I think, but I'm fae, and—thanks to you—I've got magic. I'll be healed by sunset."

Lore made to remove her hand, but Finndryl pressed his own to hers, keeping it there. "Hmm, don't just yet. Your hand is so cool. It feels nice."

Lore would never argue with Finn when he asked her to touch him. Even if it was just her hand on his forehead.

Syrelle stood, glancing away from the two of them, his jaw suddenly tight. "I've got to check on my room. It's across the hall if either of you need me." Syrelle slipped out and shut the door behind him.

"I thought I killed you."

"You didn't."

"Yeah, but . . . I mean, for a bit there you looked pretty close to death."

He laughed, clutching his chest. "Ouch." His smile dipped. "For a bit there, I felt pretty close to death." His hand clutched hers, the pressure pacifying. "But it was worth it."

Lore wanted to believe him.

"Don't make that face. I mean it. You gave my family something back that we thought lost forever; not just my connection to my grandfather's legacy, but the chance to do magic. Isla never cared that she didn't have magic. But it plagued me. This other life we should be living. It haunted me . . . that this was stolen from us before we were even born. Would be withheld from my own offspring." His thumb began rubbing circles on her own. "I spent years searching for ways to break this curse. Every text, anecdote, and instance that I found all said the same thing: A blood curse is absolute. Forever. Irreversible. Once done, it cannot be undone."

"I guess we'll have to write a new book."

"Alemeyu, our book would be one for the ages."

"We could call it *Is This a Prison or Just a Room, Surprise—I Broke Your Blood Curse, and Other Tales from the Deep*."

Through a grin, Finn said, "For a companion novel . . . something along the lines of *How Many Times Is Too Many When Running Headfirst into Peril?*" Finn shifted closer to the wall, turned sideways, and propped his head on his arm.

Lore wasted no time filling the space he opened. She settled onto the bed and mirrored Finndryl's pose. This wasn't the largest bed, and her lips parted slightly when she realized just how close they were. She played with a braid. "The sequel could be something along the lines of *Oops, Danger Found Me Again: A Memoir*. Quick, someone find us a quill."

Finndryl barked a laugh. "I would absolutely purchase these if I saw them in a bookseller's shop."

Lore pressed closer, marveling at the way his face transformed when he laughed. It was magnificent. He was magnificent. "You know, the only bookshop I've ever been in was my own apothecary? I would love to explore another."

"I saw one right here in Lapis Deep on the way to the palace." He frowned. "But I imagine it might be a while before the owners reopen it, and we will be long gone by then."

"We will be?" Lore yawned, the last day's events finally catching up to her now that she wasn't caught in a cycle of terror, guilt, and fear.

"Wasn't that what you said in the strategy meeting yesterday? As soon as the pearl was restored, you had to leave."

"Oh, yes. I did say that. *Auroradel* isn't going to find itself, and I have a revolt to arrange." Lore stretched as contentment settled in her chest, cozy and warm. "You're coming with me, then?"

"Of course. I wouldn't miss the chance to chronicle the next installment in our saga."

"I hope this one has a happy ending," Lore murmured as she fought to keep her eyes open.

"Lore, I'll do everything in my power to make sure your story has a happy ending." Finndryl pulled her toward him until she was curled up, her cheek pressed to his chest. He wrapped his strong arms around her and held her tight. The kiss he placed on the crown of her curls was featherlight. She could feel his magic thrumming inside him, strong and formidable. Her eyes fluttered closed as she nuzzled in, his spiced scent swirling around her.

She'd never felt so safe in her life.

Lore didn't reply, because she was sound asleep.

CHAPTER 28

Lore awoke to the gentle nuzzling of something scaled and slimy clinging to her earlobe. Eyes wide, she shook Finndryl's arm; he blinked in shock at the vision before batting a small, inquisitive suckerfish away. The suckerfish proceeded to twirl around playfully before puckering up its lips and darting forward, straight toward Lore for another smooch.

Lore yelped, flipping herself away—over Finn, squeezing in between his massive form and the wall.

With an agile motion, Finndryl seized the slimy creature, holding it in a gentle-yet-firm grip just before it reached Lore. Through a rumbling laugh, he addressed the fish, "Those are *mine*. If anyone is going to taste them, it will be me." The fish squirmed in his grip, clearly regretting its curiosity. He released the startled thing; with a flash of iridescent scales, it retreated, disappearing through the slats of a vent above the door.

Lore tittered. "I hadn't known my ears were quite so tempting."

Finndryl shifted onto his side, his body pressed against hers. She marveled at the sheer strength corralled within his lithe form. How his muscled thigh felt pressed to hers, the rock-hard feel of his abdomen. His gaze was liquid heat, and his words came out in a purr. "Your ears are one of my favorite things about you." He reached out, trailing a finger along the bowed edge of one, making Lore shiver. "I spent many an afternoon in the Exile's kitchen gazing at them, trying to keep my hands on my quill, not reaching out to feel them. It was torture."

"You're so ridiculous; I never caught you looking even once!" Lore said through bubbling laughter. She couldn't deny that his ears always fascinated her too. The pointed curve at the tips, where hers were rounded. For ages, she'd wanted to do exactly what he was doing now to one of hers: brush a finger along the elegant ridge.

Now she wondered, if she did—would it make him shiver as well?

Her breaths quickened as she lifted a hand to do just that . . .

She marveled at his contented expression. There was no hint of the grumpy barkeep as his lips danced with mirth. His shoulders were so relaxed, as though there was nowhere else in the world he'd rather be than right here, with her.

Dread coiled in her gut. She needed to tell him. She paused, then pulled her hand back just before her fingertip grazed the pointed tip of his ear. He had a right to know that the moment she found a safe place for her people, she would be closing them off to the world.

Even if it felt a little like Finndryl was becoming hers.

She took a deep breath, her eyes meeting his with a mix of apprehension and determination. "There is something I must tell you."

Finndryl stilled, withdrawing his touch from her ear. His eyes roamed over her face, unease bracing his jaw. "What is it?"

Guilt swept through her. She had ruined this moment just as she ruined everything. Here he was, barely rested after their ordeal yesterday, and she was, once again, the reason for his apprehension.

She changed her mind; she could tell him later. He didn't have to know right now . . . right? "Actually, it's more of a question."

"Ask me anything, Alemeyu."

"You never did explain how you found me that time—when I

was being chased by the royal guards in the woods—how did you know that I was in danger?" She was a coward; how was she ever going to voice the words when she wanted nothing more than to be near him?

Finndryl relaxed his striking features. "Oh, that." He leaned back against the propped-up pillows, one arm crooked behind his head, the other wrapping around her shoulders to press her against his chest. Lore's insides trilled to be pulled into him so casually, without thought or hesitancy.

She listened to the steady rhythm of his heart; it was the most beautiful melody she'd ever heard.

"It's a charm I had placed on the Dragon's Exile; it has a simple activation: The moment we fed you and housed you, you were under our protection. For as long as you were a guest in our house, you would be safe. The Exile warned me you were in trouble, and the charm led me straight to you."

Lore chewed on her lip, curiosity igniting. "You hardly knew me, though. In fact, you disliked me . . . a lot. Or does this charm mean you're required to protect all your guests?"

He raised an eyebrow, a hint of a smirk dancing on his lips. "That wouldn't be much of a charm, more a curse." He gripped her chin with thumb and finger and tilted her head to face him better. He leaned forward and kissed her lightly on the lips, the simplicity of it spreading warmth through every corner of her being. "I'll let you in on a secret, Alemeyu. At no point did I ever dislike you. In fact, you disarmed me. You were this small yet mighty little starshine that walked in the door and never once left my thoughts. From the moment I met you, all that I was, all that I had been, was undone because all that mattered—was you." He trailed a finger along her ear again, causing Lore to clench her thighs together as heat spread from her face down to her core. "So no, I wouldn't save just anyone who activated the charm, but it was nothing for me to protect you when you needed it."

She wanted to cry. She wanted to scream. How could she ever live without him?

She closed what little space was left between them, covering his lips with hers, needing to feel him, needing to be as close to him as she possibly could, and still, it would not be close enough; it would never be close enough. With a growl, Finndryl rolled onto his back, pulling her with him until she straddled his hips. His fingers danced along her hip bones before clenching the flesh of her thighs as he deepened the kiss. Lore gasped into his mouth as he shifted his hips, pressing his hard length against her, showing her exactly how she made him feel.

She wanted him. Needed him.

And, *yes*, gods, he must feel the same because there was the stiff proof pressed between them. She remembered what he tasted like. How velvety smooth he had been, clenched in her hand. She pressed against him, grinding herself against the hardness beneath her. A low, reverberating sound erupted in his chest, and he pressed down on her thighs, so she was molded against him, moving in tandem.

Just as Lore was pulling the rim of his shirt to expose the smooth expanse of skin there, her hands eager to feel the rippling, shifting muscles on his abdomen, the door burst open and multiple palace attendants streamed into the room, led by none other than Cuan.

With a squeak, Lore pressed her heated face into Finndryl's neck.

"Get. Out." Finndryl growled, his hands stilling where they gripped Lore's thighs.

"As much as it pains me to break this up, my queen's orders supersede yours. No matter how vicious your growl." Cuan dropped something soft at the foot of the bed. Lore peeked sideways just enough to see what they'd brought them. She groaned.

A mountain of clothing. Formal dress, from the look and shape of the many layers of fabric.

"The queen requires your presence at a celebratory feast."

"We can't make it—we're busy," Finndryl said through clenched teeth.

Cuan sighed, their tone playful. "Unfortunately, you are among the guests of honor."

Finndryl opened his mouth—to protest further, she just knew it—and so she took pity on Cuan. It wasn't their fault that she and Finn would rather be in here, alone, than at a feast.

"Thank you, Cuan. If you and the other attendants would leave us, we shall report promptly to—"

"Oh, absolutely not. We are here to dress you. It's only proper."

"If she needs help, I can dress her."

Cuan placed a hand on their hip. "Oh, I hadn't realized you were so proficient in siren traditional dress."

Finndryl growled.

"I thought so." Cuan clapped their hands before pointing at the mechanism that controlled the *Source*-flow to the glowshells. A fresh-faced attendant with a bright pink tail swam over to it and turned the knob as far as it would go. Lore squinted in the bright light. This was torture! "Up, up! We don't have much time before the party and have so many layers to don."

A moment later, Lore gritted her teeth as she watched them bustle about the room, laying out bundles of fabric, while another two fussed with the multiple knots she'd tied in the ribbon, extricating it from her braids with an efficiency that bordered on aggression. A party to send them off? Lore had hoped for a moment of solitude with the queen. Lore was *hoping* it would be quiet, because she had a favor to ask, and she didn't want anyone to hear what it was. It was quite a large favor. A monumental one, actually.

If Lore had known that they were going to be barging into Finndryl's rooms this early, she would've woken even earlier.

Though Lore grudgingly had to admit, as she pressed the linen flat against her thigh, as flat as it would go with so many layers of tulle, that the garments *were* beautiful. She eyed the outfits still hanging from the dressing screen—three for Finndryl to choose from and three for her . . . But her gaze fixated on the leather satchel nestled among the folds.

The leather was so dark it had a violet hue, and it shimmered iridescently, whisperings of an unknown sea creature. A design was skillfully carved into it, and she instantly recognized the coiling pattern as intricate swirls mimicking the lingering marks of a Puallas Kiss.

This wasn't just any satchel.

Finally, the two attendants finished coiling and pinning Lore's braids and moved on to enveloping her in layers of fabric. With a proud smile, one of the attendants bid her to turn toward the looking glass to see the profits of their labor. She gazed in the looking glass, biting her lip. She'd chosen a lovely, perfectly tailored gown. The cut of the emerald-green dress resembled ocean waves that formed to her curves in a way that was flattering but left room to move. She twirled a fraction, marveling at the artistry—weights sewn into various seams of the dress allowed it to flutter in the current, without floating upward. Pearl buttons and golden thread adorned the front layers and bodice, giving the impression of sunlight skittering across the ocean.

But her favorite thing was not the dress, nor how it shimmered. It was the satchel, which came with a matching belt made from the same leather. It had two straps on top that could be slid onto the belt and four crisscrossing lines around it, two of which could be adjusted for width.

Lore was just cinching the belt around her waist and adjusting the leather satchel when Finndryl returned from the bathing chamber. He'd donned his new clothes as well. His shirt was black and formfitting, his pants black, his boots black. *Tall, dark, and handsome.* A new sword adorned his belt.

He must have finally returned Cuan's spear, then.

"My gods, Lore, you are stunning." His eyes skipped across her face, lingered on her dress, and snagged on her satchel. He smiled. "Ah, you found the satchel."

"What do you know about this?" Lore asked, holding the satchel out from her hip, admiring it once more.

"I know a little." He crossed the room and ran his thumbs over the satchel in approval. "I had it made for you." He laughed at her expression of surprise and dropped the satchel so it fell gently against her dress. "The queen was happy enough to oblige my request—they were creating the Nikoryxia scale vest for you anyway, so I figured it wouldn't be too much trouble, and I've had the sketch in my pocket for ages."

"You designed this?"

Finndryl smiled as he tied a cord around his locs, cinching them tightly behind him. How had he managed to fight off the attendants from fixing his hair? Then again, he had one of those faces—one grimace from him, and she imagined they would drop the hairpins and scatter.

"I did."

"It's beautiful." Lore ran her thumb over the stitching in the leather. She hadn't noticed before, but . . . yes, those were marigolds sprinkled here and there among the tendrils of the Puallas Kiss pattern.

"It's for *Deeping Lune*. So you won't ever have to part with it. And the straps adjust, so when you acquire *Auroradel*, it will fit as well." Finndryl frowned, crossing his arms. "Well, depending on how big it is, I suppose; I am counting on it being around the same size as *Deeping Lune*."

Lore pulled the grimoire from beneath a pillow.

No more hiding it under her shirt where it was quite uncomfortable and impractical. She slipped the book into the satchel and cinched it tight. The satchel hung comfortably from the belt; she could hardly feel that it was there.

Lore crossed the room and threw her arms around him. "It's perfect."

Finndryl laughed, his torso vibrating against Lore's chest.

Finndryl closed his arms around her, holding her to him. He licked his lips. Lore followed the sweep of his tongue, unable to tear her gaze away from the view. She watched as his dark eyes narrowed, his pupils widened, and then—and then, yes, he was kissing her, hungry, demanding, as he explored her mouth as if determined to uncover everything about her, her wishes, her wants, her secrets.

They were all lips, and tongue, and sharp teeth clashing, discovering, learning. As Lore matched his energy, her need for him just as great, he slid his hands down her back, past her ass, gripped her thighs, and hauled her up. Lore wrapped her legs around his slender waist, her thrumming pulse persistent in that soft place between her thighs. She pulled away just for a moment to gasp in breath, though even that second was too long before she pressed her lips to his skin again, tasting, devouring, peppering his stubbled jaw with kisses, marveling at the sharp planes of his face.

Heat spread past the tightening buds of her nipples down to the slickness between her thighs. She ached to feel him there, needing the pleasure that only he could give her. Their passion intensified as she deepened the kiss. She wriggled her hand between them, desperate to feel that hardening length of him. She went back to his lips, deepening, moaning into his mouth. She gripped him through his pants, hating that his shirt was tucked in, that these formal clothes were so damned restricting because, gods, the feel of his lips on hers was utter bliss.

The room heated up around them, and Finndryl tightened his arms around her, closing his fingers on the mound of braids twisted at the nape of her neck, fisting it, pulling it tight, while keeping her firmly pressed against him. The slight pain of him gripping her hair made her moan into his mouth; she wanted him to pull her hair when there weren't any clothes between them.

This was how she had wanted to spend the morning with him.

Not with half a dozen attendants swimming into the room issuing orders at them while they were snuggled up in bed, finally a bed, *alone*. Lore cursed herself for having fallen asleep last night.

Heat from his hands gripping her ass, heat from his lips on her throat, the way his sharp canines skimmed the delicate skin on her collarbone . . . Lore was on fire, she was burning for him.

"Wait, wait . . ." Finndryl said between breaths as he stilled against her throat.

Lore felt dazed. "'Wait' . . . ? Oh, yes, okay." Her chest was heaving, her breaths shallow and quick. And that was when she realized the heat around her wasn't just because she was mad with desire from being so near this damned male (and yet not near enough)—the temperature in the room was quite uncomfortably hot. And it was daytime, so her book lay dormant in the satchel, no *Source* to protect her.

Fear spiked her heartbeat now.

"What's happening? Finndryl? Is it the volcano?"

He laughed before pressing a kiss to her throat, his fingers gently tucking an escaped curl behind her ear. "No, we are safe. I just . . ." He chuckled again. "I haven't quite figured out this whole 'having magic' thing. It's different having it than reading about it."

Lore blinked, clearing her head. It only took a second before a laugh burst out of her. "I knew it was hot in here, but I thought that was because of the kiss."

"I think it technically *was* because of the kiss, but also because of me."

"Heat, huh?"

"I think so. Among other things. I'll tell you about it on the road when we are away from here."

"*More?* More than almost boiling a room in seconds?" She raised an eyebrow.

"Yes." He gave her a look. *Later.* He would tell her later.

Lore frowned. "Until you have more control, should we . . ." She didn't even want to ask, but it felt necessary to force her mouth to say the words. "Keep kissing to a minimum?"

Finndryl mocked offense. "Absolutely not. Plus, what better way to awaken my power, learn control, than by these perfect lips?"

He brushed a thumb across her bottom lip before capturing her mouth with his once more. His lips and tongue explored, and his skilled fingers reclasped the top button of her dress before pulling away, his eyes glimmering. He straightened her satchel, which had become askew on her hip.

"This looks so good on you. I knew it would, but . . . my imagination couldn't do the real thing justice."

"Were you imagining me in nothing but this satchel?"

His chest rumbled. "Of course I was. I have plans to undo the clasps with my teeth."

Her cheeks burned. "Oh, we must make this a reality." She patted the satchel, checking that the clasps were secure. "It's the best gift anyone has ever given me. Thank you, truly."

Finndryl grinned, and the sight stole Lore's breath for a moment. She vowed to do whatever it took to see that smile every day she had with him. She'd lived too much of her life without it. Smiling didn't come easily to him, and that made his smile a gift, one so much more special than from someone whose grin came quickly.

CHAPTER 29

A knock came at the door, and Cuan flew through it before either of them could call out, *Please don't come in*, or better yet, *Leave us alone for once, thank you!*

"Come on, you two. Everyone is waiting for our guests of honor!"

"Cuan, tell me honestly, is this a big thing or a medium thing that the queen has planned for us?"

"It's a *mandatory* thing, is what it is," Cuan supplied with a wink. "Don't worry, it won't be too painful. The queen is usually adept at weighing what is 'too much' for people," Cuan said as they nudged Lore and Finndryl out the door.

"See, I don't like that they said *usually*," Finndryl muttered as the three of them left the guest wing.

"If it's terrible, I'll distract everyone with my charm and wit, just long enough for you to hide from whatever is waiting for us in there," Lore said as she studied a tree that swayed in the courtyard. She could've sworn this same tree was dead the last time she saw it, and here it was—its odd, white branches blooming with life. Small fish darted in and out of its blossoms. The fish resembled honeybees, drunk on nectar, as they drowsily flitted from flower to flower.

With the pearl restored, this place was already flourishing back to life; she could only imagine what another day, a week, a year would do to restore the beauty of Lapis Deep.

They'd done this. They had helped an entire kingdom of people. Next, it would be her own.

Finndryl brought her back to the present. "I'm shocked you would think that I would leave you to fend for yourself."

Lore laughed, squeezing his arm. "Your honor is not questioned, my good sir; just letting you know that I will sacrifice myself for you when it comes to social situations."

He bowed his head, mocking the nobility filtering into the courtyard all around them. "Your offer is most generous, but I think we must both admit that you are secretly looking forward to a party in your honor."

"How dare you? I am clearly dreading the very thought of it."

"Why does your step hurry across the courtyard, then?"

"Don't call me out like this! Just accept the offer of—oh *gods*."

The doors of the hall were thrust open to reveal a party in full swing despite the early hour. Apparently the sirens could celebrate at any time, day or night.

Finndryl and Lore were ushered inside by servants dressed in frilly outfits. An orchestra was in full swing on a stage. Tables had been set up all around. A buffet along one edge of the room held a feast, and there, dancing in the center of the room, were the queen and her prince consort.

Lore, wide-eyed, could not quite make up her mind where to look first, as servants ushered them toward the dance floor to greet the queen; there weren't just people, tables, and decor spread all around her but above as well. There was another *layer* of siren dancing, swimming, lilting, eating above them and even a few tables and chairs suspended with ropes, to keep them from falling or shifting, above her head.

"I thought I was going to have to send my royal guard to drag you here," Queen Naia exclaimed as she pulled Lore into a fierce hug.

She was surprisingly strong for her advanced age, and Lore *oomph*ed as a stream of bubbles escaped her lips.

"We didn't mean to be late; my apologies."

"Hush, no apologies permitted on this day when it is you that we are celebrating." The queen moved to give a squeeze to Finn, who dwarfed her completely. "And you, don't think we have forgotten your part in this." Lore grinned to see Finn blush, his expression warring between pride and humility. He gave Queen Naia a twirl; her long tail and hair swirled out behind her as she threw her head back, her laughter easily cascading over the sound of the band.

Lore couldn't believe the difference between the world now and a few days ago. This was a happy ending for the queen and her people. Their way of life, safety, and homeland were restored. Queen Naia would not have to succumb to failure, to her people being scattered to the seas.

Lore's chest felt full with joy that she had achieved this for the sirens, but goddess knew she wanted this for her own people too. She wanted to gather them together in a beautiful ballroom and celebrate each and every one of them. She wanted them to dance and eat till their bellies would be near bursting. She wanted their laughter to ring through the room, and she wanted them to feel safe when they went to bed at night. Safe, and warm, and at home where they lived.

Lore had a long way to go before that could happen, and being here was delaying the inevitable. But she couldn't leave just yet. Lore still had that favor to ask.

The morning passed with lots of food and many heartfelt thank-yous from the inhabitants of Lapis Deep. Lore was gifted with a few seashells from siren children who shyly pressed them into her hands, precious tokens of thanks.

There were a few speeches; thankfully, Lore wasn't expected to make any. When the last speech finished and the music resumed,

Lore made her excuses and reconvened with the queen, who was busy sampling the dessert table.

"Queen Naia, might we speak in private?"

"Of course, here." She pressed a small plate of yellow dessert into Lore's hands. "Take a slice of coconut custard—and, yes, some guava will pair nicely . . ." Lore grabbed the outstretched plate. "I'll acquire the spoons—we can enjoy our dessert in the east garden."

After Lore's discussion with the queen, they returned to the party for another dance, but the queen could tell Lore's heart wasn't in it. "I suppose the party will have to continue without us. It is time for you to continue your journey."

Lore sighed with relief.

"It's time." They wove through the crowd of dancing siren and departed the ballroom into the well-lit courtyard. Music from the orchestra pulsed through the walls, punctuated by bursts of laughter and the clatter of revelry. It would be a full day of celebration, one that, if siren chatter were to be believed, would likely last through the following dawn. A bittersweet pang settled behind Lore's ribs, wishing she could share in this uninhibited joy.

As though the queen knew what she was thinking, she bumped Lore's shoulder with her own and said, "Do your people celebrate as mine do?"

Lore gave a cheeky smile. "Oh, we aspire to, but I don't see how we could ever compare to this revelry." Her smile wavered. "Truthfully, we are more restrained—an inescapable aura of fear stifles our merriment."

The queen nodded and clasped Lore's forearm, her eyes shining with conviction. "Having heard your plan, I have complete optimism that it will be successful. Your people will rejoice like mine do now.

I will wear my crown with pride knowing that I helped make it so." Lore smiled and patted the queen's hand, which still rested on her arm, her long siren fingers wrapped around the markings of the Puallas Kiss.

"What will happen to the Puallas Kiss when we are back on land?" Lore had grown quite attached to the marking beyond just requiring it to survive. "It's quite beautiful, I will be sad to see it gone."

Queen Naia flipped Lore's arm over to study the mark and ran a wrinkled finger over the boldest of the swirling fronds. "Puallas Kiss is bestowed upon very few people. It is hallowed, sacred, and therefore treated as such."

"My circumstances coming here were . . . unusual, but I can say, the honor of you allowing me to live in your world has not been lost on me. I will cherish these memories forever."

"I know that, dear; I do not say this to impose upon you how rare this mark is. I simply want you to know that my decision to let you keep it, if you wish to, is not one that I offer lightly. If you and your companion wish to keep the Kiss, then you may. You will never have to fear drowning, and should you wish to return to visit me or my grandson, you will always have a place here."

Warmth swelled within Lore, and she embraced the queen. "I am thrilled. I shall wear the Puallas Kiss with pride. And should one day I have the privilege of returning, I shall do so."

Lore released the queen and called over to Finndryl, who'd been followed into the courtyard by a rowdy pod of siren—all clearly well into their cups—determined to hear his version of the volcano journey and restoring their Mother Pearl. The grimace on Finndryl's face was almost comical—you would think they were begging him to disclose his top three most embarrassing memories, not regale them with a heroic tale. Had he ever had this much attention on him in his life? Lore covered her mouth with her hand to suppress a giggle. He was about one more slurred inquiry from boiling them all alive.

The male worked in a tavern; you would think he was used to being surrounded by drunkards. Then again, once he placed their beverage in front of them, they usually shifted their focus off him and to their tankards. He'd suffered enough. "Finndryl, come here!" Finn excused himself with a quickness and hurried over.

"Thank you, if I have to recount—"

"Right, right, all very tiring being a hero and all that—more importantly, we can keep the marks! Queen Naia isn't going to have them removed after all."

"Oh, that is—wow, thank you." Finndryl dipped his head to the queen in gratitude. "I shall bare this mark with honor."

He threaded his fingers with Lore's. Where their wrists and arms touched, so did their corresponding Kisses.

"I hope you weren't planning to leave just yet!" called a voice from their left.

Finndryl shook his head as he broke into a slow smile. "Prince Hazen, I was worried we wouldn't have a chance to say our good-byes."

Prince Hazen hurried toward them, his arms clutching a large canvas bag. "No need for goodbyes. Remember when we were at the base of Mount Vatraol and I confessed I should not like being excluded from your adventures in the future?"

Confused, Lore hesitated before answering. "I . . . yes." She looked at Finndryl, but he looked as puzzled as she.

Prince Hazen beamed, glancing between her and Finn. "I will be accompanying you both on your journey!"

"You will?" Finndryl asked, not bothering to hide his skepticism.

"Yes. It will be a rewarding experience for me. And, it will ensure I am able to keep my grandmother's promise to you as well."

"I—I *just* requested that favor, I hope it didn't influence—"

The prince waved his hand dismissively. "I discussed my desire with Gran to join your quest before all that. I wish to see the world before my coronation."

Lore's mouth hung open as her mind caught up. "Sorry I missed your party, Gran," Hazen said before giving his grandmother a kiss on her cheek.

Lore glanced back and forth between Prince Hazen and his grandmother, who remained quiet, watching the exchange with an amused expression. "But we are going somewhere potentially dangerous! Perilous, even," Lore protested. It wasn't that she didn't want Prince Hazen to come; it was that she wasn't sure he knew the circumstances—

Prince Hazen narrowed his eyes, as if worried she was having a difficult time understanding him. Lore didn't think he usually had to explain himself this much, being a prince and all. "Gran agreed. She thinks it's a grand idea."

Finndryl rubbed his jaw. "I don't know about 'grand' . . . It's going to be dangerous. Extremely dangerous, Prince."

Finally, Queen Naia spoke. "The more danger the better, my grandson needs to test his mettle."

"See?" He flashed his sharp teeth in a smile.

"If my grandson couldn't take care of himself, I would've passed over him and chosen any of his sixteen siblings."

"Sixteen?"

"Yes, our daughter had quite the collection of songlings." Prince Consort Jaladri beamed with pride as he swam up beside his queen.

"So it seems."

"We would be honored to have you come with us on our adventures, brother," Finn said, clapping Prince Hazen on the shoulder.

"Can we leave, already?" Coretha called out as she exited the guest wing into the courtyard. *Disrespectful brat.* Lore noticed the mark on her arm was faded, almost gone entirely. She wouldn't have much time left before the lingering benefits of the mark disappeared and she drowned.

Maybe they could stay a little longer . . .

"Unfortunately, the ill-mannered one is right. Say your good-byes. It won't be long before she drowns down here," the queen stated, her voice implying that the thought of Coretha drowning didn't sound as awful as it maybe should have. Lore grinned. The queen turned to Jaladri. "My love, have a servant fetch my pipe, will you? I shall enjoy a puff since we are going to the surface." Prince Consort Jaladri winked at Lore before withdrawing from the inner pocket of his cloak one delicately crafted long-stemmed pipe. "Already done, my queen."

For some reason, the image of the queen puffing on a pipe did not surprise Lore one bit. This queen deserved statues in her honor, she was that dynamic. Lore wished she'd had time to hear stories from her youth. Maybe one day she would learn how the two of them met.

"I'm going to double-check with Prince Hazen that this is really what he wants," Finndryl murmured against her ear.

Lore nodded and turned, surveying the courtyard. She still had the issue of Syrelle . . . and whether or not he would pose a threat once back on land. Lore eyed him where he lingered by the tree in the center of the courtyard, his gaze not upon the lovely blooms that had appeared overnight nor the fish flitting from flower to flower, but fixed far away, unseeing. He wore long sleeves. Lore couldn't tell if his mark remained or not. Officially, without him, they wouldn't have been able to save the siren kingdom. The queen may have extended him the same offer to keep the Puallas Kiss, and why wouldn't she?

He hadn't betrayed *her*.

Syrelle must have felt her gaze on him because he turned, his eyes immediately latching onto her.

Lore crossed the courtyard. Her knees suddenly weak. She forced her arms to swing by her sides and not let her fingers lock, twist, show any of the anxiety that gnawed on her bones. She took a deep breath. "So, this will be goodbye, correct?" She aimed for lightness. "You aren't devising any last-minute schemes over here?"

Syrelle winced. "No schemes. Coretha and I return to Wyndlin."

Lore shook her head. "I'm supposed to believe that you are simply . . . letting me go."

Syrelle took a hesitant step forward, reaching out as if to touch her. Lore recoiled, eyes flashing a warning.

"Don't," she said sharply. "Just . . . don't."

Syrelle's hand fell back to his side as he nodded slowly. "I know I've hurt you," he admitted, his voice thick with remorse. "But I swear to you, I was doing what I thought was . . . was the best way to protect you from him." His gaze flicked to Coretha, who sat slumped on a bench, waiting for the siren to escort her to shore. His voice lowered, quickened as if he had to say this despite Coretha possibly overhearing. "I am rooting for you, Lore. I hope that you find *Auroradel*, bind it to you, but please, do not confront the king. Promise you won't—"

Lore gave a slow, disbelieving head shake. "Why? Why shouldn't I confront him?" She narrowed her eyes, her eyebrows pulling together. "What do you know, Syrelle? What are you not telling me?"

She could see the jagged edge of terror in his eyes and watched as he worked his jaw but said nothing.

Lore laughed, the sound hollow, derisive. He wasn't ever going to tell her the entire truth. He was never going to give her the *respect* of providing her all the information, every layer, so that she could make an informed decision.

He was *determined* to keep her in the dark—well, she was through with the dark.

Lore huffed a breath as anger bloomed within her. She balled her hands into fists. "I am not a child in need of protection—even now, you are withholding information from me. But no—" She shook her head, tensing her jaw. "I can't let myself wonder or be dragged into the *why*s of it all." She jabbed a finger at him. "I came to say this: Do not follow me. Do not stand in my way. If you try to hinder me from finding *Auroradel*, it will be a fight that only one of us will walk away from." She stepped toward him, her expression severe, her eyes blazing with determination. "Syrelle, I will *die* before I let you control or manipulate my actions again. I will die before I let you win."

Syrelle flinched as if struck. "I understand," he said softly. "But know this, Lore. If you *ever* need me, all you must do is ask." His voice wavered, and he gazed upward for a moment, collecting himself. "You won't believe me, you can't believe me, and that's my fault . . . but I will always choose you."

Lore swallowed, clenching her jaw. The only thing he was *choosing* to do was continue to withhold information from her— maintaining her ignorance and, therefore, putting her life at risk. Lore blinked back tears and simply turned away.

If he'd wanted to share his knowledge with her, they had had days when Coretha could not watch his every move. They'd trekked to a volcano and back—he could have told her then. She wasn't sure how she had expected this conversation to go as she'd walked over here . . . but she supposed she had the best outcome she could've asked for. He'd confirmed what she'd heard—he and Coretha were returning to Alytheria. The opposite side of the ocean from where she was heading. That was the most she could hope for. Did she fully believe it? She would be stupid to. But it was enough, for now, just hearing that he would not pursue her or *Auroradel*.

She left Syrelle behind and walked back to Finndryl, a sentinel of solace waiting for her with their packed bags. Lore shouldered hers. The canvas sack was light, mostly empty, save for a few outfits and toiletries that she would have to wash and dry once they were back on land.

"Ready to go?" She plastered a smile on her face, though too many conflicting emotions were roiling within her—she doubted it was convincing.

Finndryl nodded. "Are you?" His gaze searched hers, a line carved between his brows. He seemed to be asking more than whether she was ready to go: *Was she all right? Did she need a hug? There was still time—should he go over there and connect his fist with Syrelle's face?*

Lore nodded—*yes, she was ready to go.*

She couldn't talk about it yet. Not when things were this complicated.

"How did the meeting with Queen Naia go?" he asked out loud.

Lore was thankful for his distraction. "Well—after plying me with desserts she agreed to my request and then some." She held out a heavy leather purse, her smile finally meeting her eyes. "She filled this with coin."

Finndryl held up a coin purse as well, a smirk dancing on his lips. "Turns out saving a queendom has its perks."

Prince Hazen appeared beside them, a grin on his face. His facial tattoos glowed silver in the lights, his tail shimmered iridescent.

"Ready, Prince Hazen?" Lore asked.

"Please, call me Hazen. I shall not be a prince out there, I shall be . . . an explorer! And yes, I welcome danger. I crave it."

Lore laughed, shaking her head. "All right, Hazen it is."

Finndryl grinned. "I am glad to have you along, Hazen." She glanced between the two males before taking in one last look around the palace of Lapis Deep. She hoped this wasn't the last time she had the chance to visit . . . and yet her feet itched to be back on firm land. "Shall we?"

It took everything in her not to glance back at Syrelle, but she knew, without having to look, that his gaze was trained on her.

PART THREE

THE BOOK OF
SUNBEAMS

CHAPTER 30

The Empire of Ma Serach was a fortress, protected not by walls but by its own harsh nature. Water was a currency, and sandstorms were a weapon wielded by the land itself against those who dared to intrude. The vast empire spread like the rising sun across the folded map clenched in Lore's sweaty hand.

Lore was no stranger to hardship; she'd crossed oceans and braved volcanoes—the Empire of Ma Serach, with its primordial secrets and hostile landscape, was just one more challenge to conquer. Or so she repeated to herself for the eighth time as she pulled in another dusty breath of air. It was hot. The air was hot. It felt like those moments when she would lean into the fire to turn the logs, but it was as though . . . when she pulled away, the fire came with her.

But at least it was not water. Air was better than water, even dusty air. And it tasted rather sweet, hints of cactus flower and aloe overpowering the earthiness.

Through research back on the *Lavender Lark*, she'd managed to pinpoint a cave system in the Golden Cascades, a massive mountain range that spanned the length of Ma Serach, where she thought *Auroradel* might be hidden. The Golden Cascades were so vast they almost successfully cut the nation in half. There were almost no mountain passes that cut through the Cascades; trade routes and roads were exclusively left to the coastal southern border of Ma Serach, and the northernmost route—far to the east—wouldn't take them anywhere near the griffin nesting grounds.

At least, not as shown on the map Queen Naia had gifted her. Lore had hoped for a different scenario. Maps were always more detailed when originated in the country itself. And so she, Hazen, and Finn had hurried from the docks—the travel barge had deposited them in the bustling port city of Jamal—to the closest bazaar. The three of them scoured countless stalls filled with gold, multicolored textiles, mounds of spices, nuts, and handicrafts.

It took longer than Lore wished to find the ancient shop filled with maps, but when Lore compared hers to the more localized ones, her hopes were quickly dashed. There were southern routes, northern routes, and even one that traversed the base of the Golden Cascades, but there wasn't a single map showing how to navigate the mountains themselves. The older proprietor had quickly grown tired of them browsing the maps with frowning faces. When he realized they probably weren't going to buy anything, he quickly ushered them out of his store, muttering about "cheap tourists" in broken Alytherian.

Lore eyed the muddied shadows around them, furious that the sun was setting. The market was emptying. Earlier, they had had to wind through throngs of shoppers huddled around carts, sampling roasted yams drizzled with honey and salted nuts, scrutinizing rugs in every pigment as they haggled with shopkeepers for the best bargain. Now, the bazaar was shifting as the shops, carts, and stalls were closing down. Soon, the taverns and brothels would light their lanterns beckoning the late-night crowd.

"We will find an inn with a nice hot bath and look again tomorrow," Hazen said through a large mouthful of jollof rice.

"Tomorrow is too late. I know Syrelle and Coretha said they

were returning to Alytheria, but I have this nagging feeling they may actually be here as well, searching for the caves. And they can fly, remember? I want to chart our course tonight."

"They may be able to fly, but they don't know what you know. Which is the most important information," Finndryl chimed in. His shoulders were relaxed; he didn't look concerned.

Lore bounced on the balls of her feet, her gaze darting around the bazaar. "Syrelle is too damned cunning; what if I gave him clues just by the list of books and maps I requested?"

"You may have, but he was under the impression that you would lead him straight to *Auroradel.* And he doesn't even know about the riddle, remember?" replied Finn around a mouthful of food—a thick, puffed slice of bread slathered in a creamy garlic sauce folded around seared strips of spiced lamb. Damn, he was making that look delicious. Lore licked her lips. She was starting to regret that she'd forgone food to search every stall displaying anything remotely map-shaped.

Finndryl noticed her eyeing his wrap. He slung the leather pack on his back to his front and dug around. With a knowing grin, he pulled out a second wrap, offering it to her. He'd gotten one for her. Or he'd gotten himself two and was giving her one. The outcome was the same. She gave him a quick smile before pulling back the wax paper and biting into it. Gods, this was delicious. And *spicy.*

Why must Lore always be racing against time? She had a purse attached to her belt filled with gold, silver, and copper pieces—one of many gifts from Queen Naia. In another life, the three of them could've sampled from every vendor and eaten their way through Ma Serach.

As it was, Lore was at a loss for what to do. She licked garlic sauce from her thumb and surveyed the bazaar again.

It was fully dark now. A youth was skipping from lamp to lamp, lighting each in turn, humming a happy song as he went about his work.

"Hey, you there! Do you speak Alytherian?" Lore called out to him as he passed by.

"A little," he said, leaning against the long pole he used to light the lamps and surveying them, his kind eyes showing a keen intelligence.

"Can you direct us to an affordable inn?" Lore asked.

"A safe one that you would send your grandmother to," Finndryl added from where he loomed behind Lore.

The boy eyed Finndryl up and down. Hopefully, his formidable form would deter the youngling from trying to pull a fast one on them—like leading them to a troupe of bandits waiting in an alley or something of the like.

"Easy. That one." He pointed to a tall triangular building just down the road on the main stretch of the market.

"The blue one?"

"Yes. My grandmother owns it." He grinned. Well, it seemed his grandmother *would* choose to visit that one.

"Perfect. Thank you." Lore gave him a few copper pieces. It wasn't Ma Serach currency, but Jamal was a port town, and they had discovered that most places took coin from anywhere, as long as it was real. The boy would have no trouble spending it.

They turned toward the inn.

The boy called after them, "If you see a tall woman with a big smile and a high *bhearaon* on her head, tell her Simi sent you. She will give you a good room."

"Thank you, Simi!" Hazen shouted without looking back.

Lore couldn't get over seeing the siren prince on land. The moment he'd slipped out of the ocean, his tail had split in two, morphing into legs. Naked ones. Lore was so shocked she'd almost forgotten to turn away to give him privacy as he dressed. She didn't know what she'd expected to happen . . . She'd been stunned when Hazen had announced his intention of traveling with them, but she had had so much on her mind that *how* he was going to do it hadn't occurred to her. She figured, of course, he'd had a plan in place—Cuan had had legs when they'd rescued Lore on the ship, but Lore had thought that particular skill was unique to them.

But no, siren apparently could just sprout legs at will.

Convenient as hell.

And here he was, leading the way, walking so steady you would think he was born on land. Impressive, truly.

Just before they entered the inn Hazen held out an arm. "Let me do the talking. Finn—you have a permanent glower. Lore, you're sweet, but you have an element about you that makes one want to . . . how do I put this nicely . . . con you out of all you have in that purse."

Lore made a face and placed her hands on her hips. "I don't think that's what any normal person would think."

Finndryl crossed his arms over his chest. "What element do you have that makes you the one to facilitate our sleeping arrangements?"

Hazen flashed sharp white teeth and ran a hand through his wavy hair with a dramatic flair. "Finndryl, brother, I have *this* face. One too gorgeous to deny. Not even a grandmother could resist, trust me."

"Right, because a grandmother would be so easily swayed by someone who looks like they were just an awkward adolescent last month." Lore was exaggerating, Hazen *was* gorgeous, and not one thing about him said *young* or *awkward*. In fact, he'd probably skipped the awkward phase altogether, the lucky bastard. But she wasn't going to inflate his ego any more than it already was. Born a prince *and* handsome?

Some people were the gods' favorite, clearly.

Finndryl shook his head. "You have a face that looks like you would con someone as lovely as Lore without thinking twice about it. Let Lore handle this."

Finn *was* glowering, and Lore loved it. He could glower at everyone all he wanted, as long as he didn't glower at *her*.

"I do not look like a con artist!" Hazen protested in typical Hazen fashion. Lore had just spent a week with him on a travel barge, so she was well-versed in his dramatics. He was clearly offended that *they* had taken offense.

Lore raised her chin, suppressed laughter shining in her eyes. "No, Finndryl, I would like to see Hazen at work. Though how hard could it be booking a room . . . at an inn . . . where their main source of income . . . is from renting their rooms . . . because this is an inn?"

Hazen swung the door wide and held it open for them as he replied, "You would be surprised—in port cities, an establishment as nice as this one can have its pick of clients. If they don't like the look of you, they'll send you on your way."

"Isn't this your first time away from Lapis Deep?" Finndryl asked, his tone dry as his eyebrow quirked upward.

"I am well-traveled. In my dreams." He placed a hand over his chest. "And my heart. My heart is well-traveled. Now it is time for my feet to be as well."

"Whatever that means." Lore pressed a fist to her lips to keep from laughing lest she disturb the tranquil atmosphere of the inn's common room. "Go on, acquire us a couple of rooms, handsome."

The inn was glorious. Tall ceilings decorated in deliciously vibrant tiles. Large, oversize chairs were positioned throughout the room. Three tall bookshelves packed with novels lined one of the walls, and various board and card games were dispersed on low tables for patrons to utilize. An inviting glass pitcher of water with sliced lemons stood in the center for guests to partake of. The clean, gleaming hardwood floors were covered with thick, artfully woven rugs. Oil lamps burned low, and the roaring fire in the hearth made for the perfect cozy atmosphere.

Lore wanted to *live* here.

She hurried to catch up to Hazen. "Make sure mine has a bath in it!"

Her clothing was caked stiff with salt, and the smell of the sea clung to Lore like a second skin.

The travel barge had only allotted one bathing day for the entire week aboard and a single bucket and tiny chunk of soap per traveler to wash with. It hadn't been enough to remove the salt deposits that had grafted to Lore's skin from days in the ocean.

The leftover salt and dusty desert air were threatening to turn Lore into walking ash. Her elbows and knees were proof. Lore might actually die if she couldn't submerge herself in scalding, *fresh* water within the hour.

Simi's grandma was seated behind a desk reading a book. Glasses perched low on her nose, and a beautifully beaded string connected to both arms rested against her ample bosom. As Simi had said, a blue scarf, her *bhearaon*, was wrapped around her hair and stood tall on her head.

Though, the smile he mentioned was missing.

"Hello, beautiful. Your grandson, Simi, was most gracious and directed us to your fine establishment. He said it was the finest inn to be found in all of Ma Serach, and I see that he was not exaggerating." He was laying the charm on heavy. "I am Zane. These are my companions, Fuba and Lara. We are humble travelers hoping you have a place for us to lay our heads."

"Fuba?" Finndryl hissed under his breath to Lore. Lore held in her giggle. It was a terrible name.

The woman furrowed her eyebrows. "Simi, you say? He is my least favorite grandchild. He has a personal issue with veracity." The older woman sniffed, cutting her eyes in distaste at Hazen. "I suppose my establishment is fine enough, but to boast that it is finer than any in our magnificent empire is just that, a boast."

Innkeeper: 1. Hazen: 0.

"Ah, but beauty is in the eye of the beholder, and If I may, this is the most beautiful inn I have ever stepped into."

Not to mention the first and *only* inn the siren prince had probably been to. On land, anyway.

There, the innkeeper cracked a small smile. "All right, traveler, I'll take the compliment." She took his offered hand, over which he bent low and placed a kiss upon her knuckles. "I'm Svalja, innkeeper and owner." She grimaced and wiped the knuckles he'd kissed on her dress. Lore stifled a titter at Hazen's appalled reaction that someone should not cherish his kiss as if it were a ruby necklace. "I feel compelled to mention that flattery won't get you a discount if that is what you are after." Humor glinted in Svalja's brown eyes. "In fact, as I've been told I run the most beautiful inn in all of Ma Serach, I have a sudden urge to charge you double."

"Double?" Hazen sputtered, obviously shocked to his core that flattery and his dashing good looks could not, in fact, get him everywhere.

"I won't, of course. I have what many in this town lack . . . integrity. As you can see, the prices are there on the wall, and they do not vary no matter how many compliments . . . or unsolicited kisses . . . my patrons bestow upon me."

And indeed, there the prices were, posted for all to see, written in neat, swirling handwriting on a chalkboard. Single rooms, double, family. One could pay extra for a bath to be filled, more if you want breakfast brought up to your room, less if you eat it in the common area. The innkeeper set her novel down and opened a tall ledger that sat before her on the desk. This place must be run as tight as a ship.

Not that she was an expert on ships, considering one had had a mutiny and the other was the slovenly barge that had deposited them a whole two days later than promised, and the awkward-shaped monstrosity hadn't had any sails. She never did quite figure out how it traveled the seas.

So this place must be run tighter than a ship.

Yes, Lore thought, she could live here happily.

"What can I do for you three?"

"We require two rooms, please. A double for my friend and I, and a single for the lady. We shall all require baths and breakfast in our rooms, I think." Hazen, subdued and, Lore thought, *almost* humbled, spoke without his earlier flair.

She almost felt bad for him. It made sense that being raised a beautiful prince would make one think that everyone would fall at your feet. Queen Naia was right to require the male do some traveling before taking the crown.

"Just the one night? Or are you staying awhile?"

"Yes, just the one night, thank you."

The innkeeper wrote all this down, added the sums in her head, and gave them the total, which matched what Lore had added up. Integrity indeed.

"You are welcome to have a seat while my granddaughter readies your rooms and baths. There is only one bath in each room, so you two will have to take turns unless you plan on sharing. The common area is open all day and night should you choose to use it. The kitchen is closed, as we don't serve dinner on Sunday, but you will find a pamphlet with recommendations within walking distance."

Lore dug out the coin and handed it to her. Simi's grandmother quickly placed it in a box with a mighty-looking lock. She tucked the key, which was strung on a cord, into her dress.

Svalja didn't balk at the coin, but once they left the port city, they should find a bank to exchange it. If one wasn't listed in the pamphlet upstairs, Lore would inquire tomorrow.

"Joya will collect you when your rooms are ready. Checkout is promptly at ten bells. If you are late, we charge you for every quarter bell that you linger."

"Thank you, my Lady." Hazen bowed unnecessarily, as she had already returned to her book.

Lore shoved Hazen as they made their way back to the common room. "You, my friend, are outrageous."

"I admit, she was quite impervious to my charms, but no matter, we acquired the rooms!"

Small victories.

The boys dropped their packs on the floor and collapsed into the nearest chairs within the common room. Lore dropped her pack beside *Fuba*'s and crossed the large room to browse the book-shelves.

She was happy to see that there was a variety of languages here, and a few were in Alytherian.

She was flipping through one when a shadow fell over her, blocking the light.

Lore glanced up to see a female orc—incredibly tall with a broad, kind face, ivory-colored tusks, and twin braids that hung down to her knees, possibly a fellow traveler by the size of the pack on her back—looking through the books as well.

"Oh, I'm sorry, am I blocking the light?" The orc's voice was pleasantly deep.

"It's no matter; I don't think I'm going to read this one anyway," Lore said as she placed the small book back in its spot on the shelf. It actually looked really good. An assassin romance—the love story was between an assassin posing as a girl in a traveling theater troupe and the princess of the neighboring kingdom, who she had been contracted to assassinate. If only Lore had the time to eat and read and live her life at leisure, she would have asked to bring it up to the room and read it during her bath.

Maybe she could purchase the book from the innkeeper? It was not like she hadn't the gold. Lore didn't know quite what to do with all the coin the queen had bestowed upon her departure.

"You haven't seen any maps on the shelf, have you?" asked the orc.

Lore was startled out of her musings as she stroked the spine of the assassin's love story longingly.

"Maps? I—uh, no, I haven't." She hadn't even thought to look for any maps on this bookshelf. It had seemed to be filled with novels and, on the bottom shelves, picture books for little ones.

"Too bad." The orc offered a massive hand to Lore. "I'm Pytheah, a treasure hunter. I've found maps here before."

"Oh, I'm, um, Lara . . . traveler," she finished lamely, taking her offered hand. Would she ever learn how to come up with a backstory? At least they had decided to use false names while on the barge from hell. It had been Finn's idea. And he definitely hadn't suggested that his name be *Fuba*.

"Traveler, huh? All right, I *am* a stranger, no need to spill all your secrets."

Lore laughed. "I've never met a treasure hunter before."

Pytheah smiled as her ears turned red. "I'm not surprised, there aren't very many of us; it's not really something that pays the tax collector."

"I suppose that would depend on how successful of a treasure hunter you were."

Pytheah laughed. "You're right. Depends on the treasure hunter." Pytheah leaned in, her voice dropping even lower as she wiggled her eyebrows. "I think after this score, I'll never again have to hide in my pantry, pretending I'm not home when those bastards come knocking on my door."

All right, Lore was intrigued. "I probably shouldn't ask; I'm not sure about the etiquette with treasure hunters. Do you not already possess a map? One with a dotted line and a very convenient *X* on it?"

"I wish it were that easy! No, I haven't come across any ancient pirate maps." Pytheah rubbed her chin. "Not yet, anyway. But I just arrived in Jamal; I should think it would be obvious what treasure I'm after."

"Not obvious to me—I'm not from around here."

"Oh, right. We are in an inn. I can be so daft sometimes."

Pytheah grinned. "I'm looking for the Ayred Stash. It's hidden somewhere in the Golden Cascades."

"The Ayred Stash?" The Golden Cascades? Lore saw Finn and Hazen perk up from where they were both slouched in their seats.

Pytheah's eyes widened. "You really aren't from around here." She began nodding with excitement. "It's a prominent legend in these parts. One hundred years ago, Ayred De Luatha buried his entire treasury somewhere in the Golden Cascades. No one has ever found it. And those who go looking don't usually come back whole—if they come back at all."

"I hate to even ask, but . . . what exactly happens to them?"

"Oh, all kinds of things can happen." She began to list them, ticking them off finger by finger. "I think most probably die of thirst. Or get lost in the mountains and never find their way out. Or fall off a cliff. Or get crushed in an avalanche of boulders as large as this inn. And then, of course, there are the dragons." Pytheah said all of these horrible prospects with a delighted grin on her face.

Lore felt ill and pounced on the one thing she hadn't thought would kill them when they eventually made it to the Golden Cascades. "Dragons are a myth, aren't they?"

"Dragons might be a myth where you're from—which, by the way, is that under a rock? Oh, sorry, I didn't mean to offend, I thought it would be funny—but, uh, yeah, dragons are *definitely* real, and it's known that at least three documented Reddies, that's what we call ourselves, those looking for his treasure, that at least three documented Reddies have been burned to a crisp. Or at least had a hand taken off by a dragon."

A loud snort came from behind them. "Dragons are about as real as Ayred's stash, Pytheah." Lore swiveled to see a young version of the innkeeper standing behind them, holding two keys. She was lovely, with warm brown skin, short-cropped curly hair, and delicately pointed fae ears.

"Agree to disagree, Joya," Pytheah retorted. But she wasn't angry; the smile Pytheah shared with Joya was a sweet, lovely thing.

"You've spent months combing the Cascades, and you've never seen any evidence of a dragon, let alone *multiple*."

Pytheah snapped the book she was holding shut. "I told you, last time I was up there, I saw one!"

Svalja's granddaughter huffed. "And I told *you*, that was probably just a griffin. You said yourself it was in silhouette against the sun and you couldn't be sure."

"I've since made up my mind. It was definitely a dragon, not a griffin."

"You've seen a griffin? In the Golden Cascades?" Lore couldn't help but interject.

"Well, yes, I've seen tons of them. But I've also seen a dragon. I think."

Joya rolled her eyes before putting on a pleasant smile and addressing Lore, Finn, and Hazen. "Zane's party, your rooms are ready. You'd better hurry and follow me before the water gets cold."

Hazen, who had been pretending to doze in the oversize chair, leaped out of it and hauled his overstuffed pack onto his back. "Finally. Your words are music to my ears."

Lore was beginning to think he wanted a bath more than she did. Wasn't he used to the salt?

Finndryl and Hazen began to walk with Joya to the rooms, but Lore's gut was telling her *not yet*.

"Pytheah, it was lovely to meet you. I would love to talk more with you about this dragon you saw. Will you be having breakfast in the common room tomorrow?"

Maybe Lore could eat with her and pick her brain about the griffins she'd seen.

Pytheah's jaw dropped momentarily before she snapped it shut. "That is so kind of you to ask. It's not often one finds a friend when traveling. But." Pytheah's shoulders slumped. "I'm actually leaving tonight. I just stopped by to see if there were any new additions to the Reddies' stash."

Tonight? Shit.

"Reddies' stash?" Lore asked. She didn't want to keep Joya waiting, but she had to see . . . Hazen began to tap his foot impatiently and checked the timepiece on his arm. Lore ignored him; the prince could go another five minutes without his bath. Finndryl was watching Lore and Pytheah, his eyes inquisitive.

"Us Reddies are sort of an unofficial guild. I mean, there aren't enough of us to make an official one. I realize it sounds odd that we share our knowledge. Are we in competition? Yes. But a lot of us do this for the hunt itself. Finding the treasure would be wonderful, but we aren't going to hoard our knowledge when we *don't* find it." Pytheah jutted her chin toward the reception desk, her words coming faster and faster. "Svalja was one of the first Reddies back in the day. She's retired now, of course, but in her prime, she was *fierce*. I'm convinced that if she hadn't gotten so old, she would've been the one to find the treasure. But anyway, us Reddies practically *worship* her, and when we are in the area we always visit, pay our respects. Over the years, we've started leaving each other notes, pages of our Reddy journals, and stuff like that. There is something sweet about finding new pages, tips, or newly discovered Ayred lore. Almost feels like you've got a friend with you."

"Why don't you team up and hunt together?" Lore ignored Hazen as he dramatically checked his timepiece again. "Then you wouldn't have to hunt alone."

Pytheah barked a laugh. "We are friendly, but not that friendly. I don't plan on splitting the treasure with another Reddy. And anyway, I don't trust anyone that much. They could murder me in my sleep and take it all for themselves!" Pytheah dropped the book she'd been perusing haphazardly on the shelf. Lore winced, itching to find the correct spot for it. "It's common knowledge that treasure hunters are notorious for doing that."

Lore nodded her head. Was it common knowledge, though?

"So you are leaving tonight, then?" Lore tried to sound casual as she asked, "Are you heading out to the Golden Cascades?"

"She is," Joya chimed in, her innkeeper face and voice replaced with a scowl. "No matter how many times I tell her it's dangerous to hike the Cascades, she always goes back out there."

"I'm an explorer, Joya. A Reddy. I'm not afraid of a few dry peaks."

Joya sputtered. "'A few dry peaks'? Pytheah, the Cascades are *treacherous*. I'm just waiting for the day you don't return." She crossed her arms. "And I won't be the one going to look for you."

"I'll be so pissed if the only time I get you on those mountains, you aren't with me."

"You won't be anything; you'll most likely have become griffin food."

Pytheah winced at the thought. "You've made your stance clear, but you won't be complaining when I come back with three camels loaded with gold."

"I don't want gold. I want you to be *alive*."

"Can't have one without the other."

"This is nonsense." Joya turned her back on Pytheah and addressed "Zane" and "Fuba." "Guests, I've supplied your rooms, and we've even included a few complimentary bottles of soap, creams, and lotions. Please don't throw the bottles out; they will be cleansed and refilled after you leave."

Joya turned her back to head upstairs, where a warm bath and a clean, cozy bed were waiting.

Lore winced internally. She couldn't believe she was about to say this, but . . .

"Pytheah, would you be interested in guiding a few travelers safely to the Cascades? That's where we are headed, in search of griffins, and it seems like fate that we've run into such a skilled and knowledgeable adventurer."

Pytheah stiffened, narrowing her eyes in suspicion.

Lore rushed to appease her mind. "We will pay, of course. And we don't care about gold. You won't have to worry about us trying to steal any treasure." Lore pointed to Hazen, who looked absolutely crestfallen that he might not be getting his bath. "This one's a prince. He's got *heaps* of it."

Pytheah's gaze shifted to Hazen, her eyes wide and sparkling. "A prince? I've never met one of those. I did meet a demon once disguised as a lamp." Pytheah twirled a braid around one hand, thinking. "I wouldn't be opposed to the idea. And it would be nice to have some conversation on the trip. One can never have too many friends. But you all will need supplies." She eyed their packs, which—if you didn't count Hazen's, which was bursting with outfits—were, admittedly, quite flat.

Lore smiled. "Just point us where to go, and we will buy it! And we can stock up your supplies, too, if you're low on any."

Pytheah nodded. Lore could see her thoughts racing as she pivoted. Lore imagined she was planning all the things a group that size would need—a group who had never been to the Golden Cascades . . . and who didn't know enough about adventuring to have heard of Ayred's treasure. "I know a guy. His shop is closed by now, but he lives above it, and he's always at home, and anyway, he owes me a favor." Pytheah grinned. "I introduced him to his husband."

"Joya, it looks like we may have to cancel those baths we ordered," Hazen said, his voice grief stricken.

CHAPTER 31

The shop owner, an orc with a black-and-gray unkempt beard, chipped tusk, and a permanent scowl etched onto his lichen-hued face, grumbled as he tossed supplies into a sack. "Pytheah, you couldn't have come at a more convenient hour?"

Lore swallowed a sigh. Pytheah had assured them that the proprietor was indebted to her, but he clearly hadn't received the message. At least Pytheah was right about one thing: He had everything they needed. Enough food for a week, maybe two, depending on rationing. Lore's eyes darted to the water skins for the fifth time in the past minute; water was the most crucial item on their list. Beyond the city walls, between them and the Golden Cascades, lay the Demon Wastes, a desert as unforgiving as its name suggested.

Pytheah, a wide grin splitting her face, slapped a reassuring hand on Lore's shoulder. "Don't worry, I know every watering hole in those wastes like the back of my hand."

Lore gave her a weak smile as she dug into her purse. Finndryl and Hazen hefted the biggest of the three packs onto their shoulders, and Lore winced as she handed over a hefty sum of coin. The moment the coin was in his hands, the proprietor practically shoved them toward the door, slamming it shut behind them with a resounding crash.

"Well," Finndryl muttered, his voice laced with wariness, "that was . . . pleasant."

Lore shot him a wry look. "Pytheah did say he owed her a favor." And yet, she could swear he'd charged almost double for everything—there was no way that woolen bedrolls cost a gold piece *each*.

As they made their way out of Jamal's northern gates, Pytheah's cheerful demeanor faltered. "Ah, about that favor the shopkeeper owed me . . . turns out the male I'd introduced him to . . . may have absconded with his life savings, every last one of his Reddies maps, and his favorite camel."

Hazen raised an eyebrow at Lore, his expression a silent echo of her own thoughts: *This is who we're entrusting with our lives?*

Lore could only shrug, because it was too late; they were already in the desert, Pytheah leading the way with a confidence Lore wished she felt.

A well-maintained road with plenty of Ma Serach patrol safeguarding it stretched out of the city, but Pytheah promptly abandoned it, opting instead for a direct plunge into the Demon Wastes. Lore's boots slipped on the shifting sands as she followed as close behind Finndryl as possible without treading on his boots. Her human eyes were struggling to adjust to the darkness, and she stumbled more than once, saved each time by Finndryl's quick hands.

"Fae speed comes in handy, eh?" he said with a chuckle, his voice a comforting presence in the moonless night.

Lore grumbled under her breath; it was so damned dark—she couldn't imagine why Pytheah had decided to make the first leg of her trek at night. They could be tucked into bed in the world's most beautiful inn. (Despite Svalja's insistence that it was *not* the world's most beautiful inn. Lore bet the bed was like a cloud. She imagined you lay on it and were swallowed whole until morning, when you would greet the day utterly refreshed . . . no waking up from a sore shoulder or hip, a lumpy piece of hay that refused to flatten no matter how much you shook out the mattress or pressed it down . . . and she assumed that surely one would not wake up in the middle of the night clutching their heart from a nightmare.) And then they could have left in the morning fed, clean, and well-rested.

But then again, Lore quickly learned that almost nothing Pytheah did made much sense to her.

An eternity later, she was cursing Pytheah in her head for insisting they travel at night, turning her into all kinds of unsavory animals with spells she didn't actually know, when their guide finally announced it was time to set up camp.

Lore collapsed onto her bedroll, exhaustion pulling her under almost instantly. She slept soundly, oblivious to the rock that somehow found its way beneath her hip during the night.

The next two days were a blur of sun, sand, and the distant peaks of the Golden Cascades—behemoths whose giant, foreboding bodies didn't appear to be any closer, no matter how many miles they covered.

They passed no one (demonic wastes, indeed), but on the third night, Lore swore she heard the cry of a griffin, a small thrill amid the monotony. However, Hazen complaining about the dirt under his nails for the thousandth time immediately soured the situation again.

Pytheah had been sure they would reach the basin of the mountains the following day, so on the third night, Lore laid out her bedroll next to Finn's, excitement thrumming through her bones. There had been no sign of Syrelle. Could he really have just gone home to deal with matters there and given up? Lore didn't believe it. He'd dedicated his entire life to finding the set of books his grandfather had made.

He wasn't going to give up that easily, but still, he was nowhere around. At this moment, Lore was free of him.

Hope stirred in her belly.

She lay awake long after the others' breaths had softened into the rhythmic sighs of slumber, marveling at the boundless expanse of sky. It was so different from home, where the stars above Duskmere, though swaths of bright, swirling constellations, were always framed by the shadowy silhouettes of trees. Here, nothing obstructed her view. Lore felt an unexpected closeness to her ancestors, a yearning for *Ziara*, the sacred skyglass. The stars' formations were unfamiliar, their positions shifted, and she could swear there were entire constellations she'd never seen before. How she longed to map this sky for her people, to bring it home for them to see.

Finally, she drifted off.

Lore dreamt of *Auroradel*, the Book of Sunbeams, which felt contrary to its name.

Its haunting voice whispered in her ear, telling her tales of griffins and their sharp beaks that could snap a human in half on a whim. It whispered of the power of dragons, whose ability to breathe rock-melting fire derived from the sun too. And it pushed darkness onto Lore's mind. A suppressing weight of the earth. Lore tried to pull in breath, but when she opened her mouth, gasping for air, it filled with the taste of decay and mildew; a thousand insects slithered inside, scampering on her tongue and scuttling down her throat.

Lore tried to scream; she tried to snap her jaw closed, to stop the horde of disturbing, swarming insects, but there were so many of them, and her jaw was lodged open even as eras passed, and the earth crushed her. The insects filled her belly, laying their eggs in her organs. She tried to scream as larvae hatched and began eating their way out through her rotting flesh.

Lore jerked awake.

Finndryl was crouched by her side, his grip soothing, unwavering on her shoulders.

"Lore! Alemeyu, wake up."

Lore opened her eyes to the dusky violet hues of the desert just before dawn.

She was not trapped under the earth being devoured from the inside out by insects. She was on her back underneath the sky as the stars winked out one by one to make room for the day.

Frost clung to Lore's blanket, and her breath was a cloud that mingled with Finndryl's.

Her hands were clutched at her throat as if she had been screaming outside of her dream, clawing at her throat.

"I had a nightmare," Lore choked through a sob, the relief that it was all a dream flooding her system.

"I know." Finndryl's presence was so calm. Steadfast and sure. Had he ever had a nightmare?

"Thank you for waking me."

"Do you want to talk about it?"

Lore shook her head. But then she confessed, "I dreamt I was dying." An understatement, but close enough.

"I won't let that happen. I promise."

Lore believed him.

She scooted over on her bedroll, and Finn slipped in beside her. She molded her body to his, and he cradled her to his vast chest. His large hand clasped her head and looped in her hair. She breathed him in, letting the steady drum of his heartbeat calm her own.

Despite the warmth and safety of his arms, she dared not fall asleep. Instead, she recited stories to herself, the few she knew with happy endings.

An hour later, the sun blazed bright, chasing away the cold and the others' sleep. Today was the day she would find *Auroradel*, despite that ominous dream warning her away. She pushed down the worry, hoping the nightmare wasn't a portent of things to come.

They banked the coals of the fire and ate a breakfast of hardtack, a brick of nutrients that tasted like ash on Lore's tongue but filled her belly nonetheless. At least it wasn't remotely slimy, a small mercy considering the phantom sensation of bugs still crawling on her skin. No amount of water could wash away the taste of rot.

Finally, in the early afternoon, they crested a dune, and Lore's breath caught in her throat as she saw it: the land rising steadily until it became the first mountain of the Golden Cascades.

This was where the hard part began.

It would be another full day's hike before they would reach the griffin nesting grounds. Lore's calves were sore from traversing the desert. Most of the ground was rock hard, but there had been a few dunes they'd had to climb. Soft, deceitful powdered sand that threatened to trip her up. More than once, she'd skidded back down the dunes, the sand slippery, and she'd had to make the climb back up.

When they finally reached the top of one slope, they had to climb down the other side before reaching the next. The mountain itself was layered rock. Stripes of golds, pinks, and oranges. It would be beautiful if Lore wasn't close to tears.

Pytheah, who was trying not to show her frustration at Lore's slow pace, had begun to fill the hours with stories of her travels. She'd been all over the world. She'd explored continents Lore had never even heard of and fallen in love with towns so small they hadn't earned their spot on a map yet.

Pytheah's stories got Lore through the worst of it.

The second day was easier; when Finndryl saw the sorry state of Lore's palms and fingers (she dared not use the book in front of Pytheah, though she could have healed herself with magic), he fashioned her a pair of gloves from one of his vests. He hadn't had much time before even his fae eyes had to stop sewing due to the darkness as the fire was banked and the clouds covered the moon and stars. But the next morning, he fit the gloves around Lore's hands, and she was able to climb more easily.

Pytheah didn't have to wait as long for Lore to catch up.

The third night in the Golden Cascades, Lore curled into the fetal position, pulling her legs up to her chest. Her monthlies had started, and fierce throbbing cramps were attacking her insides. She was glad that she had prepared for this time of the month with cloth strips sewn together, but she wished she had remembered to bring ginger and lemon tea to help with the cramping.

She'd asked Pytheah during their bathroom break (they usually went together for fear of some desert monster choosing that time to eat them) if she had any, but Pytheah was an orc and bled very rarely. She wasn't due for another half-decade or so.

The fae and their magical cousins had it better in every damned way; even their uteruses treated them better.

So here she was, biting her lip, curled up with her back to the fire, trying not to appear as miserable as she was.

Without prompting, Finndryl slid in behind her, molding his body to hers.

"You are in pain," he murmured into her ear. It was not a question.

"Yes, my body chooses to betray me once a month. I have half a theory that it's punishing me for not getting pregnant."

"Where does it hurt?"

"My stomach, mostly. Here." Lore moaned, squeezing her eyes shut as a particularly bad cramp attacked her. She felt a little like her insides were being twisted with knitting needles.

Some months were worse than others. Some months she barely cramped, barely felt her emotions change at all. And then there were times like this. When everything made her want to cry, rage, or shout. Fatigue weighed her body down; doubts clouded her mind.

Finndryl reached around her and placed his hand on her belly. His hand was warm, hot from his magic even, and the heat immediately helped her muscles relax.

She sighed into her bedroll.

"When my sister's cycle comes, I don't usually see her for a week. But I know that heat helps her, so I thought . . ."

"Yes, you thought right. Can you make your hand even hotter?"

Finndryl used his newfound magic to push more heat into her—guiding it beyond her skin and threading it through her muscles. Lore sighed with happiness. Her cramps had turned to a dull pain, one that anyone with a uterus could manage without a second thought.

Lore whispered, "Finn?"

"Yes?" His breath tickled her ear in the best way.

"Can you sleep with me tonight?" she asked. "Unless this makes you tired."

Finndryl tightened his hold around her, shifting her closer to him. "This is easy for me; I've been practicing control over my magic while we walk."

Lore huffed a quiet laugh. "Of course you are. I'm trying not to fall to my death, and you act as if you are on a casual stroll."

"Stop complaining; this adventure was your idea, remember?" His chuckle sent vibrations through her back. She nuzzled closer. "But as I was saying, I've been practicing, and warming you up shouldn't tire me out at all. Only let me know if it gets too hot—I don't want to burn you."

"I would gladly accept burns, I think. If it meant I didn't have to feel that pain anymore."

"That . . . is concerning."

She couldn't see his face because her back was to him—she could picture his frown in her mind's eye. That natural frown of his would have deepened, turning farther down at the edges. "I'm kidding. Mostly. I'll let you know, promise."

"Get some rest; I'll stay."

Thankfully, the cramps were gone in the morning, and Pytheah led them to a stream. They refilled their water skins, and Lore bathed and washed the blood from her monthly cloth. She tacked it onto her pack to dry for use the next day.

Nothing like hiking in the desert and being on her monthlies.

Life was grand.

CHAPTER 32

The griffins' wingbeats alone made Lore want to turn tail and run. She held her place crouched behind a boulder, surveying the nesting grounds. She shielded her eyes with a hand and squinted into the setting sun. There were at least a dozen nests filled with eggs and squawking fuzzy chicks the size of full-grown ponies. A swift breeze kicked up dust, and feathers the size of torches floated around her. A screeching call made Lore flinch backward, and she almost lost her footing and tumbled off the ledge. She shifted, holding on to the root of a large bush. Goddess, she prayed that the scent of her fear wouldn't set them off.

She had no doubt they knew she was there. Shadows from griffins scouting from the sky had fallen over them as they climbed higher, each crest of the mountain closer to the nesting grounds. She just prayed they didn't think she was there to steal their eggs or hurt their babies.

With a deep breath, she crawled out from behind the boulder and inched forward, keeping to the perimeter. Another ten feet closer, and she should be able to see every inch of the space.

A chittering alarm call erupted from one of the griffins, announcing her presence. Lore stiffened, holding her breath, but all they did was ruffle their feathers. A few sentries raised their wings, digging razor-sharp talons into the ground, and peered at her, their round dark eyes curious but wary.

But none took flight or lowered their head in warning.

Lore exhaled a shaky breath and chanced another few slow steps forward. A little more chittering, but none took flight.

The moment she could see every inch of the nesting grounds, she stilled.

Short, squat tree . . . berry bush . . . oddly shaped boulder . . . enormous bones of an animal picked utterly clean . . . sheer cliff face rising at their backs . . . there! A sliver of black amid the reddish-gold rock of the cliff.

The entrance to a cave!

Damn it. But there was a problem with *where* the opening was. Numerous nests surrounded the jagged maw of the cavern, and one particularly massive griffin was asleep on its nest, blocking the opening.

A curious griffin, a juvenile from the looks of it, cheeped (if you could call it a cheep, it was *so loud*) and took a few steps toward her, the muscles in its lion body contracting with each step. It snapped its beak a few times, turning its head from side to side, watching her with glassy black eyes.

Lore retreated.

"I found what we are looking for," she huffed, collapsing by the fire. She *may* have run back to camp the moment she was out of that juvenile griffin's sight.

Finndryl, who had been sharpening his sword, slid the weapon back into its sheath and placed it across a muscled thigh. "Welcome back. Any longer, and I was going to come find you." He passed her the water skin. Lore thanked him as she grabbed it and began to take large swallows. "Remind me again why you insisted on scouting alone?"

She wiped her mouth with her sleeve and handed the water

pouch back to him. "Because if anyone was going to become baby griffin food, I wanted it to be *me*."

He huffed a sound of displeasure. "I figured it was something like that."

Lore narrowed her eyes at him. "I'm surprised you didn't argue with me."

"They don't usually attack unless provoked. And I've seen you under pressure. I know you can handle yourself."

She raised an eyebrow at him. "And yet, you were about to come searching for me."

"I figured you had gotten lost," he said as he handed her a cleaned stone with still-steaming rock hare and a few foraged mushrooms.

Lore scowled. "Their nest is only a few hundred feet up from here!"

Finndryl smirked. "Exactly."

Lore rolled her eyes and took a giant bite of the rock hare. "Oh—that's hot!" she said, huffing on the food, attempting to cool it down.

"It *just* got done," Finndryl said, his lips twitching upward. "Slow down."

"It's too good," she said as she took another large bite. "This is exactly what I needed after days of hardtack. I can't believe you caught three of them so fast," Lore said as the stirrings of an idea came to her. Possibly a way to make it inside the cave without being ripped apart by talons.

Finndryl stilled where he was plating another stone with sizzling meat and mushrooms. "Honestly, it's been a while since I've hunted—the land here is so dissimilar to back home . . . I'm a bit surprised as well." He glanced sideways at her before turning once more to his task. "It helps that there is more game here on the mountain than in the wastes."

"Is that for me?" Hazen called across the fire from his bedroll. Lore had thought he was asleep. "Or wait, Pytheah, do you want that serving?"

Pytheah stood up from where she was rummaging around in her pack. "None for me, thanks. I think I'm going to head out, actually."

Lore stopped chewing. Pytheah wasn't rummaging around in her pack; she was packing it. Lore placed the makeshift plate down and stood up, wiping her hands on her dress. "So soon?"

"I did what we agreed to. Got you to the griffins safely. Now I've got to do what I set out to do: find that treasure."

Lore nodded.

"Well—" Lore was cut off by Pytheah hoisting her into a fierce hug. Lore squeaked as the orc's tree trunk–size arms squeezed the breath out of her.

Pytheah's booming voice rumbled in her ear. "Goodbyes are most difficult when they are with a friend." Lore squeezed her back, though her arms didn't quite reach all the way around her torso.

"I hope . . ." Lore wheezed, ". . . this won't be goodbye forever!" Lore patted her back, gasping for air. Pytheah, realizing she was crushing the human, dropped her. Lore pulled in a breath, shaking with laughter. "Maybe we will see you back at Svalja's."

Pytheah was laughing too. "If the gods will it. But I still have days before I reach my next hunting location. I think this will be the one. When I'm rich and famous, I'll let you know of my success."

"I wish you many successes. May you return to Joya triumphant, with more than three camels' worth of gold!" said Lore.

Pytheah laughed before patting Finndryl on the shoulder; to his credit, he did not go flying into the mountainous wall but held his ground. Hazen squeezed Pytheah next.

Lore began to rummage through her purse; they hadn't ever agreed upon a price, now that she thought of it. How many coins should she . . . But Pytheah placed an enormous hand on her own and said gruffly, "Don't you dare think of paying me for guiding you here. It was my pleasure to get to know a human; you will make a fine addition to my stories."

"Are you sure? I can't thank you enough for being our guide and—"

"I'm sure. We are friends now. It is the least I could do."

"Well, friend. You will also be a great addition to my own stories. I can't wait to tell everyone I met the fiercest Reddy of all."

Pytheah's olive-green cheeks pinked with pride. She grinned, her tusks flashing in the sunlight, before flinging her pack over her shoulder and starting back down the mountain.

Lore watched her retreating form. She would miss her stories. *If the gods will it*, Pytheah had said. She'd gotten them here safely . . . strangers she'd met in an inn—it did feel as though someone was looking out for Lore.

"I hope that isn't the last time I see her," Lore mused aloud.

"Oh, it won't be," Hazen said, munching on a mushroom. "I invited her to my coronation."

Lore grinned. "You did? Wait, does that mean we are invited too?" Lore wouldn't think about the fact that, one day, she might be isolated behind a wall. That was too depressing, and right now, she craved hope and happiness. And another piece of rock hare.

"Of course."

"I can't wait to see how she fares underwater," said Finndryl with a smile.

Lore cackled. "All right—but imagine the treasure she could find with a Puallas Kiss!"

Hazen lightly bounced in place. "There are *so* many shipwrecks that I can bring her to."

"I hope she brings Joya," Lore said as she began to clean up dinner. She would have to dispose of the bones well outside of camp, lest they tempt a monster of some sort.

Hazen took a pull of water. "Me too. They make a cute couple."

Lore was about to agree when Finndryl cleared his throat.

"What is it, grumpy?" Lore asked, beaming at him.

"Cuuute." He leaned forward. "Not to wreck the mood . . . but when exactly are we going to the cave?"

Lore sighed, scooping up the last of the bones. "I was thinking . . . tonight. When I can use my powers."

"That works for me. That leaves time for a nap," Hazen said, cozying back onto his bedroll.

Lore paused on the edge of the campsite, animal bones in hand. She chewed on her lip, deliberating. "Actually, I was going to see if you and Finn would go hunting. A griffin is blocking the entrance to the cave, so we will need to draw it away with something."

A groan sounded from deep inside Hazen's bedroll. "You're messing with my beauty sleep, Lore!" Hazen whined as he unrolled himself with a huff, splayed out in dramatic fashion in the sand. "It takes more than genetics to reach this height of beauty."

"Stop complaining. It will build character," Finndryl said as he gathered supplies.

"I see why they call her a witch!" Hazen mock-whispered to Finndryl, though he winked at Lore.

"What was that?" Lore asked, faking offense.

"I said, I hope we catch something without a hitch!" the prince singsonged over his shoulder.

※

The males were hunting. Pytheah was gone. The quiet of the camp pressed in on Lore as she settled against the cliff wall at the back of their campsite.

Lore busied herself rolling up the bedrolls.

What would she find in the cave? What if it was a trap? Lore tightened the buckles on all three packs. Would she set foot in there and be buried alive? Lore poured sand over the burning coals of the fire. If so, she would never see the sun again, feel the wind on her face, or marvel at the shine of stars overhead. Lore collected a sprig of herbs, the roots of a bush, the leaves of a purple flower, and the venom of a red snake and stashed them in vials, hoping she would not need them.

It took forever for the sun to set, and yet it set too quickly. Lore walked toward the nesting ground, Finndryl to her left, Hazen to her right.

The day's activity was over, and the griffins lay on or around their nests, basking in the moonlight. Some preened their feathers, others nipped playfully at their young.

Hazen handed Lore the weasels he'd hunted. "Let's make this quick. Those beaks look fucking sharp."

"Lore, are you sure about this?" Finndryl asked as he unwrapped his own bundle of bloodied furs.

She hesitated, then met his gaze. "It should work." She eyed the griffins, whose hulking forms were utterly terror inducing. "I think." Lore coaxed *Source* from the grimoire, urging the breeze to kick up around them, hoping the scent would draw the griffins away from the cave entrance.

Finndryl, ever graceful, took the lead, his movements as silent as the desert wind. They crept along the cliff's edge, staying low to the ground as the griffins' cries grew louder.

Lore flung the first weasel into the open. The griffins' cries intensified into a hungry chorus as they descended upon the bait. She tossed another, its limp body tumbling toward the cliff's edge. Lore watched, a pang of guilt mixed with relief as a griffin swooped down, its sharp beak snatching the carcass midair.

Finndryl threw a third and fourth, igniting a frenzy of wind, feathers, and flapping wings.

With a smile playing on her lips, she whispered, "Distraction successful," gesturing toward the abandoned cave entrance.

Hazen eyed a carcass being fought over by two juveniles. "We had better be quick before the others realize how tasty we look."

Finndryl nodded, his expression turning grim. "The longer we delay, the higher the risk."

As Lore prepared to throw another, a movement caught her eye. A small, scrawny griffin chick, barely more than a fledgling, was pecking at the ground where the first weasel had fallen. Clearly the runt of the litter, its feathers dull and patchy, its pecks weak and listless, desperate hunger in its eyes. As Lore watched, one of its siblings snapped at the smaller chick before giving it a rough kick. It tried once more, but its sibling repeatedly shoved it to the side, denying it even a scrap of the feast.

It didn't have enough strength to even *fight*. Lore's heart ached for the outcast.

"Look," Finndryl murmured, his voice tinged with sympathy.

She couldn't let it starve. With a quick glance at Hazen and Finndryl, she made a split-second decision.

"Throw the rest," she whispered, "then run for the cave." Before they could protest, she moved forward with the last remaining weasel while chaos ensued as griffins jostled toward the feast. Lore carefully approached the chick, her movements slow and deliberate. It watched her with wary eyes, its beak slightly open in a silent plea. With a gentle, underhanded throw, she tossed the last weasel right to it, and it snatched it up with surprising speed. Lore held her breath as she watched the runt devour its prize, waiting for the inevitable backlash, but to her surprise, the other griffins seemed to have forgotten about the runt as they squabbled.

When the chick had eaten its fill, Lore gently stroked its ugly bald head. It leaned into her touch, a soft coo warbling from its beak. "There you go, little one," Lore whispered. "You deserve to eat too."

A shadow fell over them, and Lore looked up to see one of the adult griffins hovering above. Its keen eyes were fixed on Lore— its expression unreadable. Lore held her breath, unsure of what to expect.

But instead of attacking, the griffin dipped its head in a gesture of respect before flapping its powerful wings and launching into the sky.

Lore exhaled a shaky breath and raced toward the cave, her boots kicking up sand and feathers behind her. Her triumphant shout as she skidded into the cave was drowned out by the sound of the griffins' cries behind her.

CHAPTER 33

"It worked!" Finndryl shouted as he scooped Lore up into his arms. She kicked her feet up behind her as he spun her around, her laughter ringing through the cave.

"Save the celebration for later," Hazen's voice called from somewhere within the pitch-black cavern. "Can someone light a torch?"

Finndryl set Lore down, raising a hand. With a whoosh, his hand burst into flame—it was as though his hands were not flesh and blood and tendon but burning embers.

"Impressive." Lore grinned, widening her eyes as she mirrored his gesture. With a whispered word, her palm began to glow with silvery moonlight, illuminating Hazen's silhouette as they approached.

The cave wasn't very tall or wide, and Lore was thrilled to see that it didn't fork or branch off—a straight path. At least for now. However, the elation of making it safely past the griffins was beginning to wane as their footsteps echoed in the darkness.

Lore led the way, through tunnel after tunnel, always heading down. A few times, they had to squeeze through passageways one by one, turning sideways and sliding through.

Sometimes, they had to drop down through pitch-black holes, trusting Lore's faith in the book to guide them safely.

One less thing to worry about.

The deeper they walked into the twisting labyrinth of caves, the more *Deeping Lune* began to stir. It began to glow where it sat in Lore's satchel on her belt, and she could swear she heard it singing as if calling to its sister, *Auroradel*.

Lore placed her hand on the edge of the book and could feel it vibrating. It wanted to be reunited with its sister. Lore was happy that one thing wanted to be in these caves, because Lore did not.

Eventually they began to hear water dripping, and soon it puddled at their feet and trickled from stalactites hanging from the low ceilings. They had to maneuver around stalagmites, some as tall as Lore herself.

At a sudden skittering touch, Lore screamed. Finndryl's sword flashed, a low growl rumbling in his chest.

"What do you see?" Hazen demanded, a pair of curved daggers appearing in his hands.

"I'm sorry, it was just a bug," Lore stammered. "Or something. It scurried across my boot."

"A bug?" Finndryl asked, his voice deadpan.

"I hate them," Lore admitted, her skin crawling.

"I see." Finndryl sheathed his sword.

"It had about a million legs."

But Lore hadn't told him about her visions. Or the dreams that came to her every night now. Were they a cry for help from the grimoire? Or a warning?

Lore scratched at her arms. There were no bugs on her, but the feeling of just that one on her boot made her hair stand on end, and she could now feel phantom creatures.

They pressed onward.

"Do you hear that?" Hazen's voice came from behind Lore. She knew he was right behind her, but the echo in the cave made it seem as though he were far away.

Oh, goddess. "Hear what?" Lore squeaked.

"Singing."

Lore strained her ears. "Wait, yes. I hear it now."

A lilting tune was coming from farther in the cave. It was haunting yet comforting.

"Lore." Hazen's voice trembled. "Please tell me the singing is coming from your book and not a being luring us to our deaths?"

Lore cocked her head. Listening. She couldn't make out the words but . . . "I think it's the book. It's guiding us."

"Well, I wish it wouldn't." Hazen shuddered. "It sounds like a ghost."

"You are a siren and you don't like the singing?" Finndryl quipped.

"Our songs don't sound like this."

"Nothing natural sounds like this," Finndryl agreed.

But to Lore, the song was a beacon, a promise of the grimoire's proximity. And that, in this unsettling labyrinth, was a comfort.

They trekked. The passage of time seemed not to exist here. They could not see the moon as it traversed the sky or feel the sun's rays as they awakened the earth.

They walked in the dark, the weight of the earth oppressive above them. When they reached a tunnel large enough for them to sit, they rested. When they grew too tired, they dozed off for a bit, taking turns to keep watch. But never for long; always they pressed onward.

It must be day, but her book did not slumber as it usually did. Her magic continued to light their way. Was it because of the proximity of the sister grimoire? Could her *Deeping Lune* gift its sister's magic to Lore despite the moon being at rest? Despite her not yet making a bargain?

The tunnel they traveled began to narrow. The air grew humid, the sound of water droplets echoing louder. The rock snagged on Lore's tunic, and when she turned sideways, it squeezed her chest. Lore was small, and she could hear Finn and Hazen struggling behind her.

Finally, just when they all thought they could go no farther, the tunnel spat them out into a vast chamber. Moonlight, impossible moonlight for they were so far underground, spilled through a fissure in the ceiling, illuminating smooth, obsidian walls that shimmered with an ethereal glow like polished mirrors.

"Enchanting," Hazen breathed, his wide siren eyes reflecting the silvery light.

Finndryl, ever vigilant, drew his sword as he scanned the cavern. "No immediate threats," he reported. "Beautiful, but deceptive. I sense magic woven into this place."

Lore nodded, her gaze tracing the intricate patterns formed by water droplets clinging to the walls. "Moonlight and mirrors," she murmured. "An alchemist's playground."

A faint hum resonated through the chamber—the magic whispering.

Finndryl began to sweep the chamber, looking for a way out. "The corners are seamless," he remarked, running his hand along the wall in the far corner. "It's as though they were carved from a single block."

It was then that Lore's breath caught in her throat. The slim tunnel they'd just entered through was gone. It was as though it never was. In its place was a wall of unbroken obsidian.

"This must be a puzzle." Her heart drummed in her chest. "We are meant to find our way out." With a flick of her wrist she summoned her magic, the moonlight intensifying as it flowed through her. The water droplets quivered, shifting, morphing into tiny, shimmering mirrors.

Hazen swung around to look at Lore. "Whatever you are doing, it feels right. I can feel that the droplets are eager to join—become one."

The person who designed this chamber—this test—was the same person who made the grimoires. Lore unclasped her satchel and slipped out her grimoire. She turned it this way and that, studying it. What would Syrelle's grandfather have wanted when he built this chamber? There was a reason that moonlight filled it, not sunlight . . . though it was the sun book that was hidden somewhere in this cave system. Maybe it was a test only someone who had already procured the grimoire of the moon could solve.

"I wonder . . ." Lore directed the water droplets, weaving them into a complex arrangement on the far wall—a familiar pattern began to appear. A crescent moon, then below, a waxing moon, with the full moon in the center, only for the pattern to start over again in reverse, ending with a mirrored crescent moon at the bottom. Surrounding the moons was a circle of vines with small flowering buds. Moon moths circled the flowers in perpetual flight.

A perfect replica of *Deeping Lune*'s cover.

The moment the last droplet in the room settled into place, the obsidian wall began to shimmer as though it were made of water. All at once, the wall dripped down like liquid tar, revealing a corridor cloaked in shadow.

"Well done, Lore," Finndryl praised, his voice a warm caress in the cool air.

"Something tells me the book won't just be waiting for us when we walk through there," said Hazen as he followed Lore into the passage.

"Something tells me you are right," said Lore, the hairs rising on her arms as she spied a hulking form waiting for them at the other end of the passage.

A towering figure blocked their path—a sentinel between them and another cavern. Eight or nine feet tall, its skin was tree bark, its limbs branches. Lichen and mushrooms sprouted from its head. Its ears were elongated, pointed at the tips like daggers, twitching slightly as if listening to the silent screams of its victims. A cloying aura of decay clung to its bark, a smell of damp earth and rotting leaves, hinting at the unnatural power lurking beneath its skin.

"Don't bother turning around; the obsidian wall is back in place." Finndryl's voice was quiet beside Lore.

"Forward it is," she said and stepped onward, her gaze unwavering.

"To pass," the creature rumbled, its voice echoing through the cavern, "you must answer my riddle."

"We seek *Auroradel*, the Book of Sunbeams," she declared, "to restore balance to our world."

The creature's lips curled into a sardonic smile. "Pretty words, little witch, but you will not find what you seek unless you can answer my riddle."

"How many chances do I get?"

"One."

That wasn't very many. Lore wasn't even good at riddles! "What about my friends here? Do they each get a chance?"

The creature blinked eyes of unfathomable depths. "Only the one who seeks *Auroradel* may answer. Only the one who seeks *Auroradel* may pass through."

Lore squared her shoulders, preparing to get on with it, when Finndryl pulled her aside. "Lore, what do you know about this being? A reverie?"

"This is the first time I'm hearing about them."

"This creature is ancient and rare. I've only known one person who has ever even seen one . . . and lived to tell the tale."

"Oh, lovely. Wait, what happened?"

"My aunt Caia, my father's sister, was determined to make a name for herself—she wanted to be a legend. So Caia and her closest friend went searching for a pawa, a creature similar to this one— only if you answer its riddle correctly will it gift you one of its many ears. With one of its ears, you will be able to hear people's darkest secrets and greatest desires."

Lore's throat went dry. "What happened to your aunt Caia, Finn?"

"She answered the riddle wrong, so the creature ate her. It grew two more ears that day."

"I thought you said she lived to tell the tale!"

"Her friend is the one who lived to tell my father how his youngest sister died."

Lore felt queasy. "I see. So what you're saying is, if I answer this wrong . . . I won't just get turned away. The creature gets to eat me?"

"Yes. That is the bargain you make when you deal with reveries."

"Maybe we should turn back. There could be another way. We haven't even looked!" Hazen whispered.

Lore shook her head. "There is no other way." Without the grimoire, there was no way to save her people. There was no way to fix all the wrongs in their lives. *This was the only way.*

"Hazen is right. Lore, it is one thing to solve a puzzle; it is another thing to risk being *eaten*. Even with my new magic, even with a thousand swords, I would not be able to defeat this creature and save you."

Lore closed her eyes. This felt impossible, though she knew that *impossible* wasn't enough to stop her from trying.

And then a thought struck her. Was this why *Auroradel* had spoken to her in riddle form? Was it preparing her for this moment? If she could not solve its riddle, then she would not be ready. But she had, she had solved it. And here she was.

"And I would not want you to risk trying. Who else will tell my story?" She leaned up and pressed her forehead to his, breathing in his spiced scent. "I need you to trust me. Nothing in this world will stop me from reaching *Auroradel*."

"Come back to me, Lore." His voice was gruff, thick with emotion. "I am no writer; I can't tell our story without you."

Lore laughed, somehow, even though she was scared shitless right now. "Just as well. Nobody would read it if you wrote it. It wouldn't be funny at all."

His answering chuckle filled her with warmth. "I would write the facts and nothing more. Imagine how terrible it would be."

"It would put anyone to sleep who even dared read the first page. I'll *have* to come back to help you."

"Exactly. I want to write our story, as we live it—together."

She kissed him. He parted his lips, allowing her to explore

him, and she did, gripping his hair, pulling him down to her level, needing this, needing his strength, his pride, his confidence. When she came up for air, she felt as though he had imbued her with all of his best attributes.

She turned back toward the reverie. "I am ready."

The creature's answering smile wasn't one of joy or amusement; it was the leer of a predator, promising pain and suffering to its prey.

I am a mystery, a void profound. I am where silence resonates. I am avoided by youths, embraced by ancients. What am I?

Immediately, two answers came to mind, which was the worst thing that could happen when dealing with a riddle that had only one right answer. Lore wrung her hands.

Sleep?

She pictured the kiddos back home, how they hated bedtime and naps most of all. They pulled every trick in their cache to prolong the inevitable. And yet, the older one became . . . the more *ancient* . . . the more one longed for sleep, relished naps. But sleep was not a void. Sleep healed, it brought wellness and rest, and more importantly . . . it was filled with dreams.

So that left *death*.

Death was a mystery. For every species and every culture, there were a thousand answers to what death brought. And for many, it was as simple as a *void*. Ancients, tired of living, longed for death, while the youth avoided it at all costs. And yet, something in the back of her mind was screaming at her—that this answer was not right.

Her mind raced through her memories, through every late-night conversation with Grey where they pondered the complexities of life. She thought back to *Auroradel*. Did the answer lie there? It had given her a clue about the riddle. Prepared her for it, in a sense . . . she just hadn't known it. Had it tried to help her in another way?

The reverie licked its lips, it tasted her fear, hungry for her flesh.

Lore thought back to when she'd connected with the grimoire while scrying. It had shown her a vision . . . she had thought it was just showing her where it was. In a cavern, far beneath the earth. The reverie took an impatient, lurching step toward her, raising claw-like hands that dripped with decomposing filth, ready to grab hold of her the moment she uttered the wrong answer. Lore closed her eyes, blocking out the beast. There had been bugs . . . the stink of decay . . . the taste of rot . . . exactly how the reverie *smelled* . . . no, don't think of that now. *What else had it shown her?* She'd lost all connection with herself; she'd been cloaked, trapped in an impenetrable . . .

And then she knew the answer. Goddess, please let her guess be right. Please let *Auroradel*'s desire for freedom have led it to help her find the correct answer.

"Darkness," she gasped, opening her eyes. Her chest rose and fell with heaving breaths. The creature had closed the distance between them; it was poised right in front of her, its claws inches from her throat. She tensed, ready to call forth her magic, ready to *run*. She didn't care what bargain they'd made; she wouldn't be eaten without a fight.

The reverie retracted its claws, its leer falling from its face. "The witch may pass."

She'd done it! She'd answered correctly!

Lore found herself crushed between Finndryl and Hazen as they hugged her, jumping up and down with her.

"I hadn't been worried for a second," Hazen lied as he stepped back, his smile wide.

Finndryl said nothing, only kissing her on the mouth, his sword still poised in one hand. Lore kissed him back, salty tears wetting both their lips. If she had answered wrong, he would have died trying to protect her. Lore knew this. Lore hated herself for putting him in this position.

At least they would be safe out here in the corridor while she went forward and claimed her prize. She broke away, though it felt wrong to ever stop kissing him.

"It's time. When you see me next, I will be twice as powerful."

"I'm expecting you to blast a hole above us and carve stairs, so we don't have to find our way back through that labyrinth," Hazen joked.

"Twice as powerful doesn't mean I'll be a god who can mold the earth like clay, Hazen."

"A prince can dream."

Finndryl pulled Lore into his arms, enveloping her. Lore pressed her cheek into his chest, inhaled the spiced-bourbon scent. Finndryl's arms tightened around her. "I'm not sure what you will find in there, but you're the most resourceful person I know, and you're so damned smart. I know you will be successful, but more importantly, I need you to return to me, Lore, all right? I will be waiting for you on the other side." He pulled back slightly, his eyes searching hers, alighting across her face. He brushed a thumb over her cheek, her bottom lip. "I can't wait to see you in all your glory."

Lore swallowed back a sob. She wanted him with her. She wanted him by her side. But if this was something she had to do on her own . . . then so be it. Lore squared her shoulders and swiped a stubborn tear from her eye.

Finndryl dipped his head. Their lips met, the press of his lips tender and gentle. Lore wound her arms around his neck, pulling him closer and closer. She wanted to linger in this moment with him forever. But that wasn't possible. She broke away, her chest heaving, the threat of tears once again a battle. She pressed her cheek to his chest, inhaling his scent one last time, as though she could keep it with her.

Finndryl pressed one last kiss to her cheek, his words a choked whisper. "You're a marvel, Lore Alemeyu. You *can* do this, there isn't a doubt in my mind."

Lore sniffed and turned away, though putting space between them was one of the hardest things she'd ever done. She stepped back toward the sentinel and paused in the doorway, turning to look at Finn once more. "I will come back to you, Finndryl. I promise."

CHAPTER 34

Lore walked into blackness. Silence rang in her ears. She whispered a spell, but the light in her hand barely glowed. She tried again, urging it to brighten, but her *Source* was weak, as though suppressed by something.

Lore pressed deeper into the cavern, her breaths coming fast and shallow. The air was stale, as if there wasn't quite enough of it. It was heavy with the musty scent of stale earth. And something else . . . There was something rotting in here.

Something and not *someone*, she hoped. She couldn't handle another reverie.

The sound of dripping water echoed every now and then, each plop amplifying the silence that otherwise pressed against her ears. The silent flow of an unseen river rippled over her boots, a caress that sent shivers down her spine. The cave floor, slick with algae, threatened to betray her footing at any moment. Each step was a calculated risk, a gamble with the threat of a twisted ankle and a lonely demise.

She held her hand high above her, casting what little light she could. She glanced down and froze in place.

She was not walking in a river.

Insects covered the floor.

They crawled over her boots in a steady stream. She yelped and kicked them off. Her fear helped her light grow a little brighter, but these bugs did not have eyes to see, so the light didn't scare them away.

There were beetles whose exoskeletons shimmered in the light. Centipedes the size of her arm with hundreds of legs. Slippery, colorless salamanders that slurped up the bugs with ease. Lore wanted to scream. She wanted to run. To slip back into the corridor and tell Finn and Hazen that she couldn't find it. She'd failed, and gods, could they get the fuck out of here?

But no, she could feel *Auroradel* calling to her from beneath the earth. How it longed to be rescued from this hellscape. Lore blessed Finndryl in her mind and donned the gloves he'd made for her—though they were made of thin material and not, unfortunately, armor—and then she began to dig. The ground was soft clay; it dislodged easily. What wasn't easy were the bugs that clung to her fingers, pinching them or trying to crawl up her wrists.

The bugs had sensed her, and they were hungry.

They crawled up her legs, and onto her back. She brushed them off, but when she did that, the clay would fall back into place, filling the area she'd just cleared.

The clay was bitter cold, and it wasn't long before her fingers were numb.

Lore began to sob.

There must be a spell; there must be something she could do to keep the insects at bay; but her brain was barely functioning, such was her desperate, primal need to *run*.

A spider dropped down from the ceiling and landed on her cheek. Lore brushed it away along with hot tears.

As long as they stayed away from her ears and her mouth, she would be fine. She would find the book and get out of here. This would all just be a bad dream.

But the hole in the ground was getting quite wide and deep, and she still hadn't found the grimoire.

The bugs were more determined. One tried to crawl into her shirt collar, but, gagging, she squished it between her jaw and shoulder. She heaved, the contents of her dinner almost coming up.

The thought that this *was* a bad dream—another one of her nightmares—wound its way into her mind. This was futile. She wasn't ever going to find the book. The bugs would burrow their way into her clothes, tunnel into her skin, slither into her mouth.

Lore began to claw at the clay, not caring when a sharp stone jammed into her already broken and bruised nail beds. She ignored the pain and kept digging.

Finally, her knuckles rammed into something solid.

Not stone, nor dirt or clay.

She dug around it. Wood. A box. She brushed a bug with pincers away from her ear. She shook off a centipede that tried to wrap itself around her wrist.

With a groan she heaved the box up and out of the dirt.

It was bound with a silver chain, locked. She muttered a spell, hoping the mechanism would spring open. It didn't even tremble.

She flicked a bug off her ear and squinted in the low light of her glowing hand. The keyhole was obnoxiously small.

Syrelle's grandfather was damned thorough.

Survive hungry griffins, not die in a labyrinth of caves, solve a magical puzzle, answer a fucking riddle, not die from the terrifying bugs . . . and now she needed a key. Lore held in a wail.

She could do this, she could do this. She glanced around the cave. Was the key hidden somewhere in here? Maybe one of the bugs was key-shaped? She forced herself to look down at the swarming mass. With her luck, it was probably the one she'd squished. Its juices still clung to her jaw.

Just then, she heard a sound other than the slippery bugs. It sounded from above. It sounded again, and all around her the bugs scattered and fled, disappearing into gods know where.

Lore was almost too scared to look. She hadn't scared the bugs, but this did? Slowly, she lifted her gaze upward, not knowing what she would find . . . a spider the size of a dragon? Shit, at this point, would she really be surprised if it was a dragon?

Lore lifted her gaze up, up, up . . . and then she laughed. "It's you."

Perched on a jutting piece of granite was a griffin. A too-scrawny, underfed fledgling with a patchy coat. The runt.

It squawked at her, tilting its head back and forth before flapping ungracefully down to her. It landed on her outstretched arm, and she winced. Its back talons were quite sharp. She ignored the minor discomfort and petted its bald head. "How in the world did you get down here? Did you follow us?" It nipped playfully at her hand. "No, there is no way that Finndryl missed that. He would've smelled you." She supposed it was magic of some kind.

The griffin began to preen what few feathers it had while Lore rummaged in her pockets for jerky. When she looked back at it, jerky in hand, the chick held a feather in its beak. "Here, I'll trade you, some jerky for this fine feather." She tossed the jerky into the air and the griffin leapt off her, its beak open. She snatched the feather from the air, brushing her finger along its edge. The quill . . . she gasped.

The tip of the quill was shaped just like a key.

The griffins had been another test.

With shaking hands, she slid the quill into the lock and twisted. It opened with a *clink*.

She ripped off the chains and pried open the box. Inside was something wrapped in faded cloth.

She pulled it out with shaking hands. Brushed away a red spider that had tumbled from her shoulder onto the fabric.

The string was tied with an elegant bow.

All she had to do was untie the bow, and she would have her prize. Her fingers shook with cold, numbness, and terror as she gripped the edges of the silken bow.

Until Lore retched, gagging on . . . oh goddess. No, no, no.

That cloying, rotting stench that lingered underneath the smell of roach dung, of stale cavern air and mineral-rich clay . . . it tripled, quadrupled.

It filled her nose and mouth. Rotten flesh. Decomposing organs and muscle and sinew.

The smell of death is singular.

The smell of death was here.

Lore dropped one length of ribbon to cover her nose and mouth.

Beneath her knees pressed into the dirt, Lore heard a scraping sound. She scooted backward.

Could she run? Could she . . .

The hole she'd just dug began to tremble, the earth spreading on its own, a ravenous maw.

CHAPTER 35

Lore was a hairsbreadth from the exit to the corridor when a door slid out of the wall and slammed shut. One moment it was there, she was running straight toward it . . . She could practically see Finndryl and Hazen on the other side of the hulking reverie . . . and then . . . and then it was gone.

Just a wall.

"No, no, no," Lore mouthed as she tucked the book under one arm and began to swipe at the damp, mildew-covered walls.

Rough stone, slick muddy water, mildew, moss, algae.

Her exit was gone.

Hadn't she passed enough tests? Hadn't this been enough?

Lore heard a gasping, grating sound, something rattling, something viscous from behind her.

She spun around, holding her glowing hand up above her, casting it over the circular cavern.

And that's when she sensed Syrelle's powers. The dark, raw magic that *he* commanded.

"Syrelle?" she whispered, hopeful. She didn't want it to be him . . . but at the same time she did. She knew him. As much as one could know the enemy.

He must have followed her here. Maybe he got here first, hid himself from her somehow . . . Maybe the disappearance of the exit was just a glamour of his. All she had to do was convince him to make it reappear, let her free.

The rasping sound came again. Lore whipped her head side to side, searching the darkness.

"Syrelle, I can sense your magic . . ." *You're scaring me.* "Show yourself," she commanded, failing to conceal the fear in her tone.

There was something awful, terrible, in here with her, but where?

The light she cast wasn't bright enough to see more than three feet in front of her. Darkness pressed in from all sides.

"Mine . . . all mine . . ." the voice said.

This wasn't Syrelle's voice.

It was something *other.* It grated against her ears; shivers slithered up her spine. She ground her teeth as she backed into the cavern wall.

"Wh . . ." And then she saw it.

A decomposing body lumbered toward her. Its movements were *wrong.* It jerked and shook, halted and stumbled. Rotten flesh hung from bones like ribbons. Its eyes had decomposed long ago, or more likely had been eaten by the insects who made this cavern home.

She broke out in a cold sweat; shallow breaths burst in and out.

The thing . . . It had no lips, only hints of flesh that once were cheek, forehead, chin. Its hair was long, spun in braids that had sprouted moss and lichen. A cockroach slipped out of its gaping mouth and crawled up decomposed flesh to enter the hole where its ear should be.

Lore's eyes shuddered closed for a moment. She had to close them, for she was on the verge of retching from the scent, the sight.

This, like the bugs, was also a creature that made this cavern home, though it should not have a home.

It was obviously long dead. She felt faint. She held her breath, trying to stay quiet.

Go away, go away, go away!

Its haltering, shuffling footsteps stopped.

She steeled herself and opened her eyes once more, pleading to the goddess that it would be gone.

It was closer. Too close.

"Stay away from me," Lore gasped out. Gods, she had no room left to retreat.

Lore needed her dagger.

But one hand was her light, and the other gripped the book. She wouldn't have time to store it safely in her satchel. Her fingers numb and clumsy with terror, she hastily untucked her shirt, shoved the book beneath it.

"Who has come to steal what is mine?" The voice was clearer now. Less grating. Still, each word pierced Lore with terror.

Lore opened her mouth, working her jaw, but no sound came out. Finally, she uttered, *"Auroradel* called to me. I have come to claim it."

"Who has come?" The creature paused. It surveyed her, finding her wanting, despite its lack of eyes.

Lore cleared her throat, blinking rapidly. "I am called Lore."

"I do not recognize your scent." It could smell without a nose. How? "What species are you?"

"I am human."

"Huuumaaan." It stretched the foreign word. "You are not from this earth; I have traveled every continent, every ocean. I've never heard of your kind."

"I *am* from this earth. I was born here."

It remained silent. Pondering her response.

"You were born far from this cave, though."

"I . . . yes." What did that matter?

"And yet, this will be the place of your death."

The fuck it will! "I have no intention of dying today."

The thing jerked its shoulders and made a hacking sound. It took Lore a moment too long to realize that it was *laughing.*

"I suppose it will be a few days before you perish unless I am merciful and end you myself."

"Open the door. Let me go."

The thing twirled its hand. Dark magic swirled around the bones of its fingers. "I think not."

Lore sniffed the air. That magic. It was *his.* His scent . . . his signature. "Syrelle . . ." she whispered.

The thing tilted its head.

"That is a family name of mine. Why utter it now?"

Suddenly, Lore's eyes bulged. She straightened her posture as she realized with horror *who* she was conversing with. "Are you . . . Matleus?"

"Of course. Or were you not aware whose grave you were robbing?"

Lore quelled the urge to laugh or cry or throw up.

"I hadn't known that this was a grave at all, Matleus."

"Are humans often liars?"

"Many are. But I am not usually one. Your grandson, Syrelle, told me that your ashes were brought home a long time ago."

He harrumphed, not unlike an old man. "My wife no doubt spun this tale."

So, the story Syrelle heard . . . about his grandfather's ashes being brought to the widow by an owl . . . sent from an unknown source . . . was a lie. Because here were his grandfather's remains. Standing up. *Talking to her.*

A wave of dizziness washed over her.

"I must be going mad," she murmured. The only thing—the *only* thing she knew for sure was that death was final. She placed one hand on the cave wall, steadying herself. One did not just . . . come back from the dead whenever they pleased. Unless, of course . . . that being was so powerful an alchemist they created the two most powerful grimoires in existence.

"Mad?" He rubbed what was once a chin. "Perhaps."

He reached a bony hand toward her. "Give me my grimoire now. I am weary; I wish to rest once more."

"No."

"Wait." Matleus cocked his head to the side, not unlike a griffin. "*Deeping Lune*? Is that my *Lune*?" Lore felt the grimoire at her hip begin to quiver. She slapped her hand on her satchel, urging the grimoire to still. The creature took another step toward her. "How are you in possession of *Lune*? I closed the library off from all creatures save my family." He shook his head, his bones rattling. "No, I see. Human. A creature I did not include in the curse. Clever."

"You have your descendant to thank for that. Using a human to breach the cursed library was all his idea."

"My descendant? Where is he now? Why is he not in possession of my book? Why is he not here to rob his grandfather's grave?"

"*Deeping Lune* chose me."

"Impossible. I specifically told it to never choose anyone but me."

If Lore weren't on the verge of passing out from terror, she might have rolled her eyes . . . That response was so like something Syrelle would command if the books were his creation. Lore managed to control her shivering shoulders enough to shrug. "It belongs to me now, and I to it."

The dead alchemist leaned back on his heels, somehow managing to look down his missing nose at her. "The book is not something to belong to. It is a tool, nothing more."

"It is so much more than a tool. It is a companion. A confidant." She raised her chin in defiance. "It is mine, and I am *Deeping Lune*'s."

"Very well. It is fitting that you brought it here to be with its sister. Now they can rest together. Though . . ." Lore had the impression he was frowning. "I went to quite a lot of trouble to keep them separated." He reached out both decomposing hands now. Lore had to look away from the putrid liquid dripping off his wrists. "Give them to me; there is room in the box for both."

"I am sorry to have to do this . . . but *Auroradel* and *Deeping Lune* do not want to lie here with the bugs for the rest of time. They long to be free."

"You are a stupid creature, aren't you? The books are not to be listened to. They are books. What do they know?" He gave a long-suffering sigh.

"Why do this in the first place? To lock them up . . . it's evil."

"They are too powerful to be destroyed . . . When my health began to wane, I knew there was no way I could allow anyone access to this much power. They would only use it for evil."

"So you locked your people out of their entire wealth of knowledge? You buried the Book of Sunbeams far from the sun?" That sounded pretty evil to her.

"I will have my grimoires back now, small creature."

Lore raised her chin. "I will have the exit restored."

"It cannot be restored. You are locked in here now. I designed this spell myself. It is infallible."

"Then . . . undo it."

"If you haven't noticed, I am no longer living. How am I to call on that much *Source*? All I have left is this parlor trick." He shook his hand where the dark, swirling mist lingered.

The dead could not control *Source*, and yet his magic clung to him centuries later. That was how powerful he had been in life. Lore wanted that. She *would* have that—would wield such power that when she perished, *it permeated her very bones*. "I'll just have to do it myself, then," Lore said.

"You shall not!" He seemed affronted that anyone would defy his desire to have them starve to death in this cavern.

Fucking nobility.

It was slowly dawning on her that although the sight of him made her stomach heave . . . he was harmless. He'd created puzzles for anyone who sought out the grimoire, laid one last trap, and then he'd perished.

But there was nothing else he could do. As if he could hear her thoughts, the old bag of bones lowered himself onto the box. His breath came slowly, in a rattling wheeze.

Lore pulled *Auroradel* from beneath her shirt.

"Matleus. Why was Syrelle unable to find *Deeping Lune* when he searched the library?"

"I suppose his heart must not have been pure. I knew that not all my descendants who divulged they would be unharmed by the curse would have good intentions. I couldn't risk them finding *Lune*."

"And yet . . . *Lune*"—she tried out the nickname, finding that it suited the book—"found me."

"So say you."

Curses. This damned suspicious old gat.

"My standing here is proof that my heart is pure. Or do you have so little faith in your spell casting?"

He harrumphed.

"My people are in desperate need of saving. My only hope is to use the powers of both grimoires to protect them. No innocents will be harmed by me. I promise you that."

He remained quiet, listening.

"Your legacy will be safe in my hands. I will cherish them, care for them, and I will uphold your values."

The griffin chick squawked from its perch before awkwardly fly-falling to land on Lore's shoulder. It nuzzled its sharp beak in her hair for a moment before pulling out . . . a bug and swallowing it whole. Lore gagged; *gods*, it had been in her hair this whole time.

"You did pass the first test I set. Which, I am quite proud to say, ultimately becomes the most important. Nothing would have opened that lock without a token rightly earned from helping the weakest of the griffins."

"I hadn't even realized it was a test," Lore admitted, scratching the griffin's fuzzy wing.

"Which makes it more admirable."

She untied the bow and pulled *Auroradel* from the cloth.

"I'm so tired. This fear that my creations would cause pain and suffering has long kept my soul from resting. It would be a welcome thing to entrust that burden to another."

Lore raised her chin.

"I have carried burdens before, and this one I would shoulder willingly." Matleus did not answer, only gazed upon her as though weighing what she'd said.

Auroradel vibrated in her hands. Lore could not see what was stitched on it in the low light, and she tried to touch the edges as little as possible. Her gloves were filthy. She was filthy. She withdrew the gloves and cast them away.

With shaking fingers, she parted the bindings and opened the grimoire of the sun.

The cave became awash with sunlight and warmth. Immediately her fingers began to thaw. Lore wanted to shield her eyes from the bright light, but she kept them open, ignored the burn, and gazed upon the pages of *Auroradel*.

I am free.

"You are free."

My savior. And you have brought my sister to me.

"It's time to leave this prison. Will you guide my friends and me back?"

I will give you anything and everything you desire. I have been waiting for you so long, Lore Alemeyu.

"Shall we go?"

You must pledge yourself to me and I to you, and when we are as one, I will guide you home.

"Right now? We don't need to be in the sun or anything?"

The sun is with me; can't you feel it on your face?

"I can." Lore's eyes watered in the blinding light. "I pledge myself to you, be mine, and I yours."

A wave of *Source* exploded from the book as *Auroradel* ignited, bathing the chamber in light and warmth and life. *Source* invaded her body, and Lore accepted it willingly, as her body became inflamed with the heat of a star. It overtook her entire being, as though cleansing it. It was white-hot agony. It was glorious.

The blaze lasted a single breath, a moment, all of eternity.

It was the end of all things and the beginning of everything. It was pure power.

She was power.

When it was over, when they were connected as one, Lore heaved a breath, and it felt like the first she'd ever taken. She felt new and fresh and more wonderful than she ever had before.

Lore closed the book, extinguishing the light, and tucked it beside *Deeping Lune* in her satchel.

She gazed upon what was left of Matleus. Power thrummed within her, she vibrated with it. "My friends are on the other side of that door and I will go to them." Nothing would stand in her way now. She would blast a hole through the Golden Cascades if she had to. She flexed her fingers, feeling a jolt of *Source* hot and waiting beneath the surface of her skin. It was antsy. Ready to be wielded. "I would love to leave here with your blessing."

Matleus closed his eyes, a small smile playing on what was left of his lips. "You have it, then, child. Take my blessing. I shall rest now."

The door behind her slid open, and Lore could hear shouts from Finndryl and Hazen as they tried to get past the reverie.

"Rest, Matleus. And know that your creations will help restore balance."

A beam of moonlight pierced the ceiling, encasing the ancient alchemist in a radiant circle. From this circle, a faery ring of luminous mushrooms and moonflowers bloomed. The alchemist's form shimmered, dissolving into a flurry of moon moths that filled the cavern. Lore laughed, twirling with outstretched arms to marvel at the delicate white-and-green moths flickering like candlelight.

Lore stilled a moment amid the fluttering wingbeats to thank Matleus for allowing her to gain the knowledge and power she needed.

She had done it.

Now she could free her people, and no one, not even a king, could stand in her way.

CHAPTER 36

*A*uroradel and *Deeping Lune* worked as a compass, a guiding hand, a friend whispering in Lore's ear to lead them out of the cave system. But without Finndryl and Hazen, Lore would have been doomed to wander the desert forever.

The days blurred into a whirlwind of parchment and arcane symbols. She barely spared a moment for chatter with her companions, her focus consumed by the two grimoires she carried. Every possible second, whether resting beneath the scorching desert sun, shuffling through dunes, avoiding snakes, or huddling around a meager campfire, was dedicated to deciphering their secrets. The endless sands shifted around her, but Lore's mind remained fixed on the mysticism and spellcraft hidden within those ancient tomes—which, now that she possessed both, appeared infinite.

When finally the trio stumbled out of the desert, caked in sand and dust, Lore almost cried when they arrived back in Jamal and checked into the inn.

Joya was the one to book them this time. She was disappointed to see that Pytheah was not with them but was relieved to hear that they had not encountered any deadly dragons. After coin was exchanged, Joya led them to their rooms—Lore was delighted to see the steaming copper tub. On a small table sat tiny vials filled with soaps and oils and even—Lore squealed—lotion! She peeled the clothes from her body, stiff with salt, cave grime, caked mud, and sand; piled her clothes into a cloth sack with a stitched patch labeled *to be laundered*; and placed the sack outside her door.

Lore lay a fluffy towel across the arm of a chair and sank into the tub. The hot water immediately evaporated all the tension that she carried like a talisman on her shoulders. She dipped below the water and scrubbed her scalp.

She had to wash her hair twice before the stubborn grime was completely gone. She emptied one of the small vials of hair cream and began the process of removing knots and tangles until her coils bounced and gleamed.

When Lore was done, she rang Joya and paid extra for her to remove the embarrassingly gray and grimy water and refill the tub with fresh water that coiled peppermint-scented steam into the room.

The muscles in her arms aching from the simple act of detangling her hair, she laid her head against the copper tub and closed her eyes. Lore soaked in the new clean water until her fingers pruned and the water grew tepid.

If she was ever back in Jamal seaport, she would refuse to stay anywhere else but here.

When she finished her bath, a small copper bucket filled with fresh hot water was waiting by the fire. She rinsed off with that and rang for Joya to come and remove the water once more.

By the time that was done, she had wrapped herself in a robe and crawled into the cushioned bed. She was just about to doze off when a knock came at the door.

Lore opened the door a crack and peeked out. Finndryl was standing in the hall, freshly bathed, holding two glasses and a bottle of wine. He was wearing a cloth shirt and soft sleeping pants that tapered at his ankles. How did he look this good in *night* clothes?

"I thought you might like a glass of wine before bed." Finndryl usually oozed confidence, but now he looked *almost* nervous. He couldn't really be worried that Lore would ever turn him away, could he?

"I'm not dressed." Lore squeezed the panels of her robe tighter together.

Finndryl's eyes glinted with heat as they trailed over what he could see of her robe. Was he imagining what was beneath it? "I will never complain about your state of undress. But I can come back if you want to—"

"No, no need! Come in. I would love some wine." She held the door open for him to pass through, closed it, and locked it behind him.

Lore sat down on the bed as Finndryl opened the bottle with a wine key he procured from a pocket and poured the wine into the glasses.

"When did you get the wine?"

"Svalja has a small shop downstairs for patrons; there was . . . an overwhelming selection of wine on the shelves." He sank down beside her on the bed. "Remind me to return the wine key when we check out. They charge if it's not returned, and the fine is at least six times more than one of these would normally cost."

"Svalja knows how to run an inn. I imagine wine keys went missing quite a lot before she made that rule—oh gods, this is yummy." The wine had hints of sugared black cherries with dark-chocolate undertones.

"Mmm," he intoned. "Dangerously good. I wish there was a way to serve this at the Dragon's Exile—people would go wild for it."

"Let's make a deal. When this is all over, we will come back here and stay for a whole week. When we leave, we will buy a crate or three to take back to your father's tavern."

His eyes swirled with warmth at the thought. "A week here with you would be lovely."

They clinked glasses, the sound of the crystal pealing throughout the room, and both took another sip.

Finndryl sighed and twirled one of Lore's curls between thumb and finger. "Tomorrow—"

"Tomorrow is unknown. And the thought of it . . . Let's not talk about tomorrow just yet."

Lore placed her glass on the bedside table and plucked Finn's as well, before turning toward him, suddenly shy. Her robe slipped down from her movement and her shoulder was kissed by the warm air in the room. She looked back at Finn and saw his eyes greedily drinking in the view of her exposed skin.

"I didn't come here to discuss tomorrow, anyway," he said. His voice was low, hungry.

Lore bit her lip. "What did you come here to discuss?"

"I didn't come here to discuss anything. I had other things in mind, if you're so inclined."

"Oh really? Like what?"

His reply was simple. He closed the space between them.

There was nothing gentle about this kiss. He was all hunger and need. She opened herself to him, parting for his tongue to enter, searching, tasting, reverently, like she was the nectar of the gods.

And him? He tasted like heaven.

Heat cascaded from the melding of their lips down to her core, and Finndryl placed his hands on her back, pressing her to him.

"You always have good ideas," Lore said against his lips. She couldn't help but smile. She always wanted to smile when he kissed her; the simple fact that he wanted to kiss her made her giddy.

He grunted his reply, perhaps too preoccupied with the feel of her in his arms to think of something witty to say. Lore pushed her hands beneath his shirt, searching for the smooth swath of skin there. He shivered under her touch.

She marveled at the heat releasing off him. He was burning, burning, burning for her, and she felt it too. His chest began to vibrate, a resonance building within him. She could feel her own magic responding to his. It swelled within her, this new sun magic. She broke the kiss for a moment, and yes, her hands had begun to glow beneath the fabric of his shirt. "That's new," Finndryl said, his voice breathy. His lips were swollen from their kiss, his face flushed, and his midnight eyes glistened with desire.

He was magnificent.

Lore reached up and felt her own swollen lips. Knew her still-damp hair must be wild from where he'd gripped it. But Finndryl was looking at her like she was a goddess. She'd never felt more beautiful than she did right now. His gaze dipped from hers down to her lips, where her fingers gently prodded them. A smirk fluttered across his lips for just a moment before he removed his shirt. He tossed it onto the floor before kissing her again, pulling her bottom lip into his mouth and biting it.

Lore moaned; his canines were sharp, and the bite of pain was entrancing. She ran her hands up the long sides of his torso, moving them to his chest. His skin was pure heat, molten, and it melted all thoughts from her mind save for one.

Need.

She needed him.

She needed to feel him, to have him, to be his and have him be hers, completely.

Lore rose up on her knees and climbed into his lap. She didn't care that the short robe she wore would hide nothing. He'd seen her naked in the library—well, almost naked—and here he was—come back for more.

Finndryl gripped her and guided her hips down on his lap, positioning her just right. The tempo of their kiss increased as Lore ground herself against him. He was so fucking hard; his own need was obvious, pressed up against her, straining against his pants.

Finndryl's breath stuttered when she pressed into him, and he groaned. Lore, emboldened by this, clasped the edges of her robe and pulled the fabric to the sides, letting the cloth slip to the floor to join his shirt. Revealing herself to him completely.

Her deep, raised scar beneath her breast, where a fae male far away had dug his knife into her. The slashing scar on her arm, which still to this day prickled when she touched it, the poison the guard had used leaving its mark in not just a scar but in feel as well. Finndryl had risked his life sucking the poison from that wound. He'd saved her that day, when Lore had been sure he hadn't cared about her at all. The newly healed web of slashes from the sailors aboard the ship. Her mind shuddered at the memories, all the ways that she had been cut and scarred. She didn't want to think about how he could now see all these blemishes that marred her skin, more than just the childhood scars everyone in Duskmere had. A natural effect that came with being raised poor, in a community deprived of medicine and enough to eat.

Finndryl's eyes widened, and his breath caught in his chest. He saw the pattern of wounds on her skin, and yet his eyes did not shy away. They ignited with something else, something deeper, that shone through him, surpassing even the lust. "You are more beautiful than I had imagined, Lore. And yes, I've been imagining what you look like since you walked into the Exile with that unabashed look of wonder you wear anytime you enter somewhere new. Like you're the main character in a storybook, and you are watching your adventure unfold."

"I thought you hated me . . . back then."

Finndryl growled. "I despise almost everyone, but never you." He wrapped his arms around her and pulled her to him. Her bare breasts pressed against his chest, and he tasted her, drank her in like she was the richest wine. The ripest fruit. "Lore." He whispered her name against her lips, as though she were his salvation. Goosebumps broke out across her skin, and she sighed into him.

Finndryl hooked his hands beneath her thighs, stood up, and flipped her around so her back was on the bed. He fell with her, his lithe body above her, perfectly positioned between her legs, which were spread wide, wrapped around his waist.

Finndryl gazed down at her, his ink-black eyes reflecting the firelight, making them dance. Shadows swirled around his locs, kissed his cheekbones. He was ethereal. He was beauty. She raised an arm and put it flush with one of his, forearm to forearm. Their Puallas Kisses matched up; one couldn't tell where one's lines started and the other's ended.

"You already have all of me, Lore. Would you give yourself to me this night?" His voice was low, hesitant.

Lore knew that if she shook her head no, he wouldn't press.

Finndryl groaned, pressing his face into the hollow of her throat. He breathed her in, waiting. He knew that she had wanted to keep her distance. He knew she was trying to protect the both of them. And yet she knew he couldn't help himself. He'd *had* to ask. Because she felt it too. This need. She was tired of denying herself.

Warmth spread through her body; her core clenched at the feel of him against her. The glorious weight of him on top of her, pressing her into the quilt.

Tomorrow was unknown.

But tonight, they were warm and safe. They were together. How could she deny herself this sweetness? When she had saved her people and placed them in a world where nothing could hurt them . . . memories of tonight with him would sustain her.

Her heart was foolish; her heart yearned. For him. And here he was.

"You have me, Finndryl."

"I am yours until the seas run dry and the earth dissolves to dust."

He pressed a kiss on the sensitive skin on her collarbone, butterfly light. He kissed the skin of her chest. Lore's lips parted.

She was trembling. He dragged his hand up her side and cupped one of her full breasts. He pulled one of her taught nipples into his mouth, swirling the bud with his tongue before giving it a light bite. Lore gasped and squirmed beneath him.

Her heartbeat roared in her ears and pulsed in her core. She ground against him again. *Gods, his pants had to go.*

She yanked at the strings on his pants, her fingers tingling with the need to touch him. These needed off. But the damned strings were being stubborn.

"In time, honey. Let me worship you." He slipped down, kneeling on the floor. He cupped her thighs and pulled her forward until her ass was on the edge of the bed. He cupped her ankles and gently placed one foot on his broad shoulder and then the other.

Lore held her breath as she flooded with heat. She might die at the vision of him between her legs.

He kissed her inner thighs while caressing each one with his large hands. "Tell me what you desire, Lore. I want to hear you say it."

Lore bit her lip before admitting, "I want you to taste me."

He rumbled his satisfaction. "Good girl."

He kissed his way to the apex of her thighs and tasted her with his lips, his mouth, but it was his tongue that set her ablaze. He lapped with his tongue, swirling it around her clit, like he had her nipple, before changing course; back and forth, back and forth, he worked her with a beautiful pattern. Lore began to pant.

She threw her head back, and closed her eyes, writhing with pleasure. Finndryl was on his knees, worshipping at the altar of her. She dug one hand around his soft locs and moaned. He growled with pleasure at this, liking the feel of her hands on his hair.

He pulled her bud into his mouth and sucked. Lore arched her back—hissed as vibrant sensations sent lightning bolts through every corner of her body. He did it again, tugging on the bundle of nerves. Lore clenched her thighs together against his head, her body completely out of control; she dug her hands into his hair, gripping it harder. "Oh gods, Finn," she moaned, gasping. He worked her with the rhythm of an expert musician, until Lore came apart beneath him.

She cried out as waves of pleasure rocked through her body.

He licked her, pressing his tongue inside her, lapping up her pleasure.

"You taste like marigolds and honey, honey," he said as he stood up. Lore eyed him from where she lay.

He was all long and lean muscle, but his shoulders were incredibly wide, and his physique was well-defined from years of training with his broadsword. His eyes were heavy-lidded, ablaze, and glassy with desire. They homed in on her body with a predator's gaze. Everything about him screamed *lethal*. His cheeks flushed. Corded muscles rippled in his abdomen, and she eyed the V that slashed into the waistband of his low-slung pants.

She wanted to reach for him, but she couldn't move; she was still riding little waves of pleasure that, even after her release, jolted through her.

Aftershocks of absolute satisfaction.

Finndryl swiped a thumb across his full lower lip and grinned. "Are you ready for me, Lore?"

With those words, she could move again. Because, gods, yes, she had never been more ready for anything in her life. Everything she'd done, every decision she'd ever made, had led her to *this* moment.

With his long, nimble fingers, he untied the drawstrings on his pants with a flick. Lore sat up, looped her fingers in the waistband of his pants, and pulled. His length sprang free. It stood at attention, hard and glistening. Her mouth watered at the sight. His girth was substantial. She'd only ever been with human men, and they were unimpressive compared to him. He was going to fill her up. Stretch her out.

Lore gripped Finndryl's hips and tugged them toward her.

"I'm ready."

He stepped out of his pants. He let her pull him down onto the bed with her. He covered her body with his. His strong arms enclosed her.

She felt sheltered beneath him. He was her shield, her defender, she had never been safer than in this moment.

He gripped his length in his fist and stroked it absently as his eyes raked over her naked body. He licked his lips, and from the look in his eyes, Lore knew that he was tasting her on them.

"I'm ready, Finndryl," she repeated, just in case he hadn't heard her. Gods, she needed to feel him inside her. She wouldn't have to imagine it anymore when she was alone at night, as she slipped her fingers beneath her dress. This was going to be a thousand times better than her waking dreams because this was *real*.

And the anticipation was *killing* her.

He positioned his head at her entrance and pressed the velvety tip of his length against her, rubbing it against the sensitive bud, her wetness that was glistening in the soft curls there. He shuddered with pleasure at just the *feel* of her.

She wriggled her hips and spread her legs wider. Was she going to have to beg? She *would* beg.

But still, he was resisting.

Not giving her what she wanted—which was *him*. Inside her. Now. He swirled his head on her bud again. Lore wriggled her hips, lifting them, and pressed down on his hips, trying to guide him inside her.

"You're so wet for me, honey. You want this, don't you."

"I need it," Lore gasped.

He growled and spoke in a low, stern voice. "Say please, and I'll give you what you want."

Lore melted at his words and wasted no time. "Please. Please, Finn."

He growled his approval, soaking this moment in, before finally, he conceded.

He pushed into her slowly. Was he afraid to hurt her because of how big he was? Her body accepted him eagerly. He slid inside without any resistance at all—she was so wet. She felt her body stretching eagerly to accommodate his girth. He leaned down toward her, pressing his face into her hair; a groan of pleasure rumbled in his chest.

"Gods, Lore, you feel so *good*."

He pushed until he filled her to the hilt and held himself there, relishing the feel of her. Lore could feel the strain in his body; he wanted to pound into her, shove himself inside, but he was being so careful with her, like she was precious and the last thing he would want to do was let her break in his care.

He slowly pulled back and then entered her again, another groan of pleasure rumbling through his chest. Lore moaned at the sensation and wrapped her legs around him, drawing him closer. He began to thrust inside her, picking up a steady cadence.

The feel of him inside her, around her, above her—this might be what they meant when the elders spoke of heaven.

"Faster, Finndryl," she panted between breaths, "you won't hurt me." Lore gripped his shoulders, pressing her nails into his skin, raking them across his back. The sensation of her nails on his back, and her insistence that he wouldn't hurt her, broke all his resolve. His mouth crashed into hers, he kissed her long and hard. He shifted her, pulling her thigh up, which allowed him to go even deeper. She began to move in time with him, relishing the feel of him. He was through with being gentle. They needed this, they needed to feel this, to be this close.

Closer.

Closer.

She could hardly breathe. All she knew was the feeling of where their bodies met, how she was whole. This was what it meant to feel complete.

"Harder," she begged.

"You want me to go deeper? You were made for me, Lore." He groaned, increasing his thrusts, pounding into her, and she opened wider for him, demanding all of him. "You take it so well. Such a good girl." He reached a hand between them and pressed gently on her lower stomach, and Lore cried out because the feel of him inside her became even more delicious, more intense; gods, this was *everything*.

"You're taking me so well," he growled. "You feel so good, Lore, I don't ever want this to end," he said, his voice thick with emotion.

His words and increased friction balanced her just on the edge of bliss; all thoughts fled her brain. He shifted his position slightly, and oh *gods*, his shaft was stroking her bud now with every thrust, and this was it, this was—

The world turned to stardust.

Lore became undone beneath him. She cried out his name, not caring that they were in an inn with people on either side of them; she didn't care about anyone else on this entire earth right now, because she had lost herself to wave after wave of pleasure.

He continued to thrust into her and reached down, swirling his thumb on her bundle of nerves. Lore cried out; it was so sensitive, but, oh gods, *oh gods*!

"—give me one more, honey, let's go together."

And they did. They crashed together.

Lore cried out, tears burning her eyes, soaking into her hair, as her body shook with waves of pleasure so intense her fingers and toes went numb. He cried out in pleasure as he tipped over the edge with her, letting his own release envelop him.

Lightning bolts shattered her mind.

Finndryl shuddered above her, his length throbbing inside her as she pulsed and tensed with waves of pleasure around his girth.

He pulled her to him, pressing her into his chest, his hand gripping the back of her head, and Lore went limp beneath him as a sob rocked through her body.

She felt utterly complete, whole.

Finndryl kissed her tears, and Lore cupped his face, running her thumb along his cheekbones. His own cheeks were wet with tears.

"You don't have to pull away anymore. I won't hurt you. I'll never hurt you, Lore." He kissed her lips and nuzzled into her hair. "I've been lost for as long as I've been alive. It wasn't until I met you that I realized where I was meant to be."

"And where is that?"

"At your side. You're my guiding star, and I've been lost at sea." He pulled back until he could see her. "Everything that I cherish dwells in your eyes. You're all I need. All I want."

She couldn't let fear limit her anymore. This was it, this was . . . "You have me. Every part of me. Forever."

Joy radiated from him to her; from her to him. It swirled in the air around them, kissed their glistening skin, and settled into them.

He rolled onto his back, and Lore nuzzled into his chest, listening to the steady beat of his heart.

The love she felt for him was written on her bones. This she would fight for with her every breath. She would give up everything on the quest to save Duskmere—save this.

She would never, could never, give him up.

CHAPTER 37

The following morning, in the dusty air of Jamal market, Lore pushed through throngs of early morning shoppers, stepped around overfilled stalls, and avoided eye contact with hawklike merchants ready to haggle with her until they were blue in the face. She'd emptied her pack at the inn—donating her supplies to the designated Reddy bin, a basket in the library filled with provisions for Reddies just starting out on their journeys, or others who might have found themselves at the wrong end of a bandit's sword—and now it sagged on her shoulders, filled to the brim with food that, with the help of a spell from *Deeping Lune*, would keep until her arrival in Duskmere.

She heaved a sigh of relief when the crowd thinned enough for her to spy the docks.

First light had barely breached the unending expanse of sea, and already teams of travelers roamed the wooden docks, loaded down with valises, packs, and crates. Sun-stained fishermen sang bawdy chanteys as they wrestled with ropes and hauled their cargo up and down gangways. Traders and skilled artisans hawked their merchandise at passersby in a dozen tongues, the cacophony of languages and dialects a song when paired with the creaking of ships, the flap of sails, and the piercing cry of gulls overhead. The smells of smoke, fish, citrus, and spices mingled with the salt-laden air.

When Lore arrived at an empty bench, she heaved the over-stuffed pack from her shoulders and plopped down to people watch. But as the minutes ticked by, all she could focus on were the grimoires nestled in the satchel at her waist. She checked and rechecked both books. Then she tested that the leather straps were secure—that they had not warped or frayed. Then, the golden clasps.

And then she verified it all over again.

Lore couldn't shake the feeling that she had a target on her back. That thieves were lurking in every shadow, behind every stack of barrels. She felt like she was walking around with a golden chain or a crown studded with rubies and sapphires on her head. A sign lettered on her forehead that said: *"Hello, I am wearing items more precious than gold—please rob me."*

These thoughts ricocheted through her mind.

Fisting her hands in her skirts and stopping herself from en-suring that the books were there was a constant command she had to relay to herself again and again. Because if she drew any more attention to them, then everyone would know, right? How valuable these were. How precious.

And if a group of hardened criminals snuck up behind her and cut her belt with the sharp end of their knife, would she be able to get the books back?

Yes, she reminded herself. Lore was powerful now—even if the books were taken from her, she would find them.

Lore scanned the seaport, letting the salty desert air calm her nerves. Finndryl had secured passage on a ship for the three of them. Another bell remained until boarding. The *Constellation Weaver*—the colossal vessel before her—the one adorned with star-studded sails and gargoyles so realistic Lore wondered for a moment if her unease came from their stone-eyed stares.

It wouldn't be long before Finn and Lore would be in their private cabin. Hazen had requested his own. Camping with them the last week had been enough for him, apparently. She didn't blame him. One more bell and they could board. Then, two weeks of travel. Two weeks and they would be on the same continent as Grey and Eshe and Milo.

No, Lore knew it wasn't the gargoyles giving her nerves. She was filled with trepidation because soon she would be home, and she had no idea what awaited her. She had no idea what state Duskmere was in. Was everyone safe? Duskmere was still clouded in an impregnable fog, and even with *Auroradel*, when she'd tried scrying that morning in the washbasin at the inn, Lore could not break through the spell. She prayed that everyone was safe. That the king had not retaliated against them.

Of course, if everything went according to plan, in a month's time, Duskmere would be long behind them. Duskmere would be nothing more than a bad memory—a nightmarish tale the children of today could one day spin to their grandchildren.

Two weeks and Lore would be there with the power of not just the moon but the sun itself. She would ignite the humans' fury, defeat the King of Alytheria, and together the humans would make a bright future.

One more bell. Two more weeks.

One more bell . . . two more weeks.

Why, then, did she feel as though everything would go wrong? If not bandits on the wharf, then a faction of pirates could appear out of the blue and attempt to take them. She'd heard stories of slave traders capturing entire ships and selling them to the lands in the west, where flesh was still bought and paid for.

Maybe a goddess would decree Lore's plans too lofty for a human and descend from the heavens just to smite Lore where she sat on this very bench waiting for Finn and Hazen to return from the harbormaster's office.

Lore checked the sky. No enraged goddesses to be seen. Just circling gulls. And it appeared that there was about . . . three-quarters of a bell left to boarding. Already the wharf had quieted a bit as the fishermen sailed their boats out to sea, off to catch a day's worth of fish.

A travel barge was heading out. It had the same look as the one they had arrived here on. Lore shuddered at the thought. The *Constellation Weaver* would be much better—no cramped quarters or rats. Soon, Lore, Finndryl, and Hazen would walk up the ramp, hand over their papers, and find their cabins.

Lore couldn't help but wish she had a coffee. With regret, it dawned on her that she'd neglected to inquire about purchasing that assassin romance from the inn's library. Anything to help her pass the time and stop her from checking for the thousandth time that her books were there. Her bag was on the wooden deck at her feet. Nothing was missing. Everything was going according to plan.

Lore leaned forward and placed her head in her hands. Her nerves were going to flay her alive. She decided to practice Uncle Salim's breathing exercises.

Inhale. Exhale. Inhale. Exhale.

Half a bell.

And then two weeks.

That was it. Half a bell . . . and then two weeks.

Where were Finn and Hazen? They should be back by now. Finn was quiet in the mornings; it took him longer to wake up. Even with a cup of strongly brewed coffee or an entire pot of tea, he remained stoic. But Hazen awoke with a grin on his face, no coffee needed. The siren prince could have two bells of sleep and still arise ready to take on the day. Lore needed that kind of energy around her right now. Hazen would distract her.

Where was he?

Gnawing on her lip, she searched the crowd for a tall male with shaggy hair and swirling tattoos on his face. Or Finndryl, who would no doubt be leading the way, his long legs eating up the distance of the dock, oozing confidence, parting the travelers as water eddies around stone.

Nobody stood in his way; it just wasn't a thing people did.

Lore didn't even think Finn noticed he had that effect on everyone. A crowd of people, sea-hardened sailors, merchants carrying stacks of ledgers, a gaggle of high-class ladies on a shopping splurge. Everyone naturally parted for him to walk through.

And then Hazen would be at his side or, more likely, slightly behind Finn because he'd gotten distracted by something—a pretty male or female who caught his gaze, a shiny necklace that just *had* to be added to his growing collection of jewelry. He was going to have quite the hoard to show off upon his return to Lapis Deep. Screw finding a small painting of each location during his travels to bring home; he would possess a piece of jewelry from every city.

Lore's gaze skimmed over countless faces. She liked this port city. There was every type of being here. Big, small. Light fae, dark fae, water sprite, siren, tree nymph, orc, everyone living, working, and traveling in peace.

One day, if the humans chose to leave their new home, some might choose to live here.

She continued to scan the dock, when something caught her eye. Not something—*someone.* Lore froze as dread filled her belly and her heart leaped into her throat.

Fight or flight.

Flee, and maybe he wouldn't catch her.

Freeze, and maybe he wouldn't see her.

But of course Syrelle had already seen her, and within a breath, he was looming above her, his gaze a heavy weight.

He'd come for her grimoires.

"Hello, Mouse," he murmured. "I see you've survived the Golden Cascades."

"How did you—"

"Did you think I would not be watching over you?"

"I don't understand. You said you were going home."

"Home?" His face twisted on the word, like it had a bitter tang to it. "No, I didn't go 'home.' I've been in Ma Serach. If I had shown myself before now, I would only have served as a distraction. The only way you would succeed in finding *Auroradel* unscathed was if I held to the shadows."

He stepped closer to where she sat frozen on the bench. She felt like a mouse, indeed, too scared to run and hide when faced with a lion about to pounce.

The salted breeze picked up and swirled her curls. Lore pushed them back from her face.

Syrelle's nostrils flared. He sniffed the air, and his face shuttered. His eyes widened, and then . . . they darkened. His lips spread into a grimace.

"You smell like *him*." His voice was a growl. Lore flinched back from the fury emanating from his eyes.

She raised her chin in defiance. "As I should. I woke up beside him this morning."

Syrelle's hands, which had clenched into fists at his sides, relaxed, and his expression went cold. "I see."

His words had a bitter sting to them that Lore rejected on principle. She threw up her hands in exasperation. "What did you expect? That I would forgive you? Even now, another lie, as you continue to make decisions for me, manipulate me, keep me in the godsdamned dark. Even now, you are here to take from me." She gripped her satchel as if that would stop him from cutting her belt and taking the books from her. Or using his magic to freeze her in place once more, his deft fingers unlatching her belt and taking the books as unhurried as he wished.

Syrelle followed the movement of her hands and, for the first time since he'd surprised her with his presence, his gaze dropped to the satchel on her belt holding the two grimoires. He barked out a hollow laugh.

Lore shivered at the sound. There was something *off* about it.

"Here to take from you? These grimoires that are my birthright?" He narrowed his eyes at her; his voice dropped low, thick with emotion that she couldn't quite pinpoint. "If you had let me, I would have been the salvation of your people and mine."

What? If she had *let* him? Why was he pretending that this conflict between them was in the past? Maybe he felt so close to having what he wanted that it *was* over for him. Her mouth screwed up in confusion. Why was he pretending he'd been here the whole time?

If he had known she'd found *Auroradel*, he would have cut her off the first chance he'd gotten and taken the book for himself.

He'd been clear that that was his plan—she would lead him to the grimoire, and he would bond it to him, harnessing that power. He would use it to overthrow his uncle. Crown himself king. Then he would fix the fertility problem of the Alytherian fae while slapping a useless bandage on the hindrance that was Lore's entire community. Her entire world.

So, was him being in Ma Serach all along the lie? She wanted to scream in frustration.

Syrelle was playing a new kind of ruse, or game, and Lore couldn't parse the rules. She shook her head, feeling irrational.

"You are mistaken. They could not be your birthright, because you called *Auroradel* and *Deeping Lune*, and they denied you. They *chose* me."

A muscle in his jaw pulsed. "Yes. They chose you. And you chose him." Syrelle ripped his gaze from hers and looked out at the sea, running his hand across his short hair.

"His scent is twined with yours, as if . . ." His voice faltered for a moment. He swallowed. ". . . as if you are one being."

Lore had failed to best him. Again and again she failed. Despite her tries, Syrelle . . . he had always been stronger than her. More cunning. He'd held power over her since the beginning. Always putting his wants above hers. And yet, she could see that despite him baffling her now, he was hurt by Finndryl's scent being tied to her own.

Truly hurt.

She was furious with him for pushing his feelings on her. She could not have chosen him after what he'd done.

She ignored his confusing words and focused on the one thing she could control when it came to him. And, yes, at this moment, she relished his pain, and she wanted to hurt him more. "Yes, I chose him. I *choose* him." She spat the words, wielding them like poison-coated daggers. She wanted them to cut him, peel away his confidence. "The choice was easy, as you were *never* an option." She huffed a laugh, checking her nails. "You've turned bitter, Syrelle, and I've just gotten better."

He flinched away from her as if her words had indeed harmed him.

"Easy?" A hollow, humorless laugh of his own cleaved free from his chest. "You claim that there was 'never a choice,' but you loved me once." His gaze swept away from hers, over the wharf, but his look was distant. He wasn't truly seeing the commotion of the port. "Just know, I wouldn't have made you choose." When his gaze landed back on her, hurt and fury and something else—something Lore refused to acknowledge—churned in his eyes. "I wouldn't have made you choose. If you had wanted, you could have had us both."

Lore shook her head, her own mirthless laugh tumbling from her lips. "In another life, maybe I would have chosen Asher and Finndryl. But Syrelle? Syrelle was never a possibility." She wanted him to feel this pain. For once, *she* was doing the hurting.

Lore frowned. She just wished that this felt like she thought it would. Since she had seen him last, something had changed within him. It soured her desire to wound him.

Syrelle's gaze locked on hers. He worked his mouth as if to say something else to her, but then he closed it, drawing his lips into a rigid line. His eyes searched her face, alighting on every corner. Snagging on her freckles, her riotous curls that had tumbled into her face. Her lips and, lastly, her eyes. As if memorizing her features, as if he wanted to be able to picture her later.

Lore's brows drew together in bewilderment. And then she saw him, really saw him.

The bones of Syrelle's wrists jutted out beneath the sleeves of his shirt. His cheeks were hollow; his normally lustrous, deep-mahogany skin was sallow, and his eyes were ringed by dark smudges. He'd lost weight.

Worry tightened her chest.

What was going on with him? She didn't know how to react to this adjacent version of Syrelle. This frightened Lore. She revisited their conversation.

Had he *not* come to gloat before taking her grimoires by force? She had not had time to master *Auroradel*, and her magic during the day was unpredictable, too powerful at times, and nonexistent at others. She'd almost boiled herself alive this morning when she'd tried to raise the temperature in the bathtub a fraction. She was sure he suspected this. He was a proficient alchemist. Was terrifyingly strong and adept at wielding *Source*. Right now, he could overpower her with a thought and take them—if she fought him off, she risked killing them both, and possibly everyone on this dock. And he knew her. She would not risk it. Not here. Not now.

No, if he had not come to gloat and take her books, then . . . he'd come for something else.

Lore's grip loosened a fraction on her grimoires, her knuckles stinging with how tightly she had held the clasps, and she stood up, her heart leaping into her throat. She opened her mouth.

"Syrelle." Finndryl's voice cut in, his tone shards of jagged ice from behind Syrelle. "Step away from her at once," he ordered.

Syrelle steeled his shoulders against Finndryl's harsh tone. Syrelle tore his gaze from Lore's and turned to address a frightening-looking Finndryl, whose stance was wide, battle ready, his jaw set—rage burned within Finndryl like a beacon. The siren queen had given him the pick of her expansive armory before they left. Finndryl had forgone a broadsword and opted for a smaller weapon that drew less attention and hung nicely from a loop in his belt.

Finndryl clasped the hilt of his sword; he'd drawn the weapon partway out of its sheath, and the silver metal glinted threateningly. He was prepared to fight Syrelle if he tried to take the grimoires from Lore, and she had no doubt that if it came to it, their clash would be violent, bloody, and end with one or both of them dead.

Syrelle, who normally would have relished the chance to goad Finndryl, ignored the threat.

"Save your strength, Hwraeth, you will need it more than ever. And"—he addressed both her and Finndryl—"for gods' sake, master your magic by the time either of you set foot on Alytherian soil. There is a price on both your heads."

"We expected nothing less. Why are you wasting our time—"

Syrelle held up a hand to cut Finn off. Lore's eyes narrowed in on a slight tremble in his fingers. "That's not all. I received news from Alytheria this morning."

Lore gasped, taking an involuntary step toward Syrelle. News? Her gut felt like it had turned to lead.

"When our ship went down, and we lost contact with Alytheria, the king made new plans for Duskmere."

"What plans?" Lore was almost too scared to voice this question. Syrelle did not turn to look at her; still he directed what he had to say to Finndryl.

Finndryl looked uneasy at this revelation, but he did not take his eyes from Syrelle, nor his hand from the hilt of his sword.

"My cousin and I parted ways when we left Lapis Deep. I inquired where your travel barge was headed and worked out where you would dock. I arrived before you to ensure that I could keep watch over Lore. Coretha went home and told my uncle everything that we said in the sunken garden."

"The argument we had?" asked Finn.

"Yes," Syrelle hissed. "My emotions caused a lapse in my judgment. I forgot that my cousin was . . . Anyway, she overheard my intentions to use the books to aid Duskmere and, more importantly, that I planned to overthrow the king." Syrelle cleared his throat, raising his chin. "I am to return home at once to be tried for treason."

"Why would they send a messenger to warn you of this? Better to have you arrive unaware and apprehend you then."

"My uncle is an impatient man; he would not want to wait for me to return on my own, potentially successful and with the power of *Auroradel*. His terms are clear. I must arrive within six days or he will execute my aunt Maple and her children. He already has them in his custody . . ." Syrelle shuddered. "Which is not where anyone wants to be. Trust me, it's better to be dead than his captive."

Lore thought of the children running through their house, slipping and sliding in their stockinged feet. How safe they had been. How warm and loving their home. "Six days? That isn't enough time! It will take weeks for you to even cross the sea."

"If I depart at once and fly continuously, my magic should allow for my arrival with days to spare. My uncle is brash and impetuous. He may choose to end their lives early. Regardless of his word, he may not let them live anyway, just to punish me further."

Lore pressed her hand to her mouth and swallowed back bile. She didn't think she could despise anyone more than she did the King of Alytheria.

Finndryl's voice was grave when he asked, "What news of Duskmere?"

Darkness shimmered around Syrelle as if he had already eased the clamp on his magic, preparing to take flight, to use all his power to cross an ocean, to save the only real family he had left.

"As I am now an enemy of the crown, he did not permit his messenger to disclose his plans for Duskmere to me, but I fear whatever he has prepared will be most catastrophic. It will take all your combined strength to save your people."

"Well, that sounds ominous. Can't you give us a bit more than that, Syrelle?" Hazen said from where he'd appeared behind Finn-dryl. He must have arrived just in time to hear Syrelle's warning.

Syrelle ignored the prince.

He took one last look at Lore, his face displaying a vulnerability she had not seen in him since he'd been her Asher. His emotions were raw, exposed, and shone clearly on his face. His eyes, glinting in the daylight, revealed a silent mourning.

Syrelle was devoid of hope.

"You can't return. Not with him intent on killing you." She wrung her hands, panic tightening her chest.

"I don't have control of the sun magic yet. I need more time." Lore fought back tears. "We need more time to fix this."

"We are out of time. You are a powerful sorceress, Lore Ale-meyu. You have endured and thrived despite the poison poured on you relentlessly." Syrelle smiled softly at Lore. "If anyone can triumph against him, it is you."

"What if we ran? Now that I have *Auroradel*, I know I can break the curse on the wood surrounding Duskmere; we will find a way to get my people out—to save Maple, your niece and nephew . . . there would be no need to—"

It was her fault. Her fault that the king would punish Dusk-mere. Her fault that he had Maple and the children in his clutches. Her fault, all her fault.

"No! My uncle is a predator—run—and you will just whet his appetite. You *must* find another way."

Syrelle stretched his wings, shaking out his feathers, preparing for flight. "I wish I had more time. If we had only had more time . . ." His voice faltered, broke.

Lore opened her mouth to beg him to *wait*, to see if they could devise a plan, together. They could board the ship together—stay up all night making plans, like they did back in the Exile in Tal Boro. He had so much information she needed, about the king, about . . . about everything.

But she knew he did not have time to waste if he wanted any chance at all to save his aunt and the children.

And her magic was not yet something that he could rely on.

"Remember, Lore. The grimoires did not give you their magic; they were simply the key that unlocked the magic within you. You *are* magic, Lore. You can harness the power of a million stars in the sky, a million suns. Craft your own paradise."

Syrelle bent his knees and, with one powerful beat of his wings, took flight.

Lore called after him, but within moments, Syrelle was out of sight. She shouted his name until she grew hoarse, collapsing on the dock, her body racked with sobs.

CHAPTER 38

L ore paced the cabin on the *Constellation Weaver*.

She'd thought she'd have two weeks to plan and prepare before she faced him. Yet now she had mere days before the King of Alytheria would unleash his plans upon Duskmere. And less time to save Syrelle, Maple, and her children.

She reached the wall and turned back around with a frustrated huff. She couldn't think in this stuffy, windowless room. She thrust open the door to their cabin and slipped into the hall.

The *Weaver* was *filled* with passengers. Families, traders, merchants. She walked not ten feet before a giggling child clutching a rag doll ran under Lore's foot, and she had to skip out of the way. Children never did well when cooped up. Only hours into the voyage, the children, most of whom had started this journey as strangers, had become friends or enemies, and they ran through the halls at top speed, playing their games of make-believe, heedless of the other passengers. The children's laughter sounded like home.

Lore spun around, maneuvered her way back to the cabin, and closed the door behind her. She pressed her forehead to the wood, urging herself to breathe.

She would find a way.

She sank onto a chair and slipped *Auroradel* from her satchel. Opening the grimoire on a ship was a risk. It pulsed with power in her hands—intoxicating, petrifying, magnificent.

Lore put everyone at risk by even considering this. But she had to. She had to be there in time.

If she had to, she would carve the very ocean in two in order to save him.

She couldn't fight it anymore. She would be adrift in a sea of darkness if she were forced to live in a world without Syrelle. She couldn't help but love him, even though she'd tried not to.

Had tried and failed.

Syrelle and Finndryl. Her heart had expanded to fit them both, beating like a drum song for them, and that was the only truth that she knew. In the war of head versus heart, her heart was victorious.

The moment she spread the binding of *Auroradel*, power surged into her, eager and waiting. Wanting. She laid the book across her lap. It shuddered with untold power, vibrating between her clutched fingers.

Two weeks to Alytheria. Over a week *too long*. She would dock and find nothing but tragedy on those shores if it took her two weeks.

Lore spread her hands across the page and coaxed the power, letting it flow through her. When she'd begun practicing magic with *Lune*, she hadn't known what magic truly was. She'd thought she needed to follow spells, translate them, recite them perfectly, find just the right ingredients, weigh them, cut and burn and mash them, and add them to the spell exactly, like a recipe. Too much of something, and it wouldn't work. The spell would be wrong, twisted.

But now, months later, she knew that the grimoires were simply *Source*, mobile ley lines, permanent swells of radiance, her own personal Mother Pearls, and Lore need only be the conduit of their *Source* to bend it to her will.

Lore pictured her people in her mind's eye. Duskmere, nestled in a forest, surrounded by enemies. Enemies of their freedom, their bodies, their hopes and dreams. The king had never seen humans as people. They had been little more than animals to him. Worthy of less than his prized horses.

Now that he knew they could wield magic, he would wipe them off the face of the earth.

Lore closed her eyes and let the power of sunbeams alight over her. Light, heat, and magnanimous *Source* filled her from her toes to the coiled ends of her hair. She let it simmer within her.

She was magic, she need not be afraid.

She thought of this ship. A monstrous vessel designed for long-distance journeys, not speed. Intended simply to traverse the ocean, journeying from one place to another and then back again.

She focused on the wall to her left. This wall connected all the wood of the ship: the hull, the masts, and the sails, which even now caught the wind and harnessed it.

She followed it. She felt the ice-cold water around the bow of the ship.

Haste.

They needed swiftness.

She called for Hazen, whose very blood flowed with a song of the sea. He'd promised to use his own magic to urge the tide to carry them along, but it wouldn't be enough.

Hazen poked his head through the adjoining door that connected his room with their own, his eyes curious. "What are you up to in here?"

"I need your awareness of the sea."

Hazen didn't hesitate. "How can I help?"

"I may need you to use your song on the captain. I'm about to take over control of the ship, and I don't need them standing in my way."

"I can't use my song while in this form. Not unless I am submerged in water, at least partly."

Damn it.

"Then use your sword. Tell Finndryl."

"No need to tell me, I'm here," Finn said as he slid the door farther open and peered in. Lore nodded, hoping that he knew how thankful she was that he was always there for her. When this was over, she would tell him. She would whisper it against his skin as she worshipped his body.

Lore grasped Hazen's palm between her own two hands. "On second thought, how fast can you swim?"

Hazen's only response was to grin.

Hazen was not just a siren, but a siren prince and the ocean his playground. He knew the sea; it was as much a part of him as the blood in his veins.

"All right, I'll need you in the water. Stay close to the ship, you'll know what to do in a moment."

"You two do what you need to. I will take care of the captain." Finndryl's lips quirked up, and he clenched and unclenched his hands. He was itching to use his magic, Lore could tell.

She knew that feeling well.

Finn hesitated.

"I'll be in the hall," Hazen said before slipping out of the room.

Finndryl crouched so his eyes were level with Lore's where she sat on the chair. He placed a warm hand on her knee. She leaned into his touch. "We will return to Duskmere in time to save them, Lore, I know it." Lore nodded. How she needed to believe him. His gaze softened. "And we will save him."

Lore nodded again, her eyes stinging. "You know I choose you, right? I will always choose you."

"I know, my love." Finn closed his eyes and kissed her gently on the lips. Lore's heart swelled with the depth of his love. "Now let's put our magic to use."

Lore laughed as he stood to leave. Maybe she should rethink unleashing the overly powerful, grumpy fae on the *Weaver*'s captain. "Don't burn the ship down," she shouted after him as he slipped through the door.

"Don't sink us," Finndryl quipped over his shoulder before the door closed behind him. She heard a curse, followed by a peal of childish giggles.

Their first task would be surviving the horde of children in the hallway. Lore smiled as she closed her eyes, directing her concentration onto the ship.

Her senses extended once more, tracing the grain of each plank until she could feel every inch of the ship within the grasp of her magic. She felt the magnificent balance the ship held, how its design was true ingenuity. She felt the stitching in the sails, the pots of simmering water in the galley. The hull complained to her as it pushed through a particularly large swell. The keel showed her the barnacles that had attached themselves to its surface. The mizzen-mast whispered its secrets to her. Lore and the ship were one.

She sensed the moment Hazen's form changed within the water. His now-webbed fingers pressed onto the hull. Through his esthesia of the ocean, she saw water with a new light; it was no longer a terrifying force that would pull her under and drown her.

It was his *home*. It was malleable. And Hazen was agile and fast. He was a prince of the ocean who drew power and life from the water itself; he would never tire, never slow.

She urged the *Constellation Weaver* to cut through the sea like it was a hot knife and the water, butter.

She heard bellows from confused parents as they called their children to come to them. Alarmed shouts as the crew ran to and fro overhead, trying to determine what, exactly, was occurring.

Lore shut them out. She ignored everything but her need for swiftness.

She urged the boat faster and faster. She could feel the wood as it stretched and groaned; it was not designed to reach such speeds, but she used her power to reinforce the joints and planks, and she pushed the ship faster and faster.

She used her second sight to delve deep into the sea, watching for obstacles, outcroppings of land, islands, low spots, rogue waves, and she steered the ship clear. They need not steer or navigate, for Lore was as the sea turtle using instinct to travel to a nesting ground thousands of miles away. She was the salmon jumping up waterfalls, driven by instinct. *Home, home, home.* She felt the pull and knew the way.

CHAPTER 39

The crossing should have taken them two weeks. They arrived in just three days. Finndryl must have been successful, because no one, not even the captain, had disrupted Lore's focus.

Now she stood on the deck as the ship steered into the northernmost Alytherian harbor; Lore scanned the dock. She hadn't slept the entire journey. As they approached, she'd found a pitcher of water and a plate of food set beside her, and she gulped the pitcher, scarfed the food, and ran up to the deck, though her muscles protested her every movement. Protested their neglect, their fatigue.

She had not been afraid of what she would find on the deck. Possibly a crazed sea captain and their crew ready to call the watch and have them imprisoned—they would have been delighted to find that there was already a reward on their heads.

She could deal with all that easily.

She was afraid the king already knew they were coming and a host of Alytherian soldiers would be waiting to capture her, Hazen, and Finndryl.

She was even more terrified of finding the corpse of a misguided noble who, despite her every attempt to harden her heart to him and expel him from it, had never quite managed to vacate it. She was afraid she would see his body with sightless eyes, his wings fluttering in a breeze, never to fly again.

But the harbor was quiet, and the docks were almost empty at this late hour.

The captain of the *Constellation Weaver*, however, *had* been waiting for her on the deck.

She was young, younger than Lore would have thought a captain to be. Her skin was a brilliant shade of blue. Her build was slight and short. Shorter than Lore even—though a vibrant set of dragonfly wings made up for it. They shimmered in the moonlight as they flicked with fury or fear. Lore didn't know which.

The pixie stood with her arms crossed, her chin tilted toward the sky. She appraised Lore, her face giving nothing away. Behind her stood six sailors, a few of them taller and more muscled than Finndryl.

She tapped her foot, waiting for Lore to speak first.

"I'm sorry I took over your ship. My people, every last one of them, risk a fate worse than death if I do not arrive in time. I might be too late, as it is."

Lore glanced between the pixie and the harbor. She still couldn't see an army waiting for them. Could they really dock and walk to Duskmere?

She felt so distant from her body. From this ship. From this moment. She was already in Duskmere, preparing her people to fight. She was saving Syrelle and Maple and the children. She was arming up for battle. She was ripping the king apart with her mind. She was anywhere but here.

Could an army be hiding? Maybe the king had come himself. Maybe he didn't even need an army.

Lore was startled out of her thoughts by the captain's voice. "At first, I was pissed." Her voice was steady and clear, with no hint of fear or fury. Maybe the pixie just swished her wings out of habit;

she probably didn't even realize she was doing it. She continued, "Finally, I have a ship of my own to command. My own ship! Do you know of any other pixies who have control of their own ship? No? Neither do I. Well, a few weeks in, and lo and behold, your friends barged into my quarters, magic out, swords swinging . . . I almost had them thrown overboard for their insolence in thinking I'm too stupid to have protections in place. I am a pixie who commands her own ship. Everyone thinks me an easy target." She thrust her thumb backward toward the six hulking fae males behind her. Lore eyed them warily.

"I must admit, your two might've held their own against my cabal here, but Vel . . . he has a unique talent. He can create a shield from the air, encase you in it. Any power you try to use . . . it bounces right back to you . . ." She blinked at Lore, tilting her head to the side. "See . . . fae and siren I can handle. I wasn't aware I had to be prepared for a witch."

The pixie raised her eyebrow at what must be a shocked expression on Lore's face.

"Oh, I know who you are. There isn't a sailor on these seas who hasn't heard of the new phenomenon. The human sorceress. The witch." The pixie tucked her thumbs into belt loops and tapped one shining black boot against the polished deck of her ship. "If I had known the Grand Witch, First of Her Kind, would be booking passage on my ship . . . well, a different captain would have denied you passage, but me being me . . . I at least would have introduced myself when you boarded my vessel. Especially because in the stories you are eight feet tall with limbs that slither like noodles, or a shrieking ghost with miniature cauldrons for hands." She shrugged, her lips quirking up into a smile. "Depending on who tells it—you can't always trust the drunks in a tavern."

The pixie stepped toward her, looking up at Lore, though Lore had an uneasy feeling she was looking *down* at her. Lore eyed her uneasily. She couldn't quite get a grasp on this creature. Was she going to let them go without a fight or not? Or was she keeping them here, stalling until the guard was alerted? It would be the smart thing to do.

Lore's eyes widened as she realized the captain didn't just *appear* to be looking down at Lore, she *was*. Just barely. Her boots were no longer on the deck but hovering a few inches above it. *Impressive.* Her wings fluttered with such efficiency they now appeared to be stationary.

Lore met eyes with Finn and Hazen, who stood by, waiting for the gangway to be lowered. For the ship to be tied up at the dock. Finndryl and Hazen were tense as well. Ready to fight. All three of them hoped they wouldn't have to.

The captain dropped back onto the deck. "Imagine my surprise when I discover you have fingers just like me, regular eyes, though on the smaller side compared to a pixie . . . but you are *barely* taller than me!"

"Sorry to disappoint," Lore deadpanned. The rumors surrounding her were alarming, but maybe she could find a way to work them in her favor. Gods, she was tired. The muscles in her thighs were twitching. Her mouth felt desert dry. Lore dipped her head in apology once more. "Like I said, I'm sorry. I had to. I wonder if we can come to some arrangement . . . and quickly. We really are in a hurry." Lore really didn't want to have to hurt the captain. Despite everything, she liked the pixie. In another life, they could have been friends. Still, she stroked the grimoires with her mind. Coaxing them both awake. Just in case.

"A hurry, you say? You know, I gathered that." The pixie laughed—a tinkle of bells. "Look, I won't grill you much longer, I promise. And if you are wondering if I'll report you to the watch, I won't. Though I am sure you've broken a dozen laws at least, and I still don't like that you didn't come to me first."

"If I had, would you have agreed to let me do what I had to in order to arrive here in time?"

"Absolutely not. But my pride would have liked it more than these two demanding my compliance."

"I see."

"They were surprisingly polite. You've got some good ones."

"That I do." Lore nodded, her gaze flicking back to the shore, searching for an army.

"I'll let you and your friends leave before alerting the harbormaster of our arrival. This quiet of a port, this late, he's no doubt asleep in his office."

The ship eased into a space within the empty harbor. Moonlight glinted on the ropes the sailors tossed down to wrap around massive metal spokes.

Lore nodded her thanks. Too weary to speak anymore. Gods, she hoped Finndryl had water on him. Her mouth was so dry.

The gangway was being lowered. So close. She was almost there. Please let her be here in time.

"And, Lara?"

Lore had almost forgotten the fake name they'd used to book passage. She almost didn't turn around as they walked down the ramp, Finndryl's hand warm and familiar, holding her up. She felt a little dizzy. She called on *Auroradel*'s power, just to get her safely off the ship. The book complied. Immediately, her focus cleared; her muscles eased.

"If you are ever looking for work, come find me—we could become rich by offering a three-day trip from Ma Serach to Alytheria." The pixie dipped her head in respect.

Lore's jaw dropped for a moment before she snapped it shut and grinned.

"If I'm ever looking for work, you'll be my first stop."

"Good. Now get off my ship."

The pixie's laugh followed them down the gangway.

CHAPTER 40

The frosted forest floor crackled beneath Lore's boots as she, Finn, and Hazen left the pebbled shoreline and ventured into the viridescent stretch of woods. The air hummed with a familiar aura as the trees, lively in their splendor, swayed in the wind, stirring their branches, showering them with velvety needles that smelled of evergreen life. Lore picked her way over roots and brushed a hand along lichen and moss that painted a tapestry upon the tree trunks. A smile spread across her face, crinkling the corners of her eyes.

Suddenly, Lore's breath caught in her throat as a flash of russet darted through the undergrowth. Could it be? A heartbeat later, a sleek orange fox emerged from behind a mossy boulder, its eyes shimmering like amber in the dappled moonlight.

Time seemed to stop as Lore and the fox locked gazes. The fox's bushy tail swished excitedly, its entire body radiating an energy that echoed Lore's own, as she could swear she heard the fox within her mind say, *you are here at last you are here*. It was Ember, her coconspirator, whom she'd thought lost to her a month ago.

Lore sank to her knees as she felt a wave of emotion surging between them. Ember yipped and pounced onto her lap, pressing her snowy paws to Lore's chest and nuzzling her cheek. She smelled like damp earth and moss, sun-warmed leaves and blooming herbs. Lore pressed her face into the fox's coat, inhaling deeply.

"I thought you were lost," she murmured into Ember's fur. Lore sensed the connection with Ember weaving stronger between them. She didn't know what it meant to feel such a kinship to a shapeshifting fox, but it felt right in her bones that she should be here to meet her upon her return.

"Will you stay by my side this time, little one?" she asked with a smile, trying to calm Ember's vibrating body by stroking her fur. *Always*, the fox seemed to say as she yipped excitedly before racing away and then back again. A moment later, Ember was sniffing at Finndryl's boots and then Hazen's, waiting for them both to give her a scratch on her tufted head.

It might be a trap—how easily they arrived in Duskmere.

There were no sentries guarding the forest, no signs of fighting, and the portion of woods right outside of home—she could pinpoint the exact moment the woods changed. It was the malice interlaced within the spell—it was a dark thing, oily and wrong. It sent shivers down her arms, but her shield protected her body and mind; she could sense the spell, but it slipped from her like water on a seal's back. One word from Lore, and the dark woods that had been the Alytherians' most useful tool for keeping them trapped would dissipate. It would be nothing but a forest. But Lore had better wait. She didn't want to break the spell; it might announce her presence to the king.

Ember seemed to feel her unease, and she shifted into her moth form, fluttering around Lore's head for a moment before settling onto her shoulder, soft wing beats tickling her jaw.

But even if it had been a trap, Lore didn't know what it had been set for, because they walked into Duskmere without a hitch, although Lore was so exhausted by the time they entered the village she wanted to crawl.

It was a ghost town. Eerie how quiet it was. There weren't any shops open. The burg's tavern was closed. The morning was heavy with fog and the promise of rain; the clouds were thick, the sunlight weak. Lore had a moment of pure fear that everyone was gone. That she was too late. But then she spied candlelight within one of the sagging cabins that had survived the shake. She could see movement inside. A figure in a window peered out before shutting the curtains tight.

People were here, but they were inside.

As if they were scared to come out. She was planning on telling the first person she saw to call the village elders. To gather everyone in the town.

Lore frowned. There weren't any sentries out here. Why was everyone shut away? Lore was with two fae, but they should recognize *her*.

She spied a sliver of Amaha's farm, which was the closest to the village center. Lore slowed her steps. It looked like there was snow on the field, but why would there be snow only here and nowhere else?

She hurried off the road and slipped behind the buildings to walk to the field. Amaha owned this land and the only two cows in Duskmere. He and his four sons should be out here now, despite the weather, to tend to the field. Spring was coming, and it needed to be turned. And yet . . . Lore knelt and ran her hand across the soil, picking up the white substance and rolling it between her fingers.

This wasn't snow. It was salt.

The Alytherians had salted the field, which would cause the plant roots to wither and die. Not only that, but this much salt would ruin the soil for *years* to come.

The Alytherians were starving them.

"How could anyone do this?" Hazen asked, his voice quiet. You didn't have to be a lander to know that this field had been purposefully ruined.

"The king has had no problems keeping my people under his thumb for centuries. Now that we have a chance to fight back, he will do everything in his power to weaken us before making his final move."

"We will flay the putrid flesh from his bones." Finndryl's words were a promise.

Salim and Eshe's vineyard was salted as well. The grapes they had so carefully cultivated for decades had shriveled up and died. Their grain and vegetable plots, as well, were covered in salt. Salt was precious, expensive. Wars had been fought over salt. Entire trade routes were founded on salt. Empires had clawed their way to power in the past because of salt. It kept meat long after it would have festered and decayed. It gave flavor to food during poor harvests when there were no other spices to be had.

The Alytherians had decimated any chance for the people here, with a product more valuable to those of Duskmere than gold.

The insult was repulsive. The results devastating.

The door to the shelter, her childhood home, was barred shut from the inside. Lore struck the bell and pressed her forehead to the door, closing her eyes.

She was so afraid of what she would find behind it.

Right now, she was on the other side of the door, and everyone she loved was alive and whole, but in a moment the door would be opened, and her greatest fears could be realized: that for all her trying, she recovered the book too late. That there would be no one that she cared for left to save.

But she heard a noise, and when she looked at the window, a small face appeared, accompanied by a distinct cry. Within a moment, answering shouts could be heard inside.

When the many locks were unlatched, and the door finally wrenched open, Lore was greeted with the smiling faces of her loved ones.

"I told you, Salim, I told you she was all right! I could *feel* it!" Aunty Eshe screamed. She was a blur of beautiful dark skin, layered fabric bursting with colors and patterns, and a swish of long, silvered braids as she pulled Lore over the threshold and into a fierce embrace. Lore had a single moment to breathe in the lovely, familiar scent of Eshe before she heaved a sob of relief into her aunty's ample chest. Aunty Eshe was crying with her, rocking her back and forth in that way only those who loved their children could do; without a thought; it was natural.

Salim, taller and broader than Aunty Eshe and Lore, enfolded them both into his chest, and the three of them cried together. But they didn't have long before the children were vying for Lore's attention. Their little hands were running over her arms, pulling at her dress, as if making sure that she was real. That she was here.

Even Milo, who normally avoided any commotion, had shoved his way through the throng of children to cling to Lore's leg through her skirts.

Lore picked him up, saving him from the sharp elbows of the bigger kids and the sticky hands of the toddlers, and pressed his sweet face to her shoulder. He was here, alive and well. Milo didn't have to speak to show how much he loved her. He already had his fingers threaded through her hair, his face pressed to her neck, breathing her in as his little hand patted her tearstained cheek.

Through the shouting, the questions, the laughter, and the tears, Lore heard a voice cut through the rest.

"About damn time, Lore."

"Grey!" Lore exclaimed, laughing through her tears.

She couldn't bear to put Milo down just yet, and she didn't think that, even if she had wanted to, he would have let her, as his small hands were tightly wound in her hair, so when Grey pulled her into a hug, Milo was squeezed between them. Lore expected Milo to give a squeak of protest, but he didn't seem to mind.

Lore broke from the hug and asked, "What are you doing here? I thought I was going to have to find you at your house."

"We moved in here. Our house didn't survive the shake, and Eshe and Salim needed help with the kiddos, anyway."

"Plus, there aren't enough houses left standing for anyone to live on their own. Everyone still with a house has at least a few neighbors living with them," Violette, Grey's mom, said, before tugging Lore (and little Milo) into a quick hug. Grey's little sister was next. Something loosened in her chest when she saw that his family was well, that they were here. And then Katu, who she thought should have grown a foot in her absence. He had been growing like a weed before all this started—but she could see the effects of undernourishment on him and all the children. They hadn't enough to thrive; they were skin and bones.

Finndryl was not one to hug, and Grey, despite being the definition of a hugger, knew this, so he clasped Finn on the shoulder in greeting. Finndryl, however, surprised Lore by pulling Grey into a hug. "I'm glad to see you here, brother," Grey said, through a surprised laugh.

Finndryl sobered as they separated. "As am I. We were both worried. The last we saw you, we were making plans to invade the castle."

"Last we saw the two of *you*, you were supposed to meet us at the rendezvous to help guide the women and children back home. Instead, Asher led them to us alone. He told us that plans had changed, to go on ahead, that you three would be following shortly. And then you never came."

"We have a lot to catch you up on . . ." Lore said.

"Isla talked to a friend—a stable hand at Wyndlin. He told us enough to know that you hadn't been murdered and buried somewhere on the castle grounds, but we would all like to know what happened." Grey looked around. "Where *is* Asher?"

"We can explain later. Where is Isla? Is she still in Duskmere?" Finndryl's jaw was tight. He was worried about his sister, as was Lore.

"Isla will be back tomorrow or the next day. She's been in and out of Duskmere; if she's not hunting for us, she's on her way to Cher, a few days' walk from here, to gather supplies. She has a friend there who's been collecting medicine and the like for Isla to smuggle back to us." Grey's smile faltered. "We never had much outside trade to begin with, but the king made it illegal for anyone to trade with us or provide aid."

Of course he did. Starving everyone in Duskmere would be hard if the neighboring towns could still come here and trade. Lore imagined he wanted as few people as possible to witness his plans.

Though she doubted many would care; they'd never tried to help before, despite things always being bad here.

Salim stepped up to Finndryl, his eyes shrewd, studying him and his proximity to Lore. "I gather you are Finndryl, Isla's brother. Without your sister's unwavering courage and selfless actions, Lore would have returned to a lot less of us," Salim said with a somber nod. "I'm Salim, Lore's uncle. This is Eshe, her aunt."

Eshe was distracted, trying to stop the toddlers from pulling on Ember's ears and tail as she scampered and yipped excitedly at the children, but Finndryl had Salim's full attention. They clasped hands in greeting.

Lore's stomach did a little flip.

To see two of the most important males in her life meeting . . . she felt like she was in a waking dream. Any other time, she would have stressed for days knowing that Salim would be meeting and placing judgment on Finndryl, but the thought had completely slipped her mind during their journey here. And yet, here Uncle Salim was, sizing Finndryl up and appearing to approve. Salim gave Lore a soft smile, his eyes glittering, when Finndryl turned to introduce them to Hazen, who had been diverted and cloistered into a corner by Grey's aunt Avarie, who was currently marveling at the ornate tattoos on his face with a little too much giggling.

Hazen was attractive, but still, Lore didn't expect even Avarie to have been reduced to fits of giggles. She was just glad that Finndryl exuded *don't touch me, or talk to me, or even look at me* energy, because Avarie's daughters, Grey's cousins, were indeed eyeing the two males from afar, whispering behind their hands.

Lore bit back a laugh. She wondered if they knew that Finndryl and Hazen had ludicrously impeccable hearing and would definitely be able to hear what they were whispering. She knew those admirers, whatever they were saying, would no doubt make Finndryl, who worked in a tavern and had seen some shit, blush. If he had been listening to them, and not giving Salim his full attention.

Or at least, Lore thought he hadn't been listening, but Finndryl met her eyes over the children's heads—and gave a quick glance at Grey's cousins before smirking at Lore.

She grinned. Oh, she would have to beg him to tell her everything they were saying later. She bet it was *scandalous*.

Aunty Eshe broke the amused gaze that Finndryl was giving her from across the room by extracting a protesting Milo from Lore's arms and handing him to Levia with instructions to corral the kiddos into their dorm while the grown-ups talked. Levia was twelve, half a year younger than Katu. Too young to be out here for the critical conversations they would have to have soon, but old enough to help with the kids. With a smile, Lore pressed a bag full of sugared sweets she'd picked up in Ma Serach into Levia's hands. "This should help to quiet the little ones' protests, at least for a short while."

Katu and Lex were sent to fetch the village elders and others with sway within the community.

The adults and older teens, who no longer had the privilege of childhood, gathered in the family room by the hearth. The fire wasn't lit, and despite the growing number of bodies and people filing in from all over the village, Lore's breath bloomed from her lips like a ghost of her past mocking her. She just didn't know if this ghost was her former self, or if *she* was the ghost, an echo of the girl she'd been when all she'd ever known was this place.

She eyed the stack of firewood in the corner, which should be piled higher, even this late in winter, but had dwindled to only a few skinny logs and stacks of twigs. Finding firewood had always been a problem. Forbidden from hunting or gathering in the forest proper, fresh meat and firewood were precious, but there *were* a few groves within Duskmere, and so the people had always had just enough to burn. Cookfires and heat in the winter had been one of the few things they hadn't had to go without.

But Lore could see that this, as well, had changed.

Uncle Salim, who, like an old owl whose large, intelligent eyes saw everything, noticed her eyeing the meager stack of sticks that would be devoured by the fire too quickly to provide lasting warmth. "They burned Dorren Grove and Ndulu's Thicket on the day they salted our land and withdrew their sentries. We only light the fire to cook now, and as you can see, soon that won't be enough."

"I stopped everyone in the town from burning your books, hon. Don't worry," Aunty Eshe said, patting Lore's shoulder from where she sat behind her. Lore patted her hand back, conveying how grateful she was, though in truth, she would rather they burn them than have the children shivering or without a hot meal, and leaned back into her skirts, settling in against her legs, feeling oddly like a child for a moment. She had sat just like this countless times growing up, but now she was not settling in to listen to stories during a winter storm or to listen while Aunty Eshe and Uncle Salim demonstrated skills to the children; she would have to speak.

The elders trickled in, sitting in the few chairs positioned throughout the room, and everyone else whose hair hadn't yet begun to gray or whose body allowed it sat on cushions on the floor. Lore was glad to see the chairs still *existed* for them to sit in and hadn't had to be used as firewood yet. They were too old to be sitting on the floor.

And it was entirely *too* cold in here.

Lore flicked her hand and muttered a word in unison with Finndryl. Lore felt Finndryl's magic being cast beside her. They'd had the thought simultaneously, and their efforts were doubled for it as a fire *whoosh*ed in the fireplace, almost setting fire to the rug, as the others gasped around them.

His own form of power had become familiar to Lore, his *Source* unique to him, but they had never cast a spell together. Their two powers had woven together on their own, for neither of them knew that the other was going to be casting, and yet their two powers merged instantly, combining to become one.

Lore's fingers jerked back in surprise, and she slowed her current of *Source*, feeling Finn do the same with his. They played with the levels until their fire was less likely to set the place ablaze and was a sensible height.

More cozy, less . . . *burn everyone to a crisp.*

She winked at Finn, who sat on the ground beside her, his long legs pulled crisscross. The room was cramped with so many people within such a small space, and he and Hazen took up a lot of space compared to the humans. Lore had never seen Finndryl sit like this before, and for the first time since she'd met him, she could almost imagine what he was like as a child.

The room began to warm, and people sighed, shifting in their seats, relaxing their muscles. Lore was glad to bring warmth to them. Who knew how long it had been since they'd felt warm enough? This fire would burn as long as she or Finn tended to it, and it would never consume the logs in the fireplace.

She nudged Finndryl's arm with her own, wishing she could kiss him, but kissing him . . . or anyone, but especially a fae male, would *not* be appropriate in a room that was slowly filling with elders.

While they waited for the rest of the elders and unofficial village leaders to arrive (they were forbidden by the king to elect official community leaders), someone brewed tea and passed cups out to eager hands. Though there wasn't any cream or sugar, and coffee stores had apparently been exhausted weeks before, it was enough to gather with a hot drink clasped between their hands.

The room hummed with restrained excitement. Her return had kindled a spark of hope within her community—hope that the king had ruthlessly sought to extinguish. Though it had flickered and wavered, the embers of defiance still glowed within her people. It could never be banked.

Conversations flowed in hushed tones, punctuated by the clinking of cups, as everyone tried to avoid overtly staring at Finn, Hazen, and Lore herself. She had returned to Duskmere transformed, as foreign to them now as the fae themselves. The women and children who had been abducted and imprisoned, while their suffering was undeniable, were more familiar to the villagers than the concept of a human willingly venturing out, only to return on her own terms, accompanied by two imposing fae, and wielding newfound power.

They were uncertain of what it meant that a human could do magic.

Was she going to save them like she had their grandchildren, children, siblings, or even themselves? She recognized a few of the women sitting on the floor with her as former tower prisoners. Their eyes held a haunted look, and the famine seemed to have ravaged their bodies more than most. They were grateful, yes, but a gnawing fear lingered within them. Did Lore bring false hope—or were they doomed to watch their loved ones succumb to cold and starvation?

But, despite this, all waited patiently and refrained from bombarding Lore with questions before everyone had arrived—which Lore was thankful for, as she hadn't the strength to repeat herself tonight.

She hadn't slept for days, she'd used an enormous amount of power forcing an entire ship across an ocean in three days, which should have been impossible, and then she'd had to trek unseen across leagues to get from the harbor to Duskmere.

All the while worrying that she wouldn't arrive here in time.

She knew that the only reason she was still coherent was because of *Auroradel*, which even now was furnishing her with a constant stream of vitality. As far as Lore could tell, its magic was bottomless, and the more magic she drew from it, the more powerful it felt. It was as though the *Source* of the *Auroradel* begot more *Source*. It was a never-ending well. The more she drew from it, the more it held, the deeper it descended.

This concerned Lore, as the one constant in her life was that everything had a price. Nothing came free. *Deeping Lune* had been difficult for her to pull magic from at first; the spells had been complicated and out of reach, and it had avoided permitting her to discover its secrets. At first, she'd only been able to harness its power when she was terrified or stressed. And after that, with Finndryl's help and weeks of study, she had only managed trivial spells that hadn't worked very well and often didn't provide the result she was after.

But this grimoire was different.

Auroradel was eager to provide, not just to sustain her but to envelop her. Lore had been tapping into the *Source* of the book since Ma Serach three and a half days ago.

If she was honest with herself, for the entire journey to Duskmere, she fretted that she wouldn't have the strength to detach.

The well of power was filled with sweet, fresh, life-giving water, but she wondered if she could halt the flow or if the well would give out instead. She would tumble head over foot, swallowed whole, in a bottomless well with no way out.

Lore stopped gnawing on her lip when she realized the room had quieted around her.

The last of the villagers had arrived. So many squeezed into the room that the floor was packed, every chair filled, and people now stood, filling every space.

And they were all looking at her, waiting for her to speak.

Lore resisted the urge to twist the travel-stained fabric of her skirts between her fingers. She missed the rock that Grey had gifted her; its absence was a constant ache, and she would love to grasp it now for strength.

She gently placed Ember into Finndryl's lap, and the fox nipped lazily at his hand before curling up and immediately falling asleep.

Lore didn't have her rock with the moon-shape hole anymore, but she did have Grey, who sat on the other side of her. She had Finndryl, whose gaze never left her face. A line was drawn between his brows, like he knew every worry racing through her head, every anxiety-inducing thought, every fear zipping through her mind in a loop. She had Hazen, who was here to fight for strangers to carve out a better life for themselves, for no other reason than because it was the *right* thing to do, which was something she had done for his people just weeks before, a kindred spirit. Lore had her aunt and uncle behind her, who took her in and loved her when she'd thought she was alone in the world.

And within the books she carried, she had strength from the sun and the moon. So she drew might from her family and friends and from *Auroradel*, enough to heave her exhausted body off the cold ground, ignoring her protesting bones and tight muscles that were imploring her to rest after hours and hours and hours of weaving magic, into a standing position, to address her community, who placed their very lives in her two hands, which did not feel large enough to carry them all.

Even Ember, the small fox who had somehow become a friend and companion, woke up and brushed her fluffy tail against her ankle, a show of solidarity.

If Lore was honest with herself, it was *Auroradel*, more than all else, that gave her that last push to convene with her community without collapsing under the weight of responsibility. It gave her the strength to stand and stay standing and to speak without her voice faltering, or wavering.

And despite her worries, it was more important that Lore *had* this bottomless well.

She could figure out how not to drown within it later.

When they had won.

CHAPTER 41

Lore's tea was cold by the time she'd told her story, explained all she had been through, all she had seen and discovered. And when all was out on the table, it was time for the brightest minds of Duskmere to devise a plan of action.

One that *wouldn't* end with the king eradicating their entire race.

Lore had begun the evening feeling separate from the people in Duskmere. But telling her story, having them listen, and hearing from the others . . . cemented in her soul the most important yet simple of all her truths: Her voyage was not solitary; she need not traverse the path to freedom alone.

At first, they'd wanted to run. She had discovered the spell surrounding Duskmere and could break it; surely they could pack up and leave tonight. "What if the sentries come back tomorrow?" they cried. But Lore had to tell them, *running would only provoke the king.* He was too powerful. He had too many sentries, not to mention winged, *flying* guards.

They had two options when it came to the king. Fight or outwit him. They argued when she told them how she knew that. Hadn't this Syrelle betrayed her? How did she know that his information could be trusted?

She didn't. But she believed him in this. This went round and round.

Finally, one of the women who had been taken to the tower, held within Wyndlin Castle, asked, her voice quiet, "You say we have two options, but there is a third. We could give up." Tears leaked from her eyes, and her chin trembled. "I'm tired. I'm scared. I don't want this. I didn't ask for this."

Lore didn't have the words to comfort her. She couldn't know what trauma the woman had gone through, what hardships she faced. She couldn't . . . wouldn't ask someone to fight unless they wanted to.

It had to be their choice to make a stand.

"We cannot be cynical when fighting for justice. When your cause is a worthy one, it is hope that will fuel the fires of change." Aunty Eshe spoke then, her voice ringing through the room. "Lore has not returned to us with empty words nor false promises of an unreachable dream, but with a flame to light the fires of our hope and kindling to help it burn. You need only look at her to see her strength, to see that she can lead us—not to Shahassa, our world of the past, but to a new life, a better life. Not just for the few, but for *all of us*. We deserve to be safe. We deserve to take up space. We will have that. We need only light our torches with her fire, hold them high, and *fight*."

Another woman took the crying one's hand and cupped it in her own. "It's all right to have hope . . . to allow yourself to dream again. We cannot allow ourselves to be enslaved by despair. Bare your teeth with me, with our brothers and sisters, for we do not do this alone. We have only to look around to revel in the beauty of all that we are."

Lore looked around the room with everyone else at the woman's words. Noted the gray, thinning hair of the elders. The ancient lines on their faces. The baby nursing at the breast of Shella, the goat-herd, its chubby fist twisting the too-thin fabric of its mother's shirt.

The young couple who shared one chair. Grandmothers, grand-fathers, families, and friends. Community. Their humanity was an opus of colors and textures. They were a people of fragile hearts who loved and cherished and survived despite it all. And gods, it was remarkable to behold. To hold space with her people.

Lore spoke then, raising her voice. "Finding strength in our *humanity* is how we will win." She met their gazes, one by one. "I have seen you be strong; I know you can be strong again. And then, when this is done, and our fight is won, we will heal together."

The woman raised her chin; it was no longer trembling. "I can be strong. And then"—she repeated Lore's words—"we heal together."

"We heal together!" they shouted, their voices coalescing to make one united chorus.

The sun had set long before their meeting was finished. By the time everyone dispersed, clutching flickering candles to guide them through the inky darkness of Duskmere, exhaustion clung to Lore like a second skin.

Pillows, blankets, and Lore's cherished childhood quilt, lov-ingly stitched by her mother, were brought forth. Lore curled up beside the fire, nestled close to Finndryl and Ember, and slept and slept and slept.

CHAPTER 42

Isla woke her brother with a swift kick to the ribs. Finndryl jerked sideways, clutching his side as breath expelled from his chest. "Goddess, Isla, what was that for?" he muttered into his pillow.

"That's for making me think you were dead for weeks, you bastard."

"If I'm a bastard, that would mean you are too."

"Good morning, Isla," Lore said as she pushed herself up on her elbows and yawned into the morning light.

"You're next."

Lore scooted backward to avoid Isla's boot. "That's not fair! We were kidnapped!"

"Excuses, excuses!" Isla said, even as she stretched out a hand to help haul Lore to her feet.

"I tried to find you, with my magic. But you must have been in Duskmere each time. I can't penetrate the concealing spell the Alytherians cast over this place. When I try to find it, it's like it doesn't exist."

"You should've tried harder. Where is Asher? And who is this gorgeous specimen?" Isla asked, jamming her thumb in Hazen's direction. Hazen was asleep in the corner, a bundle of blankets with only his precious sleeping face peeking out from the pile of quilts.

"Ah. Our friend Prince Hazen, from Lapis Deep."

"Lapis Deep? As in, the underwater siren kingdom half an ocean away?"

"It's been a journey," Finndryl said as he rubbed his ribs. Louder: "Which is why I don't appreciate you waking me up with your boot, you demon spawn."

"That doesn't answer my question—where is Asher . . . ?" Her voice trailed off, a flicker of doubt clouding her expression. "He isn't dead, is he?" She laughed, though her joke was laced with real worry.

Asher and Isla had been each other's family. Chosen family. In many ways, they had been as close as Lore and Grey.

And in a way . . . Asher was dead. Lore had grieved him as if he were, anyway. And now, in two days, the pretender in his place would be too. Unless they intervened.

Lore exchanged a glance with Finn, a silent understanding passing between them. "We were . . . taken," Finn began, his voice heavy. "By Asher."

Isla's eyes widened. "Taken . . . by Asher?" she repeated, disbelief lacing her tone. "Taken where? How did he convince *you* to go with him, Finn?"

Lore stepped forward, placing a gentle hand on Isla's arm. "He wasn't who we thought he was, Isla. The Asher that you know was using a different name, a disguise. His real name is Syrelle. He's a noble who is exquisitely skilled at glamouring."

Isla's expression flashed through about a hundred emotions. She opened and closed her mouth multiple times before settling on, "He abducted you both? Why?"

Finn winced. "He had misguided reasons, not all of which he has disclosed to us."

Isla's shock morphed into anger, her fists clenching. "Misguided? He abducted you! He . . ." Her voice broke. "He lied to me. To all of us."

Finn nodded solemnly. "We know. And we were angry too. But . . ." He hesitated, searching for the right words. "While we don't condone what he did, we forgive him. Mostly . . . And Isla, we believe that he truly cares for you. He just went about your friendship the wrong way. I'm sure that once we rescue him . . . his explanation will make more sense than either Lore or I could give."

Isla stared at them, her anger simmering beneath the surface. "Forgive him?" she echoed, her voice laced with incredulity. "You forgive him?"

"It wasn't easy," Lore admitted. "And I don't forgive him for everything; he and I will never . . . be what we were before he removed his mask."

Isla remained silent for a long moment, her emotions warring within her. Finally, she let out a shaky breath. "I don't know if I can," she confessed. "But I'm glad you are both safe."

Lore and Finn enveloped her in a hug, a silent promise of support and understanding. Whatever she decided, they would respect her decision.

"Whether Syrelle is forgiven or not . . . we must ask ourselves, do we care for the Asher we knew enough to rescue him from a fate worse than death?" Lore asked quietly, gently, as she stepped away. She, of course, had already come to her own conclusions. Nothing would stop her from rescuing Syrelle before his time elapsed. Two more days, the king had given him. But Lore wouldn't apply pressure on Isla. The undertaking would be treacherous, and if Isla were to risk her life for someone she never truly knew, it would be up to her to make that decision.

Isla shook her head. "What, exactly, are we rescuing him from?"

"We?" Finn asked Isla, his eyebrow raised.

"Of course *we*. I'm not going to let him be killed before I have a chance to beat the shit out of him and demand answers."

Finn smiled. "Thought so."

"We are still finalizing those details," Lore said as she headed toward the door, her baby quilt wrapped around her. "Is it too early for wine?" Lore called over her shoulder.

"No such thing as 'too early' when it comes to wine!" Hazen rasped from the corner.

"Yes, I will take some wine, Lore. Finn, explain everything to me once more—and I know how you can be—do *not* leave out a single detail," Lore heard Isla exclaim, muffled as Lore descended the creaking stairs into the cellar.

Lore lit a stub of candle with a striking stone and perused the shelves.

Uncle Salim carved the shelves in here directly into the stone before Lore had even been born, and his craftmanship had proved its worth. They had shielded nearly all his stores during the earthshake.

She ran a hand across the dusty bottles, a sneeze escaping her as dust motes danced in the candle's flickering flame.

The cellar, nestled underground, maintained a constant temperature year-round. It was cool, yet warmer than the house had been last night, before Lore and Finn had lit the fires in the dormitory, her aunt and uncle's room, and the family room.

The familiar smell of the cellar, with its comforting blend of dust and age, enveloped her. She picked up a bottle and blew the dust off the label. Some of these were old. This one had been bottled the year of her birth.

A fitting coincidence, as her nameday was approaching. Lore hoped she would live to see twenty-two.

As she prepared to leave, her gaze lingered on a row of reflective bottles that hadn't yet had time to gather dust. These would be the last bottles of wine Salim would ever make here.

But when they settled into their new home, he could make more, explore new flavors, and do it all without the constant fear of being slain by an arrow-happy sentry for some imagined offense.

"Breakfast is in the kitchen. You should eat something before we head to Wyndlin Castle." Grey's voice drifted down from above Lore, his footsteps creaking on the stairs.

Lore hugged her chosen bottle to her chest. "Do you remember that time we pilfered two bottles from here and drank them by the lake?"

"Seven years isn't so long; how could I forget?"

That night, the wine had been sweet, and Lore, then, had fancied herself mature enough to drink. There hadn't been a breeze to be found, and the lake had been still as glass. The moonlight reflected off the surface, illuminating Grey's face. It lit him up on the outside, matching the light within him.

That year had been harsh for everyone. Cold and wet—many of their food stores had had to be disposed of due to mold. Everyone was hungry, but that year was particularly hard on Grey.

His uncle, who had stepped up to fill his father's role, had just been murdered in cold blood, going the way of too many human men—careless brutality carried out by a sentry who never had to fear facing consequences for his actions. Grey saw that sentry every day that year, as he was stationed on the edge of the wood right near his house. He had to look upon his face, walk past him, deal with the cruel jokes they tossed at the human children like poisoned candy, and there wasn't a thing he could do about it.

It was made worse because that was how his own father had died. Lore's too.

They drank their pilfered wine straight from the bottle, pouring a splash in the tall grass that had been pressed down by their bodies as they lay under the stars, a pour for each of their fathers and now one for his uncle. They downed the maroon liquid to the dregs at the bottom of each bottle, the sediment clinging to their teeth because they were not yet fifteen and didn't know any better. The wine muddled their thoughts and softened their grief, so it didn't feel as jagged edged and dangerous; it was, for the moment, an accustomed ache, manageable, not all-consuming.

Aunty Eshe, who had a sense for these things, came roaring down the hill to the lake, her footsteps like thunder. But Lore and Grey, by then, were holding each other, their arms clasped fiercely, as if any moment they would be ripped from each other and their hands left empty, as their loved ones had been.

The wine had allowed them to laugh, something that hadn't happened often that year. They found themselves laughing through their tears, and even Eshe didn't have the heart to scold them too badly for stealing the wine, for their attempt at experiencing what little they could reclaim of their stolen youth.

After that, though, Eshe had Salim install a lock on the cellar and kept a better tally of his stores.

"I see you have access to the cellar's key now."

"*Finally,*" she said with a dramatic huff. "I'm planning on having a glass with breakfast. Steady my nerves."

"One glass. Everyone knows you can't hold your liquor."

Lore pouted, her face theatrical. "Not when I was fifteen, sure. But I can now." She wriggled her eyebrows. "Do you want to join me?"

Grey eyed the bottle, his face pulling into a grimace.

"I'd better not. When I have a glass, it reminds me of Queen Riella's wine. The craving for it becomes more prominent, harder to quell."

Lore wanted to kick herself. She was so stupid for even offering him a glass. "I see. I'm happy you are managing it, though."

"Being kept as a spectacle, an oddity for her court to gawk at, a sort of 'pet' of hers was terrible, but the worst of it is just this damned craving . . . this constant ache for her wine, her food . . . It helped that once I set foot back in Duskmere, I literally couldn't leave again. Takes away some of the urge to go off and drown myself in it." His laugh was wry.

Lore placed her hand on his shoulder. "I wonder if there is a spell I could—"

"It's fine. I mean, it's not fine, but I'm handling it."

"Let me know, all right? If it becomes too much to bear. I'm sure I can help."

Grey smiled, pulling her into a quick hug. "You returning is help enough."

Lore squeezed him back.

She was afraid again. Afraid that their plan wouldn't work. That Grey would be killed, another person in her life to leave her arms empty.

✸

Later, Isla, Finn, and Lore slipped out the back door and entered the field behind the shelter. They sat upon the earth in a circle, nestling between two rows of spindly grapevines that, even in death, clung to their trellises.

The air thrummed with anticipation as Lore, her lips pressed tight in concentration, carefully turned the pages of *Auroradel*. Sunlight streamed through the leaves of the vines, painting dappled shadows across the diagrams and texts. Isla sat opposite Lore, her ethereal beauty heightened by tentative hope.

"Are you sure about this, Lore?" Isla asked, her voice a whisper laced with trepidation. "We don't have a volcanic deity to help break the curse."

"Now that I have the sun book, we do not need one. If you want this, then I have to try," Lore replied, her voice firm despite the imperceptible tremor in her hands. *Auroradel* pulsed with heat, its soft light glowing beneath her fingertips, as if wanting to assuage her worries, as if telling her, *Believe it will be so, believe in me, in us, and it will be.* "Like Finndryl, I can feel the magic lying dormant within you, bound by the rotten film of the curse. Your magic is strong. It's time it was set free."

"This might be painful, but Isla, it will be so worth it. Trust Lore," Finndryl murmured to his sister.

Isla nodded. Her eyes flicked from Finndryl to Lore, her gaze unwavering. She squared her shoulders. "I trust you, Lore. I'm ready."

Lore found the page detailing a ritual of luminescence, a spell designed to cleanse. She took a deep breath as she studied the page, committing the ancient Alytherian to memory, before letting the book rest on her skirts and taking one of Isla's hands in hers, Finndryl's in the other. She would use the feel of his magic as a map to help guide the spell within Isla, as their magic was connected, not just by family, or the curse, but because they were connected by more than that, they were formed together in the same womb.

Lore began to chant the incantation, her voice rising and falling, the spell sounding songlike as she wove it, pressed it into Isla.

Isla gritted her teeth, her body trembling with the intensity of Lore's spell as warm, bright light enveloped her. Lore closed her eyes as she continued chanting, no longer needing the spell to guide her as she poured all her hopes and adoration for Isla into the spell.

Isla gasped, the sound choked, agonized. Lore's eyes flew open. Her resolve faltered, what if she was hurting Isla as she did Finn, but this time the spell wouldn't take?

But then, she *saw* the curse. A rust-red mist began to seep from Isla's pores, writhing and hissing as it met the light. She couldn't stop now. It was working!

Lore maintained even as Isla cried out, her body beginning to convulse as the red mist grew denser. It encircled Isla like a tornado, overpowering the light as it fought against the cleansing spell. Finndryl tightened his grip on Lore's hand, and she knew that he was clenching Isla's tighter, sending strength to his sister.

With a final surge of power from Lore, the light expanded, erupted, banishing the red mist, which dissolved into motes of dust that scattered in the wind.

Isla's eyes sprang open, just before she gave a shudder and collapsed forward into Finndryl's outstretched arms, her body suddenly racked with heaving sobs.

"Isla, tell me, what do you feel? Are you all right?" Lore asked, terrified that it had gone wrong. That she had caused Isla pain for nothing.

"I . . . I can feel it," she whimpered into her brother's shoulder. "It's lifted. The curse is lifted."

CHAPTER 43

Hazen left after breakfast, having his own part to play in their uprising. Their future settlement depended on Queen Naia keeping her end of the bargain that Lore had struck with her back in Lapis Deep. Lore had faith that she would keep her promise. The goodbye with the siren prince was swift, as Lore and Finndryl would see him soon.

The inhabitants of Duskmere gathered, each person with a bowl from home, at the open-air church, which stood defiantly nestled within a copse of trees, as the sun rose toward its zenith. Lore's footsteps were silent on the creeping alyssum that covered the ground as she wove through the crowd of humans. Dappled sunlight illuminated the moss-covered stone altar at the front of the church, casting shadows upon *Ziara*, the sacred skyglass they used to search and track the stars. Generations of hope were stored within the magnificent skyglass, as countless gazes peered through the eyepiece searching for Shahassa.

The elders chanted prayers over the people who crowded into the church, spilling out through the open windows, the entrances. For the church, not built to contain, was more a collection of lichen-covered stone pillars. Their voices wove in and out of the pillars, the trees, as they chanted—imploring the gods to guide them to victory. Many hugged their loved ones close. Lore's gaze clung to the people, trying to memorize everyone's face. Some she might never see again.

Heat from the black behemoth of a cauldron warmed her cheeks, and she placed the pack of ingredients she'd brought from Jamal market onto the pew beside her. The oil was ready. Lore scooped the chopped onion from the cutting board and dropped it into the sizzling oil. When those softened, she added the garlic that Finndryl had just finished chopping. One minute for that; she didn't want the garlic to burn. Next, she added salt—for protection—then handfuls of cumin, coriander, turmeric, and a pinch of fiery chili— the added warmth would help to strengthen them. The fragrance wafting up from the cauldron made her mouth water.

"Just in time," Lore called to Lex and his partner, a long-haired boy with kind eyes and a cheeky sense of humor, as they hauled in the last bucket of water and set it at her feet.

"Smells good, Lore," Lex said with a grin, threading his fingers through his partner's.

"I'm hoping it will taste even better," she said as she poured the buckets of river water into the cauldron. The broth began to boil immediately, a perk of having Finn there to tend the fire, so she needn't wait before emptying both bags of lentils and barley into the pot. "Finn, can you add the sausage?" She cut her eyes at him, daring him to make a joke about the "sausage" he would rather be handing her, but he refrained, though his eyes crinkled at the corners as he slid the knife across the cutting board, adding the pile of sausages to the broth. Lore snatched an end piece of a sausage just before its descent into the broth and slipped it to Ember, who was weaving in and out of her legs.

She added in the dried herbs, the last of the ingredients, before stirring with a large wooden spoon, imbuing each pass around the cauldron with intention. This wouldn't be a simple meal; this was communion, it was health, and love, and cherished memories, and hope, so much hope.

While the stew simmered, she and Uncle Salim opened bundles of sticky, sweet dates, sliced fruit, beeswax, and chocolates onto a table.

A few months ago, she passed the fae farmlands of Alytheria and dreamt of bringing wagons filled with food back to her people. She hadn't managed a wagon, but at least she would be able to fill their bellies and hearts this day. Wagons would come later.

When the stew was ready, she filled every single person's bowl. As the first spoonfuls were tasted, a murmur of appreciation arose. Lore watched, her heart swelling with a fierce tenderness. As the last bowl was emptied, a newfound resolve settled over the villagers. Their eyes, dulled with resignation and hunger before, now burned with determination.

Finally, when the sun reached its zenith, every willing person kissed their loved ones goodbye, buttoned their coats, tightened the laces and buckles on their boots, and headed toward the forest that had been their prison wall since before they were born. Since before their grandparents had been born.

Lore took the lead. With every step, she cast her magic wide, searching the barrier for fractures in the spell. She pressed her own magic of the sun, locating each fissure, widening the fractures until the spell fell apart as though she were swiping at a spider's web.

Lore was the first to step into the forest. To show them that she had indeed broken the spell. There was nothing here to fear anymore, not even any sentries.

For almost everyone, this was their first time stepping into the woods.

With every tread of her boots over the frost-covered ground, Lore spooled her magic, drawing on the grimoires' power.

Their plan was simple: a show of force.

Lore did not know what the king planned to do with the humans, why he had pulled his sentries back and in preparation for what . . . She hoped with her return that the humans were no longer defenseless and planned on fighting back, that he would not want to risk his precious soldiers on them.

They hoped he would let them go. Lore wanted to fight him. To try every one of the Alytherians responsible for their crimes, but Lore was no stranger to sacrificing her wants for the greater good. She could put her anger aside if it meant they could leave Alytherian land unharmed, uncontested, for good.

The king had plenty of warning to prepare for their arrival at his castle. A host of palace guards stood in front of the gates. Overkill, as anyone with eyes could see that the gates were barred shut and the humans were not carrying any weapons that would breach the thick wood of the gates.

Many of the soldiers wore the blue stripes of sentries, their uniforms pressed, their stripes shining with superiority. The sneers on their faces and their jeers were familiar to Lore and slid off her back like water.

The humans arrived at the gates. Finndryl and Isla came with them but stood behind them. This was not a time for the fae to speak for the humans.

Lore prayed that she had not led them to their deaths.

"We have come to request an audience with the king," Lore said, projecting her voice for all to hear. She was glad that it was loud and clear, not a hint apparent of the fear that clogged her veins.

The commander spit on the ground at Lore's feet. Some of the spittle landed on her boot. She felt Finndryl stiffen behind her but prayed he did not make a scene.

"I am Commander Arelas, voice of the king. He declines your request," he said to Lore, his tone haughty, infuriating. The commander stepped forward and addressed the rest of the crowd. "Your king views this display as blatant insurrection." He paused a beat, letting that sink in, before continuing. "But he is a merciful king. He will not end your lives for this mistake, but instead, he has most graciously decreed that you shall return to Duskmere at once. However, his mercy has limits." The commander grinned, sweeping his hand out toward the sun, which had almost dipped below the tree line. "Anyone found outside the forest barrier by the time the sun has set will be regarded as a dissenter and will, as such, be put to death. On sight."

One of the sentries in the back called out, "Do as you're told, humans!"

"Better hurry!" another shouted through a peal of cruel laughter.

"Go home to your mud. Your kind aren't welcome here!" This was voiced not by a sentry but by a citizen . . . a female fae wearing an apron, holding a fuzzy cat in her arms, leaning over the balcony railing of one of the houses that had cropped up on the outskirts of the castle wall.

Lore clenched her jaw so tightly she was half afraid her teeth would crack.

Instead, she looked behind her at her people's shining, beautiful faces and drew courage from them.

They may be quaking in their boots right now, but you wouldn't know it by looking at them. They stood, backs straight, their chins in the air, pride in their eyes. Pride in who they were, in each other.

Uncle Salim, who stood tall beside Eshe, winked at Lore and motioned with both hands toward his chest.

Inhale.

Exhale.

Lore raised her chin, turning back to the commander. "If he is truly our king, then he will meet with his subjects." She clenched her fists at her sides. "We have come to *demand* an audience. We will not leave until then."

Commander Arelas's face went red with anger, and he sputtered, "*If* he is your king? Little girl, you speak treason quite boldly for a human." He pointed a long finger right in her face; it took every ounce of strength in Lore not to flinch away. "Let me clarify this for you, since you seem to be too stupid to understand even simple commands. *You* 'demand' nothing because you *are* nothing." He raised his voice once more. "Go home, all of you. Before I set the dogs on you."

There were indeed a few vicious-looking dogs to the side, strong, bulging necks pulling at their leads. A few snapped their jaws like they were eager to take a bite out of them. A shiver of fear rolled through Lore.

It had been *years* since the king had used his hunting dogs on them. She'd never personally been a witness to it. But she'd heard the stories.

She'd seen the scars. The disfigurements.

Anyone who was lucky enough to avoid having their throat ripped out and only suffered a bite was lucky to survive the infection, let alone keep the limb.

With so many eyes on them, the dogs whined and began to paw at the frozen ground, pacing back and forth. Then they began to bark.

Lore was afraid. If they let the dogs loose, she wouldn't be able to protect everyone from them, and someone would be hurt.

"We demand an audience with the king," Emalie, an old friend and one of the women she'd rescued from the tower, called out, taking up for Lore. Her voice pealed through the frigid air but could barely be heard over the howling of the dogs.

"We demand an audience with the king!" Lore recognized

Uncle Salim's voice, though he was a calm man. A quiet man. She'd never heard him raise it before.

Others took up the cry until they were all chanting in unison, their voices drowning out the barking of the dogs and the howling of the winter wind.

Lore glanced at the gates. Surely their cry would reach the fae ears of the king. They would open, and he would treat with them now.

Commander Arelas seemed unsettled. He had obviously expected them to turn and race for home, trying to reach Duskmere by sundown. He'd probably imagined they would run over one another, pushing others out of the way to get to the front, to be the first home.

For he was aware, just as they were, that at this distance, even if they had left the *moment* he'd demanded it of them, sprinting the *entire* way, only the fastest of them would make it home by sundown.

If the soldiers acted on their threat, almost every last one of them standing here right now would be slaughtered, no matter how much they tried to comply.

Hope stirred in Lore's belly as a small, seemingly insignificant door cut into the wall swung open, spitting out a messenger like an olive pit. The messenger hesitated for a moment, almost tripping over their feet, clearly alarmed by the size of the crowd. They had probably never seen a human, let alone two hundred of them, but they had a job to do and hesitated for only a moment before running straight to the commander and handing him a note. They waited, bouncing from foot to foot. When a confirming nod came from the commander, they raced back, slipping once more through the door.

Commander Arelas crumpled the piece of parchment in his hand and placed it into one of his many pockets before spitting once more on the ground.

"Witch." He pointed at Lore, his finger stabbing toward her

face like he wished it were a knife. "Your king will meet with you." He spat. "Your . . . people may wait for you here without being harmed until your return."

This was one of the scenarios Lore wanted to avoid. She didn't want to leave them. Without her, the few knives and cudgels hidden under their coats would only delay the inevitable—if they were lucky and could delay it at all. With the way the soldiers and some of the townspeople looked at them, they might be better off turning their knives on themselves before the soldiers could get to them.

But they had known this was a possibility, and they had planned for it.

That was why there were not truly hundreds of humans who had marched with her here, but only fifteen. That had been all she needed. The rest, she had memorized their clothes, their faces, their footfalls at the church. She had replicated them in her mind, then formed the glamour like clay, multiplied them until she had an army behind her, but only fifteen, really, to protect.

She'd begged Salim and Eshe to stay back, but they had insisted.

She reached behind her, feeling for Finndryl's hand. He grasped it between both of his. They said all they could to each other with that one short clasp.

Lore's gaze pierced the commander's. She would take him out this day, if she had the chance. She would bend him to his knees and make him beg her for mercy, and then she would give him the same "mercy" that his exalted king offered her people. But for now, she just gave a stiff nod. "Take me to him."

CHAPTER 44

L ore knew this castle. She knew these halls, torches, and polished floors . . . until she didn't. She'd had no reason to visit this wing of the castle and would have been punished by the steward if she had snuck in, even if only for a peek, even if it were empty. Lore reached for *Auroradel* in her mind and told it to hold the stored power for her. Afraid there was a spell that would alert the king in the throne room, she would not enter with active magic. So she promised to use it again, knowing that it hated to be cut off from her, and she cinched the connection closed, tying once and then twice the knot in her mind.

Stepping through the double doors of the Wyndlin Castle throne room felt like being doused with frigid water. But still, she reminded herself, this was not the first throne room she'd entered. She'd infiltrated Queen Riella's, saved her best friend, and survived that ordeal. And she'd been *invited* into Queen Naia's and left her throne room with a new friend.

She would survive this one too.

Her footfalls echoed in the cavernous space, making her feel so incredibly alone. She brushed the grimoires with her wrist. Yes, they were there, she reminded herself. Both books nestled in their satchel on her belt, tucked in beneath her coat. The guards hadn't even searched her. They apparently hadn't cared if she carried a sharpened axe to their king, for they never in a thousand years would think that she would use it on him. And they apparently didn't care if she carried deadly grimoires on her person either.

She could feel the weight of countless eyes upon her, each no doubt finding her wanting. Chitters rose up from the crowd. The king was evidently holding court today; raised seats on either side of the throne room were filled with courtiers—a poisoned sea of silks and brocade, lush skin dripping with glittering jewels. Wicked grins flashed, hidden behind delicate hands that had never had to lift a finger in their too-damned-long lifetime.

Perfect. She'd hoped the king would want an audience as he denied her everything she asked for, because she needed hostages to exchange for Syrelle and his family.

The antiquated king sat upon his throne, a selfish lion lording over his dominion. Despite being fae, time had not been kind to him. His balding wings had lost most of their feathers and sagged behind him like a kite ravaged by the branches of an oak tree. His skin hung from his skeleton like clumps of wet paper. Lore was almost grateful when the commander pressed hard on her shoulders, pushing her to her knees with bruising force, because she couldn't stand to look upon the vile king a moment longer.

Lore bowed her head in supplication, waiting for the monarch to speak first. He took his time, allowing the silence to press on her ears, making her want to squirm.

She flinched at the sudden bang of a door being thrust open at the back of the throne room. Followed by the soft shuffle of slippers as someone walked across the hall before stopping beside the king.

"Why have you brought this mess to my door?" the king finally demanded of Lore. The king might look old, but his voice was strong, robust. The juxtaposition startled Lore into glancing up at him before he'd permitted her to. She had a moment to glimpse that it had been Coretha who'd just entered and now leaned casually against the gold back of the king's throne before Commander Arelas shoved Lore's head back down.

"Do not look upon the king unless given leave to do so."

Maybe instead of forcing the commander to his knees when she had her turn, she would one-up him and break them instead.

"Oh, Your Majesty, do let her look upon us. Your visage is a gift no human has ever seen before. And I do so like watching her squirm," said Coretha.

"You may look upon me but stay kneeling, human. It's only proper," the king acquiesced, leaning forward on his throne. Lore was surprised she couldn't hear his bones creaking or collapsing into dust with the movement.

His curiosity had been piqued. Maybe Lore provided a novel experience for him. Could she use this somehow?

"Your Majesty, I bring you the wishes of my people."

"Oh?" He feigned surprise. "I was not aware your kind *could* wish." Chittering laughter from the crowd of courtiers. He knew they wished. That they dreamt and loved and sought more than he would allow them.

He may view them as worth little more than the weakest nag in his stable, but the king couldn't live as long as he had and not be privy to the intellect of the humans. And, due to their intelligence, how truly atrocious an existence had been forced on them.

For it was true, they might wish, but when had their wishes ever come true?

Only, Lore's had. She had wished for magic, and she had gotten it.

Lore swallowed her pride and bowed low until her forehead rested on the floor of his throne room. At least it was clean; his servants were an effective bunch. Rude, but efficient.

"We wish not to burden you anymore with our presence in your great kingdom. If you would let us, we would depart—make our way so far from here you need not ever think of us again."

"Did you hear that, Uncle? They wish to unburden us and *leave*."

Gods, Lore was ready never to have to hear Coretha's haughty voice again. She'd hated it before, but now that she knew she'd betrayed her own cousin, put in jeopardy his niece and nephew, who were innocent children . . . she despised the sound even more.

The king barked a laugh. Lore recoiled. He had a monstrous sound to him. Lore imagined for a moment what he would have been like in his prime. Dragon eyes gleaming from his face. A desire to bite, and rip, and smash, and grind her bones.

She pushed the disturbing thought from her mind.

"Do you know why I called the humans through the portal to my land?"

What did he mean . . . *he* called the humans here? The room spun as a wave of dizziness washed over her. Could the king really have been the cause of her ancestors' displacement? How could one being, unless a god, be so powerful?

The king continued on, "Your life force, human. You burn with it. Humans are dumb, filthy things, but you live such short lives; your life force is like a beacon. Your passions, emotions, all of that sustain me. It empowers me. It has kept me young. I called your kind here as a *Source* of my own. I draw on your people as we speak. Your own life force, little witch . . ." he licked his lips ". . . will be delicious."

Rage thrashed within her like a writhing den of serpents. "Our lives are not for you to consume. They belong to us," she hissed.

"You are the weak, I the powerful. What you have will always belong to me." Suddenly, he looked bored with the conversation.

"Heir Coretha, it would be wonderful to have that land free of vermin . . . but why do they think that we would ever let them go? It would be a truly daft leader to kill the fathers and not expect the children to rise up as soon as their back is turned."

"You're right, Uncle. They would come back eventually and

having to squirrel them out of their hidey-holes to annihilate them would be terribly dull, when we could do as we planned, finish them now."

Lore's blood froze in her veins. She had to implement her plan to bind him and the courtiers with her magic now—demand Syrelle's and Maple's locations, then hold the royal court long enough for the rest of her people to meet with the siren waiting at the docks. She had to distract the king while she unleashed her magic. "Your Highness—" she started, but Commander Arelas was quick, so quick, she had no time to see him move before a backhand blow crashed into her face. She felt the cold sting of brass knuckles, then arresting agony exploded through her head as the bones in her cheek cracked open like an egg.

The force flung her backward like a marionette; she slid across the freshly waxed floor. Lore pressed her hand to her cheek, trying to contain a whimper, but it slipped unbidden between ruined lips. She covered her face; afraid another blow was coming.

Coretha stepped over to where Lore lay on the ground. "Stupid girl. I don't see why you returned at all. You had the grimoires; you could have gone anywhere. You could have been free."

"I am not free until we are all free." Lore fought back against a wave of nausea. "While my people remain shackled in Duskmere under your uncle's rule, and soon, your rule, I cannot be free. I cannot rest." Lore gritted her teeth against the pain of speaking. Her mouth was filling up with blood again. "I *will not* rest." Lore spit blood and saliva at Coretha's feet, daring her with her eyes to say one more insipid thing to her.

"Insolent witch," Commander Arelas shouted, stalking toward her. Lore tried to dodge the hit, but he moved like a cheetah.

The world went dark for a moment as her lips shredded against her teeth, and her jaw made a sickening popping sound. Lore cowered, covering her head with her arms.

When no more blows came, she peeked out through spread fingers.

Arelas had shifted, making room for the king, who rose from his throne like a god.

No, a demon.

Lore shrank back from him in horror as he changed form with each step toward her.

His skin contracted, the pallid color warming, turning brown and smooth with youth as it formed over rippling muscles. His hair turned black as night, thickened, his coils shining. And his wings—gods, his wings—lifted, fanning out behind him like death, his feathers as oily black as a crow's. Beneath his skeletal disguise was power incarnate.

It was a sham to trick his enemies into underestimating him. And Lore had fallen for it. She should have cast her magic out the moment she was in his presence. It would have been the only way she could have had a sliver of a chance. But instead, she'd seen only his facade, and she'd walked right into his trap.

His eyes tripped delightedly across her face, soaking up her pain as if it were a decadent feast.

For a moment, all she could see was the yellow glow of his irises.

He *was* a demon.

And she was his prey to be devoured.

CHAPTER 45

Lore forgot that she had battled sea monsters and braved a volcano. Had faced griffins, a reverie, and caves bursting with insects. That she had done all this to become powerful, more powerful than *him*.

She couldn't remember any of that as he pinned her with his gaze.

His pupils were blown wide, but his yellow irises were all she could see.

She was only a twenty-one-year-old human. Her feats were *nothing* to him, whose age was unknowable. Her life was a blip. He would blink, and she would be gone. *He would sleep, and her children would be dust.*

He would crush her skull beneath his boot and then devour her whole. And when he was done with her, he would hunt down every single person that she loved and consume them too.

For her kind were toys to him. Something to pass the time, and now his playthings had grown unruly. They needed to be crushed.

The king said all of this with a look in the span of one step.

He did not need to speak aloud for his thoughts to be known. He was a king; what he wanted, he got. He need not worry about how, only that it simply *was*.

His thoughts conquered her mind, and he impressed onto her visions of what he planned to do with the vermin problem up north.

Lore rolled onto her back, scrambling away from him—or she tried to. She couldn't make her body listen.

I'll show you what became of Syrelle first. The king's voice was mind-shattering in her head—she was swept into a vision.

—He'd arrived at the castle days ago, collapsing to his knees at the king's feet from exhaustion. He was on the brink of death from the journey already, but Syrelle had mustered up every last ounce of life remaining to plead for his family's lives, to beg for mercy on Lore and the people of Duskmere. The king had laughed in Syrelle's face, and then the king's hands changed; claws sprouted from where his fingers had been; and with one swipe, he'd shredded his nephew's beautiful, feathered wings. Syrelle convulsed, rolling back onto his ruined wings—

Syrelle's howl of agony ripped through Lore's heart like a saw. The only thing she could do was blink away tears as they rolled down her cheeks, mixing with blood and bone and tissue from her crumbling face.

—The king crouched over a writhing Syrelle and slashed through his leathers and his shirt, parting his skin and bones—

Gagging, mind staggering, she tried to avert her eyes from this horror, but the king controlled what she saw; the king controlled everything.

—Syrelle's scream abated abruptly as the king shoved his clawlike hand inside his nephew's body and pulled out his still-beating heart. Syrelle's silence was heartbreak. His silence was torture. Then the king bit into his heart, slurping up his life blood—

Lore had come here to rescue him, but she'd been too late.

I've shown you what was, witch. Now witness what follows.

His cruelty leached into her skin as he encased Lore in viselike magic; it was unbreakable and fluid simultaneously; it slipped over her body, glued her to the floor. She tried to fight against it, but she was no match for him. Then, with one last look of contempt, he turned his back on her and left the room. But she was not free of him; she would never again be free of his control. She saw everything he saw.

—The king had combed through her mind the moment she'd set foot in his throne room, so when he stepped outside the castle gate . . . he knew exactly who to start with.

Finndryl Hwraeth was easy to spot—

"Run," Lore screamed, but she was not there with him, she was trapped on the floor, writhing in agony. "Run, my love."

—The low-class nonentity who dared defy a king was standing at the front of the huddle of vermin. The half-breed should have dropped to his knees and groveled before the king the moment he'd appeared, but the clanless one was foolish, and when he spotted the king, he had the arrogance to shout the witch's name. As though he'd truly expected her to return victorious. When it was clear to Finn that Lore was nowhere to be seen, he shouted to the humans to gather and ignited an arc of fire around them, as if that would slow the king while he left to find his witch—

To the king, inside her mind, she begged him to stop. She would do anything. She would give him anything. *Please don't do this. Not him, please, gods, not Finn!*

The king paused for a moment to remind her: *She would have nothing to give once he'd taken everything.*

Something had taken over her mind before. Something had done this before, and she had survived. She had beat it. She had lived . . .

The cave.

Auroradel!

Lore twitched her fingers. All she had to do was use her magic. She could burn him from the inside out. She could cleanse the scourge of him with her light.

Lore reached for the sun book with her mind; she called to *Auroradel*, and to *Deeping Lune*.

—It was nothing to step through the arc of fire. The king could not

even feel its heat. He deflected a blow from Isla, the sister, as though she were a gnat buzzing in his ear. With a flick of his wrist, he shoved her so she fell into her own brother's fire—

Lore called to the grimoires. *Unleash the spooled magic! Unleash it so I can save him. I was too late for Syrelle, please let me save Finndryl!* But there was no response. Something was wrong.

All that magic she had spooled and put on reserve . . . it should have obliterated the hold the king had on her. The pain in her cheek, in her jaw, was like pulsing fire. But pain was good. She should really worry when it went away.

Lore squinted her eyes through a haze, seeing double vision. The king was encroaching on her mind again, stealing her ability to think. She fought it off. She needed her fucking books, she wasn't going to let them die! She shook her hands, urging the black, inky stains to spring awake with her power, like on the ship. This reserve of *Source* . . . her black stains were still, lifeless. *Source*less. Lore looked around, squinting. There was something wrong with this room . . .

There wasn't any *Source*, not a drop of it glittering on the windowsills, not a collection of it swirling in the corners, none flowing in an air current from under the doors; this room was a void.

Magic could not exist here. Unless it was his magic.

—Finndryl roared his sister's name, quelling his fire immediately—

She felt her coat brushed aside. Someone unclasped her belt and ripped it free, satchel and all.

"Thank you for bringing the grimoires to us." Coretha's sing-song voice broke through.

Lore shook. Finndryl—she had to get to Finndryl and Isla!

Coretha continued, "I have to admit, I've been curious about them. If they were worth my cousin throwing away his future on them, they might be worth something to me."

—Finndryl's fire had been too hot; Isla's skin and hair had melted, and she wasn't breathing as Emalie pulled her into the circle of humans.

Roaring a battle cry, Finndryl lunged at the king, his sword flashing like lightning—

"Cor . . . th . . . a, plss . . ." she gurgled. Swollen tongue. Too much coppery blood.

Coretha huffed, standing up. "There's *blood* on my slippers. I'll have to throw these away now." Lore's belt, which held the grimoires, dangled from Coretha's hands. She turned her back on Lore and walked calmly toward the door, her braids swishing behind her.

She was leaving her here. Lore's vision spun, Coretha turning her back on her on the ship, and again, now, in the throne room. Only this time, she was taking her hope.

—The king gripped the halfling's sword by the blade; the metal, even being of siren make, was not sharp enough to cut him. The king ripped the blade from the halfling's grip. It was then easy to wrap his razor-sharp claws around his throat. To haul the struggling male up until his boots lifted off the road. Finndryl's eyes were wide with fear. The king used his power to shoot that same viscous substance from his free hand into the halfling's mouth. He guided it, pushing more and more into the halfling's lungs—

She had to save him. This couldn't be happening, this couldn't be. Lore wept as she burst the blood vessels in her eyes trying to claw free of the king's control. She choked on bile that mixed with blood as she gnashed her broken jaws together, fighting with everything she had to—

—A sick squelch ricocheted through her mind—the sound of Finndryl's lungs bursting—

Lore's mind splintered.

—The king smiled when Grey found him. He elongated a single claw and—Lore's mind couldn't process what she was seeing. Grey's head was too far away from his body. Her mind shuttered, trying to protect her, but it was no match for the king. He demanded she watch, so she was forced to watch. Next, Eshe and Salim, but who to kill first? Which would hurt who more? For Eshe to see Salim die, or Salim to see Eshe die? He decided on

Eshe first. A stab through the throat; then, he waited a beat to make sure Salim saw his wife die before he sliced in through the heart. Lore watched, her mind frozen with shock; it stuttered, it stopped, it started again, as though it had forgotten how to be. It was nothing for the demon to leap into the air and fly to Duskmere. Minutes. It took minutes and then he was there, with the children. They screamed and screamed—

Lore vomited.

—Lex, almost nineteen, first. Silvia, Katu—

She was choking on bile and blood because she couldn't move.

—Milo—

There was no one left.

Surely, he would come for her next.

Please. Let her be next.

Again? chimed the cruel voice in her mind.

The vision assaulted her mind again.

It started with Syrelle.

It ended with Milo.

Over and over, Lore watched them be cut down until she lost the ability to plead, to weep, until she lost their memories, their names.

All she knew was the weight of his violence, the insatiable hunger.

It consumed her.

CHAPTER 46

She had to call for her books, because they would come to her, wouldn't they? When she called them? They would be disappeared and reappear in her hands, and she could burn this place to the ground . . . She had tried that last night. And again, this morning. She had practiced it, just in case they took them from her . . . Finndryl had even run, so fast, he was so fast, and beautiful, he'd run with her books to the other side of the village, and they had still come when she called them.

But Finndryl was dead, wasn't he?

She'd seen him die.

He'd been in pain . . . so much pain . . . His lungs had burst, frothy blood had spilled out of his mouth and nose, it had splattered onto Grey's face; Grey was screaming, screaming, he was screaming *so* loud. *Please stop screaming,* Lore wanted to say. *It hurts,* she tried to say, but she couldn't say it because it was she who was screaming. She was clawing at her skin, clutching her hair, pounding on her head with her fists; she needed these memories out of her head. She would do anything not to see them anymore . . .

The books, her books. She called out for them. She had to save them. She had to save them all. She called them. She didn't feel that pull, that tug that had been so easy to gather into herself until her books appeared right there in her hands like they had been there all along. Milo had been laughing, delighted at her display of magic. Poor Milo, he had . . . he had . . .

She was moaning into the floor, no, she was screaming again, her body racked with sobs. The screams were being torn from her throat. They would never stop . . . until the sound finally did, cut off as she coughed, hacking, until she vomited onto the floor.

CHAPTER 47

O h, Arelas, I do believe the human's strength is giving out. Disappointing. I was led to believe that she was special, but she's just like the others, isn't she?"

A *humm* of agreement. "She doesn't have long left."

"I'll leave you to clean up the mess. Order the humans back to their hovel. We can't have so many bodies on our front step; better to do as originally planned and orchestrate the culling in their home. Yes. Gather the troops." A laugh. "In a few years, the forest will have made it like new again; we won't even have to dispose of the bodies . . ."

Lore couldn't make sense of the words; her world was a muddled, incomprehensible thing. She covered her ears. She didn't want to know what they were saying, for it would bring only more torment.

"Throw her in the dungeon."

The voices faded.

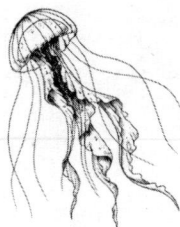

CHAPTER 48

Lore peered into the dim, wavering light. She rubbed at her eyes, removing clumps of reddish-brown flakes that had dried onto her lashes.

Blood.

Lore grimaced, and the pain in her face amplified a thousand-fold. She gingerly pressed on the swollen, crusted, weeping mess that was all that was left of her right cheek and hissed in pain. She tapped gently on her right eye—swollen shut. Tried to work her jaw, but sharp, piercing pain resonated through her skull.

Lore rolled onto her back. Her shoulders were bruised and scraped, her entire body racked with shivers. Shock, or the cold of the dungeon floor that had already seeped into her bones, she didn't know which.

Yesterday she had woken up beside Finndryl. Hazen and Isla had been there. Grey . . . they'd been so filled with hope.

They'd been so meticulous. They had planned for everything.

Except, she failed. She hadn't noticed that she couldn't use her magic in the throne room until it was too late.

Moonlight drifted in through a window she couldn't see, but fingers of light reached through the bars of the cell. The shimmering, dancing dust motes seemed to be laughing at her. If it had been

Source dancing in the light, she could call her books, melt the bars of this jail, and leave. But there was no *Source* here. Like the throne room, this was a void as well.

Yesterday she had hope.

Today she had nothing.

There was no one left.

Lore moaned, her grief a physical pain.

She clenched her hands into fists. She could feel their emptiness. They would never again hold Milo to her. Feel Eshe's warm hand in hers. Feel Finndryl's beating heart while she laid her head on his chest.

She'd gathered everyone that she loved, and she'd marched them straight into a demon's clutches. For the king was just that . . . a demon. He may have been born a person, a thousand years ago, but whatever empathy or civility or mortality he'd had . . . he must have exchanged it for evil. For whatever monstrosity she had encountered yesterday . . . he could not be beaten.

She'd killed them all.

And what had he said as he'd walked away?

Her brain shied away from the memory of the throne room as if to protect her.

But she needed to remember. The pain she was feeling was just punishment for her incompetence.

She pressed through the mental block, her own mind's attempt at kindness. She didn't deserve kindness of any kind. She was the worst sort of person . . . the type who lost everyone and was the only one left alive.

He'd said . . . he'd been giving orders. Instructions. Dungeon . . . force the humans back to Duskmere . . . a cull. They had already been planning on killing them all.

Even if she hadn't brought them here, he was going to kill them. But none of that mattered, because if she had never wanted to change their circumstances, the king would probably have continued on for who knows how many more years being cruel, but from a distance. If she hadn't shaken things up, he wouldn't have decided to end things.

But she hadn't been the one to shake things up. *He* had orchestrated an earthshake. That was what had been the beginning of their end. She just didn't realize it. And despite her attempts . . . her desperate search for the books . . . it hadn't been enough.

She was weak. Useless. She had never stood a chance. Not really. And now, they were dead.

All of them.

Lore rolled over onto her side, gagging. But she had vomited up everything, because all she did was heave, painfully; unsatisfactorily, nothing rose to the surface.

She was empty as a void.

Why was she cursed to be living?

The commander had been ordered to throw her in the dungeon, and then he was supposed to ensure everyone returned to Duskmere.

Her face screwed up in confusion. Order who? Weren't they dead? Hadn't she seen the king systematically murder them all? One by one he . . .

Lore wanted to shake her head, clear the fog, but she couldn't move her head or neck; every minimal movement was a sharp, jabbing pain. A sob rocked through her chest anyway; tears slipped down her face. It hurt to cry. Good. She deserved to hurt.

Why wasn't she dead too?

Because, a voice told her, *death for you would have been a mercy. You do not deserve mercy.*

They kept her alive so she could flounder in this gut-wrenching agony.

Their torture was working, then.

Lore heaved a breath, pressing her right cheek into the cold dungeon floor, relishing the physical agony.

The memories of their violent deaths played over and over, she saw their tormented ends, heard their screams of agony, their cries for help, expecting her to save them. Again and again, they played on a loop.

Syrelle.

Isla.

Finndryl.

Grey.

Eshe.

Salim.

One by one all the children . . . She was forced to see the light leave their eyes. Their bodies become empty husks.

These memories replayed in her head for minutes

or days

or years.

CHAPTER 49

Lore must have fallen asleep, but she protested weakly as hands slid beneath her body and lifted her.

The demon, it was the demon come back for more.

She cried out when her face pressed against fabric. It hurt. *Everything hurt.*

"No more . . . let me die, please." She didn't think her words were comprehensible, but she tried to speak again. She would beg and plead if only the demon would let her die, but her jaw froze shut, too swollen and damaged to form speech.

Lore smiled through the hurt. There was no freedom, save death. Maybe this was her savior, and he had come to set her free.

Please let her death be swift.

She would meet them in the afterlife, soon.

She would see them all again.

CHAPTER 50

Lore's face itched.

She didn't bother to scratch it. If her face was itchy, then she was still cursed to be among the living.

"Wake up, Lore, we are running out of time."

She knew that voice.

For some reason, she'd thought he had been lost to her too.

Death. What sweet relief.

Lore thought about scratching her cheek again. The thought was nagging at her, a fly buzzing around her, insistent. But she couldn't be bothered to alleviate the irksome annoyance.

"Lore, please, open your eyes. Look at me, Mouse."

Something else was nagging at her. Something she should be recollecting. Remember? Lore didn't want to recollect anything. She didn't want to *be*.

Gods, her eye was stinging too. Her lips burning.

Something pressed to her mouth. Something cold. She coughed, sputtering, as she choked on water. She would have ignored this, too, if her body hadn't rebelled, as instinct made her rise, hacking until she cleared her airway.

She wiped her mouth, coughing more.

"I'm sorry, I wasn't trying to cause you to choke, but hey, it got you up."

Lore looked around, eyes bleary. Her face still godsdamned itched. She scratched at her cheek. Her nails were cracked, her fingertips shredded, bruised, like she had clawed against something coarse. A reaction like surprise flickered through her mind. Hadn't there been something wrong with her cheek? Something dark and awful . . . But no, she wouldn't think of that.

That way lay madness.

Detachment and emotional agony had synchronized within her now, and she did not wish to disturb this cocktail of safety.

A ghost came into focus. He was crouched on the ground beside her, clasping a cup of water.

"You look like shit for a ghost." Lore's voice was hoarse. She swallowed painfully.

Syrelle smiled, running a hand through his hair. His hands were covered in dried, flaking blood. So was his face. It was splattered with it.

"I look better than you."

"Probably not hard to do." She closed her eyes, leaned against a shelf behind her. She felt a few books slide back under the pressure of her weight.

"Lore, you can't go back to sleep. We have a battle to win."

"Not sleeping."

"Why are your eyes closed, then?"

"Waiting to die."

"I just healed most of your injuries with a pilfered vial of phoenix elixir. You'll be waiting awhile." Why had he healed her injuries? If given enough time, they would have festered. She would grow hot with fever. Then weak with infection. She could slip away like Mama had.

That wouldn't be so bad.

Something heavy landed on her lap. "This might cheer you up."

She failed to reach for it, and it slid off her thigh, landing on the floor with a soft thud.

"I know it's hard, Mouse. But I need you to open your eyes."

He pressed the heavy object against her chest.

She ignored it.

"Lore!"

By reflex, Lore flinched away from the sharpness in his voice.

"I'm sorry, I won't raise my voice again. Just, please, look."

Would that shut him up? Would he go away and leave her in peace then?

She opened her eyes and saw something impossible. Well, two impossibilities.

"Someone took them from me."

"That's right," he said slowly, concern flooding his face. "My cousin, remember?" He tapped the binding of one of the books.

Lore supposed they wouldn't burn a ghost, would they? That must be how he was holding them.

She wanted to be a ghost too.

"These saved us, Lore. Coretha . . . she . . . came to my cell to gloat, not knowing that I've been tortured by my uncle before— I was . . . She assumed I was in no state to fight back, but . . . this being tortured by him . . . was my normal, for a while, when I was younger. She was always one of his favorites; she never knew what it was like to be . . . his focus . . . I was able to overpower her and pilfer the books." He pressed them into her chest again, waiting for her to take them from him. "For you. I got them for you."

His . . . uncle? Lore's mind closed off against it. She shouldn't follow that train of thought.

"Is the blood hers?"

A shadow fell over Syrelle's face. He didn't have to nod for Lore to know that it was. The pain in his eyes at what he'd had to do was answer enough.

Lore pushed the books away.

"Don't want them."

"What do you mean? They're yours, remember?"

"They are nothing but a false hope. There's nothing for me anymore." An idea occurred to her. "How about, they can be yours? Take them and go."

"I'm not leaving you. Not ever again."

Lore frowned, a slight shiver of terror coursing through her. "You should leave. There's something after me—a monster." She looked at Syrelle, met his eyes, which were creased with worry. "It will take you from me again," she whispered, afraid it would hear her if she spoke too loudly. "I'll have to watch it eat you."

"The monster can't come into the library. No one can but us. We are safe here."

"Safe?" Lore didn't know that word. She thought, at one time, she might have. It represented something nice.

Confusion tangled her thoughts. Her mind was a spider's web, broken by a demon passing in the night. Her thoughts were ripped apart, blowing in the breeze.

Lore was somewhere safe, the ghost had said.

She looked around. She knew this place. Had known it. Once. Long ago.

A library.

The library.

The one that changed everything.

Syrelle had brought her to the library. He'd hidden them in a stack near the back, one that she had spent days putting to rights. Every tome was in its place, as she'd left it. Each shelf still wiped clean, free from dust or debris. The spines of the books on the shelf behind him had been some of her favorites. Almost all decoratively, artfully designed and ornamented with gold leaf, the lettering of each title rendered with strokes of pigmented paint. Designs had been pressed into the vellum along the bottom of each spine. A collection of toadstools on one, an ornate key on another, a silly frog holding a teacup on a third. Each spine had a different impression to represent one of the stories within.

A collection of children's tales made by a loving hand for a child who must have been very cherished.

As all children should be.

Her hands had placed them on the shelf, rendering order where there had been none. This, once, had been a joy, to spend her days among these books. Lonely, these books had seemed like friends to her, with their occasional murmurs and vibrations.

Or what she'd thought had been loneliness back then.

She wished, almost, that she could put her thoughts to rights, organize them like she had these books. Each memory could be a story with a rightful place upon the shelf of her life. She reached out a hand toward one of the books before lowering it back into her lap. There was a reason her mind was hesitant to remember. It was protecting her from something.

Someone? No, something. A monster.

Pain lanced through her chest, and she pulled in a ragged breath that rattled in her lungs. She didn't want to be here. She didn't want to remember.

"Please just leave me be . . . I can't . . . do this . . . anymore." Lore was sobbing, and Syrelle pulled her into his arms. She folded in her legs, wrapped her hands in his shirt, leaned into him, and wept. He enveloped her, holding her to him.

"I know it's hard, but there are people who *need* you. Finndryl and . . ."

"Don't say his name!" Lore heaved in between sobs. "Don't say any of their names; I can't bear it." She pressed her face harder into his chest. His arms tightened around her.

She thought that if he let her go, the fragile seams stitching her together would tear, and she would fall to pieces like rotted fabric. "I can't bear this, Syrelle, I need it to stop."

"I know he hurt you so badly that you think that his visions are your reality; I've been there. It took me years, learning to discern between his will and what was real. Whatever he showed you, it wasn't real. There is still hope."

"What do *you* know of hope?" she asked, her mouth filled with bitter regrets.

All Syrelle did was lie. He was still lying to her, even now.

She wanted to shove him away, but her body rebelled, and she clung to him and his beautiful lies as though he were a life raft.

Syrelle shifted her a little so that he could place a hand beneath her chin. He peeled her face from his shirt and lifted her chin until she was blinking at him through tears. "I knew not of hope, until I met you, Mouse. You *are* hope. All our hopes reside within you." He brushed his knuckles against her cheek. "And right now, the others don't know where you are or what has happened to you. But I trust the knowledge you are coming to save them is keeping them alive." Syrelle swallowed, and Lore tracked a tear as it spilled over and slid down his cheek. He didn't bother to wipe it away, choosing instead to search her eyes, to push through, even if his voice was thick with emotion and threatened to break. "Even now, you *burn* with hope. They tried to take it from you, but I can see it kindled within you. Let it burn, Lore."

"Hope for what?" Lore wiped at her eyes. She'd been full of false hope before. But there was only darkness within her now. It whispered at her to give up. She wasn't enough. He was lying. He was lying to her again. She couldn't trust him. He couldn't be trusted.

"We have one bell to get to the woods. By tonight there won't be any of them left, but as of right now, they are alive, and they are waiting for *you*."

Lore shook her head. "I can't protect them against the monster. I tried, I'm not—"

"He outwitted you. He learned that you had magic, and he

turned his throne room into a trap, so he was the only being who could wield it within those walls."

Lore's mind still shied away from memories of that room. She tasted bile in her throat; her eyes shuddered. "He's too powerful. I am nothing, he is—"

"You. Are. Everything! He is nothing! He *has* nothing. He has no one. You have family waiting for you. So let's go." Syrelle pulled her up to a standing position. She felt weak, exhausted to her bones.

"They are alive?"

"Yes. Arelas, the king's commander, fucked it all up. He was supposed to bring your corpse to them, break their spirits. But your little Ember got there first. She shifted into a godsdamned griffin, caused a disruption; Arelas had to join his troops before he got the chance. By the time he got out there, the humans had fled to the woods, where Finndryl and Isla put up a spell around them, but they can't hold it forever."

"Isla . . . I cleansed the curse from her. This morning."

"Good. You remember. You did well. She is a natural. She and Finn singlehandedly defeated the troops outside the gate."

"How do you . . ."

"Ember found me, with a note explaining all of it attached to her fur. She led me to you too."

"Where is she?"

"I wrote a note on the back and sent her to Finndryl. He knows that I have you, that you are coming back to him."

Lore's mind was reeling. That voice was trying to sow doubt in her again. But here was Syrelle, in front of her.

He was warm, his face flushed with emotion. He was very much . . . alive.

And he'd come back for her. And he'd brought her grimoires. If there was good in him . . . if he had hope that she could free him, free her people . . .

"Maple!" Lore gasped. "The children?"

"I have a small group of loyal soldiers. They smuggled them out yesterday. They are in a safe house in town."

Lore wiped the last of the tears from her face. Her fingers lingered on a raised ridge of flesh. A worthy scar for a worthy cause. She didn't care what she looked like, only that Syrelle had healed her at least enough to see . . . because she couldn't wait to see the look on the king's face when she annihilated him.

CHAPTER 51

Lore knelt on the floor of the library, flipping through *Auroradel*, her eyes skimming over pages and pages of looping script, drawings, spells, recipes, notes, everything that made this book as powerful as it was. She muttered under her breath, urging the grimoire to show her what she needed. It listened; the parchment fluttered and then warmed to the touch. Lore ran her fingers along the vellum. Animal skin of some kind. This page had a hole in the bottom-right corner, where the arrow had shot the beast whose skin was used to make these pages.

A spell to go from here to there.

She memorized the spell as best she could in the span of a few breaths. She need not have it perfectly, just enough to know that performing the spell was possible. Once she knew that, she need not recite the spell at all, only form it to her will.

"Hold on to my arm, Syrelle. We are going to the woods."

"Are you sure this will work?"

"It has to."

He nodded, his jaw firm. His eyes held no fear as he gripped her arm, his fingers wrapping around her bicep with care.

He trusted her, and she him.

She looked around at the library. She'd done a fine job fixing it up, and now it had saved her life, providing sanctuary for her and Syrelle.

Lore uttered a word, evoking the magic from the book. She blinked. A flood of power filled her being; she pushed it to flow through Syrelle as well, from his bloody boots to the tips of his hair. The world went sideways; it dipped, swirled. Her stomach lurched, and Lore clenched her teeth together, focusing on the spell.

To go from here to there.

She opened her eyes.

Syrelle and Lore were no longer kneeling on the marble floor of the Wyndlin Royal Library, but upon the earth, shaded beneath an ancient spruce.

She could hear the murmurings of her people, where they huddled in the forest against the cold, trying to figure out what to do next.

She'd done it.

The vivid orange of Ember was a blur as she raced to close the distance, her *yip yip* excited as she neared Lore. Lore snapped the grimoire closed and squeezed the wriggling fox, who'd saved her again. She pressed a kiss to the fox's head.

When she opened her eyes once more, they landed on him.

Him.

Finndryl. Was alive. Alive, alive, alive where he knelt, tending to the wounds of a man, though his hands had stilled as he saw Lore appear in the forest. His face was stricken, and the haunted look in his eyes, worry for her, she knew was because nothing had gone to plan.

Finndryl murmured something to the man he was helping, excusing himself. Lore didn't have time to blink before she was in his arms. Before his heartbeat, his beautiful, perfect *beating* heart, was thrumming against her ear.

"I'm sorry. I'm so sorry." She cried into his shoulder, clinging to him, barely letting herself believe that this was real, that he was real.

He lifted her up, pressing her to him as if he, too, couldn't believe she was really here in his arms. He kissed her, briefly, before murmuring in her ear, "No time for pointless apologies, my love. Your people need to hear from you."

Lore sniffed.

"Okay, put me down, but don't go far."

"Never."

Lore looked around her at the four hundred in the woods, who had traveled here in the night as they'd originally planned. She'd let them down yesterday—gods, was that just yesterday? It felt like a century had passed since she'd willingly walked into that snare.

Now wasn't the time to explain what had gone wrong or to even apologize, Finn was right. So she kept it short. She pulled Finn's sword from his belt and held it aloft, pointing it toward the skies. "I am hungry for justice. Shall we feast?"

Lore's cry rang through the forest, reverberating through the trees, lichen, and winter breeze until her words landed on everyone's ears.

The ground shook with their answering cries, their pounding feet, the rings of siren-forged swords and spears against sturdy shields, for Hazen had done it, and here were the weapons she'd asked the queen for, in the hands of her people.

She hadn't wanted to use the weapons, though she'd known she'd had to ask for them, even back then. The queen had them made for humans, smaller and lighter but sharp as anything, so that they could wield them even though they were farmers and not soldiers. She'd had them deposited as close to Duskmere as possible without the Alytherians knowing; Hazen had just had to grab them.

But she hadn't wanted it to come to this. She'd tried, on her own. The Alytherians had an army of guards, though most were down south. Focusing on protecting their borders from the southern queen, not knowing that this threat would come from within.

She knew that if they went to battle, many would be killed, because they were just people, starved and tired and cold . . .

So she'd tried; she'd tried to do it alone. To take out the king and his advisors herself . . . to suffer as few casualties as she could. And she'd almost lost everyone because of it.

But here they were, willing and ready to put their lives at risk, to stand with her, to fight for a life worth living. To fight for their children and grandchildren to breathe free air. To run in the light, to grow up with their heads held high.

Lore raised the sword and shouted, a wordless battle cry. She stamped her feet, she shook her sword, she threw her head back and screamed her rage.

To Lore it seemed that the very trees themselves shook their branches in celebration.

Today, they would win, or they would die.

CHAPTER 52

The air crackled with Lore's raw power as she raised her hands, unleashing a torrent of magic that ripped the gates of Wyndlin Castle apart. A wave of splintered wood and metal crashed down upon the unsuspecting sentries and guards, their cries of alarm swallowed by the deafening roar of Duskmere rebels surging through the shattered entrance.

"First we fight!" roared a voice from the horde.

"Then we heal!" hundreds of voices responded to the cry as they charged the castle grounds, a relentless tide of rage and defiance against centuries of fae oppression.

Once inside the castle, Lore, Finndryl, Syrelle, Isla, and Hazen moved like wraiths, their combined powers a force of nature unleashed upon the unsuspecting royalty. Finndryl's flames danced in his eyes; his flaming locs soared behind him as his every step left scorched stone in his wake. Isla, with her newfound connection to the ancient stones of the castle, tore chunks of masonry from the walls, hurling them at the fleeing courtiers with deadly accuracy.

"The throne room!" Lore shouted, her voice ringing with authority as she led the charge. The king and his advisors had barricaded themselves within, their faith in the king and his throne room's magical defenses their last desperate hope.

Outside the heavy oak doors, Lore paused, sensing the thrum of the king's magic woven into the very fabric of the room. She had let herself be led into his trap, and while it had nearly been her end, the knowledge of it now was all she needed to obliterate it—but why obliterate it when she could turn it back on them? After having spent eons in her mind being tortured by the king, she knew the rotten signature of his magic, and this would be his undoing.

She twisted the fabric of the spell, morphed it so only the five of them would be able to wield their magic in the throne room now. This might not be enough to hold the king forever, who had a thousand years to practice breaking spells, but it would hold just long enough to beat him. With a surge of concentration, she peeled back the layers of enchantment, her fingers tracing the intricate patterns of the spell. A wave of power coursed through her, and with a final, decisive gesture, she flipped the spell.

Syrelle was first in the throne room, his eyes glowing in the eerie light as he stepped forward. His dark magic reached out like strokes of ink to ensnare the king, queen, and their advisors. They froze midmovement, their faces contorted in terror as their bodies refused to heed their commands.

The king struggled against the bonds, his yellow eyes glowing with fury.

"I can't hold him for long," Syrelle gasped, the veins on his neck popping out from his efforts. Lore channeled her own magic into Syrelle, her light magic weaving with his darkness to form an unbreakable seal.

The king's struggles weakened, his defiance fading as he succumbed to the overwhelming power of their united effort.

"The curse of your people is that your hearts have shriveled to stone from indifference." Lore stepped closer to the king, raising her chin and voice in defiance. "Justice is the only thing that will set you free." Lore turned and paced back and forth in front of the nobles, watching them squirm. "You bowed to a king of darkness. You are as complicit as he in the crimes against my people, and for that, I condemn you all to death."

Lore raised her hands before them, calling on her magic—she would kill them slowly, inflict as much agony as she could, so that they would feel her pain.

Lore turned her hands around, the backs of them completely ink black. There was darkness in her too. Rage, envy, greed. She'd wanted power, not just to save her people but also to cease bowing in supplication before a populace who harmed her kind for sport. Baba had been taken from her by the violence of sentries. Mama by neglect—from withheld medicines and malnutrition.

This rage boiled within her. Ignited her desire for vengeance.

But Lore had light too.

She could see, below the black ink of her fingertips, her palms, the streams on her wrist, the silver glow of *Source*. How it came to her when called, danced in her presence. And the purple Puallas Kiss, it glittered in the light of her *Source*, evidence that she had saved an entire empire, because it was the right thing to do— because she was incapable of walking away from beings in need. And how the queen had gifted her with the Kiss, a permanent monument to her triumph.

She had her friends who had become family. The joy of watching the children at the shelter live and breathe and mature. No longer would her loved ones' growth be stifled from forced starvation.

Love for them . . . it kindled the fight within her just as much as rage.

Lore was dark, and she was light, and only by balancing the two could she do what needed to be done.

She pinched her fingers together and pulled forth a thin string of light, so thin it was invisible to the eye. Translucent but sharper than any steel. She would not prolong their deaths. She would not torture them as the king had. She flung her hands out, propelling the string out before her. Even with their superior fae eyes, they didn't see it coming, not even when it sliced through all their necks at once.

Finndryl whooped, and Syrelle sank to his knees, his eyes watching his uncle's head roll. She did not smile as she watched their decapitated bodies collapse, blood spurting out of them in rivers to form a lake at her boots.

But she did feel at peace when the deed was done.

CHAPTER 53

A small armada awaited Lore in Alytheria's western harbor: six imposing navy vessels and four nimble merchant ships, all gifts from the new King of Alytheria. For now, this would be enough. Enough to carry Lore's people to their new home, along with a handful of skilled fae who had volunteered to share their knowledge with the humans. Blacksmiths, carpenters, weavers, healers—masters of crafts long forbidden to the Duskmere folk.

The ships' holds bulged with the promise of a new beginning: bountiful stores of foods, seeds ready to sprout in fertile soil, stacks of lumber, tools of every kind, livestock, the gentle hum of bees, bolts of colorful cloth, and crates filled with healing herbs and remedies. Everything they would need to build a thriving community, to carve a life of freedom and prosperity from the wild embrace of the islands.

And Lore had a new grimoire in her satchel—the defeated king's own spell book, taken from his rooms. One day, when she felt that her shields would be strong enough to withstand his corruption, she would study it to find out how and where he called the humans from—so that those seeking answers, or who wished to return to Shahassa, would have the chance.

Lore glanced away from the bustling harbor and cast her gaze toward Wyndlin Castle, whose towers peeked over the tree line.

Ah, there he was.

King Syrelle had his work cut out for him.

He had sent a trusted few to the new steward's office where the records were kept. They were compiling a list of every single fae who had been a sentry at Duskmere. Whether they were long retired and living elsewhere or had been active when the king had withdrawn them to prepare for the slaughter of her people.

One by one they would be hunted, collected, and tried for their crimes.

The merchants, too, who funded the king's evil deeds.

The winged royal guard who had been on duty while the humans were imprisoned in the tower.

The royal advisors.

Everyone complicit would be brought before a tribunal, tried, and made to answer for their crimes.

In the meantime, he had a million other things to do as well, but for now, Lore needed him to do one last thing for her before she left him to rule his kingdom.

She eyed his form as he walked toward her where she stood in the Alytherian harbor. Massive wings. Purple robes. Gleaming golden crown.

Lore heard a peal of laughter coming from the dock behind her. She glanced toward it for a moment, and then cast her gaze back toward the new King of Alytheria.

She gasped. Standing before her was not the king, but Asher. He wore a simple tunic and breeches, his antlers displayed proudly. The scar on his brow, that full bottom lip.

"Asher," she breathed out.

His mouth quirked.

"This form seemed the most fitting for our goodbyes." His eyes glistened. He tapped his antlers. "I can't bear to think that this is it. That you will leave me and never return to Alytheria."

"If you can bear your uncle's 'punishments,' you can bear anything, I think." Lore winced. She was trying to make light of the horrifying ordeal they'd gone through, but it would be a long time before she could truly be carefree about it, and she learned now that she was not quite there, yet, to make jokes and laugh about it. "Truly, though, you have so much on your plate, you won't even notice that I'm gone."

"Oh, I think I will," he murmured, his voice thick with emotion as he took another step toward Lore. He gently lifted a stray curl, twirling it around his finger as if savoring the last strands of their connection. "The world doesn't feel quite as bright when you are not here to add your light."

A bittersweet smile played on Lore's lips, her eyes shimmering with unshed tears. "I'll send a letter once we're settled. We still have those trade agreements to negotiate . . ."

"Please don't tell me you will only write to me of exports and imports, Lore," Syrelle pleaded, a playful lilt returning to his voice.

"Perhaps I'll slip in a note about Ember's latest antics," Lore replied, a warmth spreading through her chest as Ember, the sly thing, wove her way in and out of Syrelle's legs.

"She really is rather like a cat, isn't she?"

"I have a theory that she was once a plump bookshop cat who dozed off in a mushroom circle that gave her the ability to shape-shift," Lore shared, her voice filled with fondness for the animal that she'd begun to think of as her familiar.

"That seems probable," Syrelle agreed, his laughter echoing through the harbor. "I believe I can feel her purring through my boots."

"Oh, you most assuredly can," Lore confirmed. "She purrs louder than any fox ought to. That is, at all. I don't think foxes *do* purr."

A poignant silence settled between them, the weight of their unspoken feelings hanging heavy in the air. This was goodbye, if not forever, then for a few years at least.

Syrelle, his voice catching in his throat, whispered, "I will love you until they put me in the ground, and even then, my love will endure."

Lore swallowed a thick lump in her throat. In another life, on another world, maybe he would be climbing the gangway along with her and Finndryl, and they would be heading for their new home together, the three of them. But they both knew that too much had happened. Too many lies. Too much hurt and pain. Syrelle had grown so much, and Lore had grown to love him, even as she had Asher . . . But his place was here, leading his people to greatness.

Her heart ached and rejoiced at the same time.

She pulled his hand between her own and held it "And you, who stubbornly refused to leave my heart, though I asked it quite nicely to let you go . . . well, a piece of it will always belong to you."

And she belonged to the people formerly of Duskmere as much as she belonged to herself. In a few years, when they had settled, and their fledgling empire could stand on its own feet without her magic to prop it up, she could leave and travel . . . but for now, they would be half an ocean apart, and that would just have to do.

"Safe travels, Archivist, First of Her Kind, First Grand Witch, Lore Alemeyu. Be well."

"Be well, King Syrelle Asher Gylthrae of Alytheria."

They embraced. She breathed him in, his blackberry and honeyed scent. She felt her power long to mingle with his, to dance, her light with his dark, and she let it do so, one last time, for just a moment, one moment more.

Then she stepped back from him and went to meet Finndryl on the gangplank.

"I don't think he'll last a month without you here to keep him humble," Finndryl uttered softly, his eyes filled with warmth as they gazed at Syrelle. They weren't friends, exactly, but they shared a mutual respect.

"Oh, he'll be fine. Besides, he's got Isla to do that."

"Chief Royal Advisor . . . what a career my sister landed for herself." Finndryl bent down and scooped a waiting Ember into his arms. She settled in her favorite spot—propped on his shoulders, concealed beneath his locs, and curled around his neck. "Never would have seen it coming," Finndryl said as he placed his arm around Lore, tucking her into his side—Lore's favorite spot.

Lore brushed her hand along the ship's railing as they stepped onto the boat, their strides in sync. She couldn't believe she was willingly stepping onto another boat. "I think it suits her. Isla's got a head for strategy, she's cunning enough to survive any court politics they try to throw at her, and she can travel. She'll never grow bored—I can't wait to see her next month."

"You make a good point."

"The only kind I ever make," she remarked with a laugh as she shut the door to their cabin. This would be their dwelling for the next four weeks as they sailed to their new home.

Home would be a cluster of five islands on the far eastern edge of Queen Naia's realm. Queen Naia had initially offered them as a "housewarming present," a ridiculous proposal. Lore insisted the humans purchase the land outright. It took Prince Consort Jaladri's pragmatic intervention to convince the queen that her grandson might one day have wanted the islands for himself. Hazen, of course, was laughing in the background—he and his grandfather had obviously conspired to help Lore, who was beginning to sweat at how Queen Naia was not giving in. A compromise was finally struck, and the islands were sold for a nominal fee, a fraction of their worth. Lore tried her best, but the queen was as stubborn as they come.

It was great practice in diplomacy, honestly. As far as Lore was concerned, the weapons Queen Naia had supplied for their rebellion had been payment enough for Lore's help with Anuya's pearl.

As Archivist, one branch of the six councils the humans had elected, she could not advocate they start their civilization in anyone's debt. Help from her neighboring empires was wanted and welcomed; handouts from them, however, were not.

Of course, the gold she'd purchased the islands with had come from Alytheria's immense reserves. Reparations for four hundred years of subjugation of every single human who'd lived and died in Duskmere under the demon king's rule.

Lore kicked off her boots, placed a treat in Ember's bowl, and collapsed onto the bed.

"I think I could sleep until next autumn," she mused into the blanket. Which, she just realized, was her baby quilt. "When did you put this on here?"

"Lore, you've been so busy these last two weeks, I think I could have hidden an entire camel in here and you wouldn't have noticed upon walking in."

"Oh, I have always wanted to ride one." She scooted over to the wall, allowing Finn to slide in beside her. "Though I've heard they bite."

Finndryl, instead of lying next to her on their bed, pounced on her and wrestled both of her wrists above her head, easily grasping them both in one of his hands. His lips quirked upward into a smirk. "I bite, and you have no qualms about riding me."

Lore laughed, turning her head in what was—even she could admit—a very sorry attempt to maneuver her neck away from his teeth, which were now nibbling their way down the sensitive skin of her throat to her collarbone.

Her core turned molten at the hot press of his lips.

"That's different. You are considerably better looking than a camel."

"I wouldn't tell any camels you plan to ride that; they would bite you for sure."

"You know, I've never even ridden a horse. How would I ever ride a camel?"

"Easy—I would be in charge, and you would simply ride at my front. That way, I could keep you from falling. Or from steering both yourself and the camel off a cliff." He sucked on her throat, eliciting a moan from her. "And I could do other things too." His voice was accompanied by a low, guttural growl as he pressed his kisses down, down, down.

Lore gasped as his mouth closed around her nipple through the fabric of her dress. He was so damned hot, the sensation was delicious. "Oh really? What sort of other things?" She ran her hands over his broad shoulders. They were wearing entirely too many clothes for being the only ones in their room right now.

"Well, it's common knowledge that anytime the heroine in a story must ride on the same . . . camel . . . as the dashing hero, he must slide his hands up her skirt when no one is looking." He trailed his hand up her skirt now, slowly, the *tease*.

"Sounds rather—oh, yes, right there, my love—sounds rather like that would be distracting for the two of them as well as their camel . . ."

"The camel doesn't mind, trust me; it's just living its best camel life, and so is the heroine, because she would be making the same sorts of sounds you are right now, love."

"Stop talking about camels *right now* and kiss me, damn it."

"Your wish is my command, Lore Alemeyu."

He granted her wish and kissed her.

She marveled at the way her stomach did a little flip at the feel of his lips on hers; the taste of spice and bourbon and happiness was intoxicating. She deepened the kiss, needing him closer.

He growled when she tried to pull away to lift the fabric of his shirt over his head.

"This isn't about me right now, this is about you. I'm training you for our first ride on—"

"If you make a camel joke instead of . . . oh yes, doing *that*, harder, faster—" She clinched her hands around his wrist, where it lay between her legs. She rode his fingers, bucking her hips. "I will throw you out of, oh gods, Finn, I'm going to—"

Her release was a cascade of sensations; it trilled through her like lightning from the buds of her nipples down to her core and back. She shuddered with each aftershock as her muscles tightened and released around his long, skilled fingers.

"That's it, honey, you sound so lovely when you cum for me."

Lore gasped in little pants, pressing her face into the muscles of his chest and—damn it, why was his shirt still on?—trying to catch the thoughts that had tumbled out of her head when he'd picked up the pace.

"Okay, I've given you what you want, now it's my turn."

"Your turn?" he asked, smiling over the two of his fingers he'd just pulled from his mouth, tasting the sweet flavor of her release.

"I haven't felt you inside me since last night, and that should be a crime; in fact, I might add it to our list of laws we are drawing up . . ."

"No, no need, I think I can comply with this one, no need to threaten me . . ."

He lifted her dress all the way up past her breasts and slid her underthings down her thighs. She helped by flinging them away with a graceful arch of her foot.

"I will never be tired of the sight of you. So damned pretty, lying beneath me all flushed and ready." He used one arm to pull his shirt up over his head before he kicked off his pants, throwing them onto the floor, and climbed above her.

She spread her legs for him, all jokes flown out the window, lost to the wind, because the only thing she could focus on was the long, thick length of him. It jerked when her eyes alighted on it, so hard, eager, ready for *her*.

"Please," she rushed out, before he could tease her and make her beg.

Finndryl huffed a laugh, deep in his throat, his desire shining in his eyes as he gazed down at her pretty brown lips, lining his length at her glistening entrance. "Mmm, you know just how to please me, don't you?"

Lore couldn't respond, because he'd given her what she craved with one solid thrust, filling her up to the hilt, and the feel of him was, oh gods, it was everything. She closed her eyes, holding back happy tears. This right here was all she would ever need to live blissfully ever after.

He slowly pulled out, and thrust into her again, and she moaned as her body stretched to accommodate him.

"Honey, my love, you feel so damned good. You were made for me, you know that?" he groaned into her ear, increasing the speed of his thrusts.

She cried out at his praise, whispered in her ear with each thrust. The grip of his hands on her ass as he held her to him, as he pulled her as close as she would go, as if he wanted to mold their bodies together . . . to fuse into one being. She cried out, not caring that tears were sliding down her face now, tumbling into her curly hair. She couldn't fathom this love, this need to be so close. It encompassed all of her being; it was bigger than her, bigger than him; it was the whole of the black sky, the swirling stars, and distant moons, this love they shared. Here, around them. This, between them.

The feeling of another release built up within her core. Climbing, climbing. Finndryl increased the speed of his thrusts until he found the perfect rhythm, just for her, hitting that spot he always seemed to find, again and again. She clung to his back, her nails carving half-moons into the deep mahogany flesh. He grunted in pleasure, loving the scrape, the burn of her nails, caused by her pleasure.

Her release crashed at the same time as his; he growled when her core clenched around his length, over and over as waves of ecstasy surged through her. His legs straightened out as his length throbbed, shooting his own release into her.

When it was over, he collapsed onto her, just as she liked, the feel of him above her, her safe place, her favorite place to be.

They slept like that until morning, when she woke before dawn, sliding her hands beneath the sheets, ready to explore, to feel him again.

EPILOGUE

We arrive at the first of the islands in just three days, and we still do not have a name for our new home yet," Aunty Eshe mused over the tinkling sound of a spoon hitting the side of a porcelain cup. She must be stirring honey into her tea.

Lore opened her eyes from where she sat dozing in an oversize armchair by the fire. The comforting sound of her friends and family chatting in the Lantern Room, the gathering space of the ship, melding with the crackling of the fire, had put her right out. She stretched before pulling Finndryl's knit sweater tighter around her and padding over the plush carpet to take a seat at the table between Hazen and Finndryl.

Finndryl slid a clay mug over to her. She tasted it, sighing when the flavors of coffee with maple syrup and fresh cream danced on her tongue. He sipped his own black coffee, the corners of his mouth turning up in satisfaction. He took pride in making her the perfect cup of coffee—not too sweet, not too creamy. She'd had to admit, for someone who preferred his coffee black, he was truly an artist when it came to crafting her a cup.

"About our name. I have the perfect one," Grey said around a mouthful of bread and butter.

"Oh, this ought to be good." Hazen snickered behind his hand.

Grey guffawed. "You sound sarcastic, Prince, but it is."

"Why does *Prince* sound like an insult when it's coming from you?" Hazen quirked an eyebrow.

Grey opened his mouth to retort *something*, but Lore interrupted before the two of them could start bickering again. "Please don't keep us waiting," Lore said from behind her mug.

Lore had been wondering what they should name their realm as well. Duskmere was a name imposed upon their village. It had not been one they had chosen. Their previous home, well, that name had been lost to time, along with so much of their history. Wiped clean when her ancestors appeared in Alytheria hundreds of years ago, so they'd chosen Shahassa as a filler. But it didn't feel right for their new nation, their new home. This name would be one of the most important things they chose. And the task was more than a little daunting.

"All right . . . prepare to fall in love." Grey looked around the room, pausing for dramatic effect. Uncle Salim gave an impatient *harrumph*, and Lore had to hide her smile behind her hand. "*Dawnmere.*"

Grey's grin was proud as he met everyone's eyes.

"Dawnmere?" Aunty Eshe asked.

"Yes, because we are at the *dawn* of a new age. The start of something new. It's a play on Duskmere."

"I get it, boy."

"Seems a little on the nose, don't you think?" Lore asked, her own eyebrow quirking upward.

Grey laughed. "That's the point!"

"Maybe we hear some other ideas before deciding," Uncle Salim said, patting Grey's shoulder.

Grey looked at his hand with mock offense. "No need to coddle, Unc. No one will have a better idea than me."

"I'm pretty sure we can ask a toddler to choose, and they would come up with a better name," Hazen choked out through a fit of cackles.

"Well, out with it. Let's hear some more ideas," Aunty Eshe ordered, giving each of them a hard stare.

Finndryl held his hands up before him. "Don't ask me. It's not my place."

She nodded her head and moved on to the next person.

Which happened to be Lore.

Aunty Eshe smiled encouragingly. "Lore, it's only fitting that we hear yours next, since the council gifted you with the honor of making the final decision on our new name."

Oof.

Did she want to even voice an idea when everyone was in this kind of teasing mood? Yes, because she had an idea. She'd been thinking about it for weeks now . . . and every time she did, she couldn't think of anything but this one name. She glanced toward the skyglass by the window. Their sacred skyglass, the one each and every human looked into on their eighth nameday ceremony. There was no chapel on any of the ships, so they had decided to put it in the Lantern Room. One entire wall was windows; if you angled it right, you could see the sky at night.

All eyes were on her when she turned back to the table.

"I was thinking . . . we could call our new country *Ziara*. After our skyglass." She bit her lip, suddenly shy as she waited for ribbing, or something snarky to pop out of Hazen's or Grey's mouth, but the only sound was the crackle of the fire in the hearth.

Aunty Eshe reached out and clasped Lore's hands between hers, her eyes glistening with unshed tears. "It's perfect."

One by one everyone nodded, even Grey.

Uncle Salim's voice was gruff with emotion. "Ziara. For our refusal to keep our eyes cast to the ground."

"Ziara. All our searching of the celestial, and it would lead us home after all."

Finndryl squeezed Lore's thigh under the table, his grin filled with pride for his lover. "Let's toast." He lifted his glass. "To Ziara."

"To Ziara," they cried, their glasses clinking.

ACKNOWLEDGMENTS

I have never written a sequel before, so at times, *Lore of the Tides* felt daunting—herculean even. It takes a village to raise a child, and this duology felt like giving birth, twice.

Firstly, I would like to thank my husband, Lamarr, my partner and best friend. Thank you for being my biggest fan, my unwavering support system, and the inspiration for all my characters' sweetest moments. Thank you for the surprise cappuccinos, snacks, and dinners that fuel my words, for always being willing to take over parenting so I can travel to live out my dreams as an author, and for picking up the slack without ever complaining whenever I am on deadline. Without you, I am lost.

To my mother, Robyn, thank you for reading every version of Lore's story and for being the most supportive mom an author could ask for. Your willingness to discuss plot points and debate the nuance of a single word or sentence is invaluable. My writing is better because of your artistry and your love.

To my daughter, Delilah, my delightful Delilah, you are the motivation for every good thing I do and the light to my life.

I am eternally grateful to my publishing team: Thao, my agent, for singlehandedly championing my dreams and making sure they all come true; Tessa, my editor, for believing in my visions and making sure they are realized in the best way possible; and Harper Voyager, for supporting my books and my career. I am so thankful and lucky to be an author at my favorite imprint! To Jordan, my cover artist, for designing the most incredible covers any author could ever have. Your art brings my words to life. To Guthrie, my sensitivity reader and friend, for reading *Wilds* and *Tides* and for ensuring that my books are a safe place to be.

To my lovely friends: Roxie, there aren't words to express how much your friendship means to me. You are my chosen family. Danielle, my unwavering friend, for supporting me not just emotionally, but for being my hype girl and celebrating all my wins, no matter how small. Jolie, for spilling alllll the tea with me, for being an inspiration within the bookish community, and for our writing sprints that genuinely helped this book be written. To the Books are Magic girlies, my life would be dismal without our group chat. And to Jules for all those quotes of *Tides* you saved—they truly let me know that I might just be good at this.

To my siblings, I love you all.

And to my lovely readers, *you*. Thank you for not only reading *Lore of the Wilds*, but for trusting me enough to finish Lore's story. This is the story of my heart, and without you, I would've never been able to finish it.